Dear Reader,

It's been fifteen years since this book marked my debut as a
fiction writer. *The Long Road Home* was first published in 1995.
Reading it again, I was amazed to see the similarities of personal impact
between the bank scandals of the nineties and the scandals that have
made headlines in the past year. The old adage is true: what goes
around comes around. Yet, the struggles and triumphs of the heart
remain ageless.

I chose not to revise the novel, rather to let it stand as written. I did,
however, change a few anachronisms for this reprint. It was amusing to
remove the Walkman cassette and public coin-operated telephones. No
matter how much time passes though, this novel will always be special
to me. It's my first novel. I began writing it when I was put on bed rest
during the pregnancy of my third child. When I finished writing the
story, I had given birth to both a book and a baby. It was an amazing
journey, one in which I learned that what is at first perceived as an
obstacle can be a serendipitous turning point.

I hope you enjoy reading the timeless message of love and second
chances in *The Long Road Home*.

Mary Alice

The
LONG ROAD
Home

Mary Alice Monroe

MIRA®

Recycling programs
for this product may
not exist in your area.

ISBN-13: 978-0-7783-2755-4

THE LONG ROAD HOME

Copyright © 2010 by Mary Alice Kruesi

Updated from original publication by Harper Paperbacks, 1995

For questions and comments about the quality of this book please contact us
at Customer_eCare@Harlequin.ca.

www.MIRABooks.com

Printed in U.S.A.

First Printing: November 2010
10 9 8 7 6 5 4 3 2 1

I dedicate this book to my mother,
Elayne Monogue Cryns.

For he hears the lamb's innocent call,
And he hears the ewe's tender reply;
He is watchful while they are in peace,
For they know when their Shepherd is nigh.
                    —William Blake, "The Shepherd"

PROLOGUE

———

THE DAY HAD BEGUN as so many others. An early arrival at the bank, quick signatures on urgent papers, Mrs. Baldwin presenting the day's schedule; nothing unusual. Yet outside the Manhattan skyscraper, the weather had turned. Blue skies had grown black, and an arctic wind was blowing in an unseasonable cold front. It was still early on Wall Street. Lights flickered through the dark morning mist like candles.

On the streets below, a drunk peed on the corner of the bank. Above, the sky did the same, releasing a pelting rain that left angry streaks against the windows and sent the people below scurrying into buildings, ducking under newspapers, or disappearing, shivering, down the pavement.

Charles Walker Blair looked out from his window at the gray sky and the gray-cloaked figures on the pavement and had the singular thought that his whole world had turned gray. It was a rare, trivial thought for the level-headed banker, owner of the Blair Bank.

From the hallway, angry shouts seeped into his office: the low drunken slurs of a man and the shrill opposition of his secretary. His mouth tightened in annoyance. Suddenly, the door flung open and the drunk lurched in.

Charles Blair turned from the window and stared at death in the eyes of Michael MacKenzie.

MacKenzie wobbled at the entry, his arms outstretched in a steadying gesture and his feet spread eighteen inches apart. He was a big man: broad shouldered, wide jawed, and ham fisted. His usually impeccable suit was soiled and had probably been slept in, his customary red tie with the corporate logo had vanished long ago, and his thick ruddy-brown hair was as unkempt as the hair on his cheeks.

"So this is where you're hiding out, eh, Blair?"

Charles Blair rose from his polished mahogany desk and discreetly indicated for his secretary to leave. Her large frame hovered at the door, looking expectantly at the angry drunk, then she lowered her head in resignation and silently closed the door behind her. Charles knew that she would race to the phone as fast as her arthritic legs could get her there and place a call to security.

Charles eyed the weaving drunk suspiciously. The man reeked of sour booze, and MacKenzie's sneering face made it clear he was a mean drunk. Charles casually walked around to the front of his desk and lightly tapped a green leather chair with his long fingers.

"I'm not hiding anywhere, Mike. You always know where to find me. Sit down. Let's talk."

"Talk!" shouted the other man. MacKenzie staggered forward and grabbed the opposite side of the high-backed chair. "You don't want to talk to me. Last week, you wouldn't even see me. Sicced your army of lawyers and execs out to do your dirty work, didn't ya?"

Charles Blair leaned against his desk in a leisurely stance but kept a wary eye on the other man. MacKenzie had a reputation for being a mean mule with a hard kick. With a will of iron and the genius of a maverick, he had built his financial empire up from a single grocery unit in New Jersey. He was young. A man of action. Which made his drunken state all the more foreboding.

"I don't know what you're talking about."

"You're a liar."

Charles narrowed his eyes. He wasn't lying, yet MacKenzie was convinced. Every instinct in his body screamed alert. There was too much hatred here for mere confrontation; too much anger for reason. Michael MacKenzie wanted blood.

"Mike, sit down," Charles tried again, speaking slowly. "It's obvious you're upset."

"Upset?" Mike slapped his knee and laughed till he coughed and spit out upon the oriental carpet. He rubbed the spittle into the wool with his dirty heel.

A muscle twitched in Blair's cheek, but he neither spoke nor moved. He watched as Mackenzie, with halting steps, paced a muddy trail across his office, eyeing the diplomas, trophies, and personal photographs on the walls.

"Well, look at you," he slurred. "Got yourself a picture with every president since you were in diapers. Now ain't that sweet. An' lookee here." Mackenzie pointed to a wall of diplomas. "Harvard... Harvard again... A Rhodes scholar? The old-boy network oughta love that."

Suddenly the young man twisted to face him, a small pistol grasped in his fist. Blair snapped to attention.

"Give me the gun, Mike," he said, holding out his hand. His voice was low and deliberate. He dared not even blink. "Give it to me, then sit and tell me more."

MacKenzie waved the gun in front of Blair. The metal shone in the artificial light. MacKenzie's lips twisted into a sinister grin.

"Why?" Charles asked, realizing the death he saw in Mac-Kenzie's eyes was his own.

Michael MacKenzie teetered, pointing his free hand toward the diplomas. His voice fell to a flat tone. "When did I get the chances you got, huh? I slaved in the back of a grocery store since I could walk. Chased rats as big as a cat. My dad didn't hand over a bank. The only thing he handed out was a cuff to the ear." He winced as though the slap had just now reached his head. "Oh, Ma." He moaned, and his whole face contorted.

Blair's muscles relaxed as he watched the burly man bring his hands to his face and release his death grip on the pistol. He no longer saw a dangerous, belligerent drunk. He saw a broken man. Although he did not know what had broken him, he did know that he had refused MacKenzie any loan from his bank. He'd protected his bank from a high risk. Now, for the first time, he questioned whether his prudence was worth the price.

"Look, Mike," he began. His voice was conciliatory and he took a step forward. His mistake was to reveal pity.

"Get your goddamn filthy hands offa me!" shouted Mac-Kenzie as he swung his shoulder away from Blair's reach. Blood-red anger rushed to MacKenzie's face and his eyes bulged, making him look like a bull on the charge. Suddenly he swung around and with amazing speed slammed the pistol against Charles's face.

Charles saw the blow coming, but not soon enough. He heard the crack of metal against bone, heard a rush of air expel from his own lips, and felt a blackening pain that sent him catapulting against his desk. Blood flowed from his nose and he knew that it was broken.

The force of his swing threw MacKenzie off balance and sent him reeling into a crumpled heap in the corner.

The Long Road Home

The room was silent except for the muffled, drunken moans from the corner. Charles drew himself up, one hand leaning against his desk, the other holding his nose with a handkerchief. The stale smell of whiskey singed Blair's raw olfactory nerves, but it was his own bile that made his stomach churn. Staring at the defeated man, the only pain he felt was shame. How many businesses had he crushed, he asked himself? So many he had lost count. They had all been figures in a ledger, pawns on a chessboard. Until now. The human predicament had never figured in his calculations. Until now. And now, the rules of the game had changed.

He was about to tell MacKenzie that he'd get his loan. He was about to reach out a hand to a fellow man. But he was too late.

The world seemed to slow down in those tragic few moments. Blair saw the pistol rise again, but this time it pointed not at his head, but the other man's. MacKenzie's eyes rolled up to meet his, red and goggling—like the desperate eyes of a fish on a hook. Blair reached out and lunged forward, his mouth open in a silent scream.

A roar sounded in his ears. Blood spattered across his face, blurring his vision of Mackenzie's body jerking its lifeblood across the priceless oriental. The red staining the gold silk-papered walls, blotching the gilt-framed portrait, splattering the green leather chairs, and tainting forever the soul of Charles Walker Blair.

1

—

NORA MACKENZIE SLIPPED a complacent smile on her face. It was a look that she had mastered over the past year. A mask she donned to protect herself from the horde of lawyers, accountants, and other corporate hit men who had invaded her life since Mike's death. Most of them were here now, assembled around the massive oak conference table in Mike's office, shuffling papers, murmuring, jotting notes. Their work was done. Like jurors, they were poised to deliver a verdict.

She sat alone at the far end of the table, one against so many. Nora felt the bulk of her dark wool suit, the high blouse collar like a cinch around her neck. She had chosen the respectable outfit deliberately. Despite the gossip, she would show them that Michael MacKenzie's widow was a lady.

There was a chill in the morning air. No one had offered her coffee. Clasping her hands tight in her lap, Nora peered from behind her mask to study the men and women who would decide her fate. A few had the air of pompous boredom that she long ago discovered hid incompetence. She recognized those that had played the role of her supporter and those that had taken the attack. There were more of them. A few she had talked to daily for almost a year. Today, however, she was universally ignored. Dismissal was clear in their eyes.

Ralph Bellows sat across the length of polished wood, his gray hair flowing from his broad forehead like a periwig. Nora knew he would act as judge. Bellows relished the role. A clearing of his throat served as a gavel, and he called his court to order with a firm "Shall we begin?"

Nora's shoulders tensed. She had no doubt Mike would be found guilty in the eyes of his peers. He had committed the worst of crimes: bungled his finances, destroyed his businesses, and left them without a profit. Yet the one to serve the sentence would be her.

Straightening in the stiff leather chair, Nora appeared calm and dignified. She offered Bellows a gracious nod.

"Mrs. MacKenzie...well, we are not strangers in this room. We have endured together a long, arduous year. May I address you as Nora?"

His smile revealed teeth the color of ripe bananas. Nora nodded again. They'd endured? Nora clenched her hands in bitterness. *She* had endured. They'd conducted business as usual. No matter how disastrous her estate, they would be assured their pay before creditors got a dime.

"The untangling of Mike's business dealings has been more complicated than we originally envisioned," Bellows began gravely. "Our work is not yet completed."

A short gasp escaped from Nora's lips. It had been a year since Mike's suicide. What more could they need to accomplish before settling the estate?

Reading her frustration, Bellows continued in a conciliatory tone. "No one realizes the futility of further delays more than I. However, to put it bluntly, Michael MacKenzie left behind a mess. No one, least of all family, understood the extent of his holdings. We are doing our best to put together the pieces of his myriad dealings, but some critical bits of information are still missing."

From under his bushy brows, Bellows's pale eyes searched hers intently. Nora felt like the prey of an owl. She paled, yet steadfastly returned his gaze with the wide eyes of innocence.

You bet they're missing, she thought from behind her mask. There wasn't a man or a woman at this table who hadn't rifled through every nook and cranny she and Mike possessed. Who hadn't read every personal letter they could find. Who had bothered to ask her permission. There was a frenzy to their search that raised her suspicions and her ire. Even the break-in at her New York apartment disturbed her less than their blatant disregard. Nothing had been stolen, but Mike's desk had been ripped apart.

"Don't trust anyone." Those were Mike's final words to her, whispered urgently the night before he died. Nora had heeded his words and hidden every paper she could find on his desk.

Bellows cleared his throat again with a frustrated staccato, glancing at the papers on the table. When he looked up again, his gray eyes were as cold as the rainy sky outside the windows.

"Even without further information the result is clear." Bellows tapped the report with finality.

Nora leaned forward, focused on his lips.

"The bottom line is, the estate is bankrupt."

Nora blinked. "You mean his *business* is bankrupt."

Bellows screwed up his lips under his red bulbous nose.

"No, I mean *you* are bankrupt. For all that we loved Mike, he did a stupid thing. He made himself personally liable for his debts."

Bellows's voice ended abruptly, leaving everyone to finish his thought: *and then blew his brains out before pulling himself out of it.*

"What do you mean, personally liable?" Nora asked, reality taking hold. She was fighting to maintain her composure. Suddenly she loathed the alcoholic nose that Bellows peered over.

"Mr. MacKenzie put up his personal estate as collateral for loans," contributed a young clean-shaven accountant. His voice shook and he fingered his papers nervously. "The family's seventy-five percent stake in MacCorp., personal property—he pledged it all. Mike was so deep in hock he was unable to make the repayment schedule."

Nora did not acknowledge him. The family's stock? What family? There was only her. She had a name. Nora remained rigid in her chair and continued to stare at Bellows.

"Ralph, what does this mean to me?"

Bellows's features softened as he laced his fingers together and rested them on the stack of papers before him. Nora wasn't fooled for a moment. Bellows had nothing to lose by offering kindness now.

"What this means, Nora, is that Mike left you with nothing. Worse than nothing, actually. We have paid back as many of the loans as possible, but you still owe a great deal of money. You will have to sell everything—and even then you may still owe."

"Owe? If everything is gone, how will I pay it?" Her voice was a whisper.

"The company is in receivership. Your goods will be auctioned off in October by a reputable house. Fortunately, your antiques and art collections are quite rare. Properly managed, the auction should bring in a satisfactory amount."

"Enough to pay off the debts?"

"Hopefully. With enough left over to give you a start. These are estimates," he said, opening up the collection of papers in front of him. Immediately, the dozen other people opened their packets. With dread, Nora followed suit.

"If you direct your attention to the bottom of page three," Bellows continued, "you will see the amount I believe we can salvage for you from the estate."

Nora quickly flipped to the third page and read, then reread the dollar figure they had allotted for her. It was less than she had imagined, and she had imagined a scant amount. Surely there was an error somewhere. She scanned the other fourteen pages of notes carefully, ignoring the impatient sighs and tapping fingers. The report listed, with astonishing accuracy, her personal possessions and their estimated worth: houses, cars, jewels, furniture, art.

"You even list the few personal possessions that I brought to the marriage." She indicated the report with an exasperated flip of her hand. "My grandmother's jewelry, for example. It may not be worth much monetarily, but to me—" her voice almost cracked and she swallowed hard "—to me, they are priceless."

"I'm sorry, Nora." Bellows shrugged, running his fingers down the columns. "Maybe we could take out a few…less valuable items." He seemed embarrassed now.

"This is wrong," Nora said, deeply feeling the injustice.

"It was Mike's doing."

A familiar ache gripped Nora's heart. Her feelings lay somewhere between anguish and anger. They made her breath come short. Calm yourself, she told herself. Get through this last step and you will be free from the lot of them forever.

"I don't blame Mike," she lied. "What I don't understand is how he could appear so successful and suddenly I learn he is bankrupt. How did it get this bad?"

Bellows's look implied all that he did not say, all that everyone already knew. That she had left Mike. How, their eyes accused, could she expect to know about Mike's finances after she walked out on him? Left him in his hour of need? Nora knew they saw her as the New York socialite who collected antiques and art. A pretty blonde who couldn't be bothered with bank balances.

Nora looked at the accusing eyes and despite her vow, shrank inward. Guilt was an unwelcome shroud for a widow to bear. It kept one mourning without resolved grief. Deserved or not, it was a heavy burden. If Mike had died naturally, perhaps she could have escaped it. He had chosen suicide, however, and with that final act he had completed his seven-year campaign of verbal abuse. Nora's hand moved to rub her brow, but she arrested the gesture in her lap. She tightened her fists and raised her chin.

"He took a new direction in his last year," Bellows explained.

"This 'new direction' is not detailed in the report," she replied icily.

Bellows raised his brows. "Quite right. The purpose of today's meeting is only to explain the status of your estate prior to settlement."

"Since my money seems to have been lost as well, I should think I am entitled to a full disclosure."

Mumbles sounded at the table. Nora still focused on Bellows. Always work at the top, Mike had said.

She sensed a new appreciation in Bellows's eyes. Up until now, her encounters with him had been purely social. Despite his gentlemanly facade, his hand always seemed to find a way to her waist. In what might have appeared a mindless motion, the broad expanse of his palm would caress her ribs while his long thumb would nudge upward toward her breast. Beneath his fastidious apparel, Nora always found him dirty.

"I'd be happy to set up a private meeting to outline Mike's past projects, Nora." Bellows's voice projected the cooperating attorney. His rheumy eyes spoke of another project he had in mind, and to emphasize his intent, he presented her with a magnanimous smile. Be good to me, the smile said, and I'll be good to you.

"That won't be necessary," she replied firmly. "A report in the mail should suffice. I plan to leave town as soon as possible."

Thirteen pairs of brows rose in unison.

"Leave? To where, my dear?" Bellows asked.

Truth was, she didn't know. Anywhere but here, Nora thought, her gaze traveling across the impassive faces surrounding her. She'd had enough of false friendship. She'd had her fill of dismissal and rejection, of sympathy with strings attached. Somewhere along the line, she'd lost sight of her values. Looking back, she couldn't remember what it was she had hoped to achieve by thirty.

This was a turning point. Nora wanted to go somewhere she could work hard, earn her own living, and reevaluate her values. Somewhere, she wanted to build a life that mattered.

Nora's hand stilled in her lap. An entry from the report came to mind with a flash. Such a place existed, she realized, a smile escaping from her rigid control. Excitement bubbled. She knew exactly where that place was.

Leaving Bellows's question hanging, Nora dove into the report and began flipping quickly through the pages.

"I assure you we went through everything thoroughly," an attractive woman lawyer commented.

"I'm sure you have," Nora replied tersely. She remembered the blonde from the "attack" team. Nora ran her finger along the listed property, unconsciously holding her breath. When she spotted what she was looking for, her breath exhaled with a satisfying gasp. The estimated value was fairly low.

"Looking for anything in particular?" asked Bellows, his interest clearly piqued.

"Just one moment, please," Nora replied without looking up. Grabbing a pencil she made notations, referring back to page three. Always facile with numbers, Nora reviewed the estimated values, made a few more notations, and calculated an alternative plan.

When she looked up again, the twelve lawyers and accountants were slouched in their chairs in exaggerated poses of boredom. Their noses seemed to have grown inches, the way they peered down at her from behind them. Nora coughed back a laugh. Only Bellows viewed her with intense interest.

"I'll take the Vermont farm instead of the cash," she announced.

Twelve chairs creaked as the men and women snapped to attention and shuffled through their papers.

Bellows seemed both amused and curious. "The sheep farm? But why, Nora? It is a small operation, risky at best. Its only purpose for Mike was as a tax write-off."

"All true," she replied, holding back her excitement.

His eyes narrowed. "I believe the house is unfinished. Have you and Mike ever lived there?"

"No," she said emphatically. "Never."

"I see," he replied, leaning back in his chair. His eyes never left her. "Then why the farm?"

"Why not?" She wasn't about to confide in Uncle Ralph. "I want it," she said bluntly, "and according to my calculations, I can have it—plus enough to establish an interest-bearing account of about three hundred thousand dollars. That should give me enough to eke out a living."

"A meager living, to be sure."

"I'm not afraid," she lied again. As he went through her figures, adding a few of his own, Nora maintained her icy composure. She could not let on how much this meant to her.

"I don't want any surprises," she said. "Not without a cushion. I assume your calculations are correct?"

An indignant *harumph* sounded from her left as an accountant's face mottled. Nora focused only on Bellows. This was between the two of them, Mike's personal lawyer and his widow.

She could sense the growing surprise and antagonism of the men and women around her. These were Mike's people. She, his wife, was the outsider.

And that was the way she wanted it. Her foot began tapping beneath the heavy table as she put together the pieces of her new, even radical plan. In her mind she could envision the farm the last time she saw it—what was it—three years ago? The verdant lushness of the Vermont mountains, the fat red raspberries hanging ripe on the bush, fields of oxeye daisies, Queen Anne's lace and clover sprouting up between rocks, dark woods with cool breezes, and the bucolic bleating of the lambs. It could all be hers. She could make something of her life there, she felt sure of it.

A heady kind of enthusiasm raced through her no-longer-complacent veins. An excitement that ran slipshod over her rational constraints, delivering a new confidence. The kind that in the past had inspired her to impulsively buy a piece of furniture, or a painting. Though based on knowledge, the decision was instinct. She was born with what some people called "a knack."

She had to have the farm, she thought with quiet desperation. It was right. And it was all she had to hold on to.

Bellows cleared his throat, once again bringing his court into session. "Well," he said with both resignation and mirth. "I see no reason why this can't be arranged."

Amid the grumbling of disapproval at the table, Nora beamed.

"Only one more contingency," he warned.

Nora stiffened.

"Remember that nothing is final until after the auction. That gives you two months to determine if you can make a go of it at this sheep farm of yours. And even if you do, you can still lose it to Mike's creditors."

"But that is unlikely. You said yourself the auction should be a success."

"Should be and will be are worlds apart." Like a consummate judge, he glared at every man and woman that sat around the table, no one longer than at Nora herself. "The status of the MacKenzie estate is confidential. This is absolute. Should word of MacKenzie's bankruptcy leak out, the auction will be ruined. Mrs. MacKenzie cannot set a minimum bid. And if the auction doesn't bring in the bacon—" he paused to close the report with grand effect "—then all of you go home hungry."

Not a paper rustled.

"That's it," Bellows concluded. Instantly the table was covered with expensive leather attaché cases of every color considered understated yet elegant. As papers were shuffled in and people shuffled out, Bellows came around the table and offered his hand to Nora.

She took it warily.

He held her hand for a moment, looking at the lone gold

band on her ring finger, then said with surprising sincerity, "Good luck, Mrs. MacKenzie."

Nora detected none of his earlier lecherousness. A small smile eased across her face. "Thank you, Mr. Bellows. I'm sure I'll need it."

Bellows released her hand with a glint of amusement in his eyes. After an urbane nod of his head, he strolled from the room.

Relief flooded her. Good-bye, old boy! she mouthed as she watched his retreating back. Good-bye all of you, she thought, addressing the empty chairs around the table. The images before her changed. Instead of furniture, Nora envisioned mountains. Instead of oak, she saw maple.

I'm going home, she realized, still not believing. *Home.* The word felt strange upon her lips; distant yet full of promise. It was fall; the farm would be ripening with color. Warm days and cool nights. Harvests coming in. New lambs.

So much new. So much to learn. Instinct would carry her only so far. Could she manage? What did she know about farming or caring for sheep? No one would be there to pull her out of trouble. To casually write the check. Her hand hesitated on her bag as doubt pressed. It would take hard work, tons of it, and daily prayer to pull this off. Was she up to it?

Nora raised her chin defiantly and gave the zipper a firm tug. She'd better be. The farm was all she had left. She was on her own. If she didn't make it there, she had nowhere else to go. Hoisting her purse, Nora took one farewell look at Mike's office.

The recessed lights cast small shadows upon the cleared oak table and the empty credenza. It gave off a ghostly sheen. Memories stirred, producing goose bumps along her arms. Nora rubbed them quickly, brushing the memories away.

"Good-bye," she whispered, taking one last look before

turning out the light. The words sounded hollow in the empty room. As she closed the door tight behind her and hurried away, Nora had the ominous feeling that Mike's ghost was right behind her.

2

———

DAWN ROSE OVER MANHATTAN. Its reach stretched for miles in reflection against steel and glass. The morning light pressed relentlessly against rows of window shades, curtains, and blinds closed as tight as eyelids. They seemed to squint against the brightness.

Forty-four stories up, Nora stood, arms folded, coffee cup in hand, allowing herself a farewell to her city. She could feel the heat of a new day against the glass. She leaned her cheek against it. How quiet the city was at this hour, she thought. A sleeping giant. Yet Nora could feel the energy awakening beneath her. The sun was stirring the beast, and soon, within the hour, it would be fully awake, belching out the sounds of shouts, honks, and whistles. A hungry city.

She shuddered. This city had always intimidated her. Only her wealth had protected her from the harsh realities of the streets below. Now, she'd lost her cocoon, she thought. She'd been booted out.

Oh well, she decided, gulping her coffee and closing the blinds with a snap. "Sweetie, it's time to fly." She said it aloud, encouraged by the sassy tone in her voice. If she wanted to be out of the city today, she had a lot of work to do. The auction house people were due here soon.

At the thought, her stomach churned. This was it. She was really leaving the city. Even though she wanted to go—was eager to go—the leave-taking was hard.

She surveyed her home with a critical eye. The rooms she had hated yesterday were comforting today in the memories they held. The apartment was gracious and inviting; eight rooms full of rare antiques, intricate oriental rugs, and paintings that museums coveted.

Things, she told herself. They're just things. Trappings of a lifestyle. Yet, she loved them. Over the past several years, each time she walked through these rooms she would get a small thrill of delight at the sight of these beautiful things. Not that she was greedy, or even cared for the dollar value of any of them. No, she simply enjoyed being surrounded by the intrinsic beauty of the pieces. The flair of a Chippendale, the vibrant color of a rug, or the focus of a Satsuma ware pattern. The art touched her, and her life had been so hard the past several years that she sought simple pleasures wherever she could find them. So she had pursued her art and antiques collections with a vengeance, earning for herself a reputation for a keen eye and a handy checkbook.

Nora ran her hand across the French high-gloss finish of a table. Her unpolished nails seemed so mortal against the ageless wood. These things, these precious things, she thought with sadness. Now they were her champions. It was up to them to bring in enough cash to pay back the debts and to keep her going. She had depended upon Mike for so long, and in the end, it would be her own abilities that could save her. How ironic life could be, she thought.

From one room to the next, Nora strolled through memories.

In here, she thought, gazing at the Sheraton dining table, at this table she had presided over countless dinners. Seemingly effortless soirees that displayed Mike as the successful financier and herself as the stable dot beneath the exclamation point. Her husband used to smile his approval from across the long damask-covered table. His Irish blue eyes had sparkled beneath his heavy dark brows. He'd seemed so handsome then, so powerful, so hers. In recent years, she remembered with a pang, he had awarded his approving smile to the lovely lady he had selected to sit at his right.

In those Victorian chairs, she thought, entering the morning room, she and Mike would lean back and read the newspapers. In the early days of their marriage they'd blurt out comments and questions that always sparked remarks or laughter. Later, however, only she would persist, making comments that never brought a response.

Her heels clicked upon the polished parquet as she completed her rounds. The coordinating patterns of fabrics, the dominating pieces of art, the soft-hued paint and carpet, and the lemony smell of polish and soap enveloped her in their security. Each room was perfect.

Mike had hated them all. He hated every detail of the small, well-appointed apartment. He wanted a house as big and brawling as he was. Full of unruly children, a basketball hoop in the driveway, and a big hairy dog in the yard. He had expected a family in the suburbs—he had demanded an heir.

"If you spent as much time trying to have a baby as you did buying furniture," he'd mutter, cutting her to the quick.

Nora paused, the pain as sharp now as it had been when spoken. So many mean comments, so many slurs. She shook her head, loosening pain's hold. Oh yes, it was time to go.

Nora went directly to her bedroom to gather her suitcase.

She had to get out of here. Let the movers fend for themselves. At the door to her bedroom, however, Nora froze. The trip through memories was not yet over. A farewell was due to this room as well. This room, where dreams had been dashed, battles waged, and a marriage lost. Her eyes roaming over the heavy four-poster, Nora wondered for the hundredth time how so much love could have engendered so much hate? Despite her resolve, old questions nagged. When had Mike begun to loathe the sight of her? To find her too repulsive to touch? In how many ways had she failed?

Mike was everywhere. He haunted every room in this place. Still mocking, relentlessly accusing her.

"Please, Mike," she muttered. "Let me go."

Nora heard the front door unlatch and after a hasty wipe at her eyes, she checked her watch. It was only 8:00 a.m. Could the movers be arriving so soon? She peeked out from behind the bedroom door. Down the hall she spied a stocky, robust figure impatiently jerking her arm from a too-long coat. With a sigh of relief, Nora flung wide the door.

"Trude, what are you doing here?" Nora walked swiftly down the long hall to take her maid's hands. "Yesterday was your last day. I thought we said our good-byes."

Trude puffed herself up. "I no could stand think of you, here in this place, by yourself." She looked around then jerked her shoulders. "He still here, you know? Bad feeling. You go through too much." She sniffed loudly. It had never been any secret how Trude felt about Mike. Trude stepped back and surveyed the coffee cup in Nora's hand. "You have no breakfast, right?"

Nora smiled, knowing it was futile to argue. "I've been busy. I'll catch something on the road."

Trude took the coffee cup. "I know you. You forget. Look at you. All bones. I go make something."

"No, really. I couldn't eat. I've got too much on my mind."

Trude shook her head and Nora read worry rather than irritation on the older woman's face. In fact, Trude couldn't be more than forty-five, but she was the type to mother, regardless of who or what age. Nora had been her special project for seven years.

The intercom buzzer rang.

"Oh boy, look out. Here they come now!" Trude called with hand raised. "I go get some coffee going." Trude's answer to all problems was a cup of coffee.

The apartment was soon crowded with men and women of all shapes, sizes, and nationalities. Nora could smell the different spices, as well as the common scent of fast food, in the close air of the apartment. There was no more time for sentiment. It was time to pack up and go.

The day sped by as she worked alongside the crew. Some of the men were efficient, others had to be hawked. Nora cataloged her furniture, checking it without emotion against the computer list. She watched, impressed, as the men slipped her heavy glass-front antiques into specially constructed, padded crates as easily as a hand fit into a glove. Trude backed her up, offering fluids and snacks and cleaning floors as soon as they were bared. Room after room was emptied, leaving emptiness behind.

"You wanna check this out?"

Nora bobbed her head up toward Mike's breakfront desk where a mover was waving her over. "We were lifting this top piece off when this panel here broke open. We didn't do nothin'."

Nora stuck her pencil behind her ear and hurried over to the desk, disassembled now for the crate. One side panel, disguised as molding, had popped open to reveal a thin niche. Nora hid her shock. Mike had purchased this desk, and all these years she had never known this hiding place existed. She knelt beside the open panel and, turning her body, reached far in. The wood was raw, unfinished, and dusty. Something was in there, she realized with a sudden intake of breath. Grabbing hold, she eased out a burgundy leather notebook. She stared at the leather volume, worn in spots to a dull luster, and knew with every fiber in her body that this held secrets.

She looked over her shoulder at the two men huddled together, staring in curiosity. "Oh, my goodness. My diary! I forgot all about it."

She tucked the notebook under her arm, then forced an airy laugh. "Thank God you found it. I'd hate to think of some stranger reading it!"

"Yeah. Bet it's loaded with good stuff," one of the men jeered. Nora cast him a wary glance, unsure if he was complimenting or insulting her. Without response she turned heel and immediately hurried to her bedroom and closed the door. The furniture had already been removed and the carpets rolled. Only her suitcase sat square in the middle of the floor, under a brass and crystal light fixture. Nora plopped down Indian-style beside the suitcase and looked long and hard at the notebook. Around her, she could feel Mike's presence, hear his voice inside her head. "Open it. Read it." She obeyed.

The notebook was filled with pages and pages of numbers; more a bank ledger than a diary. Notes were scattered here and there in Mike's distinctive, heavy script. Leafing through the pages, a pattern of desperation emerged. Neat lines and columns filled the early pages. As the pages progressed through the months, the nature of the writing changed. Instead of neatness, quick notes were scribbled in an illegible hand. Crossed-out computations and many underlined words and dashes scrawled across the final pages. An artist, Nora recognized the design of mania.

She closed the book and rested her hand upon it, as though to force quiet memories of the last months of Mike's life. He had gone through a period of marked deterioration. Although he had once taken a vain interest in his appearance, he became unkempt. In the few weeks before he died, Mike grew argumentative, obsessed, even erratic.

The parallels with his handwriting were too strong. She needed time, away from prying eyes, to decipher the message held here. Time to hear Mike's final words and time to decide if she should give this notebook to Ralph Bellows. Bellows was Mike's closest colleague. Executor of the estate. And it was clear he was searching for something.

Three short raps sounded on the door. Nora scrambled to her knees and stuffed the notebook into her suitcase just as a high nasal voice sang out from the doorway.

"Oh, there you are!"

Nora bristled. Whoever it was didn't have the courtesy to wait to be allowed in. Turning, she saw a tall, emaciated-looking man with pale skin and the brightest, most unnatural shade of red hair she'd ever seen. Another player in today's circus, she thought with a sigh of resignation.

"Can I help you?" she asked. Her tone would, she hoped, give him a clue to her mood.

"I'm from Sotheby's," he replied, as though that was enough introduction. "I'm glad we caught you before you left."

"Caught me?" Something in his tone raised her ire.

"We went over the inventory of your jewelry for the auction and a few things are missing." His singsong voice implied *naughty, naughty*.

"Whatever are you talking about?" Nora's voice was brusque as she rose.

He began flipping through the pages clipped to his board. It was filled with computer entries. Did she really own that much jewelry, she wondered? She hardly ever wore it.

"Here it is. A square-cut diamond. Antique setting."

"My grandmother's engagement ring. It's not to be sold. Didn't Mr. Bellows notify you?"

"No, he didn't. Apparently he changed his mind." The cynicism in his eyes stung. "The ring's on the list. Sorry, dear. I have to ask you for it."

Nora choked. "It's mine. It's all been arranged."

"Apparently not." He tapped the papers a tad too loudly. "It's on the list."

Nora's lips tightened. "How much is it worth? I'll buy it now."

"Look, dear. I'm sorry, but no can do. You can talk to Sotheby's about it, I guess, but I have to collect that ring now—and a few other items." His voice trailed as he searched the papers.

I'll bet you're sorry, Nora thought, steeped in bitterness. So, Bellows didn't come through for her after all. A simple kindness was beyond him. She couldn't trust him.

Blind rage colored her thinking. She flipped up the lid of her suitcase and pulled out her zip cloth jewelry bag. Without opening it, she held it out to the nameless man with the red hair and papers.

"Take it."

"Certainly not all of it," he moued, his blush making him look like an elongated carrot.

She jerked it toward him. The thin man stepped forward to retrieve the small bag, then stepped back again. He pulled out some Victorian beaded necklaces, a yellowed pearl necklace and earrings, a large cameo pin, and the solitary engagement ring. It was a pitiful show compared to the many-carat diamonds, rubies, and emeralds on the list.

"So much fuss about so little," she said softly. Her shoulders slumped. "It doesn't matter. Just take it and get out. Please."

The man paused, then selected out the pearls and set them delicately upon the suitcase. "I don't see those on the list," he muttered as he rushed out the door.

Nora picked up the pearls and rubbed them against her cheek. "Oma, I miss you," she said. She slipped the pearls around her neck and placed the earrings in her ears.

In the mirror, the burgundy notebook was visible in her bag. In that same bag, beneath wool sweaters, nestled a shirt box. And in that shirt box was a stash of personal letters, memos, and a pocket diary that she'd found on Mike's desk the day he died. Papers that were scattered next to an empty bottle of bourbon and a loaded ashtray.

Mike had called her to New York from her house in Connecticut, yelling over the wire that it was urgent. So she had come, against her better judgment, only to be ignored once again. Until that night, before he died.

"Don't trust anyone," he'd told her, roughly awakening her. He was drunk, again, and the sour smell of bourbon and smoke descended upon her like a winter cloud.

At first she was afraid. Something in his voice had changed; she heard it even in her sleepy stupor. The anger was gone. The arrogance was gone. In its place she heard desperation and fear.

"Don't trust anyone." That was all he'd said. That and a firm shake and an intense stare. So intense. Telling her in that gaze that he was leaving. Warning her that she was on her own now. Perhaps, too, that he was sorry. She liked to think that anyway.

Nora closed the suitcase, zipped it, and locked it. Whatever secrets lay hidden in that notebook, she'd uncover them later. On her own. One thing was certain—she would keep her secrets from Ralph Bellows.

"Mrs. MacKenzie?" Trude stood at the door, arms akimbo.

Nora could tell she'd overheard the entire exchange. "Well, I'm all set to go," said Nora with false enthusiasm.

Trude clenched her lips and nodded. "Well then, let's get you go."

Nora walked over and touched Trude's shoulder. "I wish I could take you with me."

"I not ask for much," Trude replied, opening the door once again for an offer.

Nora sighed and shook her head. "I couldn't pay you. I don't know how I can take care of myself, let alone anyone else. And what about Roman and the children?"

"They love mountains. Live good. Cheap."

For a wild second Nora considered it. How good it would be to have them nearby. Friendly faces and support.

"I wish I could," she replied, looking into Trude's disappointed face.

Trude nodded. "I know. I had to try, though."

Nora hugged Trude in a rush. Trude faltered, standing stiff in awkwardness. Nora felt awkward too at this rare show of physical contact. Suddenly, however, Trude responded and Nora felt true affection in the Polish woman's bear hug.

"You're the only family I've got left," Nora whispered.

"You take care of yourself, hear?" Trude said, pulling back and revealing a flash of tears. "Here. Piroshki for the car. I make them. You be sure to eat them."

"I will, I will." Nora laughed, moving back.

She picked up the suitcase. It was unusually heavy. With his papers and notes, Nora was taking Mike with her.

"I will carry for you," Trude said.

"No," Nora replied. "I have to carry this."

She took one last look at the apartment. The sun was setting now and poured in through the slats of blinds, creating vertical shadows across the parquet. Her luxury apartment never looked more the prison it had been for years.

"Don't trust anyone." Mike's last words to her sounded again in her head.

"I don't," she said to the ghost. Nora turned away, her shoulders drooping with the weight of Mike's message.

"I'll never trust anyone again."

3

___

NORA PAID THE TOLL and asked for a receipt.

Now that she was off the Thruway, she felt New York was truly behind her. In her head, she knew that a place could not make someone happy or unhappy, rather the life one led there. But her heart didn't buy it. In her heart, she believed she'd be happier once she crossed the Vermont border.

The small white sign with green lettering welcomed her to the Green Mountain State. Speeding by at fifty miles per hour she felt a rush of exhilaration as she crossed the line. "Whoopee!" she called aloud as she rolled down the window and stuck her nose out like any perk-eared dog. Fresh cool air gushed in. She inhaled deeply. Vermont did feel better. The mountains were prettier, the grass was greener, and, hot dog—she was headed home.

The Volvo hummed along on the state highway, past small towns with red general stores and lone gas stations that boasted two pumps. Nora paid attention to all the markers now; it had been a while since she'd traveled these roads. She chewed her lip as she navigated the journey. Did she turn left at this blinking light? Which way did she veer when the road split by the green warehouse?

Following both memory and instinct, she guided the car toward the small mountain she called home. A brook ambled over white rocks along the side of the road, black-and-white cows chewed lazily in the pastures. She passed Ed's syrup stand, rounded a steep turn, and there it was. She recognized it immediately. Why had she thought she wouldn't?

Her mountain. The center of the small tree-covered mountain sagged like a saddle on an old horse. A first memory flashed.

"Let's hike to the saddle," Mike said. He already had his boots on, a picnic basket packed with crusty bread, strong-smelling cheese, and a cold bottle of white wine, and in his arm he carried a red-and-black wool blanket. His eyes flashed in invitation.

Nora grabbed a sweater and Mike. "Let's go."

The saddle was a long hike up, across steep terrain, over marble and granite boulders, and through muddy valleys. But once there the grass was as soft as baby hair. Wild berries flourished and the sun shone freely up where the trees didn't grow. It was a favorite resting place of deer. A heavenly spot—divine for lovemaking.

Nora tightened her fingers on the steering wheel. "Mike, Mike," she murmured. She was afraid of her grief and the unexpected turns it took. Was it a good idea to come back here of all places? The one place they had been happy.

The road curved and led into the neighboring town, really just one long road between Victorian farmhouses that were now antiques stores and bed-and-breakfasts, a needlepoint shop, the post office, a hardware store, a pizza parlor, and, busiest of all, the corner grocery. Nora pulled in to pick up some supplies.

The Long Road Home

The small store was in fact grocery, liquor store, bookstore, and video rental shop all rolled into one confined space. The front four-square windows were plastered with local notices: the firemen were having a water show in Rutland on Saturday, Wild Bird Weekend brought a special seed sale, and a brightly colored banner invited everyone to a contra dance in October. Baskets of apples, squash, and mums bordered the store's narrow entry. Nora selected two apples and squeezed in past the baskets.

Inside, the small store was dimly lit and the precious floor space was crammed with more baskets filled with corn, potatoes, and onions. In the front of the store, the few shelves were crammed with dry goods, and in the rear of the store stood rows and rows of dusty alcohol bottles. Nora wrinkled her nose as dust tickled it. She wouldn't find everything she needed here, but she'd find enough to make do. The wooden floors creaked as she crossed them but they were well swept. A plastic mat covered the grayed wooden counter, and on it sat a shiny nickel-plated cash register with the drawer half open.

"Hello," Nora chirped.

The old woman behind the counter gummed her lips a moment and gave Nora a thorough once-over. "'Lo," she replied.

The woman was no one Nora had ever seen before. It appeared no more talk was coming, thank heavens. Nora wasn't up to questions yet. She cut a swath through the store, grabbing quickly. Coffee, eggs, milk, bread, and she was done.

"Thank you. Bye."

"Yeh-up."

If she shopped there daily for the next ten years, Nora doubted she'd ever get more of a response than that. Vermonters weren't a chatty group.

At last she made the final turn by the marshy pond. The car veered off the paved road and rumbled along a dirt town road, not fit for tourists. She stretched out her cramped legs and arms and slowed to a crawl. The meadows were on a higher plain than the road and were separated by a low stone fence bordered by pine, maple, and apple trees. She began searching for something—a barn, a tree, a pond—anything familiar.

She passed the Johnston house, her nearest neighbors. The small cape with pale green asphalt siding appeared to be slipping down. Its sills were sloped, the front porch leaned, and there was chokecherry now where there used to be flowers.

The house was close to the road but she passed without stopping. She was too near her final destination to stop for hellos. The vista opened up and she smiled seeing Skeleton Tree Pond, acres of fresh spring water so cold Mike swore it could stop the heart. She felt the first prickle of excitement along her neck.

The bumpy road curved around the lower barn where sheep stood in small clusters. In the field beyond, fifty, maybe more, lazily chewed in the sun. They raised their white faces as she passed, ears pricked. Nora smiled again, feeling an instant bond with the gentle creatures.

She was on her own land now. Four hundred acres, most of them vertical, all of them green. She was surrounded by green, interspersed now with the oranges, reds, and golds of an early fall. A few yards ahead she spotted the pair of marble monoliths that signaled the foot of her private road. The stones blended in with its surroundings, so only a careful eye could spot the entry. Mike had wanted to build an imposing brick gate, but Nora had persuaded him that, at least in Vermont, nature should prevail.

She made the turn and slowed to a stop. Her road curved gracefully and disappeared behind a small hill, but Nora wasn't fooled. She knew that beyond that hill the pastoral road made the grand prix seem like child's play. It turned and twisted sharply and inclined straight up, making it a hair-raising trip in spots where the gravel gave way to dirt.

The unanswered question was: How was the road? Did Seth put down the gravel? Did the rain wash out gullies so deep a tire could get caught? Why hadn't she stopped at the Johnstons'? Even now she could back up and travel back down the road.

Something inside of her resisted. A new independence told her to handle it herself. She was tired of asking for help. Sooner or later she'd have to deal with this road and sooner came now.

Gear in first, she let the clutch up and pressed the accelerator. On up she went, past the hill, past berry bushes long since picked clean by the birds, around big rocks that had lost hold and fallen to the road. Leaf-laden branches arched low, brushing the windshield as she passed and giving off an eerie squeak. Then the road began to incline steeply and the gravel bed grew thin. Nora pressed the accelerator a tad, scuttled up twenty yards and then felt the wheels slip.

Her knuckles whitened on the steering wheel. Her foot pressed the accelerator, yet her car slid backward down the steep dirt road. Pushing the pedal to the floor, she leaned far forward and whispered, "Go, go."

The Volvo whined as its wheels dug to dirt, spitting gravel and swinging its rear across the narrow road like a wild bronco. She headed straight for the steep bank. Nora slammed on the brakes.

Nausea swept over her as she shifted her gaze from the steep road ahead to the shallow cliff beside her. Unable to move forward, terrified to slip backward, she was in limbo. "What do I do? What do I do?" she muttered in a litany as she laid her head against the wheel.

There was no reply. She was very alone. In the density of the forest surrounding her she sensed the presence of animals—crouched and watching. Squirrels, deer, porcupines, bears, and scores of others she couldn't even identify. She heard every snap of a branch in the uneasy quiet. Each call of a wild bird seemed to say, "Go away. You don't belong here."

"Damn you, Mike!" she swore as she hit the steering wheel with her fist. A September wind caught the curse and carried it across the Vermont mountains. The echo diminished into a menacing breeze that floated through the car like the whisper of a ghost. She shuddered and closed her eyes.

Why curse Mike? It was childish—and too late. She got out a short laugh. Mike never got stuck here. He had skidded on this same road, but instead of cowering as she was, he'd grind into first gear and will that heap of metal up the mountain. Only once he didn't make it, and that was when the snow was so deep even the tractor couldn't get up to the house. Nonetheless, he had sold the car as worthless.

"Well, there's no Mike now," she blurted out as she raised her head. "This is it. Nora MacKenzie. Your first test. There's no turning back. Home is ahead."

She let out a ragged breath as reason took over. With a thrust of determination, she shifted into first then slowly, with ease, let out the clutch.

"Come on, you hunk o' junk," she said. The tires spun, whined, and slipped back a few inches. Nora bit her lip and fought the temptation to hit the gas. Instead, she yanked the wheels away from a dirt patch. With a jerk, the tires caught on the firm roadbed and lurched forward.

"Go, go, go," she crooned as the metal beast struggled up the steep incline and slowly rounded the final curve.

The Long Road Home

With the care of a captain in shallow waters, she turned the wheels away from the loose patches of gravel and rode the crest. At last, the high-pitched drone of the engine lowered as the incline flattened and she emerged from the tunnellike foliage into the light of a clearing. She hooted triumphantly.

Ahead, perched high on her mountain overlooking the Vermont mountain ranges, was a sunlit terrace. And standing proudly in its center was her house. Nora's heart swelled when she spied the peak of the redwood and brick structure looming high above the purple heather. Next appeared the large, angular windows divided by a mammoth beam and lastly, the broad wooden deck that stretched like a smile across the breadth of the house. Nora couldn't help smiling in return.

Pulling up in front, she danced her fingers along the wheel. She couldn't wait to get out of the car. She yanked on the brake and scrambled out. The air was cooler that high up and its pine-scented breezes caressed her cheeks. She inhaled deeply, tasting its sweetness. Sporting a triumphant grin, she stretched her arms wide to take into her soul the majestic Vermont mountain range, blanketed now in a homey patchwork quilt of greens, purples, reds, and oranges.

Her hands might be shaky, she thought, and maybe her knees were wobbly. So what if she didn't know what her next step would be. She felt exultant. She had made it to the top! In an inspired rush, she tugged the gold band off her left finger and threw it with desperate force into the horizon.

"I'm home!" she cried to the mountains, bringing her arms around her chest in a bear hug. The echo bounced back to her, repeating "home, home, home," in reassuring repetition.

From above came a deep, resonant response.

"Looking for someone?"

To Nora, it was thunder in the mountains. Fear struck her marrow like a lightning bolt. She jerked her head toward the second-story deck where a man, dressed only in a pair of worn, unbuttoned jeans, towered above her. His eyes glared with suspicion from under a towel as he rubbed his wet hair. Across his chest, droplets of water cascaded like a waterfall down a mountainside.

Questions froze in her throat. Suddenly her mountain seemed very small and she felt trapped under the harsh gaze of the man on the deck above her. He was a stranger—an intruder. She was alone and vulnerable. She had to get out and get out fast. Spinning on her heel, Nora lunged for the car door.

"Hey! You! Stop!" shouted the man as he threw off the towel and pounded down the stairs.

A scream caught in her throat as Nora leaped into the Volvo and punched down the door lock just as the man grabbed the handle. He shook the handle, cursing.

"Look, lady," he shouted, dipping his head to peer in. Water dripped from his dark blond hair down his broken nose. On either side, his eyes blazed. She froze as would a deer in a flash of light. Only when he pressed hands as large as bear paws across her windshield did she bolt upright and insert her keys.

"Let go, mister," she shouted. He didn't. Nora started the engine yelling, "I'm warning you."

"And I'm warning you."

With shaky hands, Nora rammed the gearshift and roared into reverse, sending the man and gravel flying. Again, she slipped into first, jerked the wheel around and hit the gas. From the corner of her eye she saw him leap out of the way of the moving car, then heard him pound the rear in frustration. Nora cringed but kept her eyes on the winding drive ahead. She knew she was going too fast as she neared the first sharp curve and hit the brakes. They locked, sending the car skidding across the gravel straight toward the steep bank. She corrected the steering wheel, but the wheels had locked. She'd lost control. Her muscles tensed, her mouth opened, and time stood still. Nora was filled with the sickening knowledge that she was going to crash.

She covered her head as she hit the tree.

He heard the crash as he reached the door of the house.

"Aw, damn," he muttered, swinging wide the door and dashing inside. Within seconds, he had grabbed his keys and jacket and was rushing toward his Jeep, buttoning his pants along the way. The gravel dug into his bare feet, but he ran without pause to the car, hit the accelerator, and sped down the road. After the first curve he spotted the blue Volvo in the ditch and sucked in his breath. The car lay buried under a broken limb and its foliage. He saw again the New York license plates.

With dread, he ran to the driver's seat and peered in through the broken glass. The woman lay crumpled against the steering wheel. Jiggling the handle of the locked door, he cursed again. The passenger door was blocked by a heavy limb. He'd have to move it but wasn't sure he could. Focusing on the limb, he grabbed it and heaved the limb away from the door, all the while still cursing the woman for showing up here at all. He yanked open the crumpled door and crawled in beside her.

She was beautiful. It was one of those futile thoughts that pop into one's mind at the wrong time. Shaking his head, he reached to pick up her wrist. It was thin and fragile, like the wing of a wounded sparrow. He laid his own large, callused fingers upon her pulse. Nothing had ever felt so good as that steady beat. The stranger was now a real person.

"Just hang on, little bird," he murmured. "I'll get you out of here." But how? Advice he had once heard nagged him:

Never move an accident victim—something about broken bones. Well, he thought as he shifted his weight, there was only one way to find out. Carefully lifting her head, he cradled her against his shoulder. Her blond hair felt soft against his bare chest, making him uncomfortable touching her. His hands clenched and unclenched in indecision.

"This is ridiculous," he said aloud. There was nothing to do but be professional and quick. He gingerly lifted her suede jacket and slipped his hand under the fabric. His fingers palpated her neck, shoulders, and traveled down her spine. Then, being exceedingly careful not to touch her breasts, he slipped his hand across her ribs. She really was like a sparrow, all bones and feathers. And as far as he could tell, the bones were unbroken.

His whistle of relief filled the crushed compartment. The rest he could handle. He carried the woman to his Jeep as gently as he would a handful of fresh raspberries. Resting her head on his lap, he frowned when he saw the purple swelling of the bruise on her head. He'd have to get her to a doctor, but her crashed-up Volvo blocked his path down the road. He'd better call Seth.

The Jeep's gears screamed as he backed up the mountain in reverse, but still she didn't awaken. He carried the petite woman into the house, thinking as he did that he'd carried sacks of grain that weighed more than she did. Without a second thought, he took her up to the master bedroom. It was quiet, private, and somehow appropriate. Balancing her against his knee, he pushed back the piles of quilts and blankets, releasing a heavy scent of mothballs. Carefully, he laid her upon the clean sheets, then as carefully, removed her fine leather shoes and covered her with a thick down coverlet.

The air was getting crisp as night set in and her hands were cold in his warmer ones. As he dialed the farm's caretaker, his free hand rubbed hers softly, noting that her delicate fingers were void of the large, vulgar rings he despised. In fact, there was no wedding ring. That struck him as odd. She looked like the type a man would marry. How old could she be, he wondered? Twenty-five, thirty? Probably divorced—then again, maybe not.

He shook the idle thoughts from his head as Seth Johnston answered the phone. In few words the old man agreed to have the Volvo moved and help sent to the house. Talk was cheap and time expensive on the farm, and Seth liked to economize. They both preferred it that way.

After laying down the phone, he covered the woman with another blanket and tucked it under her softly rounded chin. His hand moved to her cheek and patted it, then brushed a few hairs from the purple lump on her forehead.

Staring at her face he was once again struck by her waiflike beauty. Hers was not a voluptuous appeal. Her face and golden hair were delicate, like an angel's, making the ugly bruise swelling on her forehead menacing. There lay the truth of it, he thought with a frown. Her business here made her more a devil than an angel. A skinny runt of a devil.

The woman's clothes, though of fine quality, were baggy and hung loose on her bony frame. Her cheeks were gaunt and her skin color was more pale than fair. She looked as if she needed a good meal.

He sighed. He had expected a Philip Marlowe type to track him down. Leave it to Agatha to send a woman.

"Lady, lady, lady," he whispered. "Just look how your snooping has hurt us both."

He ran his hand through his hair. The evidence was clear: New York plates, expensive clothes, patrician features. He recognized the style, he could almost give the address. And her money and status made it a sure bet she knew who he was.

"Karma," he said with resignation. He could only accept it and pack. As soon as she was in good hands, he'd slip away.

From outside, the sound of whining engines and crunching gravel alerted him to Seth's arrival. He reluctantly left the woman's side to throw on a sweater and greet his boss.

Seth squeezed his great girth out from behind the wheel of his pickup truck. He looked as weathered by time and mileage as the Ford and about as rusty. In the cab sat two children, grandchildren from a marriage gone bad. Following as usual, his sons drive up in the old green Impala. He expected the whole family. This was exciting business up here in the mountains.

Seth stretched out a well-callused hand. "You be havin' friends up at the big house now, Charley?" he asked with a grin that revealed many missing teeth.

C.W. knew it was more than a friendly inquiry. Seth shared the flock and used MacKenzie's land in exchange for keeping an eye on it and the house.

"No, sir, I am not," he answered firmly. "I've never laid eyes on her before. I was in the shower when I heard the car pull up. When I tried to talk to her she sped down the mountain like a demon. Her plates are from New York."

Seth's eyes narrowed. "New York, you say?" He turned to his son. "That right, Frank?"

"Yeh-up. The city all right. Saw the plates when we moved the car. Never saw that one before, though. You thinkin' it might be one of MacKenzie's?"

"Could be. Come on, Charley, show us where she is. You two young'uns stay out here and out o' trouble. Frank, Junior, Esther, come on."

The two tall and lanky men strode with a gait so loose and close their shoulders bumped in a brotherly camaraderie. Even in their mid-twenties, they resembled lion cubs, swiping and jabbing with a youthful exuberance. They approached the house as they did everything—together.

C.W. smiled a brief greeting, then turned to Seth's eldest daughter. Esther, one of Vermont's persistent flower children, covered her long, lean body with patched jeans and a flowered shirt. At her side she carried a large straw bag. Knowing Esther, he imagined it carried a practical, well-thought-out first-aid kit.

As she passed, Esther smiled from under her floppy straw hat. As always, C.W. had to search for signs of her twenty-six years. The soft lines at the corners of her eyes accentuated her sharp mind; the thin frown lines at her mouth revealed the degree of her discontent.

He led them to the master bedroom, then stepped aside while Seth and his family filled the room. In a moment he heard them utter as one, "It's Nora!"

C.W. stood straighter and walked closer. "You know her?"

Seth turned to face him, his eyes serious. "You did right by putting her in here. This be her room...her house."

C.W.'s eyes widened. She wasn't an investigator? He looked at the woman again. Mrs. MacKenzie? She seemed too young and innocent to be the flamboyant Michael MacKenzie's wife. Realization set in.

"I thought you said they never came up here."

"They don't. Her not once in three years," Seth responded.

C.W. held his arms akimbo and his chin low to conceal his shocked expression. The Big Mac's widow. Here. He felt like he'd been punched. He studied the thin, pitiful-looking woman in the bed and hardened his heart. What the bloody hell?

He searched Nora's pale white profile. No doubt she was as cold-hearted and fast-fisted as her husband. What other kind of woman would marry Mike MacKenzie?

4

—

"SHE'S COMING AROUND, PA," called Esther from Nora's bedside.

Nora blinked once, lazily, then again as her eyes grew accustomed to the dim light. Through the lifting fog, she saw a woman's face peer into her own.

"Esther?" Nora asked in a feeble voice.

"That's me, Mrs. MacKenzie," Esther replied in the clipped, practical voice that Nora remembered. "You got yourself a nasty bump. Here, let's put some ice on it."

Nora winced as a bag of ice was plopped on her head and a thermometer was stuck in her mouth. "Seth? Seth Johnston, is that you?" she asked, removing the thermometer and holding out a hand.

"Yeh-up," he drawled as he ambled to her bedside with a rocking gait.

Nora was disturbed to see him so fat now that he panted with the effort. The only things thin about Seth were his hair and his clothes, and the latter were faded as well.

"Nice to have you back again, missus," he said, taking her hand. "Long time."

"Too long," she responded with a weak smile.

"Yeh-up." He nodded, releasing her hand. "Long time." He nodded again and shifted his eyes.

Stepping forward, Esther returned the thermometer to Nora's mouth with authority. "What the blazes sent you tearing down the mountain that way?"

"I believe I did," came a reply from the corner.

Startled, Nora followed the bass voice to the far corner of the room. A tall broad silhouette was outlined in the shadows. She slowly raised herself to her elbows, squinting in the poor light.

"And who are you?" she mumbled with as much authority as she could muster with a thermometer in her mouth.

He slowly straightened, and after a palpable pause, strode into the light. Her hand rose to her throat. It was the stranger from the deck.

"You!" she whispered.

He didn't respond, but his mouth set in a grim line. He stood before the bed, watching her every reaction in tense silence, before quietly asking, "You don't know me, Mrs. MacKenzie?"

The question was more of a challenge. She narrowed her eyes and searched the tall man in tight jeans and a plaid shirt. With his dark blond hair and hard, chiseled features, he had the kind of masculine good looks that a woman would remember. Yet standing next to Junior and Frank, he did not emit the conceit or pride that she found so offensive in attractive men. In fact, he appeared distinctly uncomfortable with her study.

"No," she replied, firmly removing the dread thermometer

and returning it to Esther. "I'm quite sure we've never met. Should we have?"

He stepped back a pace, shaking his head no. But not before she detected a distinct smile of relief. A shiver of suspicion ran down her spine. Nora quickly straightened, but the room spun, forcing her back on her pillows with a groan.

The man was suddenly at Nora's side.

"The lady needs to see a doctor. No offense, Es."

"None taken, C.W. But *there's* no doc to call."

"Well, now," interrupted Seth. "There's that New York doctor what stays in Middleton Springs. Comes up every fall for the hunting season. Redman…Red somethin' or other."

"Redden," Nora responded softly behind closed lids. "I know him. His number should be by the phone."

"A New York doctor?" C.W. asked. "Isn't there anyone local we can call?"

"No," Nora said cautiously, surprised by his antagonism. "He's our physician of choice. He'll come." She didn't add that he'd better come. Mike had given Dr. Redden full rein of their four hundred acres to hunt every fall for years, and it was time to call in a favor.

At a nod from her father, Esther headed out of the room.

"I'll give him a call, C.W."

C.W. stood abruptly, his face clouded.

"Do you have objections to calling a New York doctor?" Nora asked. His stance, the authority in his voice, the angle at which he held his head—all held an indefinable air of breeding. Strange in a farmhand, if that was what he was.

"No, why should I?" he replied, his face suddenly impassive. "Call who you like—as long as you call."

"Better watch how you throw your weight around, Charley," said Seth, laughing, "now that it's hunting season. Big bucks are a prime target."

Nora witnessed the affection in C.W.'s glance at Seth. Who was this man, she wondered, who wore his sophistication as comfortably as his work clothes?

"Just who are you and what is your name, anyway?" she asked. "C.W. or Charley?"

His smile revealed deep dimples that stretched from the corners of his mouth to the curve of his chiseled chin. "Only Seth gets away with calling me Charley."

"Never could take to calling a man by letters," Seth muttered.

"Very well, C.W.," she continued, her smile disappearing. "Would you mind telling me what your full name is and what you were doing showering in my house?"

Rather than being put off by her tone, he seemed pleased by it. He smiled wryly and put his hands on his hips. "My name is Walker, Charles Walker. I work here as an extra hand. Part of my arrangement was to stay in this house. I'm sorry if I frightened you. You see, I didn't expect you."

Nora sought confirmation from Seth, who nodded and stepped forward. "That's right. Hired him back in January to help with the sugaring and the lambing."

She returned her gaze to the tall man, then self-consciously realized it was he who was covertly assessing her every reaction.

"I'm sorry about the confusion, Mrs. MacKenzie," C.W. said, looking down at his feet. When he raised his eyes again, they held a teasing light. "I didn't mean to send you careening down the mountain."

Nora flushed and her voice rose a note. "Mr. Walker, I'm not accustomed to half-naked men running out of my house and trying to bully me out of my car!"

He made no reply. Now she read remorse, and perhaps even guilt, in his eyes. This fencing was getting her nowhere.

"It wasn't entirely your fault, Mr. Walker," she admitted with an exhausted wave of her hand. "I didn't expect you either. It was a comedy of errors."

"With a near tragic ending. Nonetheless, I apologize."

Something in his tone, sincerity perhaps, caused her to look back his way. With his hands in his hip pockets and his head tucked low, she wondered how she'd ever been afraid of him. He almost smiled at her, and she returned a half smile.

"I assume you'll be staying here for a while," he said, straightening his shoulders. "I'll get my things together immediately and find another place to stay."

"Wait, Mr. Walker. Things are going too fast." She closed her eyes and rubbed her temples. He saw the wariness slip from her face like a mask removed.

"Such confusion," she said, letting her hands fall on the bed. "I should have called—I usually do. Things have been a bit…hurried. I didn't have you down on my guest calendar and assumed the house would be empty."

"Right peculiar it is," said Seth. "I wrote them lawyers about it. But I never did hear nothing back from them." He didn't bother to conceal his smile as he scratched his belly. "I figure them fellas didn't put Charley here on that guest calendar of yours."

Nora sat still in the bed. They were laughing at her, lying there with a ridiculous lump on her head. Ralph Bellows had failed her again. Worse thing was, nothing she could say could alter their opinion. Only actions counted for much up here.

"Seth," she began, "from now on nothing, absolutely nothing, goes to the lawyers. Everything goes straight to me." The skepticism in Seth's eyes hurt.

He ambled up to her bed and removed his green cap with *John Deere* emblazoned across it. His oil-stained fingerprints were visible on the visor as he held the cap before him.

"You aim to keep the farm?" he asked with characteristic bluntness.

"But of course," she replied with emphasis. "I plan to live here. Permanently." She ventured a small smile. "I guess that eliminates my guest calendar."

No one laughed. Seth shifted his weight and shook his head.

"Don't know but you're up to it here alone," he began slowly. "Snow comes and you'll get stuck up here for days before we can dig you out. Power quits too, every bad storm." Rubbing his chin he muttered, "Nope. This house is just too high up for real living. Leastwhiles in Vermont winters." He snapped his cap back on his head. "You best know what you're getting into."

"I agree with Seth," C.W. added. "This is no place for you to live alone. It's brutal. Nobody has the time to keep checking up on you."

"I wasn't aware that I asked," she snapped back.

While outwardly she knew she appeared hard-boiled, inwardly she was thin-shelled. With no family to fall back on, Nora was truly alone. Only her optimism and blind faith spurred her hope that she could form new roots here on the farm.

"I'll manage, Seth," she said, bolstering herself up on the pillows and forcing a smile. "I know I can count on you for advice on how to winterize this place. And if Frank and Junior need the work, I'd like to hire them and get started right away. And of course, Esther," she added as Esther returned to the room.

Nora pushed higher in the bed.

"This is no longer a vacation home. It is home. My home." Nora's chest swelled. At that moment, she felt she could really do it.

"Well," Seth answered with a grunt. "It won't be any vacation, that's for sure. But it's plain you got your mind set. The boys and I will look around and see what's got to get done before snow sets in. But it won't be cheap. It's a big house."

Nora paled. "I understand. But do keep a tight rein on the budget. Nothing fancy."

C.W. looked at her askance.

Nora turned to face him squarely. "And you, Mr. Walker. What are your plans?" Her voice was as cool as the autumn air.

C.W. shook his head. It seemed to her he would laugh out loud.

"My plan, Mrs. MacKenzie," he replied in a controlled voice, "is to honor my contract and finish out this lambing. Then I'll pack and be out of here by October's end." He glanced at Seth for confirmation.

C.W.'s eyes took her measure and she felt she had come up lacking.

"My contract does not stipulate that I work on your house for this...urge of yours to live off the fat of the land. If you get a chill, you can always pack up and jet down to Palm Beach."

Nora dug her nails into her palms. She wanted to scream at him that she wasn't that type at all. That she was scared out of her mind.

Pride held her tongue. She knew that to them, she was a pitiful figure. To them, a woman without a man was sad enough, but one trying to make a life for herself alone in the mountains was an object of ridicule.

Nora took a long breath and willed her hands to relax at her sides. "I see," she replied with a patronizing tone. "Whatever is more convenient for you."

His blue eyes steamed, and by the way he cleared his throat she sensed that he, too, was swallowing his frustration.

"It's clear I can't stay in this house," he continued in a decidedly polite manner. "I'd appreciate being able to sleep in the cabin."

A sound of disbelief came from the corner. Esther was whispering furiously in her father's ear. Seth shrugged and looked away.

"There's not but a potbelly stove in there," Esther cried. "No water, no facilities. You'll freeze your you-know-what off."

"It'll do," he replied, still looking at Nora, "if you'll agree to let me eat breakfast here, do some laundry, and take a shower or two. I'll be discreet."

"Yes, I think that would be fine, Mr. Walker. Until October's end, that is."

"I think you're crazy," said Esther. "Or just muleheaded." She scowled. "Shoot, I'll fix up the cabin for you. But when that frost hits, you'll be checking to see just what Jack nipped."

Esther blushed as the men snickered.

"You quit it, you guys," Esther barked.

C.W. reached out and gave her back a friendly pat. "Thanks, Es. I do believe your temper will keep us all warm this fall."

Nora was quick to notice the commiserating glance Esther offered him. Once again, C.W. caught Nora staring at him, and a veil of distrust cloaked his features.

"I'll check on the car," C.W. called over his shoulder as he headed for the door.

Nora watched his retreating back in silence then glanced from the empty doorway to Seth, to Esther, then back to Seth with her eyebrows raised in question.

"That Charley don't jaw much," said Seth. "Keeps to himself. But he's a good man. Best I ever hired."

"Where's he from?" Nora asked.

"The east. Got references from some horse farm. Did some managing, not much handling of sheep. He's a quick learner, though."

"It's true. He's always got his nose in some sheep or farm book," added Esther. "I like him. So do Frank and Junior. Thought they'd be jealous, the way C.W.'s taking over and all, but I guess it's all in the way it's done." The look she gave Nora spoke plainly of how poor a showing she'd offered so far.

Seth's persistent nods and occasional "yeh-ups" confirmed that Mr. Charles Walker had passed the stringent acceptance test of Vermonters. Nora was impressed.

"Seth," Nora began, looking into the caretaker's wizened face, "I have to get a handle on the finances of this farm right away. Budgets, expenses, and the lot. When can we meet?"

Seth scratched his head. "Any time, as long as you meet with Charley."

"Mr. Walker?"

"Yep. Charley's the man for the numbers." He jawed his gums a moment then added, "Sure helps me out, I can tell you. Truth is, he's so good I just let him handle the whole job now. And he's teachin' my Frank the tricks, too." He hitched his pants. "If you got any questions about budget, missus, Charley's the man to ask."

Nora did not respond. She faced the unpleasant prospect of having to work closely with the stone-faced, dispassionate, opinionated Mr. Walker.

"Nothin' worth doin' around here," Seth concluded, tugging at his visor. "I'll be joining C.W. at the barn. Esther, you wait till this Doc Redman shows up."

"Sure, Pa," Esther muttered.

Seth left, leaving the two women in an awkward silence. Nora had never known Esther very well. Unlike the other Johnstons, she had always kept her distance. Esther was tall, angular, and with her penetrating green eyes, striking. She wasn't a big woman, just strong boned, and Esther never hunched her shoulders, as so many other tall women did. The effect was one of confidence, and it was imposing. Nora remembered stories about Esther, the way she'd venture off into the mountains alone.

"I'll go make you some tea," said Esther in her husky voice. "Don't fall asleep, now. You might have a concussion or something."

"No, I won't."

Nora viewed the closing door with relief. Her triumphant return had turned into an embarrassing disaster. Instead of charging in and taking over, here she was, lying in bed with a goose egg on her head. Life just wasn't fair. Tomorrow, she'd try again, Nora vowed, burrowing under the blankets. Tomorrow, she'd do better.

The mountain of blankets formed a barrier between herself and the rest of the world. She sank deeper into their warmth. Nora turned on her side and watched, transfixed, as a spider carefully spun its web in the dusty corner.

To each creature a home, she thought with hope.

5

IN THE LOWER BARN, C.W. was working up a sweat. He loved to throw hay. It was hard, backbreaking work that brought his muscles to the point of pure pain. C.W. threw at a steady pace, humming a soundless tune in his head, beating the rhythm of his pitches with grunts. Poke, lift, pitch. Down, up, and out. Down, up, and out. Over and over. Faster and faster. His biceps began to tremble, and sweat beaded his brow and pooled under his arms. He needed to work hard now. This was the one way he could blot out the questions that haunted him.

Today, however, the questions kept coming. Why was MacKenzie's widow here now? He'd thought he found the perfect haven in which to hide while he redirected his life. Seth had confirmed that the MacKenzies never came here. What was she up to? And why was MacKenzie's widow worried about old Seth's house budget? He was right about her, he realized with distaste. She'd be cheap with good, honest people and end up using them, just like her husband did.

From the corner of his eye he saw a figure move near the

barn's entry. C.W. groaned, threw a final forkful of hay, and stopped to catch his breath. Standing still now, his muscles throbbed so; he could hear the beat of it in his brain. After wiping his brow with his dusty shirtsleeve he looked over his shoulder toward the figure by the door.

Seth was rubbing his jaw as if he had a bad itch, and when he wasn't rubbing, he was hitching his pants and clearing his throat. C.W. coughed, set down his pitchfork, and met Seth's gaze. There was no delaying it. Seth wanted to talk.

"Hey, Seth," he called, slipping easily into the vernacular. He walked directly over to the old man, his long legs crossing the barn quickly.

"Barn looks good," Seth said. His smile was brief.

C.W. was always stunned to note how many of Seth's teeth were missing. "Thanks."

"Yeh-up. Can't work a farm when the tools are rusted."

"Nope," C.W. replied. He enjoyed giving the short rejoinders as much as Seth did hearing them. Seth started at hitching his pants again.

"Something I can do for you, Seth?"

Seth looked off at the ewes awhile. "You were acting strange up there with the missus," Seth said at last.

Here we go, thought C.W. "How so?"

"Like you knew her."

C.W. skipped a beat. "Nope. I never met her."

Seth screwed up his eyes.

Cagey old bird, thought C.W. with affection. He held his tongue, however, knowing his silence could outlast even Seth's patience.

"Silence is a wonderful thing, son," Seth said after a spell of watching three hens peck the corn. "But it's a far cry from secrets."

C.W. kicked the dirt and stared at his dusty boot. "I never met her," he said quietly.

Seth nodded, knowing it was the truth.

C.W. ran his hand through his hair with a long sigh.

"Well, I guess I was hard on her for a while there. Skinny New York women have a way of getting on my nerves." He was relieved to hear Seth chuckle. "From what I know of MacKenzie, she's going to be a real pain."

"What you know of MacKenzie?"

Clever man, mused C.W. "I know what I hear. Let's see, from you I heard he was ornery as a mule and late to pay his bills. From the boys I heard he was short on charm and long on demands, and from Esther..." He paused. "I get mixed messages from Esther. I gather she both hates him and, dare I say, admires him?"

Seth rubbed his jaw again. C.W. sensed an untold story there. Seth looked away for a moment, but when he swung his head back, his face flattened to a deadpan.

C.W. went back to his hay. He hadn't thrown more than three forkfuls before he heard Seth's voice again.

"You workin' up a frenzy today," Seth said.

"Lot of delays," he grunted between pitches. "Lot to get done before the sun sets."

"Lot of thinkin', seems to me."

C.W. slowed, stopped, and peered over his shoulder once again. Seth was standing with his hands in his rear pockets and one foot slightly before the other. His eyes were boring into him.

"When a boil starts to fester, it's time to stop everything and clean it. Else it spreads and ruins you. Makes you mean and ugly and you hurt bad all the time."

"Just what is it you think I need to clean out, Seth?"

Seth gummed a bit, holding back. "Reckon you know that

best, son. But I do know that you've been festering for months now and it looks like its comin' to a head. Might be time to tend to it, that's all I'm saying."

A quiet pall settled in the barn. C.W. leaned on his fork while staring at the ewes. They stared right back at him, as though waiting for his response.

C.W. shook his head and dug his fork into the ground. Festering was the word for it. Perhaps it was time to purge. He trusted Seth, both his wisdom and his silence. Running his hand in his hair, he approached Seth.

"I never met Mrs. MacKenzie," he began slowly. "But I knew Mike."

Seth's eyes widened.

"Everyone on Wall Street knew the 'Big Mac.' Mac, the big dealer. Mac, the big spender. There was this inside joke, spawned by jealousy: 'Have you heard today's Mac Deal?'"

He looked up at Seth. The old man wasn't smiling.

"MacKenzie was this ruddy, handsome fellow with a loud, confident laugh and a firm handshake," C.W. continued. "People enjoyed gathering around him and listening to the ribald stories that he told with professional skill. But his eyes were cold and calculating.

"At least he was honest about it," added C.W., kicking the dirt. "Mike wanted to make money. And boy did he. Some called him a genius. Others called him a shark. He had an instinct for the kill and devoured businesses and swallowed profits in huge gulps. And that was business." He shrugged. "I saw him as a highly leveraged con artist."

"I guess I ain't surprised you're some kind of money man, the way you handle numbers. Still, it makes me wonder. I know how MacKenzie left. Why'd you leave?" Seth asked.

C.W. flinched, hearing in his mind the revolver's retort, Mike's blood blurring his vision again. His nose burned.

His breath choked. C.W. wiped a shaky hand across his face, squeezing his eyelids tight. Then, suddenly, the answer came to him. A burst of clarity, after so many months of confusion. C.W. took a great gulp of air before speaking, more to himself than to Seth.

"I don't want a killer instinct."

C.W. didn't move; he stared out of the barn with his hands in his hip pockets, while a muscle twitched in his broad jaw. From across the barn the sound of bleating was a staccato against the quiet dusk. Seth waited, giving C.W. the time he needed to clean out the wound.

After a spell, C.W. blinked, absently stretched his shoulders, and turned toward Seth, a sheepish look on his face.

"I suspect the boil burst."

"Yeh-up." Seth shifted his weight. "Speakin' on MacKenzie. The missus, she ain't nothing like the mister."

"Oh? How is she different?"

"She's a sad one. Used to wonder what made her so. When they first came up here she laughed all the time. Sweet thing, always comin' down to the house with a gift from town or to buy more syrup from us than she'd ever use. They didn't always have that big house. Nope. Used to camp up there before the building set up...and during. Some of them nights was cold enough to freeze water in a pail."

He shook his head and chuckled. "We used to credit it to love. And them being young, 'course. Heard he got pretty rich, real quick. Money can change a man."

C.W. felt a chill. "So I hear."

"Not her though. She was sweet as ever. But she started getting that sad look on her face, like a ewe what's been left behind in the field."

"Then they just stopped coming up?"

"Yeh-up. No word, no nothin'. Just stopped coming." He

shrugged. "I guess that's the way it is with rich folks. Maybe they just get bored. Still…" Seth scratched his belly then his head, ending the pause with a slap of his cap against his thigh.

"This still be her place and she's a nice lady."

"I understand, Seth."

"Figured you would. Well, better get down to dinner before Esther starts to calling. Lord, how that woman can holler."

C.W. walked over to the hay pile and resumed a steady rhythm of throwing hay.

Seth slipped his hat on, paused, then added, "If you feel like jawin' a bit more, you know where to find me."

C.W. stopped and faced the old man. His chest swelled.

"Thanks, Seth. I believe I will."

Seth gummed a bit, then gave a brief wave. Before he left the barn, he threw a final sentence out. It seemed to reach C.W. after Seth had left the barn.

"You're a good boy."

The few words touched C.W. in a deep place that no words had reached in a very long time. It had been a very long time since anyone had called him a good boy. Or since he had thought that of himself.

C.W. sat on a bale of hay and rested his head in his hands.

The blue skies outside the great room were turning misty, signaling the end of her first day home in the mountains. Birds skittered in the sky, frantic at being away from home so close to dark. Nora went out on the deck to watch them arc, swoop, and bank turns, understanding how they felt. The warm day was becoming cool night. The sweet day songs had ceased; only the nighthawk, with its long pointed wings, kept up its nasal *peent, peent*. From the north, a wind was picking up and carrying off the first of an army of leaves. In the air, Nora could taste sweet rain.

She wrapped her arms around her shoulders. She should go in, but the cloud mist on her face refreshed her. So she stood out on the deck awhile longer to stare out at the mountains, dark purple now under lowering clouds. The clouds would soon swallow the house. Thunder rumbled in the valley.

"I'm safe now," she called back to the nighthawk. "I'm already home."

Speak them she might, she didn't feel the words in the red hush of dusk. As she stood alone in her large, unfinished, mountain home, she thought if this were a nest, she'd be wildly searching for twigs, twine, and mud to patch together a safe haven against the incoming storm. But she was a woman, with neither the practical skills nor the money needed to finish the endless projects she'd discovered today.

She had forgotten how much remained to be done. Miles and years had fogged her memory in a romantic vision of country life, leaving unremembered unpleasant details such as unfinished floors and ceilings. Memory was selective, she realized.

Esther, however, had reminded her all too clearly in her forthright manner earlier that afternoon.

They'd been walking up the short flight of stairs to the great room. On this first day, Nora had made overtures to a possible new ally. A friend, a woman friend, would be welcome. So she sought out Esther's opinions on what she'd do in the house, even though she already had her own plan firmly set in her organized mind.

Esther was not easy to approach. She was definite about her opinions and did not couch them with "I think" or with questions. She could be intimidating.

"I don't know what you're going to do all by yourself in this big house," Esther said bluntly.

"There'll be no shortage of projects to keep me busy. Besides, I'm used to living alone."

Esther raised her brows. "Well, it's going to be pretty lonely up here when you get snowed in. All those windows will make it cold too."

"I suppose," Nora replied, scanning the high ceilings and huge plates of glass that surrounded the great room. She'd look into sewing some insulated shades right away.

"All these cement floors," Esther said in the lower levels, "get icy, and there's nothing you can do to warm them up till summer—and that don't come till July."

Nora's gaze swept the pitted gray cement floors of the lower floor. This part of the house was low on her priority list of improvements.

"I'll have to get wood floors put in, someday." In the meantime, she thought to herself, a row of carpet samples might do.

"You'll probably want the upstairs john done too, I suspect."

"Not this year."

"That means you'll have to run down three flights of stairs just to pee? Long trip in the middle of the night." Esther laughed, but at the sight of Nora's face, she cut it short.

It went on like that as they toured the house, and Nora's *to-do* list grew. Esther also pointed out all the fine features of the house, like the redwood beam and deck, the slate roof, the rosy brick, and more copper piping than anyone else in town could dream of putting in.

"Not another house like it in the county," Esther reported.

Nora would have traded grandeur for economy. All she

saw was miles of unfinished floor and ceilings, rafters covered with thick sheets of clear plastic, and trapped under them, the carcasses of hordes of flies, ants, and wasps. There were no doors to the bedrooms, or closets for that matter, and all the walls, from the basement to the top-floor bedroom, were only roughed in. Electrical outlets hung from walls or frames where walls were supposed to be.

Nora's critical eye took in and calculated what it would cost to complete the five-level six-bedroom house. It was enough to weaken her at the knees.

"I'm just hoping to get done what I need to survive during the winter. And at least a door on the bathroom," she said, thinking of C.W.'s showers. "I can hold off for a while on the aesthetics." She didn't mention that once the house was finished, her taxes would also rise.

Esther stood in the center of the great room and craned her neck to view the vaulted ceilings. "Why don't you just finish it all up?" she asked. "This house has been sitting up here untended for years. In fact, every year, right about February when we're feeling pretty tight in our place, we can't help but wonder what you started this big house for, just for you and Mike and no kids."

Nora saw from Esther's expression that she envied the room.

"Why be finicky now?" Esther asked, casting a testy glance Nora's way. "Mike would finish the job in a hurry. First-class all the way."

Nora's back stiffened. "Frankly, I wish he had finished this house. But he didn't." Nora's face was pink with indignation. "Mike left quite a few projects unfinished, and now it's up to me to tidy up. I will get it done when I can, as I can." She tightened her arms across her chest and her voice was more sharp than she had intended.

Esther's eyes narrowed, studying Nora. "You really plan to live here?"

"I do."

"Why?" She shifted her weight. "Why did you move here anyway?"

Nora expelled a long hiss of air. How often was she going to have to defend this decision? She thought a moment, trying to explain the unexplainable.

"I moved here from New York to find something beautiful again. In me and out there." She saw Esther's doubtful expression and coupled her hands in frustration. "I can't put it into words."

"When are you gonna move back?"

Esther scored a direct hit that left Nora speechless. Looking at her, Nora saw the peachy skin and sweet features of a country girl—and the brittle cool of a seasoned New York socialite. Nora's face colored, then flushed as she watched a small smile of victory ease across Esther's face.

"People like you come and go from New York all the time," Esther charged. "Dreaming of the good life. Then you learn that life is life, and up here that life is pretty tough. Next thing you pack up and go. Leavin' us behind." She sniffed and looked away, squinting. When she turned back, her eyes were hard.

"We don't take much to people who come and go."

Nora stared back with eyes wide, affronted by the hostility she did nothing to inspire.

"Speaking of which," Esther swung on her heel and grabbed her bag off the floor, "I gotta go."

Nora counted Esther's steps across the plywood. "It's not like that," Nora called to her back.

Esther turned. "We'll see," she said, then left.

Nora walked out onto the deck to watch Esther as she backed away in her Impala, turned, then drove out of sight.

The Long Road Home

She had remained standing on the deck; she stood there still, recalling Esther's words as the clouds grew heavy in the heavens. Nora gripped the deck rail tightly and fought off the dark, dull cloak of depression.

"Yes, Esther," she spoke aloud in the autumn hush. "We *will* see."

6

MAY JOHNSTON STIRRED UP a potion of baking soda and warm water and set it before Seth, giving it a final spin at the table.

"Drink every drop. You need to burp."

She stood, one hand on the back of Seth's chair, the other on her ample hip, hovering like a hen as her brother grunted and slowly reached out for the brew.

"You know I won't budge till it's gone."

Seth looked up at the formidable figure of his sister. Only her stubbornness was bigger than she was.

"Don't I know it," he muttered. With a sigh of resignation, he took the cup and swallowed it down in three noisy gulps. Wiping his mouth with the back of his hand, he grimaced. Soon after, a loud raucous burp exploded from his girth.

"Good!" exclaimed May. "See, I was right. Nothin' but indigestion."

Seth rubbed his sore chest and smiled weakly. "Yeh-up, that'll be it." Another smaller burp offered him more relief.

May took the chair opposite Seth and slowly lowered herself

into it. She was no stranger to ill health but always seemed to tend to others' ills more than to her own. Diabetes had made her obese, gum disease had taken a number of her front teeth, varicose veins kept her off her feet, and every spring and fall the flowers that she adored kept her sneezing and tearing.

She cast all that off as "her ailments," and nothing more. Just crosses to bear, time off purgatory. Nonetheless, her own ailments kept her on the alert for the ailments of others. No flu bug could creep in her family's house without vitamin C and orange juice being rushed out. If a sore throat stung, a spoonful of honey, some lemon juice, and a splash of whisky flowed.

May had come to Seth's house soon after his wife took sick. She bathed, fed, dressed, and nursed Liza during the final months the doctors let her stay home. Then, after cancer claimed her sister-in-law, May stayed on awhile longer to help her brother and his five motherless children. She rented a trailer, parked it across the road from Seth's house, and in typical fashion, rolled up her sleeves and focused on "the babies."

That was twenty-two years ago. May had long since bought the trailer, planted her beloved perennial bed, and paved a small walkway from her trailer to Seth's back door. Her "babies" were grown up now, and "her ailments" kept her boxed up in the trailer most of the time. Still, she never let an ailment pass by without speaking on it.

"You sure that doctor came up and checked on Mrs. Mac-Kenzie?" she asked Seth.

"Yeh-up. Saw his car come and go."

"How big did you say that lump was?"

Seth offered as detailed a description as he could between burps, knowing his sister would settle for nothing less.

"Strange, her coming back here. Thought for sure they'd

put that land up for sale once he died. The Vermont Land Trust already made inquiries, you know. Nice piece a land. You sure she ain't selling?"

"Didn't sound like it. She wants to live here, so she says."

"Live in that big, unfinished house all alone? Without help?" Her meaty hand slapped the table. "That's just crazy."

"Don't I know it. Told her so but she's got her mind set. Me and the boys are gonna work on the house. They can use the work. Lamb prices are down again."

"I just hope she don't end up breakin' up the land into ten-acre parcels and selling them off. Like Widow Nealy's done." May made loud clucking noises. "Leaving her kids with nothin'."

"The widow's gonna be lonely someday…real lonely."

"MacKenzie's got some beauty views. Them out o' towners like the views."

"Like I said, she ain't selling. Not right away anyway. She's a funny thing. Stick-to kinda person. Remember how she planted all them blueberry bushes on the slope, then came over to get fresh manure?" He chuckled and wiped his mouth.

May laughed and slapped her hand again. "Lord almighty, I do too! I about died when I saw them nylon bags full of manure hangin' off them tiny little bushes. Bowed them right over."

"Deer came and ate them bushes anyway." Seth's eyes twinkled. "But she went and planted another batch."

"Yes, she did," said May, remembering now. "Deer ate them too, though."

Seth scratched his head. "Yeh-up. Hungry, ain't they?"

May picked at a muffin, gummed it awhile, then sneaked a quick glance at her brother. He seemed comfortable enough now that the burping stopped. She decided to venture a new topic.

"How'd Esther take Mrs. MacKenzie coming back?"

Seth's face pinched and he drummed his fingers a moment. Then his eyes met May's. They spoke in a silent code established early in childhood and nurtured over fifty years of devotion. May interpreted his pain, his worry, and his hesitancy to discuss the subject.

Seth knew she understood. May was a good listener and an even better observer.

"She's up there now," Seth finally muttered. "I guess she's all right."

"Don't be so sure, Seth. Esther's all bark and no bite. She may have a hard time seeing Nora MacKenzie move in next door. She'll have to work with her every day, too."

"As ye sow, so shall ye reap." Seth's mouth was set in a hard line.

"That'll be the day I listen to a heathen preach the Bible at me!"

"Who you callin' a heathen, heathen?"

May cackled loud and hearty. Neither one of them went to church, but they each considered the other the most honest, loving Christian they'd ever known.

"Well then," May said, pushing back her chair and hoisting her largesse out of it. She, too, panted with the effort and her legs started to throb from sitting still too long. "Ain't nothing left to do but go up and see the missus for myself. Check on her ailment. Sweet little thing, up in that big house by herself. Just hope she don't plant no more blueberries. Don't know I can stand the smell!"

May rolled up the mountain in her burgundy Buick. When May turned fifty, she treated herself to her first luxury, an "almost new" new car. It was plush: wide bodied, a cushy interior, air conditioning—the works. She even got one of those vanity mirrors, though she never used it. Today, eight years later, her beloved auto had spots of rust and a crumpled left fender from when she slid on the ice and bumped a tree. These she considered her car's mere ailments. Like her, the burgundy Buick ran rough but reliable and only clocked in at 49,241 miles.

She spotted Esther barreling toward her down the back road with dust flying at the wheels. May lay on a honk that brought Esther to a crawl at the fork. She eased to a stop beside the Buick. May made a show of blowing the dust out of her face and offered a cough for emphasis.

"We don't need no more accidents," May warned.

"Yes'm," Esther replied, knowing better than to risk a fiery scolding from her aunt. Nothing Aunt May hated more than back-road speeders.

"You just leaving the MacKenzie place?"

Esther's face clouded. "Not soon enough."

May scrutinized Esther's face. She was right, she decided. This move of Mrs. MacKenzie's back to the farm was coming hard for Esther. Esther would never let on to anyone how deeply she'd been hurt by Michael MacKenzie; she was too proud, or too ornery, to show it. They all counted on Esther to be the strong one, and she never let them down. In the process, however, she never let her hurt out. May saw it, however. Saw the hurt in the spurts of anger at all the wrong places, in the many lone ventures up to the mountains with her easel. Mostly, she heard it in the way Esther pined to leave the farm but never did.

"Your pa, he wants us to be fair with her. Don't be casting blame where it don't belong."

"I don't know what you mean." Esther looked ahead out the windshield.

May knew that tight-lipped, squinty-eyed stare. Esther was simmering and ready to blow.

"I've got something I want to take care of," said Esther, abruptly shifting into drive. "You be careful going up that road, hear? It's full of rough spots. See you."

Esther's Impala sailed away on a cloud of dust. May clucked and wagged her head. The devil had that girl's tail, she thought, and if she wasn't careful, she'd have the devil to pay. Esther sure had a tongue. May remembered Nora as the kind of girl who kept her thoughts to herself.

"Poor little thing," she murmured, thinking of what might have transpired between the two young women. That'd be like pitting a cock with a razor against a hen.

She rambled to the MacKenzie road, and remembering it, she took it in first gear all the way. The burgundy Buick had plenty of power and hummed without whining, though May did each time she spotted bare dirt on the steep incline. She veered wide, rounding the final turn, and spied the protruding deck, then the brick and the huge glass windows of the big house. It always looked to her like rock crystal jutting out of the mountain.

Getting closer she spied a slight figure standing on the deck looking out at the view. As she rolled into the drive, the figure came over to the railing and leaned over. May tried to remember how many years it had been since she'd come up here or seen Nora MacKenzie. Sure was nice, though, to see the place again and to catch up with the gossip.

She stilled the engine, took a moment to catch her breath, then pushed herself out of the car.

"Hello," called Nora. "Can I help you?"

May took a few steps, then paused to look up at the high deck. "Hey there, Mrs. MacKenzie. It's just me, May Johnston from down the road."

"May Johnston!" Nora quickly climbed down the stairs and approached May, hand outstretched. "How nice to see you again, May," she said taking her hand. "How have you been?"

May remembered how much she always liked the missus. A nice girl. Always polite. "I'm fine, except for my ailments, of course." Her wide, bulging eyes scanned Nora's face, resting on the purple bruise on her temple. Nora looked much the same as before. Only now she was pitiful skinny. No wider than a cattail.

"I'm here to see how you fare, Mrs. MacKenzie. Heard you took a lump."

Nora's hand fled to her head. "Oh, I'm fine, thank you. The doctor gave me a clean bill of health. And please, call me Nora."

May scrunched up her lips in skepticism. "Doctors, humph. What do they know? Bend your head here and let me take a look. Hmmmm. You listen to me and take it easy for a few days. Call me if you feel at all sick or dizzy. Never can tell with a head injury."

"I will. Please," Nora said, extending her hand to the house. "Come in. I don't have much to offer, but I'm sure I can at least provide a glass of water."

"Don't mind if I do."

The two women went indoors, May catching every detail of the house as she passed. The house structure seemed pretty sound, considering it'd been neglected for so many years. Few slates missing from the roof, a bit of wood rotted on the stairs. The inside's condition, however, caught her by surprise.

"My, my, but you have a lot to get done. Frank and Junior will have to work fast to finish it up by the first snow."

When they finished the quick tour, they stood before the plate glass in the great room, surveying the mountain view.

May found the view as spectacular as she remembered. The grandeur of her beloved mountain range still had the power to take her breath away. She stood beside Nora for a few moments just soaking it in. For her, the sensation was akin to a religious experience.

"The nice thing about getting old," she said, "is understanding how young we all are compared to nature. Even old May. Looking out at all this, it's plain I'm less than a twinkle in God's eye."

"I understand," said Nora, coming nearer and looking out. "Everything seems insignificant compared to all that. That's one of the things I love most about being here. It keeps me in my place." Sadness flittered across her features. "If this is my place."

"If it ain't yours, it ain't nobody's."

Nora's face lightened.

"I suspect my niece was rude."

Nora pinkened. It was obvious that straight talk was a Johnston trait. "Not rude, exactly. Maybe just honest."

"What'd she say?"

"Let's just say she has her doubts about my sticking around." Nora looked around the room, and once again May spotted the uncertainty. "You can tell her this for me, though. I'm going to give it my best effort."

May smiled, remembering the berry bushes.

"Glad to hear it. Well," she said turning from the windows and taking a step forward. "I'd best be going before it gets too dark." It took several plodding steps for her to cross the big room and several more to descend the steps to her car. She stopped at the door to catch her breath.

"Come down and visit sometime. I'm that blue-and-white trailer 'cross from Seth's. We'll have some coffee and we can plan a garden. Nothing like a garden to make a home permanent, I always say. That pasture up here would be perfect. Get some manure, some hay, throw some black plastic over it and wait till spring. Then we'll put in the seeds. Put some perennials in, too. Nice showy ones, like hollyhock, rosy daisies, and lilies. They'll give you pleasure and make you feel more at home way up here."

Her eyes softened when she saw the eagerness in Nora's expression. "Come on down, honey, and we'll talk."

Their eyes met and searched out what that innocuous invitation might mean to each of them.

To Nora, it meant a mentor. Someone who'd show her the ropes, the tricks of a woman living alone in the mountains. She was also deeply grateful to May for her first real welcome. No warnings, no threats. This invitation was as ingenuous and warm as the woman who extended it.

To May, it meant she'd found a possible ally in her campaign to heal Esther. God works in mysterious ways, she thought. Maybe he sent a MacKenzie to heal a wound a MacKenzie started.

"I will come, soon. I promise." Nora fairly beamed.

Nora waved good-bye to May and watched the older woman rumble down the mountain out of view.

The nighthawk cried and Nora entered her home just as the sun set and a deep blue blanket covered the mountains.

7

NORA WOKE TO THE persistent cry of a finch outside her window. She yawned wide then allowed a sleepy smile to cross her face as she listened to the chirps. It seemed birds were to be her only friends up here.

Bringing her knees to her chest, she looked out the far window at the morning sky. The sun shone over the fog-laden mountains, the cool green rusting to orange red. On the grass, frost sparkled like diamonds as it caught shards of the morning light. She sighed and stretched her toes against the crisp old cotton sheets. The mountain had worked its magic. Observing the power of the surrounding nature, her problems seemed somehow lessened.

Nora peered at her bedroom. This was her favorite room. Like Heidi's mountain loft, the ceiling was all angles that pitched dramatically beside long windows. Her big double bed, laden with down, was tucked in under one angle, making it cozy in the vast room. The other three fireplaces in the house were large and angular. Here, the fireplace was small, rosy bricked, and arched. A feminine touch in a masculine house. Everything about this room was charming rather than imposing; more a Swiss chalet in the mountains than a castle in the sky.

She slipped from her warm bed and walked to the window, opening it just a crack to let in the morning. The air was crisp, even cold, and carried the faint scent of pine. How she loved this view of the valley. The Danby mountain range rolled rather than jutted upward, so instead of a majestic feeling, the view was pastoral, calming. Across this valley she could see a red barn and silo, and black-and-white cows grazing in the vertical field. It reminded her of her childhood home in Wisconsin.

How long had it been since she felt this peaceful?

Three years. Yet she remembered, like yesterday, the evening she'd driven up here to surprise Mike, hoping to patch up a particularly nasty quarrel. In the backseat she'd packed a bottle of French brut champagne and a box of Belgian chocolates, very dark. She'd even brought a new nightgown of peach silk, the blatantly sexy kind that Mike liked but embarrassed her.

That warm June night three years ago, Nora had been determined to save her marriage. She had dreamed that maybe on this land that they had walked together, at this house that they had happily designed and worked on together, he'd remember, notice her, perhaps love her once again.

That dream fizzled as abruptly as the uncorked champagne. A surprise was what she had planned, and it was exactly what she got when she found Mike in the arms of another woman. In their home. In their bed.

He never even said hello. She never said good-bye.

Neither had ever returned. It was as though this house represented all that they once had valued and lost—or perhaps thrown away. This house that was filled with their heartiest laughs, their silliest dreams, their most precious confessions, and beloved possessions stood as a barren monument to their failed marriage.

She couldn't come back—until now. And now she never wanted to leave.

Nora shivered and wrapped her arms tighter across her thin cotton gown. The cool air was moist and laden with dew. She leaned her head against the windowpane. Its touch was icy and seemed to pierce a third eye into the middle of her forehead. Dear God, she prayed as she closed the other two tightly, help me to forget. Help me to get past my anger and let me heal.

From the valley she heard the broken call of sheep, then from the road came the faint sound of crunching gravel. She craned her neck to peer at the winding drive, and soon she saw the figure of C.W. emerge from the tunnel of foliage. He was trudging up the hill at a steady pace. Gasping, she quickly checked the time: nine o'clock already. She wasn't even dressed—this was hardly the impression she wanted to give.

Nora rushed across the cold plank floor to the antique cherry dresser and pulled open the heavy drawers. They creaked as they revealed their treasure of old sweaters and rolled wool socks. Most of them dated from her college days. She grabbed a pair of faded jeans and an old handknit sweater, scowling at the two small holes in the sleeve. Buy mothballs, she told herself as she pulled it over her head.

On her way to the bathroom, she slipped her feet into worn loafers and peeked out the window. He was almost at the house now. She splashed freezing tap water on her face and ran a brush through her thick hair, wincing when she grazed the purpling bump along her hairline. With a groan of frustration she set down the brush and in minutes, braided her hair with practiced hands. A final check in the mirror reflected an aura of organization.

"Looks can be deceiving," she told herself as she flicked off the light.

She reached the kitchen as C.W. walked in. His tall frame filled the doorway as he scraped his muddy boots upon the mat. In the morning light, his handsome features were staggering. Perhaps it was the layers of shirts and jacket he wore against the changing fall temperatures that gave him a broad profile. Yet underneath the layers she guessed the muscles were as solid as the mountain. Instinctively her hand went to smooth her hair.

Nora always liked the look of a man in jeans. Men in well-tailored suits evoked an image of an intellectual power. Wealth. Theirs was a seductive lure, the hint of romantic dinners and intimate talk.

Men in jeans evoked the image of a physical power. Raw and earthy. Like the jeans, they were tough, rugged—roughriders. C.W.'s jeans stretched taut from hip to hip, and she could follow the curved line of his thigh muscle up to the groin.

He straightened, stretching his shoulders wide, and met her gaze. Nora blushed and looked down, wildly wondering if he'd caught her perusal.

"Glad to see that you're on your feet," he said. "I was worried about you and wanted to be sure you're all right." His voice was low and he spoke with deliberate slowness.

"I'm perfectly all right. Thanks for checking on me. I'm fine, really." She felt ridiculous, stammering like a schoolgirl and rubbing her hands.

In contrast, C.W. seemed relaxed, leaning against the doorframe and barely concealing his amusement. This was her house, she told herself. Why was she on edge? She leaned against the refrigerator to appear equally casual, but immediately felt self-conscious and righted herself.

An awkward silence fell between them. She waited for him to say something, but he didn't. She tapped her foot, looked out the window, felt a blush creeping up her neck. Then, not able to withstand the silence or his watchful gaze any longer, she blurted out the first thing that came to mind.

"Thank you for leaving the coffee this morning. At least, I assume it was you." She laughed, then felt childish.

He straightened and headed for the hot coffee. "It was nothing." Hand on the pot, he asked, "Mind if I have some?"

"Not at all. It's your coffee, after all. Oh, and thank you for the fire, too," she added, walking in its direction. She stuck out her hands and made a show of warming them over the heat. "It was very thoughtful."

"No problem," he answered between gulps, watching her over the rim of his cup. "You'll have to keep that thing stoked up, not only for yourself but so the pipes don't freeze. That would be a real mess. And expensive."

Nora made another mental note.

"If you're cold, why don't you just turn on the heat up here?"

"Because it costs a fortune to heat this white elephant with electric heat."

C.W. raised an eyebrow. Why would the expense bother her now, after all these years? MacKenzie should have left her set for life. Well set. What was going on here? His suspicions tingled but he dismissed them. For all he knew, she was one of those tightwads who was always flicking off lights and squeezing a penny, not because they didn't have one, but because they were terrified of losing one.

C.W. looked over at Nora as she warmed her hands. No, she didn't look like the penny-pinching type. She was, in fact, his type. Simple, natural; a beauty so assertive it did not require a fashion statement. If she fattened up a bit, she'd fill out those jeans nicely, he thought. She had one of those bodies that looked great in jeans. Her thighs were long and her hips were small and firm. Soft mounds rose and fell under her baggy sweater, and beneath all that wool was the slender form that he had felt the day before. Knowing it was there, beneath all the layers, added to her quiet seductiveness. Even her feet were small and tucked in scuffed loafers. Where had she been all those years in New York? He'd have remembered her.

"Are you settled in?" she asked.

He shifted his gaze away. "More or less."

"Must be cold in that cabin."

"A bit."

"Perhaps you could stay here and—"

"No," he said emphatically.

Nora blinked hard. "I… It was only a suggestion."

He paused, then sighed and leaned against the counter. "I realize that," he said with a milder tone. "Thank you. But it's better this way."

She nodded. It would only be a matter of time before the gossips guessed which room he slept in. "I'll lend a hand fixing up the cabin. In fact, I have to go to town to buy supplies. What do you need?" She paused and put her hand on her forehead. "Come to think of it, I don't have a car."

Her eyes met his over the rim of his mug. He didn't sip, and his hesitancy revealed he anticipated her next question with dread.

"Could you drive me to town? You could pick up what you need for the cabin while I do my own shopping."

C.W. set down his coffee and tapped his fingers on the

counter. A small muscle twitched in his jaw and his tension crossed the room to grab her.

"Is there a problem with that?"

He took a deep breath. He rarely went to town, preferring a hermit's life in the mountains. Although once an avid reader of the news, these days, he barely even scanned the *Rutland Herald*.

"I can't go to town."

"Can't?"

"I'm tied up at the barn," he quickly added. "Besides, I wouldn't be a very good guide. I'll check with Frank."

Nora took in his nervous pacing. "No problem," she said. "I'll manage."

C.W. turned and looked out the window. Then, taking a final gulp of his coffee, he walked over to the sink, rinsed his cup, and set it beside an already rinsed and neatly stacked cup, bowl, plate, and spoon.

Nora watched him with disbelief. "Are you always this neat?"

"I like order. And it would be rude of me to abuse your hospitality."

"Why, thank you." An image of Mike's dishes, clothes, and papers scattered across the house flashed through her mind. He had always assumed someone—she—would pick up after him. "It's appreciated."

She tilted her head and sipped her coffee while she furtively studied him. He appeared to be a laborer: his clothes were stained by oil and iodine, his work boots were worn and muddy, and his hands were scraped. Both his hair and skin were a tawny gold, dried and colored by the elements. Yet beneath his weathered exterior Nora saw the spirit of a gentleman. Somebody had taught him manners.

"I understand you worked on some horse farm out east."

He swung his head around. "Where'd you hear that?"

"From Seth, of course."

The threat in his eyes vanished as quickly as it had come. "That's right," he replied in a friendlier tone. "A private estate for leisure farmers." He tucked the tips of his long fingers into his waistband. "Cattle, sheep, horses, a little of this and that just for their private pleasure or consumption. Not commercial, like this."

Nora knew the kind of place he meant, and the kind of wealth it required. "I see."

C.W. was relieved she let it drop. Old Abe, the manager of his family estate in New Jersey, was a trusted friend of his, and his father before him. He'd finagled references for Seth. Abe would keep his mouth shut about his whereabouts, C.W. was sure. But snoopy letters to Agatha about a Charles Walker would set the hounds on his trail. Best to keep Mrs. MacKenzie off track.

Lifting his cup, he remarked, "Nice china." Then bringing it closer and turning it upside down, he studied its provenance. "Strange to see Meissen ware mixed with Pyrex."

Nora laughed. "I guess that's the story of my life."

They both smiled, yet measured each other like pugilists sizing up an opponent. He seemed as intrigued by her comment as she was that he could identify the rare German china.

She waved her hand toward the heavy mahogany table, chairs covered in needlepoint, and tall chests filled with china. "All this came from Oma's house—*Oma* is German for grandmother." Her eyes softened as she recalled the thin gray-haired woman with the unassuming manner and endless depth of love.

"My happiest childhood memories came from her kitchen.

It was among these things here that I learned science, math, and reading. Not from textbooks, mind you, but from baking. The wonder of carbon dioxide from yeast, the fractions of a measuring spoon, and reading endless recipes in both English and German.

"That old oven over there," she said, indicating an iron industrial oven in the corner, "was always hot and filled with loaves and loaves of dark bread."

She closed her eyes and sniffed the air, but instead of fresh bread she smelled smoke from the wood stove. When she opened her eyes, she saw C.W. watching her with a strange expression in his eyes. Nora blushed and wiped an imaginary tendril from her brow.

"Anyway, that was how I always wanted my own kitchen to be. Busy and warm. That wouldn't be a bad description for a person either, would it?" she added.

He gave her a wry smile. "Nope. It sure wouldn't."

For a moment their eyes met and revealed their private yearning for a home and a family and a simpler life. Then they both quickly averted their eyes, as though they had both opened a hidden box and exposed their most private secret, before snapping it shut again in fear it would be stolen.

Glancing around, she found reassurance in the familiarity of Oma's things: lemon squeezers, metal sifters, can openers, paring knives. Near the oven, the shelves overflowed with an odd collection of battered pots and pans, large flour bins, wooden spoons with chipped porcelain handles, and oddshaped bottles and baskets. Yet, it was all surprisingly efficient.

"Function, not aesthetics," she murmured.

"What's that?"

"Oh, I was just thinking how this kitchen reflects the code of farm life."

"Did you live on a farm?"

She shook her head. "Unfortunately, no. But I'm originally from Wisconsin. My father was a baker and owned part of a dairy farm. I used to love to go out and visit the cows and hunt for barn kittens. We didn't go that often, though. Mother found it boring and Oma didn't drive. So…" She sighed, running her hands across a tall cherry armoire. "No, I love these things because they belonged to Oma. This is her legacy. Each item is more precious to me than a jewel."

The bittersweet memories of her childhood played upon her features. C.W. watched with fascination, remaining silent, listening. She had no idea of the effect she was having on him as she spoke simply about her childhood. There was no subterfuge, no name-dropping, not a hint of the pretension he was accustomed to. Nor, he suspected, did she have any idea of the sexual magnetism he felt. For under his impassive exterior he was struggling to deny it.

She turned her head away and wrapped her arms around her chest. Her wrists were frail and her long fingers with their short, unpolished, oval nails tapped gently upon her shoulders. As she stood, absently looking over her things, she invoked the image of the child she had just described. An innocent, perhaps even a timid girl. The kind of child who kept treasures in a box under her bed, who sang to the trees, and who knew the name of each of her dolls.

As he watched, mesmerized by her tapping fingers, the child became woman. Her innocence grew sensual, erotic, and he found himself imagining those fingers tapping upon his body. He stepped closer, with nonchalance, and smelled the sweet clean scent of soap. His physical response was immediate, forcing C.W. to reel back and create a distance. God, how long had it been since he'd been with a woman?

Looking up, Nora blinked, as one coming back from far

away thoughts. No, he realized. She had no idea at all how she affected him. And he was glad.

Smiling, Nora said, "I had to fight Mike to keep this stuff. He thought it was all worthless junk."

"You obviously love your grandmother's legacy—and this place. Why did you stay away so long?"

Her face clouded and she looked away. "I had my reasons."

Nora ran her palm along the mahogany table. "I knew it was all here waiting for me," she added, more to herself. "I'd never throw anything out."

"So, you're the type that squirrels away old clothes, family photographs, and chipped china."

She offered a wan smile. "That's me. I keep it all. Everything holds some memory."

C.W.'s gaze swept over her old worn jeans and handknit sweater, to her small hand arced over the table. "Then, why did you remove your wedding ring? Isn't that usually the last vestige of sentiment to go?"

Nora blanched, her hand flying instinctively to her ring finger.

C.W. watched her and cursed himself for his bluntness. It was time to go.

"I'm sorry, Mrs. MacKenzie. That's none of my business."

He crossed the room with determined strides and paused only to grab a large crate of empty glass bottles.

"Recycling is going strong in Vermont," he muttered. "I'll take these down to the center. I—I left a list of recyclables on the fridge." He cleared his throat. Work, business, he thought—the great panacea. "Just rinse them out and toss them in here. I'll take them down to the center for you every Monday."

"Yes, fine," she murmured.

She was still rubbing her ring finger and staring out the kitchen window. Seeing this, C.W. gave himself a mental kick. He had hurt her with his careless comment, and he was sorry. All his life his blunt honesty had been praised, feared, even encouraged. It was viewed as a show of power and intelligence. Good for business.

He shook his head and with a firm grip, hoisted the bottles into his arms and left the house.

What a weak excuse for vanity, he berated himself. He knew better now. Sometimes silence and compassion required greater strength.

Nora finished her morning coffee hunched over Mike's ledger with her heels hooked on the chair's upper rung. From what little she could gather, the figures involved a bank trans-action of some kind, or several transactions, it was hard to tell yet. Mike moved around unbelievable amounts of money. She munched on a piece of toast, careful to brush away the crumbs from the paper. Perhaps if she attacked it differently.

Nora flipped through to the last page. Once again she was struck by the difference in handwriting style as the months passed. In May, she could make out the notations clearly. Yet by September, the writing was erratic, a shorthand of barely legible script. Nora struggled to decipher the ledger for over an hour before she closed it and rubbed her eyes.

She couldn't glean much, yet she felt certain she could figure out what had driven Mike to suicide from these pages. In all the deals and craziness, however, one name emerged as the villain. She recognized the name; it had been carved into her heart. She had traced the letters in the ledger to be sure she got it right.

Mike may have shot himself, but the man who pulled

the psychological trigger was the man who singlehandedly, and with deliberate purpose, had brought Mike to financial ruin.

That man was Charles Blair.

8

—

ESTHER WALKED THE DUSTY distance from the mailbox to her house. Repeatedly, she glanced back again at the tilting metal box with the red flag up and the three numbers half falling down. Inside was her application for a fellowship at New York University—her whole life in an envelope. Her one shot at a dream she'd held since her third-grade teacher, Mrs. Crawford, in the town's one-room schoolhouse told her she had real talent as a painter. She'd known, even then, that it was true.

She peered over her shoulder several more times, just to make sure that bent, rusty red flag stayed up. Then the road curved and her view of the box was lost in foliage. Esther sighed and picked up her pace. There was nothing more to do now but wait.

She had walked the distance from her house to the mailbox every day for twenty years. Once in a while the mail brought a glossy magazine or a letter from Uncle Squire in Florida. Most days there was nothing much except for ads, mail-order catalogs, and bills. The dirt road lined with maples, pines, and here and there seasonal wildflowers was repetitive in its sameness, but never boring to Esther. In spring it was black with mud, in summer it was green, in fall it was orange, and in the cold of winter it was as gray as the sky. But the hues and values changed on cloudy or sunny days, or when the raindrops on the leaves glistened or when a bright red newt slithered into an ink black puddle. Esther approached the house as she always did, lost in her world of colorful thoughts.

"Hey, Es. I've been waitin' on you."

Her hand flew to her heart and she jerked her head toward the far side of the porch where a young man stretched out on the old sofa.

"You scared me, John Henry." She caught her breath, then asked with irritation, "What are you doing here?"

He was quick to respond, but not before she detected the disappointment on his tanned face. "We're supposed to go to the movies. Your pa said to wait, you'd be right back. Come on, Red, don't tell me you forgot?"

She had. Completely. Her face said so.

"We don't have to go," John Henry said quickly. "We can just hang around here."

"No, that's okay," she replied in a colorless voice. "I'm sorry. I got all caught up in getting that application in the mail."

John Henry's face fell. "So you went and did it."

"I sure did." Esther's face flushed. She didn't like feeling vulnerable, telling someone that she actually sent out the forms. Win or lose, she didn't want anyone snickering at her high hopes behind her back.

Esther looked at John Henry. His slightly dazed expression was the same one he'd worn when she beat him in a fight in the first grade. But today John Henry was different. Twenty years of different. And so was she. A lot of time and love had passed between them in those years. A lot of secrets shared. He'd never hurt her or break his word, she was sure.

"Don't tell anyone about them forms, now, promise?" She had to say it anyway.

"Of course I promise." He paused, then waved her over. "Com'ere."

Esther pushed air out through pursed lips. She just wanted to be alone right now. But she went anyway and plopped on the old sofa·beside him. The sofa creaked, complaining at the extra weight on its already bowed out legs.

John Henry lay silent for a moment. When he spoke, his voice was quiet. "What's the matter, Red?"

"I dunno." Then she said in a hushed voice, "I'm scared. What if I don't make it?"

"What if you don't? It doesn't mean you can't paint anymore. You can do that anywhere. Here."

Esther didn't reply. Instead, she tucked her hands tightly between her knees and looked off. How could she tell him that she had to leave here, soon, or she'd be so choked up she'd never paint again. Nora MacKenzie's return brought back too many memories, vivid recollections that she could not share with John Henry most of all.

It was desperation that had finally made her do what she'd been putting off for months: fill out the application for a fellowship in art at New York University. Her whole being was focused on that little envelope in the mailbox.

She felt John Henry's hands rubbing her back. Esther knew his touch so well by now that she read in his fervent strokes a plea that she love him. Any talk of her leaving made him nervous. Esther leaned over and pecked his cheek.

He held out his arms and Esther reluctantly slipped into them. He smelled of sweat and the sofa smelled of mildew. Esther lay in his arms long enough to give him a reassuring squeeze. She sensed his need like radar. Wriggling her shoulders, she loosened his hold and quickly sat up.

John Henry grabbed her back, holding her squashed close with arms like bands of steel. His kisses were hungry.

"No," she said against his lips. "Not here."

John Henry drew back and swung his leg around, hoisting them both off the sofa. His hands remained around her waist in a possessive grip.

"Come on, then."

"I can't. I've got things to do."

"Come on," he drawled close to her ear, propelling her off the porch toward the barn.

Esther allowed herself to be led off to the dark corner of the barn that they often went to when they wanted to be alone. She didn't want to make love. She wasn't in the mood, but John Henry's persistence was not to be ignored.

And she loved John Henry, in her fashion. His need of her was obvious. He wanted so much from her, more than she felt capable of giving. John Henry was one more person who needed her.

Esther relinquished all resistance by the time they reached the dark recess of the ramshackle barn. She'd give in to him, as she always did when he wanted her. He was a good, kind man—her best friend. It was the best way she knew how to show she cared.

His kisses were urgent and his hands grew rough. He pushed her back against the barn wall, hard, and his hands trembled down to her belt and started unfastening it, squeezing her waist as he jerked the leather free.

So, he was going to be dominant today, she realized. He always was when he felt threatened. That application to New York University must have really set him off.

Esther put her hand gently on his, stilling him. John Henry

sighed when he released her belt. Esther quickly finished the task and stepped from her jeans, looking over at John Henry as he fumbled with his buttons.

He was a long sideburn kind of man. With his easy manner and his handsome straight nose, not to mention the dairy farm that would someday be his, most every girl in town had set her sights on John Henry Thompson at one time or another. And he strayed from time to time over the years of their courtship. Yet, Esther always knew that John Henry would find his way back to her, so she never worried or got jealous. Some called her lucky. Others called her a fool.

John Henry looked up, caught her eye, and smiled wide. Even in this dark corner, his bright blue eyes twinkled.

Esther smiled back. She really did care for John Henry. She welcomed him in her arms.

Afterward, when they were putting their clothes back on, an uneasy silence fell upon them. Esther buttoned her shirt back up, watching John Henry thrust one leg into his jeans. His leg was long and covered with fine brown hair the same dark color as the hair that spread across his thin, well-muscled chest and massed upon his head and around his ears. Her hands stilled. How many times had they repeated this scene over the years, she wondered? How many more times till they realized that they could not go on like this forever?

As if he read her mind, John Henry shoved his other leg into his pants and said, "I'm getting pretty tired of pickin' hay out'a my butt. What do you say we make some decisions? Get ourselves our own bed."

Esther jerked her head down and her fingers began to fly on her buttons. "Don't be silly, John Henry. You know I'm waitin' on this scholarship."

"You're always waitin' on something, Esther. After high school it was junior college. Two years later you wanted to finish college in Burlington. Then your sister up and left her husband and you had to take care of her kids. Then your brother—"

"What does Tom's death have to do with us?"

John Henry looked contrite. "Nothing Es, only..." He picked up some hay, sorted it a bit, then threw it on the ground. "Only you always have some excuse for why we can't get married. Now you push this New York stuff in my face and expect me to sit back and wait some more."

"I'm not asking you to wait." She whispered it.

"I'm twenty-six years old!" he continued, not listening or hearing. "Tell me, Es. Tell me to my face. What am I waiting for?"

Esther felt more cornered by his words than the two walls she pressed against. She huddled over and hugged her knees.

"Please, John Henry, don't push me."

John Henry stood straight, his hands in fists at his side.

"It's expected that we marry."

"I've never done the expected," she snapped.

John Henry looked as though he'd been punched in the stomach. "What's that supposed to mean?"

Esther instantly regretted her temper. "You know I can't abide gossips. Oh, John Henry." She rubbed both hands in her hair with frustration, undoing her elastic and sending the curls flying. When she looked up she appeared as disheveled as she felt.

"Maybe you should start seeing someone else. I've said so before."

"Not this again."

"I don't want you waiting for me. I can't promise my life to you. It's still mine. Please, don't ask me to."

He knelt down before her and tugged gently at her hair.

"That's just what I'm asking you to do. I know there are

other girls, but I don't want another girl. I want a dreamer who has two feet on the ground. I want someone who speaks her mind, and gives her heart."

Esther looked at her knees.

"I want you, Esther. Only you."

Tears filled Esther's eyes and she reached out for John Henry. Her hand closed around the fabric against his heart.

"I don't want to make you unhappy," she got out. "You deserve so much happiness. Please. I can't marry you."

His hand quickly covered hers over his heart. He squeezed tight. "I can wait," he said urgently.

She couldn't let him do this. He'd waited so long already on the thin hope that she'd come around and marry him after all. Settle down on his dairy farm. He'd told her he liked the bachelor life, had lots of dreams of his own to live out, too. But she knew he was lying. That he'd walk down the aisle in a minute if only she'd walk it with him.

Esther raised her head to his. His eyes were open, pure. If only there was something mean in him, it would make the telling easier. It was hard to be strong for both of them.

"Face-to-face then," she said. "Don't wait."

She saw him pale. "I tell you of my dreams," she continued steadily, "but you don't want to see them. I speak my mind but you won't listen. John Henry, I can't marry you."

He dropped her hand and sat back on his haunches. His face was stricken. "Is it someone else? That C.W. fella maybe?"

"No, no, course not. There's no one else. More like some thing else."

John Henry rubbed his hands on his thighs and stared at them. So did Esther. He had long, callused hands with short, chipped nails, scrapes and fine crisscrossed cuts. A man's hands—a farmer's hands. Esther felt small inside, remembering those hands when they were short, pudgy, and soft.

Remembering how, as children, he'd always let her win at jacks.

"It's this art thing, right?" he said, tapping those man fingers now. John Henry stood up abruptly. His face had never seemed so hard. He waved his arm like a scythe cutting wheat.

"All right. Have it your way. I'm through with waiting."

He paced three steps, then angrily jutted his finger her way, his face scowling above it. "But you listen to me, Esther Johnston! While I'm off marrying some other girl, mark my words—you'll still be waiting. Waiting till they tell you they've got more than enough artists in New York already. Waiting for me to come 'round again. Waiting till you realize that all you dreamed of was sitting right here in front of you all the time."

Esther's heart was near to breaking when she heard John Henry's voice crack and watched him draw back, slam his hands on his hips and sharply lower his head.

"John Henry...don't."

He swung around to grab her arm and hoist her up before him. Holding on to her shoulders, his face reddened and his breathing came fast. Esther wasn't sure if he was going to kiss her or hit her.

"Do you love me?" he whispered, tortured.

"Yes."

"Marry me," he said, his eyes pleading.

"No."

That one word almost killed them both.

He pressed his forehead against hers and they both closed their eyes tight against the pain. Then he quickly released her, almost pushing her away. He turned away with a choked gulp and took several wild, rounding steps across the hay-littered floor, his hand rubbing his forehead.

"John Henry, I'm sorry," she said, despairing.

He stopped short and his head pulled up. "Don't you be sorry for me, Esther Johnston! You just be sorry for yourself."

John Henry turned heel and stomped angrily from the barn.

Esther leaned back against the wall, blood drained and bone weary. From the dark corner, she stared out the empty barn entrance, wishing he'd walk through it. The straw grass waved in the light outside. A few tires tilted beside a pile of scrap wood.

John Henry wouldn't walk back through that door. Not this time. Esther closed her eyes, forcing back the tears. She'd known this day had to come, but she'd never known how much it would hurt. The pain radiated from some core inside and wouldn't let up. Esther slumped against the barn wall and brought her knees up to her chest. John Henry's bitter warnings repeated in her mind. She was terrified that she'd made a mistake. Afraid that she was already feeling sorry for herself.

The bleating of lambs echoed in the valley below. Nora strolled along the road under the noonday sun, passing pastures of brown and gold that were littered with milkweed pods. Some hung fat upon their stalks; others were already bursting forth their feathery seeds, reminding Nora of days she had blown upon the seeds and sent them sailing like a fleet of white ships upon a golden ocean.

She wasn't headed anywhere specific; she was just getting a sense of where she was. Compared to the confined spaces of the city, everything here seemed expansive: the broad sky, the looming mountains, the vast acres. On her head Nora wore earphones and hummed along. Her pace slowed as she passed a field bordered by a rickety fence. The timber teetered and the wire sagged. Veering from her path, she ran her hand along the fence's splintered wood and smelled autumn's ripeness.

The Long Road Home

Nora imagined how the field must have looked generations ago when the old fence was new. It might have contained a herd of black-and-white cows that grazed on a pasture green with forage. Now the cows had long since vanished from the rocky fields and scores of thistle weed and scrubby pines reclaimed the land.

RRRRRRRRRrrrrrr. The throaty call of a chain saw was audible over her music. Curious, Nora followed the sound, trotting around the grotto called Mike's Bench. There, standing in the sun, jacket off, plaid flannel shirt rolled up at the sleeves and knees bent in a steady stance, a man was cutting away at a damaged maple. He wore goggles and large ear protectors over wild golden hair, but there was no mistaking the powerful visage of C.W. He had already cut and stacked the limbs into neat piles of firewood, but the trunk stooped over a large gaping wound.

She recognized the tree as the one she'd hit. The maple was cracked and bent. A lump formed in her throat as she spied the golden sap oozing from the flesh-colored wood.

Nora watched with fascination as C.W. cut a deep wedge into the mangled trunk. Seeing him doing chores that she could never do made her appreciate how valuable he was as an employee. Logging was hard and dangerous work; the muscles in C.W.'s forearm were rippling as he guided the chewing metal through the wood.

The throaty roar of the chain saw was an exciting sound. To people in the mountains it was the sound of man's control over the wilderness. The maple trunk began to weave and wobble. The acrid scent of fuel mixed with the sweet scent of freshly cut wood and rose up. A strong, heady odor that drifted her way. She felt the thrill of anticipation.

The chain saw droned again, longer, louder. Then the

noise abruptly stopped, leaving her ears ringing in the sudden silence.

C.W. stepped back, setting down the chain saw, and took a last check of the area. She knew the moment he spotted her, for he stiffened, whipped off his goggles and called, "Get out of the way!"

Instantly, she understood her danger and tore off her earphones. Now she heard the tree creak, wood against wood. Looking up, she saw she was standing directly in its line of fall. She had miscalculated the distance. The leaves rustled, the tree groaned, and Nora took three steps back, eyes on the tree. It was shaking, wailing, then it began falling.

Before she could run she felt two muscled arms grab her under her arms and yank her, dragging her feet in the rush, farther down the road. They hit the ground as the tree did—with a graceless thud. Birds cried, squirrels scrambled, and all around her dust and leaves scattered and filled the air. Coughing and rubbing her eyes, she leaned back on her elbows and felt the earth shake around her. When the dust finally settled and she peeked up, she realized it wasn't the earth shaking, just herself and the thin branches that extended to within inches of her head.

C.W. lay half beside her, half over her, covered with broken twigs and crushed dried leaves. He swatted the debris away with harsh, angry swipes and stood, centered between her bent knees. He stared down at her with a look of controlled anger.

"Are you all right?" he asked gruffly.

She coughed again. "Yes. My God." She coughed. "I didn't see it coming." Her breath was coming fast and her hands were still shaking. "I could have been killed. You saved my life."

C.W. ran his hand through his hair, then extended it to her. When she placed her small hand in it, he felt it tremble.

That was enough to shake away his anger and allow him to see how frightened she really was.

"Don't mention it." The lady was turning out to be a nuisance, but he kept Seth's admonishment in mind.

"And don't wear that damn thing out here," he said, pointing at her earphones. "Leave it in the city. Learn to listen to the woods," he said, placing his free hand on her elbow and helping her up. As she reeled up alongside him, he caught sight of the bruise beneath her hair.

Nora nodded, accepting his words as a given.

"Listen," he said as she steadied herself on her feet. "What is it with you and this spot? First you run your car into that poor tree, then you stand under it as it falls. If you have a death wish, please let me know and I'll stop interfering."

He was smiling and she couldn't help but laugh at the absurdity of his words. She laughed, then laughed harder, then suddenly felt herself on the verge of tears, overwhelmed by that sudden switch in emotions that comes when one is uncertain and desperately hiding pain.

He saw the shift of emotion in her expressive eyes. He heard it in her sudden high-pitched hilarity. This was a lady in pain. He recognized pain—knew it well—and felt an immediate empathy for her.

"Come. Sit down and rest," he said, lowering his voice and guiding her to a marble bench set into the mountain.

Nora crossed over crunching twigs, small flakes of wood and sawdust. When she reached the cool shadows of the bench, she settled herself in a prim and upright manner.

Remembering his rude comment in the kitchen, C.W. thought it was his company that made her so sour. "Perhaps you'd prefer to be alone?"

"No, please, don't leave me. Not here."

He raised his brows in question.

Nora scanned the marble grotto, covered now with moss and mud. Then they traveled to the surrounding slopes. Scores of maple saplings had sprouted through the rocks, and uncounted weeds and wild berry bushes bordered them. What was three years ago a hillside of fern was now little more than a wooded jungle.

"Mike built this," she began slowly. "The house we designed together, but this bench he built himself. Wouldn't let anyone help him." She gave a short laugh. "I thought he'd get a hernia lifting this thing," she added, patting the marble slab under her.

"You must miss him."

She gave him a quizzical look. "Miss him? No. Not at all."

C.W. didn't know what answer he expected, but certainly not that one. It left him nonplussed, and that was unusual for him. He kicked his toe in the dirt.

"Must have been something to build that," he said, gesturing toward the big house. "Quite a place."

"Yes. The main beam is forty-five feet of solid redwood. Half the county came to watch it go up. Mike climbed this mountain, decided this was where he wanted his house site, and bulldozed it into reality."

C.W. could envision Mike MacKenzie bulldozing any vision—though he had to admit the result of this one was spectacular. Yet, as he looked at the small frame of Nora sitting prim on the bench, still rubbing her ring finger, he wondered what else the Big Mac had bulldozed. Seeing her empty ring finger focused his attention.

"Oh, I found this on the road," he said, digging into his pocket. "Could it be yours."

He handed her the small gold ring he had found glistening in the afternoon sun atop a quartz rock.

The Long Road Home

Nora stared at the gold band lying in her open palm. Her lips worked but no words came. Was this some sign? The ring, the bench; she felt as though Mike's ghost were hovering about her. Nora sighed heavily. Memories were not something you could just throw away. They kept turning up.

"Yes, it's mine," she said, closing her fingers around the ring.

He noted that she did not bother to thank him for finding it. Stepping back, he said, "If you're all right, then I'm off to the barn. It's feeding time and those girls complain when I'm late."

Nora could hear the insistent bleats from the valley and smiled at the image of a long row of hungry, whining ewes.

"Oh yes, go on ahead."

Waving his hand, he turned his back to her.

"Oh, Mr. Walker?"

He stopped midstride.

"Would you be able to meet me up at the house when you're done? I need to get a rough grasp on the finances, and Seth says that you're the man to talk to."

"Yes ma'am," he replied in a long drawl. "Four o'clock." Without another word, he pivoted to leave.

"Mr. Walker?"

He stopped again, brows up. "Ma'am?"

"I'd also appreciate your teaching me as much as you can about shepherding. I know there's a lot to learn, but…" She let her voice trail away.

He paused. "It's really quick to pick up, if you've got the inclination. I'd be pleased to teach you what little I know."

She nodded, pleased. He turned again.

"Mr. Walker?"

What now, he wondered, scowling.

"Thank you. For everything."

She smiled, and he felt the radiance of it enter his soul. His senses tingled as he felt some kind of connection with the woman named Nora. What was that Chinese saying? Something about if you save a person's life, you are responsible for that life forever. Their eyes met and held, and in that moment, he feared that the old proverb would prove true.

The woman's name was Nora MacKenzie, he reminded himself. The Big Mac's better half. With a perfunctory nod, he turned, gathered his things, and walked swiftly down the mountain.

Nora watched his retreating figure with confusion. A nice man, she decided, but she sensed layers of complexity behind his eyes. Once or twice they had connected—a special glimmer in the eye, a half smile, before they caught themselves and turned away. She couldn't deny the attraction, but it was unwelcome. They were just two lonely people.

The wind gusted. Nora shivered and looked around the bench, as though Mike's ghost haunted it.

"This is crazy," she said aloud, opening her fist. She picked up the ring with two fingers and stared at it without emotion. Mike was dead. All that was left of her marriage was this band of gold. She was about to slip it automatically back onto her left hand, then thought again. Slipping it onto her right ring finger, she vowed that life went on.

9

———

NORA KEPT HER VOW to let life go on. Immediately, she tucked in her shirttail, wiped her nose, and headed down the road toward the barn and the sound of bleating ewes. Her heels dug in the gravel as she marched. She caught up with C.W. at the lower bend of the road and waved to flag him down. He turned and, to her surprise, waved and walked up to meet her. C.W. covered the distance in no time, his long legs easily taking the climb, and when his towering form arrived at her side, she felt dwarfed.

"I decided there's no time like the present," she announced.

"You're the boss."

"Shall we begin lesson one?" She pointed her finger to a small road, actually more a trail, that stretched up the mountain and disappeared in the thick woods.

"Where does that lead to?"

"Seth and the boys use that trail for logging," he explained, looking up to the road. "Esther uses it for berry picking, and we all use it for sugaring. You might want to hike it, to get a feel for the place again. See? It travels far into the woods to some pretty beautiful spots. Ferns, meadowsweet, wildflowers, all kinds of birds. Maybe even a wild turkey."

He stood at the ridge of a small hill, one hand around Nora's shoulder as he guided her gaze across her acres. The gentle hills of the valley curved up to meet the foot of her mountain, cragged and mysterious, and she felt excitement at the prospect of climbing up among the maples to harvest their bounty. As she gazed across its broad vista, an ancient bond to the land rekindled.

Her gaze shifted from the mountain to the man beside her. His broad silhouette mirrored the mountain behind him. From the set of his jaw and the exhilaration in his eyes, she knew that he, too, felt the bond.

"And there," he called, pointing north, "is the lower barn where we store equipment and tractors."

In contrast to nature's archaic beauty, however, man's creations aged into dilapidation. Her smile slipped to a frown. What had she gotten herself into? How could she and Mike have let this place fall so low? The barn was as gray and stooped as an old man—and twice as old. Gaping holes exposed beaten tools, tangled rope, and rusted tractors, and the whole shebang looked ready to topple over into the lower pasture. Nora chewed her lip. If anything brought to light the precariousness of her sole livelihood, that old weathered barn did.

Seth's warning played in her mind: This wasn't any vacation.

"Come on," C.W. said, giving her shoulder a shake and leading her on down the road. "Come see the new barn."

That barn was a sight better and Nora heaved a sigh of relief. It was made of new wood, straight and strong, painted dove gray, and its wide swinging doors actually worked. From within came a din of bleats. Drawn to the sheep, she passed an area of fifteen ewes corralled before the barn's entrance. Nora reached out to open the wire gate and felt C.W. pull her away with a sharp yank. She fumbled flat upon his chest.

"Careful! That's an electric fence. Touch it and you'll get quite a jolt," he warned.

She bounced away from his chest, as though she'd just gotten zapped.

"Listen up. Most of the pastures have electric fences now. Never assume you can go through it. Always check to make sure the juice is turned off."

Taking her elbow, he led her through to the barn. Inside, the cacophony of pregnant ewes was so loud that she followed his example and covered her ears. The trapped air was warm, moist, and heavy with the pungent odor of manure mixed with damp hay. All around her, the excitement of pending birth was tangible. Ewes clustered in groups, some with lambs at their side, others with swollen bellies and an air of expectancy. Unconsciously, her hand ran across her own belly, flat and taut, and she felt oddly jealous of the animals.

C.W. gave her a brief tour of the facility, set up now for the heavy lambing. While he spoke he was always busy, scooping up a birth plug, moving a trough, closing up a gate. She hawked his moves and listened attentively while he explained to her what it was he was doing and why. Her appreciation of C.W.'s knowledge grew, and more, his willingness to share it with her.

As the afternoon sun rose, the heat swelled up around them like a cocoon, trapping them in dank moisture. C.W.'s hair gathered in thick clumps along his broad forehead, which he wiped from time to time with his arm.

Once he started flipping over the large wooden grain troughs, the tempo in the barn really picked up. The full-bellied ewes butted each other in frenzied attempts to secure a space in front of the feeders. Their bleating took on a panicked note. Between the ewes' legs, forgotten baby lambs scrambled to the safety of a far corner, getting bumped and kicked along the way.

Nora watched in horror as one lamb was broadsided by a rushing ewe. It wobbled and fell to his knees. Another set of ewes trampled him as they scuttled past.

"C.W.! That baby!" Nora cried aloud. He didn't hear her and kept working while the dazed lamb lay in the muddy hay getting butted and trampled.

Acting on instinct, Nora climbed the rail into the corral and ran toward the lamb. Immediately, the startled ewes stampeded across the pen, bleating more wildly than ever. Nora froze amidst the mayhem, her heart pounding as hard as the ewes', coughing in the stirred-up sawdust.

"Stop running, for God's sake," C.W. shouted, his face dark. "You'll cause premature labor."

She could hardly hear him over the frightened bleating of ewes crowded now in the far corner. A few more skirted past her toward the rest of the flock, eyes bulging and ears pricked. Like her own, she had no doubt. She wasn't frightened exactly, but she didn't know what to do next.

"What are you doing in there?" C.W. called as he approached. His steps were slow and deliberate, his eyes were blazing again and his nostrils flared almost as much as the ewes'. Nora silently pointed toward the lamb lying alone now in the center of the pen. It didn't even try to get up anymore but lay there, its white coat muddied and looking piteously up at them. Her heart lurched and she looked with a pleading expression at C.W.

His expression softened and he gestured for her to go ahead.

"Take it real slow."

Nora slowly paced to the lamb's side. As she approached, it looked up at her with eyes filled more with curiosity than terror. But when she bent down, it struggled to rise on feeble legs.

"Hush now, baby," she crooned as she gingerly reached out to pet its fur. To her surprise, the wool wasn't soft and downy like she had imagined Mary's little lamb to be. The matted curls were wiry, and she could feel his bones beneath.

"Poor thing," Nora murmured. "Don't you worry. We'll take good care of you."

"He's a runt," C.W. said from the fence. He scrunched his face. "Don't know if that little guy's going to make it."

Nora loved the lamb all the more and cradled him in her arms. "He's a baby," she murmured affectionately. When she lifted him, he bleated weakly, and from the corner, a ewe bleated back.

"That must be his mother," said C.W. climbing the fence. He carefully took the lamb from Nora. She was reluctant to unhand it. The lamb bleated again, and again the mother responded.

"I'd like to reunite them," he said, checking the lamb, "but she's not doing such a great job at mothering. I'll have to find out which one she is. We don't need any bad mothers for breeding stock."

Nora cringed, remembering Mike's past taunts about her.

C.W. laid the lamb on a pile of fresh hay and murmured something soothing as he checked its eyes, noted its tag number, and finally stroked the lamb's back. He was confident and efficient, as if he had done this hundreds of times before. Yet there was a gentleness to his movements and she leaned against the fence to watch in admiration.

"He'll be fine here till we get back, Mrs. MacKenzie," he said as he filed past her.

She touched his sleeve to stop him. He tilted his head and waited, curiosity etched in his long dimples like question marks. She wanted to thank him for helping the lamb, for sharing a simple kindness. But all she could muster was, "Please, call me Nora."

He hesitated. He liked her, perhaps too much. And she was MacKenzie's widow. For those reasons he preferred the distance of formality. Then he remembered her confidences in the kitchen and the way she had run to the runt's defense.

"I better get to these sheep. Nora."

Her expression lightened and she smiled as he passed her. He almost winced as the smile hit its mark.

What the bloody hell, he thought as he bent low and grabbed the wooden trough. Flipping troughs down the alley he counted, one by one, the reasons to stay clear of her wide, expressive eyes and the pain he read behind them.

The offer of food brought the ewes hustling back to the grain bins. Once again, they whined, bleated, and butted each other for a better place.

"Can I help?" she called.

Straightening, he pointed to his ears. Nora walked—very slowly—to the grain bin, and using primitive hand signals, asked if she should scoop grain into the troughs. He gave a grateful nod and she set to work.

The two of them worked side by side at a feverish pace spreading grain to the scrambling ewes. Her unfit muscles began to tremble, but she refused to quit. Eventually, the bleating diminished as they settled down to chow, forming two long rows of efficient eating machines.

C.W. walked over to Nora and rubbed his palms against his jeans. "Whew. Gets pretty noisy in here at feeding time."

"So I hear," she replied, wiping her brow. "My ears are still ringing."

His gaze rested a moment on her bump. "How are you feeling? Any headaches?"

Nora shook her head. "Just tender."

He raised his callused fingertips to tilt her chin a degree upward as he studied her pupils. Nora's throat constricted and her chest tightened. She jerked her head away.

"I said I'm fine, thanks."

C.W. abruptly stepped back. "Enough work for your first day. You'd better rest, or May will have my hide."

Nora chuckled softly. "Okay. Just for a second. I'm only a little tired."

She wandered to a small stool and slumped upon its wobbly seat. What a liar she was. She really was pooped. Nora's bottom just reached the stool when Esther entered the barn with long, confident strides. Nora bolted back up as if the bench were electrified.

Grabbing a pitchfork on her way down the alley Esther called out, "Sorry I'm late, C.W." When she spied Nora, her eyes widened in surprise. They shared a look, a shorthand reminder of their earlier conversation.

"Didn't expect to see you down here," Esther said.

Nora stepped away from the stool. "Why not? This is where I work now."

Esther seemed to accept that at face value. Without another word, she threw the pitchfork into the hay. Standing on the sidelines, Nora watched the two seasoned farmers shovel impressive forkfuls of hay. She felt out of place, like a fan on the bleacher. Her gaze swept the barn, really taking in for the first time the assorted metal and wood tools, the bottles of medicine, the charts, the mysterious plastic tubes and bins. Tools of the trade. Nora didn't have the faintest idea what they were or how to use them. Esther, no doubt, could use them all.

Wiping her hands, Nora noticed that her palms were smooth and uncallused, her nails were clean and unchipped, and her jeans were old but unstained. So much to learn, she realized, and so little time. Nora grimaced under the weight of her own ignorance.

She turned to go.

"Leaving already?" Esther called out.

As though on a dance cue, Nora spun on her heel, grabbed the nearest shovel and pail, and began the dirtiest job in the barn: spotting birth plugs.

"Someone's started labor over here," she called out.

Esther stilled her fork, her face the picture of surprise. C.W. swung his head around, obviously pleased. "Great. I'll check the ewe."

"C.W.," she said when he approached near enough that she didn't have to shout. "Would you call me, sometime, to see a birth? If it isn't too much trouble, that is?"

C.W. finished his quick examination of the ewe, then paused to catch his breath and study her. Nora shuffled her feet as she waited, looked at the new scuff marks on her boots, then bobbed her head back up to meet his gaze. Well? her eyes asked across the distance.

"It's no trouble," he replied, deciding. "Nature doesn't give any warning."

"Anytime. Please."

Nodding his head, C.W. turned his back to her, grabbed his fork, and set back to throwing hay.

Nora grinned from ear to ear. As she walked down the aisle checking out the pen floors, her pail bumping her shins, she felt inordinately pleased with herself. This wasn't such a bad job after all, she decided. Maybe not her favorite job, but for now, it was the only one she knew how to do.

"Tomorrow, I'll learn another," she vowed, peeking over at C.W. and Esther talking together over a pregnant ewe.

"And then another."

10

———

AT PRECISELY FOUR O'CLOCK, Nora sat across the bare mahogany dining table from C.W., her ankles together, her back straight, and her hands tightly folded atop a neat pile of papers. If she was going to work successfully with Mr. Walker, he had to first understand that she was capable and up to the job. She had a college degree in business, had spent childhood summers on a dairy farm, was eager to learn, and had boundless energy. There was no reason on earth why she couldn't make a go of it here in Vermont.

No reason other than money, of course.

She looked across the table at C.W. and wondered how she was ever going to manage working with such a quixotic personality. One minute he seemed almost kind, the next he was critical—and it seemed to her that he was especially critical of her. What had she done to make him feel that way about her? If she was going to fit in here, she had to be one of the guys, like Esther.

C.W.'s long fingers began to tap impatiently upon the table.

Okay, Mr. Walker, she thought, clearing her throat. I'm just as eager to end this meeting as you are.

"I intend to be frank with you, Mr. Walker," she began, hoping she sounded professional. She didn't realize that to him she sounded more like an arrogant housewife giving orders to the gardener.

He bristled and shifted in his seat.

She fiddled with the corner of a paper.

"I have a net worth statement from Mike's lawyers," she continued steadily, "but I would like to verify it with your figures. I'm not sure I trust theirs."

He found that very interesting. "I can get that for you."

"Thank you. Next, I need a budget."

"Uh-huh."

They were both on their best behavior. Nora felt relieved. So far so good. She decided to dive right in. Taking a deep breath, she reviewed her numerous lists.

"In order to do that, I need a complete farm inventory, the variable and fixed costs, receipts, and," she added, stressing the syllable, "your projections for next year's budget. A profit and loss statement is necessary too." She looked up. "Can you get that for me?"

He hunched forward and she sensed he was hiding a grin of amusement. "Yes," he replied in a mildly condescending voice. "Usually this is gathered at the year's end."

The subtle tease in his voice reminded her of his arrogance the first night she met him. Nora twisted her pencil in her fingers.

"Not this year," she snapped back.

C.W.'s face hardened as he sat back in his chair.

Nora sat forward in hers. She coupled her hands and leaned forward. "Look, Mr. Walker. I'm aware that we got off on the wrong foot. Somehow, I don't know why, you got the wrong idea about me and my intentions here."

She searched his face for some change but found none. Yet she knew she had his complete attention. "I was sincere when I said this isn't just a vacation home anymore. This place means everything to me." She flattened her hands on the table and took a deep breath. "I apologize for the inconvenience you've suffered and my earlier harsh words."

C.W. considered her words for what seemed an eternity. She'd never known a man to be silent for so long. Nora pinkened but stared him down, matching his silence with stubbornness.

"Mrs. MacKenzie," he said, his face grave and his voice low, "I assure you, there is nothing you need apologize to me for. Ever. It is I who should apologize to you."

Nora slowly leaned back in her chair and dropped her hands in her lap. Her lips parted slightly. C.W. had turned the tables. She'd never expected him to apologize to her.

"Let's call it even." Nora was sincere.

"All right," he said, easing into a wry smile. "As for your other requests, I can get that information for you. But all that will take some time. Seth's records are filed, shall we say, creatively."

"I understand."

"Since we're being frank here, Mrs. MacKenzie, let me say that I don't understand. It isn't gossip to know that you're loaded. Why are you so worried about money? Things have muddled along on this place for years. A check here to cover expenses, a write-off there." His tone spoke volumes.

Nora tightened her lips. She hadn't anticipated this question, at least not so soon. The hardwood of her chair was suddenly very uncomfortable.

"Well, you see, Mike, that is, my husband had some

outstanding debts that still need to be settled. Until then, the banks have put me on a restricted allowance."

His face skewered. "A restricted allowance? Just how restricted?"

Now it was Nora's turn to bristle. "Let's just say things will be tight for a while." She wasn't about to confide all her financial details.

"Well," he said, slightly lifting his shoulders. "Banks can be like that."

"Banks nothing," she said with unexpected vehemence. "One bank—one man—by the name of Charles Blair. He's responsible for this."

C.W. almost reeled back from the shock. "Charles Blair? Did what?"

"I don't know exactly but I intend to find out, and when I do—" Nora immediately clammed up. She waved her hand, as if to brush away any further thoughts or comments about the disagreeable subject. That was her past. Now she had her future to think about.

For the next half hour, she discussed in her best business tone the groundwork for her eight-week plan: what she needed to learn and what he could help her with. She ended her presentation with a brief plea for his cooperation, knowing she needed all the help she could get.

While he seemed willing enough, his replies were monosyllabic or mere nods of the head, as though he was preoccupied with some other problem. And when she concluded, he grabbed his coat and darted for the door like a schoolboy after the three o'clock bell.

Well, she thought with disappointment as she watched him hike down the mountain road at a clipped pace. What more could she expect? He was, after all, just drifting by.

★ ★ ★

There was nothing drifting about the way C.W. headed for a telephone. Thoughts were churning full speed in his head, propelling his long legs faster and faster down the mountain to the Johnston house.

Charles Blair connected to MacKenzie's downfall? What the hell? He did no such thing! Why would she say that? It was too easy to write it off as mindless chatter. She was too sure—too angry—for that, and there was nothing mindless about Nora MacKenzie. He had been impressed with her long tables of figures and her ease with banking terms.

What the bloody hell, he repeated.

When he arrived at the Johnston's pale green house, he knocked, called, then sighed in relief that no one was home. They'd opened the house to him from the day he arrived: the Johnstons were like family now. He met with Seth and the boys here daily, and Esther had simply assumed he'd be at the family table for meals, a hospitality he was careful not to abuse. He was aware the extended family couldn't easily absorb the burden of another mouth to feed.

Entering the house uninvited was never considered an intrusion. Today, however, he felt out of place. The task at hand made him a stranger. He walked straight to the phone that would connect him to a world he'd fled ten months ago. He stared at it, but could not touch it.

Sticking his hands in his pockets, he rocked on his heels while he reviewed his conversation with Nora. MacKenzie's widow was clear that Charles Blair was connected to her financial troubles. C.W. stared out the window. Charles Blair. Charles Blair was another man. He no longer felt akin to the name or the lifestyle of the prominent banker.

The distant perspective helped. A man named MacKenzie had chosen to kill himself before a man named Blair.

For months he'd asked himself why? To be honest, he never seriously pursued it. It had always been too painful. He'd procrastinated. Now, however, Nora's presence set the clock ticking.

C.W. reached out again for the phone. His hand shook, like he needed a drink. That sordid image set his mouth in a grim line. Hard memories spawned determination that spurred him to action. Grabbing the phone, he quickly dialed a New York number. As the phone rang he took deep, cleansing breaths, mentally shifting gears. Within seconds, he heard Sidney Teller's crisp, Boston accent excitedly tell the operator he'd accept the charges.

"Charles! My God, Charles…I'd begun to think you were dead. Where the hell have you been for ten months? Not a word. Not a word!"

C.W. paused, cupping the telephone receiver, and looked around the living room. It was five o'clock and Seth and the kids would be returning from the fields within the hour. Satisfied he was out of earshot, C.W. lowered his mouth to the telephone.

"Why were you worried? I told you I'd be gone for an extended leave. I left the bank in your hands—good hands, I hope."

"Oh yes, certainly," sputtered Sidney as he tried to recollect his poise. "But damn it all, Charles. At the very least I expected a postcard from some Tahitian island."

C.W. smiled and sensed his brother-in-law's relief over the miles. "I'm all right, really. I needed the time to sort things out."

He was grateful Sidney had the grace not to press.

"How's my sister?" C.W. asked.

"You know Cornelia," Sidney replied. "She takes care of herself."

Sidney's reply disturbed C.W., but at the moment, he had business to address.

"Tell me, Sid. In a nutshell, what's going on with the Mac-Kenzie estate?"

He heard Sidney's sigh over the wire. "For God's sake, Charles. Aren't you done beating that dead horse? Let it go."

C.W. resented the bitterness he heard in Sidney's voice.

"I have my reasons for asking," he replied.

"Hard to say. There is a big mess over his finances. No one is sure even yet how his estate has settled. The whole estate is shrouded with unusual secrecy. Bad loans somewhere, apparently."

"Not from our bank, I assume." C.W.'s voice rang with a warning that Sidney didn't miss.

"Of course not. Your instructions were explicit. No loans to MacKenzie. You called that one right."

C.W. sensed Sidney's discomfort on the other end of the line. Sidney was his sister's husband and his own right-hand man. At the Blair Bank they had been quite a team: Charles Walker Blair was the spearhead, the man of ideas. Sidney Teller was the detail man, his secretary of state. Together, they had brought the Blair Bank to its pinnacle of success.

In the past year, however, everything had changed. C.W. had changed. How much, he wondered, had Sidney changed?

C.W. let the silence linger well into the discomfort zone before quietly asking, "What is it, Sid?"

Another pause, then a clearing of the throat. "On the subject of loans… Something's wrong at the bank," he blurted. "I've been searching for you for months, but no one can find out where the hell you are. You'd better come back. Right away."

"What's wrong, exactly?"

"Some bad loans have been issued. To a number of small firms. It all seemed straightforward on paper," he said in a rush, "but they've all come up short. Smells like shell companies, a front of some kind. And, Agatha's routing me."

"What's she got to do with this?"

"I'm not sure, but she's on the march, patrolling the rank and file, shooting out memos, holding court at the board meetings." He paused. "It's been tough."

C.W. frowned. That Agatha would force an attack against himself and Sidney was no surprise. His brother-in-law and stepmother despised each other with a deliberateness that C.W. found distasteful. Agatha loathed only one person more than Sidney, and that was him. But he had been able to ignore their personal animosity. It was bad for business.

"Bad loans imply bad judgment," C.W. replied in a low voice. "Could bring the stock down. The directors will be held responsible."

"Exactly."

"Here's what I want you to do. I want the names of the companies we loaned money to. I want the exact dates. And, I want the names of the officers who issued them."

"Got it."

"One more thing," he added, on a hunch. "Sniff around the MacKenzie estate. Something is off there; I can feel it." He thought of MacKenzie's widow. Was that haughtiness he read in her eyes—or fear?

"When will you be home?" Sidney asked. There was no mistaking the urgency in his voice.

C.W. sighed. Home. Where was that? "Soon. I have a commitment to finish up first. In the meantime, don't let anyone know you talked to me. Keep a low profile but dig around. Find out what's not being said and report back to me."

"Sure, Charles. Where can I reach you?"

C.W. smiled. "I'll call you."

He hung up the phone but still felt the intangible tie to the bank. Damn this cursed business, he thought. All cuts and stabs. Would he never find a way to free himself of it? Or was he bound to the bank by birth as surely as some monarch to his throne?

No, he thought with cold sureness. He'd come too far to let the machinations of the bank bring him down again. He'd give Sid a few days to dig up some information, then he'd help his brother-in-law formulate an attack. If worse came to worst, he'd head back to New York, if only long enough to throw his support to Sidney and resign from the bank. He wanted out, that much was certain.

C.W. ran his hand through his hair and let out a ragged sigh. Leaning back against the wall, he let his gaze roam the small rooms of the Johnston house. It was a modest house that had seen better days. The walls stooped with age and were covered with faded rose wallpaper. The furniture was sparse and poor, and the sofa's floral upholstery was worn bare in spots.

Yet, a bright handmade quilt was neatly spread across the fabric, and fall meadow flowers cheered up the dining table. Neat stacks of newspapers and split logs rested beside the warm wood stove. Near the front door, a long line of muddy work boots sat under a large collection of hanging jackets. Closing his eyes, he could still smell the scent of Esther's coffee and pancake breakfast from the kitchen.

God almighty, he thought, squeezing his closed lids tight. He'd give his fortune for what he found in this small, family home.

In Manhattan, in a tall building of ornate cement, up in the penthouse suite, Agatha Blair was just informed that Charles Blair had placed a phone call to Sidney Teller.

"Where did the call originate?"

"We don't have tracers on the line," replied the voice. "It's just bugged."

Agatha tapped her long red nails in irritation. Such incompetence. Did she always have to tell others how to do their job? Oh well, she muttered. What did it matter? As long as Charles Blair remained out of the picture for two more months.

Still, it rankled. What was Blair up to now? Sniffing around the MacKenzie estate after all this time. Could he be on to something? Or merely more guilt.

She pushed the intercom button. "Ask Mr. Strauss to see me. Immediately."

As she waited, Agatha Blair considered again her hatred for Charles Blair. The entire Blair family, for that matter. Everything about them, from their clipped, perfect English, their patrician manners, their worldliness, their impeccable taste, all the things that came from growing up with privilege. Even this room, she thought. She was unaware that her lip curled in distaste.

It was a man's room, Agatha thought for the millionth time. Dark mahogany wainscotting and baseboards lent the room a denlike quality. On the walls were assorted paintings of indisputable value, but of little interest to her particular taste. She found the landscapes boring and the hunting scenes ridiculous with those long-nosed, long-eared dogs sniffing about.

This had been the office of the bank's president, Edwin Charles Blair: her husband. When he died a decade earlier, at long last she'd always thought, Agatha had moved in. She didn't change a thing. Not that she kept them in fond memory of her husband. No. Each dreaded painting, every masculine appointment, served to remind others not only of her position in the Blair Bank, but in the Blair family. A position hard earned, in her opinion. Despite what the family had thought initially, regardless of the opposition she faced during those years, she had clawed her way to this office and guarded this den as fiercely as any lioness.

Agatha leaned back in her chintz-upholstered chair, her single deviation toward femininity in this horrid office. It was a man's room, she thought again. And banking was still a man's game. She knew the rules and with skill and cunning had bent them, twisted them, and made them work for her.

The buzzer rang. Her hand tightened upon her cane for a moment, then she slowly released it and moved to the telephone.

"Send him in."

The door promptly opened and stocky, stern-faced Henry Strauss marched into the office. He crossed the room with purpose, and when he reached Agatha's desk he placed his hands upon it. A simple transgression. Not a threat, that wasn't Henry's style. More a reminder of his position and seniority in the bank.

Agatha's eyes remained on Strauss's hands. Fat, peasant hands, she thought with disdain. With delicious slowness she raised her eyes, past the bulging buttons on his double-breasted suit, past the fold of flab that simply could not be contained by the starched button-down collar, inching up beyond jowls far too fleshy for a man in his fifties, to his eyes. Yes, here she could alight without that nasty taste in her mouth. Even behind those heavy black glasses, Strauss's eyes still had that clear German blue, intense and fringed with thick blond lashes. Today, those eyes were angry, as she knew they would be. She considered whether to punish him for his rudeness. Perhaps not. Next time. This time it wasn't prudent to anger Henry too much.

"Sit down, Henry." She flipped her small fingers up twice, shooing him away. Henry cleared his throat, then obediently took one of the dull green leather chairs. Agatha's eyes gleamed.

"There's been a two point drop in MacCorp.," he said.

"I know. A trifle."

Strauss's expression did not change, but Agatha's sharp eyes noted that his nostrils flared.

"Maybe not for a Blair, but that represents a significant amount of money to a Strauss." His voice lowered. "I've risked everything. You promised me a killing on this stock."

Agatha could not contain her smile.

Strauss blanched. "Oh God, I didn't mean…"

"Of course you didn't. No one imagined poor MacKenzie would take such a drastic course."

Agatha forced herself not to reveal her anger at the memory. That fool MacKenzie almost screwed things up killing himself that way. Such a mess; too soon a scandal that rocked the bank. Yet, the Big Mac's suicide did have its advantages. Not even in her wildest dreams did she think that a man like Charles Walker Blair would have reacted so radically to the suicide. Like father like son.

Another smile. It was a long, thin slit in an unnaturally tight face. "It turned out rather well in the end, no?"

Strauss, a veteran of Wall Street slaughters, sat back in his chair, appalled. "Why? Because Charles flipped out? We cannot allow family rivalries to threaten the bank's stability. Again."

Agatha knew Strauss was testing, gauging her reaction. She maintained a cool surface over her boiling point.

"But of course. Although—" she paused, folding her hands together "—it is rather late for you to be discussing integrity, wouldn't you agree?"

Henry's pale, heavy features deepened in color as he looked at his fat hands. "Where the hell is Charles anyway?" he asked, throwing his head up. "I can't believe all your private investigators can't find him. He's a goddamn Blair after all. You'd think the society pages would have tracked him down by now!"

Agatha leaned back and brought her nails to tap at her red lips. The tension was clearly getting to Henry Strauss. She had never before heard him use profanity or even raise his voice out of a monotone. Strauss prided himself in his Old World ways; he being from old money. Agatha despised his pretentiousness. She knew that the old money was long gone. They were poor as church mice, the lot of them.

"Relax, Henry," she replied, wary now. "All bad pennies turn up."

"It's not like him to run off like that. Maybe he's dead. He was a mess when he left. A raging drunk." He shook his head.

"Since when do you have sympathy for Charles Blair?"

Strauss looked up again, his pale eyes hooded. "I don't. I simply don't trust him. Charles is like a snake. One never knows when or where he'll strike. He can be very dangerous, you know, especially when riled."

Agatha's eyes narrowed. She thought of Charles's phone call to Sidney Teller. A small sense of alarm seized her. "Has Bellows turned up anything?"

"No. Bellows has come up short."

She swiveled in her chair. "He's out," she snapped. "Understood?"

"Quite so."

Agatha sat back in her chair, tapping the tips of her polished fingernails. "I hear MacKenzie's widow has left town."

"That's right. Bellows assures me she's out of the picture. A pathetic figure, actually."

"Who cares about her? It's MacKenzie's papers I want. That

conniving bastard. It would be just like him to keep a secret file on the deal. He was a double-dealer."

"We have no reason to believe he did."

"All MacKenzie would have had to do was implicate me in any way and that would have been enough for Charles Blair. He is too sharp and he loves the kill as much as I do. No, if those papers exist, I want them."

"This whole deal reeks. MacKenzie never should have died. It was supposed to be a done deal. Prop up MacCorp. stock: buy low, sell high. Quick and clean. Who ever would have thought…"

Agatha narrowed her eyes. "MacKenzie couldn't make the repayment schedule."

"We held twenty-five million in the company as collateral for the loan, for God's sake! We should have been well protected. If Charles hadn't sniffed it out and called in the loan, we could have stalled. That was the plan."

Agatha sank back in the upholstery, looking with disdain at the sulking figure. Oh no, she thought with satisfaction, that was not the plan. MacKenzie may have duped other bankers into believing his illusion of wealth, but not her. She'd known all along he was too highly leveraged; why else would she have chosen him for her plan? She felt a ripple of pleasure. Banking could be orgasmically delightful.

Henry gritted his teeth. "There are going to be some embarrassing questions if this gets out."

Agatha raised her brows. "*If?* Surely, you mean *when*."

Henry Strauss flushed along his starched collar. It had to be a first. "We have got to keep MacKenzie's bankruptcy under wraps," he said. "It's agreed."

"By whom?"

"Everyone. The banks, the auditors—everyone wants to get paid back and no one wants a scandal."

"His company is headed for receivership. It's being raided even as we speak. My dear boy. It's too late."

"It's not too late." Henry's voice rose as he did. "The MacKenzie auction can satisfy our loans, at least. We just have to allow a delayed payment schedule. If not, the shit will hit the fan. Sidney Teller is already hot on my trail, trying to call them in. He's a solid banker. Teller won't give up."

"Think, Henry." Agatha's fingers tapped impatiently over the ball of her cane. "What if the auction does not satisfy the loans?"

"The board will trace the loans to Charles Blair's office. He'll be forced out. We all will."

"Not all of us. I will not be implicated." She flicked lint from her lapel. "I will protect you."

"And let Charles take the fall?"

Agatha smiled. "He's the top man. It was always the risk."

Henry Strauss straightened his shoulders and looked Agatha in the eye. For a moment she thought the old Henry had returned. He appeared cool and detached.

"Of course," he eventually replied, a hint of the patrician air returning to his voice. "That was the plan all along. I was blind not to have seen it earlier."

Agatha looked at Strauss now, not even attempting to disguise her disgust.

Strauss's pale lids fluttered. "MacCorp. stock will surely plummet." His voice flattened. "I'm ruined."

Precisely, thought Agatha. They both knew that now Strauss had no choice but to go along.

"It's only money. We can make more," she told Strauss. "You're tired. Ask Miss Wilton to give you a set of keys to Bar Harbor. It should be empty." She flipped her thick leather schedule book. "Yes, Cornelia is in Palm Beach already."

Flipping the pages back again, Agatha assumed a magnanimous expression. "Take a few days to unwind. The next few
weeks will be critical if we are to pull this off. And we will.
Charles has no power here any longer. I hold all the strings.
We can't have you tense, now can we?"

Henry narrowed his eyes. Agatha searched them but could
not read them. He was the old, cold Henry.

"Yes, I think I will," he said. "I am tired." His florid features were immobile as he stood lifeless before her desk. His
eyes, however, were staring without a blink straight at her, or
rather, through her.

"Thank you for your concern," Strauss finally said with a
slight nod of his head. Then he turned and walked stiffly to
the door, never once looking behind.

Agatha watched him leave, an inordinate hatred bubbling
up against the younger man. Pathetic pup! How could men
be such fools? Edwin, her husband, had proven himself naive,
despite his intellect. His son, Charles, was of the same ilk. One
after the other, they were all little boys with egos brandished
like swords at play. Swagger, spin, and fall.

She pressed the intercom button. "Call Sidney Teller. Tell
him I'm on my way to his office.... Yes, immediately."

With Strauss out of town and Charles Blair on the horizon,
it was time to get things stirred up a bit. She'd leak just enough
to see how much Charles knew. In any case, the MacKenzie
estate had to fall quickly.

"Well, little Henry," she murmured, grabbing hold of her
cane and raising herself up on stiff legs. "You shall get yours.
Poor Henry. You were the biggest fool of all. For you, a brief
parry and score. But Charles..." Her hand tightened around
the cane.

"Oh, for you, stepson, I waited till the moment when you

were most vulnerable. When your mental guard was down. Now, at last, it is time for the attack."

Agatha slowly, precisely, extended her arm, aimed her cane, and after a brief swirl of the wrist, thrust the cane forward in a mock fencing ritual.

"For you, Charles, the thrust lunge."

11

———

NIGHT IN THE MOUNTAINS comes on quietly, like a thief that steals the farmer's precious light. Nora climbed from her bed and, slipping a thick robe over her flannel nightgown, padded in her slippers down the stairs into the great room. Even in the evening shadows, the room was magnificent. The ceiling vaulted to twenty-five feet at its peak over huge windows that allowed the night to flow in.

In the city, the night sky was broken by the lights of other apartments, neon signs, and headlights. Here, the wilderness poured in, thick and unbroken. From somewhere out in the silence, an owl hooted and an animal screeched a shrill wail.

She shivered and wrapped her robe high along her neck. Outside, she knew the stars shone bright in the crisp air of a country sky. She might see the Big Dipper, maybe even the Milky Way. But she couldn't bring herself to venture out into the dark unknown. Even the great room was foreboding. Its vastness mirrored the wild space outdoors.

Nora went back up to her bedroom and climbed back in bed, bringing the covers up around her ears. Snug in a small space, with the light from the lamp shining beside her, Nora couldn't remember when she'd felt so alone. Not even after Mike died did she sense her isolation so completely. She knew, with a sureness as cold as the night air, that no one really cared if she made this farm succeed or fail. That no one would celebrate her life or mourn her death.

What was she doing on this mountain, she asked herself. She had come up here with a heart full of dreams and an armful of books, but today in the barn she learned the difference between a dream and reality. Esther had walked so confidently among the sheep, doing everyday chores that she herself had only read about in one of her books.

Worst of all were the ewes. All of them with bellies swollen with life. Such a natural chore, birth, but one she had failed in. And then the lambs...the babies...

That thought of the baby lambs released the tears she'd held in check all day. Tears that were not for Mike, but because of him. Oh, how angry she was at him! He would not leave her alone. Instead of getting away, the farm carried his memory in each brick and stone.

Seven years they'd been married. For five of those years she had tried to be the perfect wife and hostess. But like the car that couldn't make it to the top of the hill she, too, had been discarded. He exacted revenge for the injustice he believed she had committed against him. A tremor shook her as she recalled the expression on his face the morning the doctor suggested he undergo sperm tests.

"Me?" he had shouted, exploding in characteristic vehemence. "There's nothing wrong with *my* sperm, Doctor. If there is something wrong, it's with my wife. *She's* the one with a problem. Got it?"

The doctor backed up and tried to regain his composure. Nora felt sorry for the frail physician faced with a big, boorish

Irishman with fists like shovels and veins protruding from his flushed neck.

"Mike," she said softly. "The doctor's only trying to discuss the possibilities. No one is saying that the problem lies with you. It's just that—"

He turned and gave her a look so threatening that she immediately silenced and shrank back into the upholstery.

"Mr. MacKenzie," began the doctor, "Mrs. MacKenzie has already undergone a long series of tests. Nothing positive has shown up. We will, of course, pursue other avenues with her, but I feel it is in your best interests to explore other possibilities."

Mike's shoulders hunched like a cat about to pounce. "Like me," he responded in a low tone. The muscle in his jaw was twitching.

She'd wrung her hands and looked from her husband to her doctor. The doctor, too, must have sensed the danger. He walked to the other side of his desk and sat down behind it. Regaining his composure, the doctor began to reel off a list of tests and procedures. His monologue included what the results would find, and finally what options they had if Mike's sperm was in fact limited, slow, or even dead.

Nora cringed.

Mike's fist slammed down on the desk, sending the pencils flying and the doctor to his feet.

"You listen to me and listen good. There is nothing the hell wrong with my sperm, and I'll be damned if I'm gonna jerk off into some bottle for you to poke around with under some frigging microscope.

"Is this what you brought me here for?" he stormed, turning his vehemence toward Nora. He was towering over her and jabbing his index finger into her face. "You listen to me, Doctor." His gaze swept between the two of them. "I don't care what you have to do, what you have to spend. But the problem lies with her," he said, jerking his thumb in Nora's direction. "Find it and cure it. Fast."

Then he grabbed his coat in his fist and stormed toward the door. Before leaving he turned his head to catch Nora's eye. She recoiled. Again he pointed his index finger at her and said, his voice ringing with bitterness and conviction, "If you can't give me an heir, I'll get a wife who can."

He left, slamming the door on any hope for her marriage she might have harbored. Nora sat staring at the door in cold disbelief and hot shame. The doctor was muttering something about "normal reaction," and how "they usually come around." She knew differently. This wasn't just about having a baby. This was about Mike and how she fitted into his world.

There would be no mutual struggle to have a baby. That was her job. He had invested time and money into her. And now, she was a commodity that had come up short.

That was when he started seeing other women. He pursued them with a vengeance. Brassy blondes, fiery redheads, sloe-eyed Asians, all with that lean, hungry look. Eyebrows had raised and tongues had wagged from Nantucket to Long Island. At first her friends rallied around her in exaggerated sympathy. Yet as whiff of her descent became apparent, invitations grew few and far between.

Mike grew more brazen about his affairs, openly displaying his latest paramour at parties she should have attended. He drank more, gambled high stakes and spent large sums of money in an obsequious display of his wealth and virility.

He was running away from a truth he couldn't escape and he punished Nora for it. After years of doing her best to dress to his liking, entertain his endless hordes of cronies, arrange his social calendar, smile charmingly at a sea of meaningless faces, have his baby, his message was clear. She had failed.

And the tragedy of it all was that she had believed him.

Nora lay shivering in her bed, knees curled to her chest, when she heard the back door open. Her memories vanished as fear sharpened her senses. She heard the door click shut, then the steady footfalls across the hall, up the stairs, then at her door. Her mouth went dry. She slid her hand across the bed to the nightstand and closed it around the handle of the kitchen knife.

A gentle rapping sounded on her door.

"Mrs. MacKenzie? Nora, are you awake?"

The deep voice was unmistakable. A thousand thoughts flashed through her mind, all of them ending with the question: What was C.W. doing here alone at night?

"What do you want?" Her voice was crisp, unwelcoming. One hand was tight on the knife while the other reached for the phone.

"Sorry to bother you so late. But you've been asking to see a birth."

Her breath exhaled with a great whoosh. She couldn't decide whether to be grateful or angry. Releasing the knife from her hand, she laughed a little at her cautiousness. This wasn't New York.

He knocked again. "Nora?"

"Yes, yes, I'm coming," she called, responding to his impatient tone. "Just give me a minute to get dressed."

"You don't have time for that. Just get your coat and shoes and come on. Nature can be impatient."

She grabbed her suede jacket and fumbled on the floor for her loafers. Then, shoving a bare foot in one shoe and carrying the other, she shuffled across the room and swung open the door. C.W. filled the frame. Even in the dark, his eyes glowed, and by the crinkle at their corners, she knew he was smiling.

"Do you even sleep in a braid?" he asked, gazing at her hair.

Her hand flew to her hair, opening her jacket over her long flannel gown.

He took a long look at her, then shook his head and laughed. "Come on, Wee Willie Winkie. You can tie up your shoes in the car." Laughing again, he turned and led the way down the dark stairs with his flashlight, muttering something about putting light fixtures in one of these days.

The ride down the mountain through the tunnel of foliage was both exciting and frightening. He wasn't speeding, but he had to be driving with as much instinct as skill to make the sharp turns in the blackness. The lights on the dashboard glowed green, barely piercing the darkness. Sitting close in the front seat, Nora found it hard not to notice his long, hard thighs as they pumped the clutch, or how long and tapered his fingers were as they molded around the gearshift. The darkness made the silence easy.

As soon as she entered the barn, she heard the laborious breathing of the ewe. C.W. left her side and hurried to the small pen, then grinning, he brought a finger to his lips with one hand and waved her over with the other. Careful not to run, Nora walked as quickly as she could to the pen where a ewe stood panting heavily amidst the clean hay. The ewe turned in her small stall and bleated. Nearby, other ewes bleated in reply, their ears pricked and their attention focused on the pen. Nora watched the exchange and wondered if the miracle of new life didn't bond all living creatures somehow.

"Not to worry, it's all quite normal," C.W. reassured her.

She felt helpless as she stood and watched the poor ewe who seemed in such pain. Yet as the low grunts increased their

The Long Road Home

pace, Nora grew inexplicably drawn to the miracle that was unfolding. All this was part of a world that had eluded her. She was desperate to learn the secrets of this natural process, somehow to become whole as a woman, if only through the efforts of a ewe. She leaned forward as the ewe bore down and a new lamb joined the world.

Nora's hand flew to her mouth as she squelched a cry of awe. Never before had she witnessed an event so excruciatingly beautiful that it touched her to the core. Tears streamed down her cheeks.

"She's a fine ewe," C.W. announced. Placing the newborn under her mother's nose, he added, "It's a shame such a good mother only had one lamb." He paused then snapped his fingers. "Nora, go and get the runt. This might work."

Nora backhanded her cheeks and carefully crossed the distance to the training pen. She approached the runt. He looked weaker and could barely utter a broken bleat when she lifted him. With maternal care she delivered the runt to C.W. Then he held both lambs in his big hands and gently rubbed one against the other while Nora watched with amazement mixed with admiration.

"With a little luck, she'll accept them both."

"You mean, she'll think the runt is her own?"

"Let's hope. Even so, that runt's going to need a bottle of milk replacer—and a prayer." He shook his head in doubt as he viewed the scrawny condition of the orphaned lamb.

Nora watched as the ewe approached the runt and suspiciously sniffed him.

"The strong maternal bond starts in the first few hours after birth," C.W. said, watching from a distance. "If she's going to accept the runt, she'll have to do it now."

"Come on, mama, don't ignore this little fellow," Nora crooned.

141

As if she understood, the ewe sniffed the runt again while he bleated and hungrily rooted for a teat. The mother held him in abeyance. Nora held her breath. The ewe sniffed once more. Then, with maternal confidence, she began licking the runt clean while allowing him to suckle.

It was too much for Nora to watch any longer. She turned and escaped to the entrance where she leaned against the frame and stared out at the drifting night clouds.

"You all right?" C.W. asked as he approached.

She hastily wiped her face and nodded, then wrapped her arms around her chest. "It was beautiful."

He moved one step closer, peering into her face, then stopped, tucking his fingertips into his waistband. "A birth is always beautiful. Sometimes brings tears to my eyes as well."

She sniffed and cast him a woeful glance. He was overcome with the sadness of it.

"Yes, but that's not it," she replied, tightening her arms around herself. "You see…" She blinked, and her pooling eyes overflowed. Wiping her cheek again, Nora collected herself with a deep breath, looking back out at the sky before continuing. It was easier to talk to the silent vastness.

"Mike and I were never able to have children. We tried— saw a lot of doctors, took lots of test—but…" She shrugged, her thin shoulders saying what was clearly understood. That nothing had worked. No baby had been conceived.

"I thought I had reconciled myself to not having a baby of my own," she continued. "But nothing prepared me for what I witnessed tonight. I never could have imagined the utter beauty of birth." She swallowed hard, a sob catching in her throat. "I could never do what that simple animal did tonight." In tempo to her fist pounding on her thigh, she stammered out, "I feel such a loss."

C.W. watched in silence as Nora struggled for composure. Her throat was constricting and her eyes and mouth were closed so tight they formed a mask of anguish.

He stood beside her, wishing there was something he could do, knowing there were no words to say. He understood now the pain behind her eyes. He understood, too, her maternal affection for the lambs. How sad, he thought. Nurturing seemed to come so easily for her. She would have made a wonderful mother.

There was more to this woman than he'd figured. In fact, he'd figured her completely wrong. Seth was right. She was nothing like Mike.

"I'm sorry," she murmured, looking at her feet as she wiped her eyes. She forced a laugh. "I'm a pushover for sentiment."

He stepped closer and leaned over her with his arm against the wall. He was so close she could smell the scent of hay and leather on his jacket, and she felt the air thicken in the small space between them. She sensed that he was studying her face. Nora kept her eyes turned away from his.

Then he touched her. His one finger wiped away a tear, and she slipped into his arms. He wrapped her snugly against his chest, like a father, or a friend. She buried her face in the warmth of his flannel shirt while he stroked her hair.

Nora snuggled deeper into the crook of his arm, rooting for security as eagerly as did the runt. As she did so, his arm tightened around her and for that moment she allowed herself the escape of feeling protected and cared for. Nora was desperate to feel the touch of human comfort. A hug.

But a hug is a two-channeled effort. As she garnered strength from him, he gathered the same from her, and in the sharing, a subtle bond was forged. They would never again look at each other without remembering this moment of closeness.

She didn't know how long they stood there like that. He

did not press her with questions nor did she offer any explanations. But as time passed, the arms of her comforter became the arms of a man. She smelled his skin rather than his jacket, and under her cheek, his heart pounded as heavily as her own.

He smelled too good, this felt too good, and she hadn't had a rush like this in so long it caught her by surprise. She'd thought that part of her died long before Mike did.

But this feeling was wrong. He was her hired hand—a drifter. If she wasn't careful, she'd confuse business with pleasure. My God, she wouldn't be like Mike.

Nora straightened and without looking into his face, released herself from his hold. The moment was awkward. It required words. She took a deep breath of the cool air and struggled for something to say. But her mind went blank and her throat went dry. So without speaking, she simply turned and walked back to the pen to peer in and feign interest as her mind cleared.

C.W. said nothing either but stood with his arms hanging at his side. He struggled to define his sudden confusion but couldn't. He only knew he felt as though someone had given him a gift, something beautiful, then snatched it away before he could even see what it was.

Nora stood at the pen, feet together and arms over the rail, and watched the two baby lambs sleep beside their mother. So, she thought. This was birth. A continuation of life, a renewal. She sighed deeply, the cycle of emotions coming full circle within her. Before her, the runt rested his chin on his adopted sister's rump and his bony ribs expanded and fell with his quick breaths. She knew he'd make it. He was a fighter. Little fellow, she thought as her chest swelled, you're an inspiration.

Her gaze swept the barn for the second time that day. This time she took in her sheep, the line of grain troughs, and the mysterious tools with a more positive perspective. They weren't so mind-boggling, they were just different. All things she could learn.

She smelled the sweet hay, the musky wool and the woodsy sawdust. Smells that she already felt akin to. This was her home. These were her babies. Deep in her core, she felt a rebirth of conviction.

"C.W.?" she called over her shoulder.

He walked to her side and raised his boot upon the gate.

"Boss?" he queried, swinging his head her way.

She almost smiled at the title. The degree to which he cocked his head, the way his hair fell over his forehead, the shine in his eyes as they met hers, rekindled the tenderness they had shared a moment ago.

"I don't know how to say this eloquently, but…thanks."

He pushed out his lips to avert his smile. "Don't mention it."

Nora released a satisfied sigh. She knew he understood. He was all right, she decided. "I hear you have a lot of books on sheep and farming. I'd like to borrow them—all of them. And anything else you've got that might help. I've got a lot to learn and I better get started." She turned her head and met his gaze. "Will you help me?"

He studied her as he considered her request. She appeared so frail, even scrawny, but her eyes shone with so much determination, it was a pleasure to witness. He could not help but admire her fighting spirit and tenacity. Did she realize how much she resembled that runt of hers?

"Of course I'll help," he replied.

She flashed a smile. The darkness could not conceal her gratitude. From the pen, her runt nickered with contentment.

This time, Nora's heart replied.

12

—

C.W. ARRIVED AT the barn early the next morning to check on any new births and to see how that spunky runt was faring. When he walked in, however, he spied Nora already sitting on the pile of hay in the corner of the barn, smiling a smile as bright as the morning sun. The runt was in her lap, lazily stretching his neck under her scratching fingers. Other lambs clustered around, curiously sniffing her shoulders and nudging her outstretched leg.

He leaned against the wall at the entry and watched with fascination as Nora pulled milkweed pods from her pocket and blew their seeds into the air. The sun that flowed through the cracks in the barn wall filtered through the darkness and illuminated her hair, giving it the aura of a golden halo. Around her, the milkweed seeds floated in a lazy pattern. She reached up and caught a fairylike seed on her fingertip, then giggling, balanced it like a tiny ballerina atop the runt's nose.

She laughed again and scratched his ears playfully. C.W. couldn't help but chuckle himself.

Nora glanced up and the smile on her face froze. Along her

cheeks and ears an apricot-colored blush spread as she stuffed the pods back into her pocket.

"I—I didn't hear you come in," she stammered.

"I'm glad. That was quite a sight."

"What? You mean… I hope it's all right that I'm in here. Willow was bleating in the corner and seemed so lost, I couldn't resist petting him. How did he get out of his pen?"

C.W. straightened and walked the distance to her corner.

"These little ones can hop in and out through the slats. It's no problem. And don't worry. The lambs love attention and we don't have much time to offer it. Besides, boss, they're yours."

She seemed to weigh his words before breaking into a wide grin. Her eyes sparkled and she heaved a sigh of relief. It was obvious she loved the lambs, and that runt in particular.

He reached the railing and lifted his foot upon the lowest slat. "Willow, you say?"

She nodded. "I named him that for his size and valor."

He mouthed an "ahh" and watched with growing respect as she rose slowly, careful not to frighten the lambs. Offering his hand, he helped her to her feet. As she brushed away the hay, he held back from picking out the stray straws from her hair.

"If you have a minute, I thought I'd show you around."

Her eyes brightened. Something about her, an innocence maybe, shook him, and he cleared his throat. "Let's take a walk toward the pond."

He led her past the hay fields, shorn now like a sheep's coat. With an outstretched arm he guided her vision across the fields, past the round bales of hay to the new line of fences, and beyond, to where the creek twisted in a serpentine pattern.

"These pastures here have been well managed," he began. "The market value of this land is relatively high. But over there—" he pointed to a hillside that had reverted to brush and wood "—that pasture is worn out and the grazing is poor. Bad for the sheep, bad for the land. Too much of America's pastureland is reverting to brush and low-value woodland."

"So I see," she replied, taking in the abandoned acres. "I really must begin to reclaim it." She frowned. "But, isn't that expensive?"

He studied her anxious expression and realized that this lady was truly worried about her cash flow. He decided to call Sidney.

"Not really," he said reassuringly. "There are low-capital methods of improving pasture. And it will improve the market value of your farmland just as open space. Besides, it's a necessary investment if you ever plan to increase your flock."

"Well, I do." She gazed across the fields. "So, I'm a grass farmer, too."

She was smiling and from the way her eyes gleamed when she overlooked the fields, it was clear that she was committed.

"You bet. I'll bring you some books on the subject. Interesting reading."

"What's that?" she asked, pointing to a line of thin green plastic tubing that ran from maple tree to maple tree.

Oh boy, he thought. She really is green. "That's a sugaring line."

"For maple syrup?" Her eyes widened. "That's another business I plan to set up."

"Good move. Seth's the man to talk to about that."

"There's a solid market for maple syrup. And I've always wanted to make it. You know, like they show on those little syrup tins, with the men in their red-and-black checkered coats and metal buckets and all. When I was a little girl, I used to eat syrup with snow. Up in Wisconsin."

"Can't do that anymore. Polluted snow's as bad as yellow

snow. And, sugaring has changed a good deal from the picture on the can."

She flushed and turned toward the hills. "I'm sure it has. You know, speaking of all that syrup reminds me I haven't eaten. I'm starved."

She looked at the barn in the distance, then ran off shouting, "Race you back!"

He found himself running like a kid, soon passing her and waiting at the small pond by the barn gate. His hands were on his hips and he sported a victor's grin. He felt ridiculous—but great. He hadn't run like that in years, and to his surprise, he wasn't winded.

She came jogging toward him, almost tripping with her laugher, and leaned against him while she caught her breath. Suddenly, he felt as ill at ease as a teenager, and the emotions that churned with his hormones were as unexpected now as they were back then.

She stood back and pulled a few stray hairs back into her intricate braid. "I feel like a kid," she said, winded.

"Yeah, I know what you mean." His voice trailed away and he thought of all sorts of idiotic things to say. Picking up a stone, he cast it with force upon the water. It skipped once, twice, three times, before disappearing in the widening concentric circles. With regret, he realized this happiness was just as elusive. "We best get back to work."

Noting the change in his mood, Nora silently matched his pace to the barn. Inside, she spotted Esther feeding Willow a bottle. Nora watched with openmouthed fascination as Willow eagerly sucked the nipple, wriggling against Esther's chest and splattering the white gluey milk down her arms and apron. Her red hair was tucked up in a blue cap to keep it away from the sticky mess, but strands strayed down her back and across her eyes. Her cotton work shirt was frayed at the collar and rolled at the cuffs and fat, black, end-of-summer flies buzzed all around her, oblivious to her swats.

Nora thought she never saw anyone look more beautiful. Nor had she ever been more envious of anyone than she was of Esther at that moment. She looked into her empty hands, then let them drop to her sides.

C.W. caught her movement. "Esther's been doing this a long time, you know," he said softly.

"All my life," Esther added plainly.

"I'd like to learn," Nora said.

C.W. smiled. "Of course. If you want to."

"I dunno," said Esther in a slow drawl, her eyes on the lamb. "Working with animals, you've got to love it. These animals will always be here, wanting to be fed. Cleaned up after. There's always something with livestock…. They count on you. You can't just pick up and go when you want to."

Nora shifted her weight. "I'm not afraid of hard work. And I have nowhere to go."

C.W. looked intently at her, then turned his attention to the loud, slurping noises from the lamb. "Now's as good a time as any. Get her started, Es. I've got to check the water supply."

Esther looked up, her eyes combing Nora's hair and clothing. Nora could feel the sarcasm in Esther's eyes as they fell on the pearls in her ears and the attention to detail in her attire. She saw herself in Esther's eyes, and saw a city girl.

"Well, get an apron," Esther muttered, pointing to a soiled denim one hanging on a nail.

Nora picked up the apron with two fingers and inspected it at arm's length. A frown crossed Esther's face and she self-consciously brushed away the hay and dirt from her own jeans.

"I don't know why you wear those expensive sweaters down to the barn. This isn't exactly a fashion show down here."

Nora looked up, stung. "It's an old sweater," she said softly, plucking at the wool.

"I should have such an old sweater."

Nora sighed but did not bother to reply. What more could she do? If Esther didn't want her friendship, there was nothing she could do to force it on her. Nora donned her gloves with resignation. She slipped on the stained apron, wrinkling her nose, but not complaining. Silently, however, she vowed to sew a few new ones.

"Over here," Esther called.

Nora trotted across the alley, chewing her lip in consternation. She sensed Esther's tension and it was creating knots in her own neck. Be calm and friendly, she told herself. She was determined to prove to Esther she could be a world-class shepherd.

Esther drilled out instructions in rapid-fire succession while Nora struggled to comply. Her hands shook as she poured the milk replacer with painstaking care into the funnel, spilling the sticky fluid down her arm.

"No, no, not like that," Esther muttered, grabbing the bottle and proceeding to fill it without a drop spilled.

Nora tucked her hands under her arms. So much for being world-class.

"Here," Esther said, shoving the bottle into her hands. "Now go get a lamb."

"How about that little one there?"

"One lamb's the same as the other."

Nora's fingers tightened around the bottle. "For the good of the farm," she repeated to herself as she marched two paces behind Esther.

Esther led her to this morning's newest lamb. Nora cajoled him out of the pen and into her lap, then, bottle firmly in hand, she tried to insert it into the lamb's mouth. She tried every angle imaginable, but no matter, he resolutely clenched his jaws and refused the nipple.

"Oh, I'll do it," Esther said, hopping the fence and drawing the lamb onto her lap.

Nora could hear Mike's ghost taunting her. "Look at you. You can't have children. You've never nursed a child. You can't even bottle-feed a lamb. You're inadequate as a woman." Her eyes stung and she turned away.

C.W. stood in the shadows of the barn's entrance watching the interaction between the two women. His brows furrowed and he shook his head slowly when he saw Nora's shoulders slump. Clearing his throat, he crossed the alley to her.

"Nora," he called gently when he reached her side. She sighed heavily and raised her eyes. Pieces of hay clung to her hair and she would have looked lost were it not for the determined jut of her jaw. There, he thought, was a clue to the real Nora MacKenzie. "The lesson didn't go well?"

Nora shook her head. "Not very."

"Let's give it another try. Give me your hand."

Nora hesitated. He was smiling. She placed her small hand into his larger one. With one resolute yank, he had her on her feet again.

"Esther," he called, "Nora wants to try again."

"I don't know if he'll take it from me." Nora balked, stepping back into him.

He nudged her forward. "Do you want to do this?"

She nodded.

"Then go get the lamb."

She squared her shoulders and approached Esther, who relinquished the lamb with a raised chin. The lamb sensed Nora's nervousness and squirmed while she struggled to keep him from jumping out of her arms.

"Here, give him the bottle before he leaps away," C.W. said, handing her the milk replacer.

Her heart began pounding. She didn't want to fail again, not in front of him or Esther, who was watching with a smug grin. I can do it, she told herself as she held the lamb's head tightly and pried his mouth open. Once again the newborn turned up his nose.

"It's no use," she sighed as the lamb scrambled to his feet and bleated piteously.

"Did you try scratching his tail?" C.W. asked calmly.

Nora looked from his smile to Esther's blank expression, then back to C.W. "Try what?"

He chuckled and bent to scratch the lamb's rump, right above the tail. To Nora's astonishment, the lamb began to simulate sucking.

"I don't believe it!" she cried.

"This little guy just doesn't know what to do." He took Nora's hand and placed it upon the newborn's rump.

"Go ahead, he'll like it. Don't we all?"

Hesitant at first, Nora scratched gently upon the wiry hair, right above the tail. The lamb quieted. Nora scratched a little harder and the lamb began rooting for the nipple.

"You better give him his bottle before he finds something else to suck on," C.W. said.

Nora chuckled as she hurried to grab the bottle, shooing away fat flies from the nipple. To her relief, the lamb accepted it eagerly and sucked away like a prize nurser. Nora's elation could not be measured by the amount of milk her lamb drank.

"Thank you, C.W.," she said in a clear voice. "I appreciate your calm manner and kindness." She gave Esther a cold stare.

"I gotta go," Esther snapped. She spun on her heel and marched out of the barn.

"I'll be right back," C.W. called over his shoulder as he paced after her. Outside the barn, he ran to catch up with Esther and grabbed her arm.

"What was all that about?"

"What was all what about?"

"I saw enough to know that you have it out for Nora and I want to know why."

Esther wriggled out of his grasp and stood before him with her back straight and her eyes looking off at the mountains.

"She's just having fun at our expense. It makes me mad to have to waste my time teaching her stuff she's never going to learn. Not really."

"That's not true," he replied.

"Sure it is. She's just another rich person from New York. I know her type. Flatlanders like her pour out of the city every summer. With their fancy clothes and hotshot hairdos. Snickering when they pass us like—like we're backward or something. Well, we have more than they'll ever have. And— and I hate them!" She swung her head around, hiding the flash of tears.

C.W. listened and understood the root of the problem. The animosity between Vermont locals and New York flatlanders was legendary, and someone as talented and bright as Esther would be particularly sensitive. He waited to let another moment pass, then took a deep breath as he formulated his answer.

"Esther, I know what you're talking about, but she doesn't fit that mold. She's not just here for a good time. I might have thought so a week ago, but since she's been here she's been consistent, eager to learn, and has done every job I've given her without complaint. And so far they've all been pretty dirty. Frankly, she's one hell of a hard worker."

"She doesn't belong. Just look at her. The color of her socks match her sweater, for Christ's sake. And her hair. Look at her," she said, pointing to the barn, "so neat and braided." Her voice carried the singsong pitch of a teasing child.

C.W. glanced into the barn to where Nora sat, grinning with contentment while Willow took a turn in her lap. C.W.'s gaze traveled down to her socks; they were the same shade of green as her sweater.

C.W. shook his head. "Esther, what's come over you? Frankly, it's not flattering. Just keep in mind that this place *does* matter to her—and she owns it. And," he said, turning her gaze back to his with his hand, "she's making every overture to be your friend. Regardless of the color of her socks, she deserves better than you've been dishing out."

Esther's face twisted in guilt. "Oh, you don't know. She's had everything—money, the city, a man like MacKenzie. What does she know about squeezing every penny dry and looking around the corner for the next trouble." She scraped the gravel with her boot. "Hell, she can just jet out of here whenever she wants," she muttered, mimicking his own words.

He grabbed her arm and his gaze bore down on her. "Don't judge," he warned. "Take my word on this one." He released his hold and patted her shoulder gently. "Give Nora a chance. Give yourself a chance."

She yanked away, then nodded curtly. "I gotta go. I want to get some painting in today."

Without another word, she turned on her heel and headed down the road. He watched her march at a clipped pace until her bobbing head disappeared behind the colored foliage.

He stared back into the barn. Nora was indeed beautiful,

in her own way. Not an applied, purchased beauty. Looking at her was like looking at a bouquet of spring flowers. Each blossom isn't especially beautiful, but all bunched together they share a freshness that lifts one's spirits. Suddenly his own words hit their mark: "Give Nora a chance."

Lowering his head, he studied his boot, considering. Then stomping it on the earth, he squared his shoulders and approached Nora.

"Listen," he said, unable to stop the words. "Do you still want that ride to town?"

"Is there a store in town you missed?" called C.W. as he lugged four overflowing brown bags from his Jeep to the house.

Nora ran to open the door, smiling as she watched him hoist up the sagging bags with his knees.

"Let's see, we hit the hardware store, the butcher, the baker, the appliance store, the garden store, and of course, the grocer's. No, I think we got them all. For today's trip anyway."

He rolled his eyes as he passed her, juggling the tilting bags. Plopping them down on the counter, he looked at the horde of bags and boxes that now littered the large kitchen.

"What in heaven's name did you buy? Or didn't you buy?"

She frowned and chewed her lip. "Just basic supplies. It's frightening, isn't it? I still have lots more to get."

C.W. cast a curious glance at her worried expression. All afternoon he watched her scout out the bargain tables, comparison shop, dicker about prices, buy in bulk the generic brands, then finally pay for the goods after a careful search through her coupons. He admired her thriftiness and the determination behind it, but something wasn't adding up.

"Did you get your errand done?" she asked while putting canned goods in the cabinet.

C.W.'s hand stilled on the paper bag. In town, he'd tried again to call Sidney. His brother-in-law had refused the call.

"Hmm?" Nora asked, looking over her shoulder.

"Yes, yes I did, thanks." He swept up the bag and carried it over to the kitchen counter next to the others. "I was glad to be of help today," he said, "but I'll just lend you my Jeep next time. Lambing is coming on strong and I can't get away."

"Uh-huh," she murmured as she unpacked the groceries.

He was relieved she let it drop. All afternoon he had dodged glances, stayed with the car whenever possible and cloaked his features with dark sunglasses and a cap. The streets were filled with "leafers," New Yorkers up for the fall foliage, and he dreaded running into someone he knew.

"Are you going to stand there or give me a hand?" she called from beside a large box.

"Nag, nag, nag," he bantered, jogging over and lifting with ease the large box from the floor. He pried open the top and began pulling out dozens of boxes of flypaper. "What every home needs," he announced holding up a strip with the pinched face, straight-backed manner of a butler. She laughed that tinkling laugh of hers and came to grab it from him with mock indignance.

"I'll have you know I've declared war against flies."

He heard himself laugh, surprised at how much he was enjoying this domestic scene.

She cast furtive glances his way as he hoisted boxes into place. He reminded her how special the companionship of a male could be.

They worked and parried as the time sped by. They were like old friends, chatting about the supplies, the farm, and other nonpersonal, safe trivia. He lifted while she sorted. He climbed stairs while she climbed stepstools. After hours of unpacking, sorting, and storing, Nora put away the final can and stood back to survey their efforts.

Night had fallen and the room held that cozy feeling of home. The pantry was filled with food and drinks, in the corner stood neat piles of linens, lightbulbs, cleaning supplies, and gear, and in the fireplace a red-and-blue flame crackled, snapped, and cheerily warmed the room. With a sigh of satisfaction, she slumped down on one dining room chair and propped her feet up on another.

C.W. strode to her side, checked her bruise, then without lifting his hands from her, walked behind her and began massaging her shoulders. His long fingers were strong and skilled, easing away, in small neat circles, all the knots of tension from her shoulders and neck.

Nora went limp in his hands and emitted a soft groan of pleasure. Up and down her neck he worked his fingers, finally caressing its small hollow base with a gentle pressure. His hands were strong and sure, and she felt her body come alive even as it relaxed. Yet, as she slumped forward, an inner voice nagged a warning: she was crossing lines again. Immediately, she sat straighter in her chair.

"Thank you, that was wonderful," she said terminating the massage. "Except now I don't think I can move."

"That's the idea," he replied, promptly removing his hands. "Care for a drink?"

Tired and limp, Nora needed all the rallying she could muster. "Sounds perfect," she purred, stretching like a cat before the fire. "Though it will probably put me to sleep."

He watched as her lithe body stretched taut, arms high above her head, briefly lifting her sweater above her navel. A perfect belly button, he thought, oval and deep. His gut stirred. Get a grip, he told himself, focusing on the drinks. He poured her a tall white wine and himself a mug of apple cider. When he handed her the wine, he barely looked at her.

Nora took a long sip of her wine, then leaned her head far back and stretched her legs far forward. "I can't remember when I've been so tired. I ache where I didn't even know I had muscles."

"You'll be sore tomorrow, and maybe the next, but sooner than later you'll tone up."

C.W. looked up again and caught sight of her stretched out like a feline before the fire. His gaze followed the firm line of her muscles from her rear all the way down to her toes, then back up again. Nora's eyes were closed and her head rested on her shoulder. He was mesmerized by the gentle rise and fall of her chest.

His own body responded with alarming ferocity and it took more control than it should have to rein it in. His face set hard as he stood there, cold cider in his hot hands, staring at her. He couldn't stop himself. Damn his needs, he cursed, glancing away, then under lowered lids, glanced back to Nora again.

It had been too long. He needed a woman. And from the looks of it, she needed a man. He gulped his cider down in a hurry, squelching any ideas that were beginning to spark. He might need a woman, he warned himself, but he had to make sure it was any woman but this one.

"I'm getting hungry," Nora said with a yawn, slowly opening her eyes.

"With all this physical labor," he said, sounding as brotherly as he could, "be careful to eat well and not lose weight. From the looks of it, you can't spare a pound."

Nora scanned her jeans and tugged at the loose waistband. Her lips pursed and she frowned. She took a final, long swallow of her wine. "Well, I guess I'd better eat some dinner. Let's see what I can whip up."

Nora swung her legs down and stood in one smooth swoop.

Suddenly she paled and reached out in a rush for the table. Just as C.W. thought she'd stumble, his hands were on her, steadying her.

"You all right?" he asked, holding her arms steady. They were as thin as matchsticks. One twist and he could break them. Nora nodded yes and C.W. caught the scent of roses in her hair.

They both knew they should draw back, but neither one did. He reached up and brushed a tendril from her face, letting his movements speak for him. She kept her eyes on him.

C.W. slowly released his hold, letting her slip back till he cupped her elbows in his palms. Her head tilted back, releasing a few more tendrils from the braid and sending them curling along her neck. Under half-closed lids her green eyes were dreamy and her lips, full and pink, parted in a lazy smile. She looked delightfully disheveled and decidedly wanton. He could have her tonight, he felt sure, and the very idea of bedding this woman sent his own head swirling.

But she was vulnerable. He had rules about such things. C.W. stretched his shoulders to shake off the sexual tension. Just like any rutting dog, he thought derisively. He determined to raise himself to the human level of decency. He let her slip out of his arms and created a distance. She weaved, then sat down in her chair with exaggerated caution.

"Too much work today," she murmured.

"Too much wine," countered C.W.

"I only had one glass," protested Nora. Then rubbing her temples, she added, "But it was on an empty stomach."

"You need your dinner," C.W. said firmly. He went straight

for the kitchen and pulled some thick slices of whole grain bread and Vermont cheese out of the fridge. In minutes, he set a plate before her next to a tall glass of milk.

Nora blushed furiously. "Aren't you having any?" she asked, eyeing the single plate.

He shook his head and went for his coat. "No, thanks. I have to go." He paused, hand on the doorknob. "See you tomorrow?"

She broke into a smile. "I'll be there. Bright and early."

His eyes lit up at her reply. "Good night. Nora."

The sound of her name floated slowly in the air between them. Their gazes locked and held. She sensed his urgency. He sensed her hesitancy. They both knew, with one word from her, he would stay.

"Good night," she replied. He nodded and left quickly, leaving her feeling like a schoolgirl with a crush.

Cold air blew in through the door and woke her from her musing. She was doing it again, allowing her feelings for this man to muddle her thoughts. Whenever he looked at her that rush overpowered her. But rather than stay clear, she found herself seeking out his gaze, hoping that he'd be in the barn when she entered.

Get ahold of yourself, she scolded. He was just passing through. He'd be gone in a month. Shaking the fuzziness from her head, she picked up her sandwich and ate every bite.

13

—

C.W. LEANED AGAINST the newspaper stand and rubbed his hands. The gas-station attendant had been friendly and offered him a cup of coffee. The night was damn cold but the coffee looked as thick as the oil on the floor and smelled as bitter. C.W. was particular about his coffee and bought a pack of gum instead. He pulled out his cell phone and stared at it. This was the first time he'd used the phone since he escaped his former life. His mailbox was full but he ignored that. Instead, he tapped in the number and the connection was made.

"You really know how to put one on the hot seat, Charles," Sidney opened.

"Really? And how is that?" C.W.'s voice was as cold as his hands.

"I've been pacing by the phone waiting for your call." He paused. "I expected you'd try me at home when I refused your call. Sorry about that, but I didn't feel safe talking to you from the office." He paused. "I think it's bugged."

C.W. didn't respond but swore under his breath. His whole

body grew more alert. He straightened again and his hand tightened around the phone.

Sidney continued in a rush. "Your instincts were right again. Something is definitely up with MacKenzie's estate. Or should I say down. Word is—and this is very inside—that his estate's bankrupt."

C.W. sucked in his breath. Incredible. That an estate as vast as MacKenzie's could go under so quickly was astonishing. But finance was a dangerous mistress, one that was quick to turn on you. His mind sharpened.

"How did you learn of this?"

"Agatha."

Agatha Blair divulge inside information to an adversary?

"When did things start to crumble for MacKenzie?"

"Sometime right before he died."

That would fit, C.W. thought as MacKenzie's desperate face flashed before his eyes. The wind sung an eerie tune between the trees, and dry leaves scattered across the empty street. Under the triangle of yellow light, his hands appeared unnaturally white. C.W. raised his collar and looked off, shaking off the specter.

"Charles, you there?"

"Yes. Tell me now about these bad loans from the Blair Bank."

There was a long pause. "I'm not sure how to tell you this but to be blunt."

"Go ahead."

"Those bad loans…there are more of them than I originally knew. They total up to millions."

Sidney squirmed in one of Charles Blair's famous silences.

"Did you find out who approved them?"

Sidney almost stuttered. "That's the mystery. On paper, *you* did."

C.W. stiffened as though he'd just been stabbed in the back.

"That's absurd."

"Of course." Sidney's voice was cautious.

C.W. felt sickened as doubt and anger churned in his gut. He knew that even in his worse state, he would never be so careless about business. Yet could he fault Sidney for believing he had? As Samuel Johnson once wrote, "All argument is against it; but all belief is for it."

There was no doubt that whatever his self-defense, Sidney, and everyone else on the board of directors, would believe that Charles Walker Blair had fumbled completely.

And that was exactly what someone had intended.

He let out a long sigh as he stared at the green-and-white neon sign in the gas station window. "Who knows about this?" he asked.

"Virtually no one, yet. Just you and me."

"And Agatha."

"Yes."

As he figured. So this was a family matter. He needed to bottle this up, and quick.

"Keep it that way. Understood?"

"Yes, sir."

He knew Sidney was sweating now. And that was good. He'd been stabbed in the back and he trusted no one.

"Charles, we need you back here. Now."

You need me, he thought. If you set me up, you're playing a damn good game. If you're innocent, then as my right-hand man, you're in as much potential trouble as I am. It was time for outside help.

"Sidney, listen carefully. We both know this thing could explode in our faces. Get Strauss in on this."

"If you think that's best." Sidney's resentment was clear.

"I do. But—" he paused to add emphasis "—under no circumstances let anyone else know you've talked to me. Especially not Agatha. My best advantage is my secrecy. I want them to think I'm out of the picture. I have a few leads here I want to follow up on. I'll call you again in a few days." He paused and considered the pressure Sidney would be under. "Buck up, Sid. We'll pull through."

He hung up the phone and exhaled a long, ragged breath. He'd have to go back to wage this war. He'd never leave the bank to his enemies. He was too much a Blair for that.

Two bits of information played in his mind as he walked to the Jeep and fired it up. One, someone had deliberately issued those loans under his name, someone close enough and powerful enough to push it through the right channels. Sidney or Agatha. The other was what Nora had let slip. That Charles Blair was responsible for MacKenzie's fall. Of course he was no such thing. But wasn't it interesting that she believed he was?

Driving home in the moonless night, he pondered the puzzle. Once or twice he veered too wide and hit gravel, but he made it back to the farm and up the road nice and slow. By the time he pulled the parking break at the big house, his instincts were making connections, playing wild cards with a loaded deck.

Maybe, if he was very, very clever, he could answer the question that rifled through his soul every morning and every night of the past year. Why did Michael MacKenzie kill himself in front of Charles Blair?

Sidney Teller paced the moss green carpet of his library for a long while after his phone call with Charles. His hands were held tightly behind his back. The comments of his brother-in-law, and more, his silence, gave him cause for concern. It was Charles's request—demand—for Henry Strauss's help, however, that really tore at his gut.

Sidney crossed to the bar and poured a liberal amount of scotch into the heavy cut-crystal tumbler. Two chunks of ice, stir, and the smooth solace flowed down his throat.

He had always known Charles Blair could be ruthless. He had seen him take apart businesses—and people—piece by piece with the cold precision of a surgeon, many times over the years. Others had feared his ability, had created legends about it, but Sidney had never feared. Not because he was married to Charles's sister. Well, maybe that accounted for part of it. Charles was devoted to his sister and fiercely loyal to his family.

No, that wasn't the reason. In all the years they worked together, Sidney had always felt that Charles trusted him. They were a team, in as much as Charles allowed himself to be a team player. So Sidney never feared Charles's wrath. He never felt Charles was the kind of man who would turn on him.

Until now.

As he took another deep swallow of scotch, Sidney considered the change in Charles. Perhaps it was time for a change in himself too, he thought. Sidney finished his drink in one swallow. The alcohol burned his throat on the long way down. In the outside hall he heard a slight scuffle. Sidney turned his head just as his wife entered.

Cornelia was deeply tanned under her short-cropped blond hair and wore none of her usual makeup. He preferred her without false color. Sidney thought her especially beautiful tonight but neglected to tell her so. Instead, he offered her a drink.

"Yes, thank you," Cornelia replied coolly.

As he poured her a scotch, neat, he said, "I thought you were off to Palm Beach."

Sidney presented her the drink, along with a chaste kiss on her cheek. Cornelia was tall, almost eye level with Sidney, and when he drew back, he saw immediately a new tension in her smooth, fair skin. A new brittleness in her soft blue eyes.

"No, darling," she replied. "I changed my mind." Cornelia took a small sip, licking her lips in thought. "I guess you could say I decided to stay." She raised her eyes and their gazes held; his probing, hers shielding.

Cornelia moved to the sofa and sat down upon the over-stuffed upholstery. "Come sit, dear," she said, patting the seat. "You look tired."

"I am, a bit." Sidney rounded the table and sat beside her, not before adding another dose of scotch.

Cornelia leaned far back in the sofa's corner to look at him better. Sidney was staring at his drink now, lost in the thoughts he could share only with the amber liquid. Cornelia felt the burn without touching a drop.

Ever since Charles had left, Sidney began closing doors. When he should have been opening them. The bank was in an uproar; it was no secret. Agatha was openly vying for control, creating division in the ranks and pitting one side against the other. Blair against Teller/Blair. Sidney was constantly under attack and trusted no one. That he didn't trust her either, hurt her, deeply.

He had withdrawn. She grew resigned.

So unlike the old days, when they had fought their wars together.

"Who was that on the phone?" she asked.

Sidney glanced over sharply then swirled his drink.

"Business."

"I don't suppose you'd care to talk about it?"

He shook his head.

Cornelia looked away. "Ahh, of course," she said, unable to disguise her bitterness.

He reached over and squeezed her hand. "Not this time, Nell." He looked at her anxiously. Cornelia's pale blue eyes revealed hurt. Sidney wished he could ask Cornelia about her brother, gauge her reaction to his comments; she who knew the mysterious Charles Blair so well. It was on his tongue to ask for her help. But Charles had been clear on the issue. "Discuss this with no one."

Across the sofa, Cornelia waited for him to say something. Her face was an open book, each small line reading, "Tell me."

"Not this time," he repeated, patting her hand. "I wish I could."

Cornelia quickly withdrew her hand and leaned away from him further into the cushions.

"I'm here," she said, forcing a sarcastic smile and raising her glass. "Whenever."

Miles away from the city, where the highest vertical elevations were the mountains, Cornelia's brother walked past the big house. The gravel crunched loudly under his feet, but Nora did not call out. C.W. continued on through the pasture, cutting a path through the tall grass. His steps cracked the long weeds, stiff from the frosty air, leaving sign and scent to the deer that man had passed.

C.W. approached the small gray cabin in the woods that was now his home. Like the big house, it perched on a bluff. But rather than a panoramic view of mountain ranges, the view from the cabin was of rolling hills and Esther's Christmas tree meadow.

As quaint as the cabin was, however, it was not built for

daily living. C.W. pushed open the door and groaned when he met air as cold as the outdoors. Esther's warnings came to mind, and he harbored second thoughts over Nora's invitation to stay at the house. No way, he decided. He'd freeze out here before he put himself in that kind of torture.

C.W. shut the door and crossed the one-room cabin to its sole source of heat: a potbelly stove. He cranked open the cold metal hatch and lit a fire with the logs Esther had neatly laid beside it. Before long, the kindling sparked and burst into flame, emitting a red glow that lit up the small room.

Esther had done a nice job cleaning, he thought as he surveyed his lodgings. Though it lacked a woman's touch. In the corner was a black iron double bed topped with his faded, avocado green sleeping bag and a worn patchwork quilt. A few paces away stood a small wooden table surrounded by two ladder-back chairs with crooked cane seats that looked like they'd endured years of service. No curtains, no rugs; just the bare necessities.

"Function, not aesthetics," he murmured, thinking of Nora's words.

It would take a while before the wood stove warmed up the room, so C.W. pulled one of the chairs close to the stove, sat back on its wobbly seat, and took out a stick of beef jerky from his coat pocket. It was so cold in the room that the plastic wrapper was brittle. He stretched his legs out before the stove, stuck one hand back into his pocket, and with his other ate his dinner.

As he stared through the open grate at the burning embers, the flames reached out like beckoning fingers, luring him inward to the realm of unbidden memories. Reluctantly he succumbed. Here, in the dark woods, in a dark moment, the ghosts of his past rose up to haunt him. He saw again the gun in MacKenzie's hand, the look of desperation in his eyes…and then blood everywhere. C.W. stopped chewing and cringed at the memory.

For months afterward, C.W. could not see past the blood. It was as though the drops that splattered across his face had left a permanent film across his eyes. Only in drink could he get past the red into black. Into a void so empty that he could lose himself. But never the pain.

That was when he'd really started to lose control. He grew jumpy and irritable. Suspicious of everyone. Nights were no better. His dreams were all nightmares, violent and horrid, and they persisted well into the day. He began to see Mike lurking in his drunken shadows. He started drinking around the clock, desperate to hide from the specter of his guilt. Days became nights then days again, rolling and rolling in a downward spiral. C.W. drank his way to rock bottom, ending up in a Vermont rehab clinic with nerves of shattered glass.

The doctors called it post-traumatic stress disorder. C.W. called it just deserts. After drying out, he followed his doctors' advice. He left his home, his work, all that he had once deemed important to concentrate on this isolated sheep farm of Michael MacKenzie. Here he did physical work to regain his strength and self-respect, he rethought his goals, and he tried to confront the ghost of Michael MacKenzie.

The doctors had been right and his exile was working. He had come to grips with his drinking, but he had yet to reconcile with Mike's suicide or his eventual return to New York. Now, after a year, he felt ready. It was time to move forward.

Moving forward, however, did not include turning back. C.W. had discovered, staring at the lifeless form of MacKenzie, that he had a conscience. He knew for certain that no million dollar loan was worth this one man's life. And knowing this, he was sure, dead sure, that he had to leave the banking business.

But how to leave? Reviewing his past as coldly as a banker would a ledger, he read without emotion that values such as compassion and pity had come up short. In the past months, he had dug deep to find those values long ignored, and once found, he had nourished them. Now, for the first time since assuming the mantle of the bank a decade earlier, C.W. could look at himself and like what he saw. In his cocoon, he had definitely changed.

But again, how to leave? That was the question he had yet to answer. The heir of a financial empire did not simply walk away. Until he figured it out, he had to remain outside the harassments of his family. No one thought to look for him on the farm of Michael MacKenzie. Everyone knew he abhorred MacKenzie's showy style and underhanded schemes, and after the suicide, it was the last place they'd look. That had been the plan, and it had worked.

He took a deep breath and leaned back. Yet now MacKenzie's widow was here and the bank was in an uproar.

A seasoned general, C.W. removed his emotion like a discarded coat and proceeded to formulate an attack. This would be his greatest battle. His enemies surrounded him. He was fighting for his life.

Somehow, this fiasco was tied up with MacKenzie. His trail was unmistakable. Somewhere he must have left records of his transactions. Could those records be here—with Nora? How much did she know?

He had always trusted his instincts. His instincts told him that Nora was probably an innocent. A lamb led to the slaughter. That knowledge made the war unsavory. For his instincts also told him that Nora MacKenzie was the key to what he wanted.

C.W. abruptly stood up and looked away from the fire and out the small four-pane window. Across the meadow the lights flicked off, room by room, in the big house. He looked at his watch; it was eleven o'clock. Nora was probably curled up with one of his farm books.

Still in his boots and coat and with arms hanging at his side, he looked awhile longer at the last light flickering in the distance. It shone, he knew, from her bedroom. He wondered if she was tired, if her head ached, and if, alone in that great big bed, she was as cold as he was.

The stars twinkled like tigers' eyes in the crisp air. The full moon illuminated the meadow between them, revealing the trodden path connecting the two buildings. C.W. sighed a long ragged breath and sat down on his bed. He was bone tired. Tired from fatigue and tired of his inner struggles.

"What the hell," he muttered, staring at his feet. His course was clear. Fate put him on this farm at this time for a reason. And that reason was to discover the link between the Blair Bank and Michael MacKenzie. To answer at last why Mac-Kenzie felt such hatred against him that he'd take his own life before him.

He knew the link existed—he just needed the proof. And the only one who could lead him to it was Nora. He didn't want to deceive her; he would try not to involve her in any way.

But keeping himself from getting involved with her—that was the trick. The timing was wrong, he told himself. She wasn't ready for an involvement, and neither was he. And she wasn't the kind of woman just to have sex with.

Oh God, he thought to himself with dismay. He had to face it. Even after so short a time, she had worked her way into his heart. Like a worm in a rotten apple, she was devouring him. It wasn't something he could understand with logic. As

Nora grew stronger and more confident, his determination to maintain a distance grew weaker. How was he going to make this work?

He stretched out on the bed and stared at the post-and-beam ceiling. In the distance he could hear the plodding, dragging sound of a porcupine. Lying with his arm beneath his head, his thoughts drifted back to Nora: her soft hair the color of cornsilk and her eyes the same verdant shade of the mountains in summer. His heart softened when he recalled how she'd struggled with the shovel that morning, how she'd sifted through her coupons, how gentle she'd been with the runt.

And how her smile made him realize his loneliness.

14

———

IT WAS EARLY MORNING. Nora stood on the bluff in the sun, one hand shielding her eyes, surveying her house, her meadow, and her fields. Before her, the morning laundry danced along the clothesline in a gusty wind. Long-sleeved cotton shirts, frayed at the collar; stained jeans worn at the rear, old white socks. Nothing fancy, nothing matched.

Fourteen days she'd been here. Just two weeks and it felt like forever. Now, she had to concentrate to conjure up the hustling pace of New York and the names and faces of old acquaintances.

Nights during the first week had been anything but peaceful. The first night Nora felt something run across her head as she slept. Sure enough, mouse droppings were found under the sheets the next morning. Nora set out scores of traps, hoping in her heart she wouldn't catch anything. But she did, two fat ones, and managed to carry the heavy rodents out to the brush then lift the metal and shake them off, all without looking once at the trap.

The second night brought nightmares of Mike.

The third night the sound of screeching and snarling hoots had her left her shivering under the covers, convinced some flesh-eating cat was crawling outside her window.

"That'll be a screech owl," Seth declared after listening to her careful rendition.

"Not a coyote?"

"Nope." He wiped the smile off his face. "That'll be a screech owl."

The fourth night a bat darted and flapped through her room. The distinct flap, flap, flap of wings batting in the windless room could be heard even with her head tucked under the covers where she remained, sweating, the whole night. Nora was sure the bats would get caught in her hair and scratch her scalp apart, like her mother had told her as a child. She blushed furiously when everyone in the barn burst out laughing at her tale.

By the seventh night she was having a hard time even falling asleep. Sometime around one o'clock she heard a distinct dragging sound on the gravel outside her window. Then came a persistent, rhythmic scraping and clawing against wood that lasted the better part of two hours. Nora had grabbed her flashlight and crept by all the windows, but the night was so black she couldn't see much in the narrow beam of yellow light. Frustrated, she picked up an old shoe and threw it out the window toward the sound. Silence followed, then the dragging sound resumed, getting fainter and fainter until it disappeared.

In the barn the next morning she started to tell C.W. about the noise but, as though on cue, the Johnston boys and Seth walked in, anxious to hear what the missus heard that night. At first the men didn't believe she'd heard anything. Frank and Junior jabbed and guffawed and mumbled comments about her crazy imagination and her "being a woman." At her indignant insistence, C.W. went up to check the house and sure enough, the plywood by the deck had a whole corner chewed right off.

"Porcupines," declared Seth. Frank and Junior nodded. "Better check your tires. Fuel line too. They like anything with salt on it."

"That's just great," said Nora with a scowl.

That very afternoon, Nora put out a salt lick on the mountain, not fifty yards from the house. She reasoned that if the varmints needed salt, they'd jolly well get it someplace other than her house and car.

After that, Nora was so tired she didn't give a hoot who or what rustled outside her window. She slept right through it.

Her nights might have been tough, but during the days her life had crystallized. The farm set roots in her heart. Each lamb mattered. Each acre counted. And at some point in the two weeks, the house became a home.

She was glad now that she and Mike had never finished it. The house's rough state allowed her dreams to soar. While she scrubbed toilets stained by hard well water or swept the uneven plywood and pitted cement floors, Nora hummed and planned what she could do given a little money. She cleaned every inch of the big house, as everyone called it, and polished it with pride. She loved each brick and rafter.

Every morning as she did her chores, Nora found telltale signs that C.W. had been in the house. He was, of course, very discreet. Only his damp towels hanging on a hook in the bathroom, his coffee mug rinsed in the sink, or a sprinkling of laundry soap near the washer, served as reminders of his presence. C.W. was always doing thoughtful things, such as having her coffee ready and stoking up the fire in the morning. But he took pains to avoid her. While she was grateful for his gentlemanly distance, she wondered if it wouldn't be nice to chat over the coffee once in a while. In fact, it had been weeks since she'd had a simple conversation with anyone and she was starved for one.

From the direction of her road came the high drone of an engine clambering up the mountain. Nora stepped away from the clothesline to move closer to the terrace's edge. Shielding her eyes with her hand, she spotted a small white van with the name Green Mountain Electric emerging from the tunnel of foliage. It rounded the ledge and came to a slow stop at the house. The gravel made a tremendous racket when anyone or anything crossed it, like a natural alarm.

Nora came around the house to meet the van, cautious as always. A compact man of medium height and build was already opening up the rear of the van and pulling out a red metal workbox.

"Hello?" Nora called.

The stranger didn't respond right away but took his time to gather a few more tools, close the door, check the contents of the box, then stroll at a leisurely pace to meet her. Before he said hello, he handed her a yellow sheet of paper with the order number and job description clearly stated.

"You're Zach Belfort," Nora said, reading the name on the paper.

"Ma'am," he replied, nodding his head.

Nora briefly scanned the man she knew to be Seth's ex-son-in-law. Former husband of Sarah. He looked more a lumberjack than an electrician with his red-checked flannel shirt worn buttoned up over long johns and all tucked neatly into dark blue jeans. He wore his pants high, like his work boots, over a full stomach. Whatever his job, he was a mountain man to be sure. All muscle, tan skin, and outdoor gear.

Most remarkable, however, was his full reddish beard. It encircled his face and met up with his full head of hair in a nonstop halo of red. His blue eyes twinkled over the bristly, full mustache, and Nora couldn't help but think that someday, when the red turned gray, Zach would make the best Santa. His friendly appearance made his silent distance awkward.

"You're Seth's relation. Thank you for coming."

Zach's face clouded. "You have some electrical work to do."

"Yes, right this way."

She led him into the house and pointed out where the circuits were and briefly reviewed what had to be done. Zach's responses were simple grunts of "sure" and "yep." It was clear he wanted to get the job done and be out of there. Nora obliged him and stayed out of his way. As the hours passed, however, she couldn't help but admire his hard work and tenacity. He didn't want water or coffee but kept to his task. When he was done, Zach brought her the form to sign with politeness and, without chitchat, started loading up.

Fred Zwinger, the pump man, who was also Seth's cousin, had been equally distant. As was Joe Ball, the pockmarked plumber from Clarendon, and Darryl Weaver, the "man to see about road work," who also happened to be Seth's cousin. They were all polite, prompt, did the work for a fair price, and never tried to sell her on another job. Whether it was because they were related to Seth and had got a warning from him, or whether it was just the way of Vermont, Nora didn't know yet. In any case, none of them was chatty. When they finished, they all hotfooted it out of her way without more than a brief comment on the weather.

Zach, however, was also her neighbor. He lived down the road where most of Seth's children and relatives had settled. The Johnston family was a tight one, and they generally couldn't stand to be off the family land. Not many went beyond the state line and only a few stepped foot in a big city. With Zach, Nora decided to try and strike up a conversation.

Nora tried the weather, the house, the new ordinance to expand the quarry, even the new hunting range, but none of them sparked. Only at the eleventh hour, when he was closing up his truck, did she obliquely mention that she was from Wisconsin. Zach's head bobbed up and his eyes twinkled.

"Wisconsin? Where?"

"Milwaukee."

"No kidding. I'm from Stevens Point."

"No kidding! I thought you were a Vermont man."

Zach crossed his arms akimbo and leaned his spine and left foot against his van. Zach Belfort suddenly appeared in the mood to talk.

He started off explaining how he'd moved to Vermont eight years earlier on a job. He missed his family in Wisconsin, but he preferred the protected wildlife in Vermont to the encroaching development in the country land of Wisconsin. Like most Vermonters, the word *development* was spoken with contempt.

Once Zach started talking it was impossible to shut him up. Nora thought it was like a floodgate that had been released.

She wasn't about to interrupt Zach. Even though she got admitted to Zach's trust only on the merit of having come from Wisconsin, she revelled in her acceptance. Nora also was politic enough to let it be known that yes, she was open to letting a "few friends" hunt her land, and no, she wasn't some typical out-of-towner who shivered under the sheets at every hoot and snarl heard in the night. Nora figured out that Zach and Seth weren't on cozy terms these days, or he'd have heard the rampant jokes about her night escapades by now.

When Zach left, he was smiling broadly and promising to lend her a hand whenever she needed it. "If you see C.W., tell him to call me about the turkey shoot. You might want to come too."

"I will," Nora called out, waving a wide arc. Plucking up her laundry baskets, she went back into the house just long enough to turn off the lights and appliances, then headed back outdoors. Today was special. She felt social and it was time for a few visits.

With arms full of freshly baked honey wheat bread, Nora managed to knock on the door of May's trailer. Very gingerly. From the looks of the rusted door, it couldn't take rough handling. May's trailer was an aqua, white, and rust-colored sorry affair with a tacked-on, tar-papered addition on the back. Beside it, under a three-sided lean-to, sat the well-polished Buick.

Around the edges of the trailer, along the walkway, and stuck anywhere sun and soil was available were garden beds of all sizes and shapes. As she waited, Nora cast a knowing eye over the garden, noting the rich, humus soil and the vigor of the plants. These were healthy gardens, made so from years of backbreaking labor, tender ministrations and heaps of sheep manure. Yet the garden had seen better days and the season was late. Mildew and mold covered long-dead leaves and the yellowed woody vines needed pruning.

It was obvious the garden was aging, like May herself. The once-sharp edges were no longer straight, brush and chokecherry had reclaimed the borders, the raised beds were tilting and rotted, and some of the perennial beds had long since given up to volunteer tomatoes. The size and scale of this garden called for a young, vigorous woman, not an old, obese diabetic. It probably pained the avid gardener every time she saw her once beautiful garden gone to seed.

"I'm coming," she heard May calling. Nora heard heavy

footfalls and a jiggle of the handle, then the door swung open. May was dressed in what was called a duster, a loose-fitting, pastel-colored kind of dress that barely covered May's shape.

"Well, hello! You finally made it!" May exclaimed. May always made declarations in a loud, enthusiastic voice, giving the impression that she didn't care who could hear what she had to say.

"Come on in. Just shoo that dog away," she said, brushing away a pepper-and-salt-colored mutt with a dish towel.

May stepped aside and Nora stepped up, squeezing past her into the trailer. Inside it was small but not cramped, and amazingly well organized. Nora expected to see a shabby room, given the run-down appearance of the outside. May's home was instead dainty. White dotted-swiss curtains with pale lavender trim fluttered at the small screened windows. Her two metal-legged chairs and her double bed were covered in the pastel multicolored quilt pattern, Round the World, that May was well known for. On the shelves, tables, anywhere she could put them, were potted plants and cactus in old tea cups, clay pots, and canning jars.

"I brought you some bread," Nora said, handing her several loaves, still warm. "I haven't gotten the kinks out of my kitchen yet, so I hope it's good. I'll bring you more, if you like."

"I would indeed. Now sit down. Wait; let me clear this wool out of the way." May huffed over and grabbed an armful of gray wool out of the chair and tossed it on the sofa.

Nora sat quietly at the small round table while May put some water in the kettle. It made her uncomfortable to hear May's heavy breaths, and she worried that she shouldn't have arrived unannounced.

"I won't stay long."

"Don't rush off. I'm just doing my spinning."

Nora noticed the small, compact wheel beside May's chair. "I've never seen a spinning wheel like that." She reached out a tentative hand to touch it. The golden wood was smooth. Instantly, Nora was mesmerized by the yellow wood black-trimmed tool that sat waist high. She wondered what it would feel like to feel wool slide between your fingers.

"It's a new design. Works like a charm. Here, I'll show you."

To Nora's delight, May delivered a brief lesson in the art of spinning. She attached a small clump of wool to the yarn by stretching the fibers out with the wheel. Pull, pull, spin, spin. The operation was amazingly easy and efficient, or at least May made it look that way. When Nora had a turn at it, her samples of yarn turned fat and irregular as compared to May's thin, even ones. Nora watched in awe as May's stubby fingers flew over the wool, nimble and quick.

"Some spinners like their wool clean, but it's easier to spin in the grease. Feel the difference."

Nora rubbed the two wool samples between her fingers. The natural lanolin did indeed have a greasy feel and looked like a clumped tail. The cleaned wool was softer, airy, like fine, brushed human hair.

"Is there much business in this?" Nora asked, already scheming.

"Some. More when you're good."

Nora made a snap decision. The instinctive, gut-level kind that she was good at. "I'm going to learn to do this," she said. "I've got the wool and God knows, up in that house all winter, I'll have the time."

May looked up and slowed her spinning. "You'll be tough competition." A smile snuck out of the folds of fat.

May's head ducked back down toward her spinning. Nora beamed. In her lap, her fingers imitated May's every move.

Gradually, as she gauged May's pace, Nora began handing her bits of wool to spin. The two women spun wool and tales over the next hour.

They talked about Nora's garden and what she should plant. May declared she would draw up the plans herself. They discussed Sarah, Seth's younger daughter, and whether she'd marry again and give those two babies a daddy. Sarah lived in a mobile home minutes from Seth. Her ex-husband, Zach, lived in their house down the road.

"Kissing distance away," May mumbled with disgust.

"Why don't they just get back together? I met him today and Zach's a great guy."

"Yeh-up, he is." May slowed her spinning and her eyes looked up with intent. "You ever seen Timmy? Her second born?"

"The one with the dark curly hair?"

May nodded gravely, pursed her lips, and went back to her spinning.

Nora continued feeding May the wool, thinking of little Timmy, always so curious and determined to get into trouble, and his sister Grace, with her carrot red pigtails. Then it dawned on her. Blond Sarah, red-haired Zach, red-haired Grace, and then little Timmy as dark haired and brown eyed as a deer.

"Oh," she replied.

"Uh-huh," May mumbled, her lips curled tight around her gums.

The spinning wheel spun while Nora thought that she still hoped it would all work out. Zach seemed mighty lonely.

"What's ever become of Tom?" Nora asked as she poured another cup of tea. Seth's eldest son had always been her favorite neighbor. Handsome and wiry, like she imagined Seth must have been when he was young. Tom Johnston always appeared with his pickup truck whenever they had car trouble or needed a spare hand. "I haven't seen him around."

When she looked up, May had ceased her spinning. She held a clump of wool in her hand and her face took on a far-away look. The sadness seemed to well up and swallow her whole.

"Our Tom is gone."

"Oh no," exclaimed Nora, setting down the teapot with a rattle. "I had no idea. I'm so sorry."

"It's a sorry tale," May replied, shaking her head. "You might just as well hear it here as elsewheres. Tom was a good boy, always workin' hard on the farm, like Seth. But times got lean so he took a job at the quarry to ease the costs here at the farm. Same as Frank and Junior done. Two years back there was this accident. Our Tom got crushed by a load of stone."

"My God, that's terrible."

May rested her hands in her full lap. "Sorrowful pain it was. Near killed Seth as well. First his wife, then his boy. Went into the mountains for a long spell. Thought we'd lost him too. He come out again, though, and when he did it was like he found himself again. A better self."

Nora leaned forward in her chair. "How so?"

May chafed her heavy arm. "Hard to explain. Seth, Squire and I—Squire's our older brother what moved out to Florida—we was always raised close to the land. Woods, ponds, fields, that's our world. But the mountains," she looked out her window toward the great timber-laden expanse beyond the windbreak. "The mountains hold a kind of magic."

"Come now, May. Magic?"

"That'll be it. The deep woods are immortal. Walk in there and see for yourself. You hitch up somehow with the wild, natural part still beatin' inside yourself. For the three of us, leastwhiles, going to the deep woods is like going to church for some folks." She cackled loudly, bursting the tension like a bubble. "Lord, Reverend Wilcox will have my soul if he hears this.

"Anyways, of all of us, Seth was closest to nature. So it was right that nature healed him. He found a small grove not far from the house. Calls it sacred. None of us is buried there or nothin'. I 'spect you couldn't dig it, it being so steep and rocky. The hills drop way far down to some rivulet of water and scattering of white rocks. Big boulders, some of them. But up high, where the sun dapples through the leaves, the grass is long and soft, like I guess angels' hair would be. A peaceful spot. A sacred spot, surely.

"Seth won't let nobody build on or around it. No human hand can change a thing. Wrote it down for generations to come. He goes to it often. Took me and the kids too. Says it's to remind us of what it was all like in the beginning. Of where we come from and where we'll all be again someday."

May sat for a moment, still looking out the window. Nora guessed May could no longer make the arduous walk to the sacred grove, but it was clear that she carried the image close to her heart, like an icon. When May swung her head back, she was her usual fiery self.

"Seth don't worry so since then. It's a relief, I can tell you. The place might be a bit let down now, but he ain't working 'round the clock and fallin' asleep at the table neither. He takes time to talk to the kids.

"And the dogs and cats. The mutts and sluts, we call 'em. Every year there's another one come crying at the door and another one leaving without so much as a thank-you. Word's got out. I think people are dropping 'em off now. He can't say no."

Nora laughed as a knock sounded on the door.

"Who in the world?" May started to rise.

"I'll get it, May," said Nora, rising to her feet. It only took a few steps to get to the door. When she opened it, she found Seth bent over three mutts, waving his glove and sending the dogs leaping one over the other for it. She couldn't tell who was having the better time: Seth or the dogs.

Seth nodded and smiled when he spied her in the trailer. Her presence seemed to keep him at bay, because he just stood there, a metal milk pail in his arms, while the dogs sniffed and scratched at his boots.

"I was just leaving," Nora said to reassure him.

Seth only nodded.

"Speak of the devil! What you got there?" boomed May from behind her.

Nora pressed herself against the door so that May could peer over her shoulder.

"That my milk?" May called. "Be a good girl, Nora, and fetch it for me. I have a hard time with these legs."

Nora did as she was asked. Seth relinquished the milk with a grunt of satisfaction and a few more nods. Underneath his visor, Nora noted that his blue eyes seemed to sparkle with some private humor that only he was privilege to. Nora carried the milk jug inside and set it on the table while May descended the three wooden steps on stiff legs, her hand tight on the rail.

"How're things over at the Thompson place?" May asked, winded.

"All right."

"John Henry?"

Seth lifted his shoulders.

"That poorly, huh? Esther ain't farin' much better. Snappin' and swipin' like a dog on a chain."

Seth grunted and looked out over the hayfield.

"It's better this way," May continued. "You can only fix a broken lamp so many times."

"Naomi Thompson's real upset over her boy," Seth said. "Worried 'bout how he's actin' so queer."

"He got an ailment?"

"Nope. Leastwhiles, not one that a potion can cure." Seth shook his head and rubbed a palm across his spreading smile. "It's a sight, that's f'sure."

"What's a sight? What's goin' on at the Thompson place?"

"Well now. John Henry just up and took his twenty-gauge and started off shootin' all his ma's whirligigs and ornaments in her front yard."

"No! All of 'em?"

"Yeh-up. Them ducks with the twirly arms, them stick-up cows, and them fuzzy sheep, too. Blowed 'em all to bits." A laugh exploded from Seth. "A real blessin', I call it."

May let loose a belly laugh that set the two of them to snickering and laughing.

"Did he shoot off the rear end of that bendin'-over lady?" May asked between guffaws.

Seth howled. "That'd be the best one."

"Praise the Lord!"

Nora stepped out from the trailer, drawn to the laughter. Not even knowing what it was about, she couldn't help chuckling herself, the laughter being so infectious. Soon enough she caught on and laughed till tears ran down her cheeks.

It took a while, but they settled down, May rubbing her belly and Seth rubbing his chest. Nora's ribs hurt.

"It ain't funny, really," May said, wiping the moisture from her eyes. The laughter fled from her voice. "That boy is hurtin' real bad. Near breaks my heart. Esther must've really broke it off this time."

That sobered Seth up real fast. "Clumsy, she is. Just like her sister."

Nora saw May's hands slam on her big hips and it was plain she was about to light into her brother with a fiery retort. Nora started back-stepping away, hoping to escape without notice.

May noticed. Her mouth was open and her finger was pointed to heaven when she spotted Nora inching away. Instantly she snapped her mouth shut and used her uplifted hand to wave Nora over.

Nora returned reluctantly. "I really have to go. Thanks for a lovely visit, May."

"You come back anytime."

"If'n you're goin' up, I got them plans for the house ready," said Seth.

"Wonderful! Then we can get started on the work. It's getting chilly up there at night."

Seth seemed quite pleased with the prospect of paying work.

"Well, I'm ready to go if you are," she said to Seth. "I expect you'll want to drive up?"

Seth snorted. "I sure don't expect to live long enough to walk up."

15

———

SETH DROVE NORA up to the house in his pickup, easily avoiding the pits and soft spots on the old road. A porcupine scuttled across in front of them, eliciting a sigh of awe from Nora and a grunt of frustration from the old hunter.

"Dang porcupines. Never remember seeing so many of them."

"Well, they won't bother me anymore," said Nora smugly. "I put a salt lick out so they'll leave the house alone." Nora leaned back in the cab, enormously pleased with her ingenuity.

Seth swung his head around to look at her, then slowed the Ford to a stop. He had an incredulous glint in his eye.

"Come on now, missus. You really done that?"

Nora guessed he was impressed. "Yeh-up," she replied proudly. It was the first time she'd used the typical Vermont response. She liked the way it rolled off her tongue. She even nodded her head a few times for good measure.

Seth's shoulders started to shake as if he was heaving. He made short, gasping sounds and hunched over the wheel.

"Seth, are you all right?" Nora asked, her voice rising in alarm.

Seth turned toward her and it was clear that he was laughing again, only his face was all red from trying to hold it in.

"Don't know," he said, pausing between laughs, "that I can take two fits of laughin' in one day."

Nora sat straighter in the cab and scowled. "What's so funny?"

"You did it now. That salt lick will attract every porcie from here to Canada. It'll be huntin' time for sure."

Nora's mouth fell open. Attract every porcie? "But I thought it would distract them from the house!"

"Nope. Nothin' a porcie loves better'n salt."

Nora slumped back in the seat and rested her chin in her palm. She imagined a long line of short-legged, spindly porcupines traveling south from Canada, just for a lick of her salt.

At first she was furious with herself. Then the whole thing seemed pretty ridiculous. Even funny. Before she knew it, Nora started laughing again. It started as short spurts, then rolled into side-holding laughter. It was fun to hear Seth let loose with another round as well.

Nothing like a good laugh to cement a friendship, Nora thought.

"Not t'worry," Seth mumbled as he fired up the engine. "My dog Zip will take care of them porcies. He just flips 'em on the back and *ziiip!* Rips their bellies clean out."

Nora blanched. "Be sure to point out Zip someday. I'd like to stay out of his way."

"Yeh-up. Good ol' Zip." Seth stretched his arm out over the wheel and eased out onto the road. The tires caught gravel and they started off with a lurch.

"Seth, May told me about the sacred grove. Will you take me there sometime?"

"Sure. Jus' let me know when."

"Would you mind if I took a few rocks from it?"

Seth's face skewered. "I would mind. I don't allow nothin' disturbed. What do you want those rocks for anyway? You got plenty of your own, lying in your fields."

"Oh, they're not for me. I just thought that since May can't get to the sacred grove, and since she loves the place, well, I thought that May would enjoy having a few of the rocks put in her garden. For sentiment's sake." Nora looked at her hands. "She mourns Tom so."

The pickup truck rumbled up the road, bumping over rocks. Seth hadn't responded. He kept his pale blue eyes dead on the road. Nora chewed her lip, worried that she'd brought up a subject still painful for him.

Seth ran his hand over his mouth and around his stubbled cheek. Then, when he set it back on the wheel, he said, eyes still on the road, "If anyone oughta bring May them rocks, it'll be me. Truth to tell, I should of brung 'em long ago."

He looked over Nora's way, briefly. Nora never knew anyone who could convey so much in so brief a glance.

"Much obliged."

Nora smiled and her chest eased as she turned her head to look out her window. Beyond in the meadow, surrounded by birch gold, straw grass yellow and maple red, a lone figure stood before an easel. Her long strawberry-colored hair blew freely in the autumn breeze. It was Esther, looking like a model in a Wyeth painting.

"Seth, stop!" Nora called.

He hit the brakes and followed her gaze to his daughter in the fields.

"Humph," he muttered with a slap on the door. "Foolin' around again. If that girl spent half the energy on her chores

191

as she did on them paints, we'd all be ahead. Yes, we would." His head bobbed in conviction.

Nora stared with her lips tight. Competent, self-assured Esther, of all people, painted. Couldn't she knit or write or something other than the one talent Nora coveted but had never mastered?

"Is she any good?" she asked.

"How would I know? Why would anyone want to paint a sky when it's right there to marvel at? God did it right the first time. Why waste time making a second-rate copy?" His voice was harsh but his eyes were soft as he viewed his daughter.

Nora's face grew somber. How long had it been since she herself picked up a brush? Two years? Three? She had buried the need, along with so many desires. Yet the yearning still burned.

"Wait a minute, Seth. I'll be right back."

"Well, don't be all day. I've got to get started on that flooring."

Nora nodded as she slammed the door shut. The walk across the meadow was a long one. The tall meadow grass that from a distance waved like silk, was brittle. It scraped against her jeans and poked through her socks as she sidestepped woodchuck holes and rocks. Yet ahead, like a beacon, stood Esther. Nora's strides were long with anticipation by the time she reached the painter's side.

Esther turned and raised her palette before her chest like a colorful shield.

"I don't mean to break your concentration," Nora said. "May I see your work? I didn't know you painted."

Esther shrugged then turned back to her work.

Encouraged, Nora stepped forward and looked past the bony shoulders to the canvas ahead. Once there, she was trapped, captured by the boldly colorful landscape. Nora exhaled a long, ragged breath.

"Esther, it's magnificent."

Esther swung around, her eyes at first wide, then narrow.

"This thing? Oh, I dunno. I like it, but something's not there yet."

"There's such vision in your work, Esther. You've captured the orchestration of the mountains, their power and color. Believe me. I've studied art, collected it. Even arranged shows. Esther, you have real talent."

Esther closed her eyes and let the palette droop by her side. When she opened them again, Nora saw a vulnerability she had never witnessed there before.

"Thank you," whispered Esther.

A silence enveloped the two women. Neither knew what to say next. In the distance, two short beeps blared from the car horn.

"Is that C.W. beeping like that?" asked Esther, turning away and squinting her eyes.

"No, it's your father."

"Aha," she said, nodding in understanding. "Can't imagine C.W. doing something like that. But Pa, well, he doesn't like to waste time."

Nora smiled. "So I understand. He thinks painting is a waste of time."

Esther smiled too in conspiracy. "Yeh-up, he does." She dabbed her brush upon the palette. "I hear you paint."

Nora almost stuttered. "Oh, I dabble. I haven't got your talent." She looked over the meadow. "I guess I'm still searching for the talent I do have. You know, you're lucky. Your gift is obvious." Her disappointment cut through the compliment and she knew by Esther's puzzled expression that she had heard it. Feeling a twinge of embarrassment, Nora looked off at the pickup.

"I better go. Your father is waiting. Sorry if I bothered you." She turned and began her trek across the meadow.

"Hey," called Esther.

Nora stopped and turned to face her.

"Maybe we could paint together someday."

Nora stood, stunned, blinking in the high afternoon sun. At last, an overture from Esther. Her own ambition to paint was pulled out of its hiding place and left dancing in her veins.

"I'd love to," she yelled back. She saw Esther nod a yes, then slowly return to her painting.

"Thank you," Nora whispered to her back.

The light from the barn glowed in the valley as C.W. hiked down the mountain to do his nightly lamb check. He was expecting a birth or two tonight. Most nights things progressed as Mother Nature had intended. Every now and then, however, a mother wasn't up to the job, and if someone didn't check, an abandoned lamb could freeze in the few hours till dawn. He was the hired hand for the MacKenzie lambs, so that someone was him.

Tonight, however, he could hear he had company. The twang of country music wafted up the road and now and then, low voices or a burst of laughter. They called it mountain noise, the way voices can carry for miles. Esther swore she knew what music he was listening to way up in his cabin.

He could use some company tonight. The day had proved too long and he needed the companionship of friends. Laughter roared out again, and catching the mood, a smiling C.W. stretched out his long legs and hurried down the road over to the barn.

Inside, Frank sat sprawled across bales of hay sipping a can of beer, and beside him Junior plucked a guitar. Esther leaned back against a hay bale with her knees up to her chest. Her face was down, ignoring the sulking glances heading her way from John Henry across the aisle. It surprised C.W. to see John Henry back with the gang and, knowing the facts, he wondered why the man would put himself through the pain.

"What's up?" C.W. asked at the door.

Their heads swung up and several hands waved him over.

"Oh, you gotta hear this," Frank said between laughs. "It's pretty good. Go ahead, Junior. Tell him."

Junior colored and shook his head.

"Aw, come on," Esther cajoled.

Junior shook his head.

"Well, is someone going to let me in on the joke?" C.W. settled on a bale of hay near Frank and stretched his legs out one upon the other. "I've got all night," he said, grinning widely.

"It's something Nora was explaining to Pa today over at the house," Frank said. He was still chuckling and coughed on his beer.

"Oh?" C.W. leaned back on his elbows. His smile faded. "What was that?"

"You should have heard her. She can talk up a pitch real nice." His sarcasm was dripping. "She's tellin'—no, teachin'—us about how to use the pastures. Like, right. We don't know. We've only been doing it for generations."

"That's not the funny thing," Esther said. "She had all these papers, jam-filled up, and she started spreading them all out in front of Pa."

Junior smiled sheepishly. "Near took up the whole table."

"There were figures, and notes and columns and columns of calculations. Pa was like to get dizzy following them graphs! You should'a seen his face!" Frank started laughing again, and this time, Junior and John Henry joined in. Esther didn't laugh. She seemed embarrassed and chugged at her beer.

"I wish I could have seen Seth's face," said C.W. in a calm voice. Inside, he was elated. His pupil was doing her homework. Knowing Nora, her report was well researched and she shirked no detail. "What did Seth say?"

"He liked it," Junior blurted out.

"Oh, he did not," Esther said. "He was just being nice to her."

"He liked it," Junior repeated, his jaw stuck out.

"Maybe he did," C.W. said slowly. "As a matter of fact, Nora and I talked about that program. The extension agent told me about it, and I suggested that she study up on it. Seems she did, in spades."

"Since when are you and the boss lady talking shop," asked Esther, pushing up from the bale of hay. John Henry scowled and threw her a sharp glance.

"Since day one."

Esther's face clouded and she leaned back again.

"Really?" asked Frank, siding up to C.W. "So, you think this plan of hers is any good?"

"I do, Frank. I think you might want to look into it for your own pastures. According to the agent, it should not only raise yield, but make your land more valuable." He looked at John Henry. "Yours too. With all your livestock, it's all the more critical."

John Henry snuck a glance at Esther's face and shook his head. "Nope. I like our tried and true methods, thanks."

C.W. shrugged. "It's your place."

Frank, however, looked interested. Frank was always interested in any idea that could increase his farm's value.

"Where'd you learn to become so expert?" John Henry asked, jealousy ringing in his voice.

A dull ache began in C.W.'s lower neck. "I never said I was expert."

"I was born to a farm," said Frank to John Henry. "I started walking beans at six and driving a four-wheel pickup by the time I was nine. That still don't make me 'expert.' You don't need to pick the beans to learn how to grow them." He looked over at C.W. and gave him a firm nod.

Like many farmers these days, Frank had to earn money off the farm to offset the rising farm costs. It'd been a tough decision for a man who loved nothing more than farming to go work with rocks and stone. Still, with being able to share C.W. part-time with the MacKenzies, Frank had made the only economic decision he could to survive.

C.W. earned the traditional package for a hired hand: a modest monthly wage, a place to live, and once a year, a freezer full of meat. And C.W. had earned their respect over the past year the old-fashioned way: with honest labor and ideas that worked.

"I never was real good in school, but C.W.'s been teachin' me a lot about money managing. Ya gotta know that stuff now to keep a farm going. You know that." He ended with a warning glare at John Henry.

John Henry nodded in agreement. Still, C.W. could see it rankled John Henry that this no-account farmhand had gained the trust not only of Frank, but of Junior, Seth, and most importantly, Esther as well.

Trust meant a lot up here.

John Henry stood and slipped on a canvas jacket over his Grateful Dead T-shirt.

"Well, it's gettin' late. Katie Beth Zwinger is waitin' for me to come over." He spoke to everyone, but he looked only at Esther.

C.W. narrowed his eyes in curious speculation. Frank

looked ready to keel over. Junior's mouth fell open and he shifted his glance from John Henry, to Esther, then to Frank with a worried look on his face. Seeing that Esther was more intent on staring at her boot than at him, John Henry waved a quick good-bye and hastened out of the barn.

The moment he left the mood of the barn lightened. Junior grabbed his guitar and started strumming. Junior was a simple, good-natured person who avoided confrontations.

Not Frank. He was too much like his pa. "What's this about John Henry seein' Katie Beth?"

Esther picked at the straw, but two small patches of pink appeared on her cheeks.

"Damn it all," cursed Frank. "He knows I've got my claim on her. I oughta give him two good reasons to back off," he said, lifting clenched fists.

"Aw, cut it out, Frank," Esther snapped. "He's only seein' her to get back at us."

"What did I ever do to him?" asked Frank, still pissed off.

"You're my brother."

"Yeah. Me too," offered Junior.

"I still don't like it," said Frank, lips taut.

"Then do something about it," said Esther in a huff. "You've been scratchin' at Katie Beth's door for years now. It would do you right, do us both right, if the two of them ran off and got married! What's the matter with us Johnstons anyway? A bunch of old bachelors and spinsters, that's what we are. Looks like that's what we'll ever be."

This time, it wasn't Esther's temper that shut Frank up, but her sadness.

Frank rubbed his neck and sprawled far back on the hay bale, bringing his foot up to rest against it with a thump.

Junior's clear, rich voice began to hum, then sing the words

of the Cat Stevens song he was playing. His voice had a soothing quality. After a few measures, Frank joined in with his
fine tenor voice and finally even Esther sang. Pick, strum,
strum. The earlier tensions melted away and faces softened as
the circle of music bound them once again.

C.W. leaned back on his elbows, perplexed by the sudden
explosion of emotion and its equally sudden demise. C.W.
allowed himself to get drawn into the music; he who never
sang. Not knowing the words, he hummed along and kept
time with the wagging of his boot.

Nora would love this, he thought, stretching out in the
circle of music and friends. He hoped she'd be included too,
someday. If Nora was going to live up here, work here, become
a good neighbor, she'd have to join this circle.

16

——

DAYS FLY FAST in the country. Not as fast, however, as Esther flew from her house a few mornings later, slamming the screen door behind her. Her long legs barely touched the ground as she traveled, straight as an arrow, to Aunt May's trailer. Taking the two steps at a single leap, she slammed against the door and knocked three times, rocking the metal, calling, "Aunt May?" She knocked again, even louder.

May swung open the door. "What in heaven's name is the matter with you, child? I'm watchin' my soaps." May took in Esther's wild-eyed appearance.

"Come on in, Esther," she said softly, as she stepped aside.

Esther slipped in, brushing against May's ample bust, and immediately slumped down on the small sofa. In her hand she carried a torn envelope and a single sheet of white paper.

"I guess you heard from that New York school?"

Esther nodded, her face grim. "Oh, Auntie May. They don't even want to give me an interview."

May took the letter and brought it close to her squinting eyes. It didn't take long to read the few lines. Lord help us, she thought, looking over at her niece blinking fast, swallowing hard, and pinching her lips, as if she was going to heave tears. So few words to throw a dream away. Esther's smug confidence would take a beatin' by this blunt rejection, that was sure. And Esther'd be more mortified to show tears.

That Esther could come here to let go touched May deeply. She understood her niece's headstrong ways. She had come by them honestly. Stubbornness could be the seed of loneliness, May well knew. It was her fervent hope to spare Esther the regret she herself felt by teaching Esther to temper her willfulness with contemplation.

"You might not believe this," May said. "I'm sorry it didn't work out. But New York is a big place. There be lots of roads to it."

"Not for me."

May watched as Esther gathered up her legs and sat as stoically as an Indian. May sighed heavily and plodded the short distance to Esther's side. There wasn't room enough on the small sofa for Esther and a woman May's size, so she eased down into the kitchen chair beside her, grunting on settling in.

"So!" she exclaimed, slamming her hand down on the table. "Let's see some tears! Where are the angry shouts? Let's hear them, get them out. Or all that anger will fester in your spleen and make you sick."

Esther shook her head. "No, Aunt. There's no fire left to belch. It's time I woke up from this dream. Get me a life."

"There ain't no fire, huh?" she said, disbelieving.

Esther stared at her hands. May followed her gaze to where the nails were stained in green and brown oils. "Esther, that paint goes deep under your skin. You couldn't wash it off in a thousand washings."

Esther chipped at the paint a moment, then her face

contorted and she brought her colored fingers up to hide the tears. May drummed her fingers on the table while Esther sobbed, her own big heart breaking. Even as a little girl, there weren't many times she could remember seeing Esther cry. Those childish tears were easy to deal with, unlike complicated woman tears. Last time she saw Esther's tears was when MacKenzie had hurt her bad. Back then, however, May'd witnessed more shame in those tears than sorrow, and her own heart didn't break as it did now. She reached out and handed Esther a box of tissues, which Esther promptly used.

"It's not just about going to New York," Esther said plaintively, tearing the tissue into bits. "I can live with them rejecting me for some reason: I'm poor, I'm ugly, I'm crude. Anything—but not my work. I don't know how much more rejection I can get past. Hell, Aunt May, I'm not even in the running. I haven't crossed the line, and until I do, all my work is just, oh, I dunno... It's considered a hobby."

"By whom?"

"You know."

"Not by me. I know how hard you work, and how good you are."

Esther shifted her weight, irritated. "I know. But everyone else will. They think I'm crazy already. And Pa...well, you know how he feels about it. He'll be glad I didn't get in. He'll say, 'I told you so.' To get married." She threw her head back and emitted a bitter laugh. "Boy, John Henry will like this. Seems he was right all along."

"Seems to be you're listening to all the wrong people, honey. What do *you* say?"

Esther ground her teeth with a determination typical of her.

"I say I'm through wasting my life. John Henry's right. I'm twenty-six years old. I'm gonna settle down, marry John

Henry if he'll take me back, and have babies. I deserve a little happiness."

An alarm went off in May. She was eager to support this turn in Esther's attitude. To have her niece comfortably settled on John Henry's dairy farm nearby was her fondest wish. But only if she really meant it. If Esther was giving up before the fight was finished, her regret would last a lifetime and snuff out any chance for happiness in the bitterness of might-have-been.

"Be sure you know what will give you happiness," May said.

"I didn't say a lot of happiness, just a little."

"That's a dangerous sentiment."

Esther straightened her long legs. "Besides, Pa needs me. The boys need me. They depend on me. I've got to stay here and take care of them. And John Henry needs me too. He loves me, even still. Everyone expects us to get married. It's just my stubborn nature that fights it."

May picked up the letter, smoothed out the wrinkles, folded it three times and neatly tucked it back into the envelope. Handing it back to her niece she said, "Esther, I'm going to ask you a favor. I don't ask many, so I hope you do me this one."

Esther took it, looking surprised. "Sure, Aunt May. I'd do anything for you."

"I don't want you to make any decisions today. Tomorrow neither. Promise me you won't go telling John Henry you'll marry him just yet. Decisions like that take thinking. Will you do that for me?"

She looked at Esther and could have sworn that she detected relief in her eyes.

"Sure. But, why?"

May rose to rinse a few teacups. Her arms filled the tiny

sink. "Want some tea?" When Esther refused, May poured herself a cup and sat back down. Once settled, she felt ready to speak.

"I wasn't always this fat and plain," she said, squeezing lemon into her tea. The tart scent filled the small trailer. May could say it now, "fat and plain," without the acute embarrassment she used to feel.

"When I was young, I had a fine full figure and a head of hair, just like your own."

"I've seen the pictures, Aunt May. You were beautiful. You still are beautiful."

May waved her hand in rebuke. "I'm not fishin'. I only mention it to remind you that a man could fall in love with me back then. One did. A fine, kindly man, a lot like your John Henry. But I had my fiery ways, even then. I got careless with something fragile, 'cause that's what love is, a fine fragile thing at the beginning, before it grows strong. We quarreled over something, I can't even remember what. I sent him away, sure he'd come back. It was expected that we'd marry, too. But he never did come back. He married another." She paused to take a long sip of her tea. The lemon puckered her lips and the cup clattered a bit when she placed it back.

"Heard tell he died a year back. Even after all these years, I mourned him."

"You think I should marry John Henry?" Esther eyed her aunt with a blank face.

"Now let me finish. Knowing what I had, I threw it away on a whim. I never had what you have—your talent and your drive. Do you think that comes every day? I'm sayin' that you don't play with the honest affections of a man like John Henry. If you love him, know it and marry him. If you don't, let him go. You can't keep bouncin' back and forth, expectin' that boy to always be there. It ain't kind."

She coupled her hands and looked directly at Esther. "Truth be told, you spend more time dreamin' about your paint than you do John Henry. Esther, that don't look like love to me. I don't believe you'll ever know the answer lest you go to New York and give your dream its due. Don't act hotheaded. Think on it."

"I will. I promise. I'm not too anxious to tell anyone just yet, anyway. I need to walk to the sacred grove and settle it inside."

"That'll be right. Go on, then. Do it now. Don't put it off. Come here and give your Aunt May a hug first."

May enveloped Esther in her arms, blanketing her in love. She wanted to protect her babies from outside harm, but she'd learned with Tom that she couldn't. She could just be here to soothe the outside ailments with salve, plasters, and potions, and salve the ailments of the soul with unconditional love.

When Esther left, May reached out for the phone and pulled it toward her. She had three calls to make. She'd call her brothers, Seth and Squire, later. But first, with her mouth set in a firm line, she dialed Nora MacKenzie's number.

Nora readily agreed to tap her contacts in New York. She couldn't promise to open any doors for Esther, but she could call in a few overdue favors. Nora didn't need to be cajoled. She was a firm believer in Esther's talent.

Squire, however, was on the receiving end of a long lecture from his little sister about family responsibilities. Him with all that money in Florida and no children to leave it to. Squire argued that he'd always planned on leaving it to his nieces and nephews in his will, but May asked him why they had to wait for him to die for them to start living? He didn't need that hold over them to get mincing attention. Didn't he know how they adored him? This got Squire thinking, and he promised to send the necessary funds to Esther right away.

Seth, well now…May knew Seth would be the hard one. There was no bullying him, or forcing him neither. Seth had his own vision of the world, a wider one than most, and he came by it after long hours of thought. She rang him up and asked him to come over and haul away her garden debris. If she asked him to help, he'd be sure to come. Seth wasn't likely to show up just to talk. 'Specially not at the close of lambing season.

Before dinner, after the afternoon barn chores, Seth drove up to the trailer in his pickup. He lived across the street, but she never expected him to walk over. She peeked out the dotted-swiss curtains to see Seth standing before her garden beds, observing them. May felt a flutter of satisfaction and pride, seeing her beloved beds freshly turned, the wooden bed boards straightened and all the shrubs pruned far back.

May tugged on a sweater and went outdoors to meet her brother by the front garden. He turned to greet her with a lively smile.

"Garden's been cleaned up real nice," he said. "Old vines took out, and them pumpkins are gonna make fine pies. Them fall greens been thinned, too."

May's gaze passed over the pumpkins and vegetables, which she grew for the family, to rest instead on the mums that she planted for color and pure pleasure.

"It's gratifying to come out here again," May said, crossing her arms in satisfaction. "I put that porch chair right smack beside the mums, just to sit and view it."

"Nora MacKenzie do all this by herself?"

"Yes, she did." May's head bobbed. "Worked for days and days, and her with all them other chores to do. It's no wonder she's so skinny, the way she hurries about. But every bone in that body is dear. Sweet thing."

"That was real thoughtful." Seth rubbed his bristle. "I got something for you, May. Somethin' I should'a brung long ago. Seeing your garden all fixed up again, well, I figured it's time."

May's curiosity was piqued and she felt like a child at Christmas as she waited. Seth climbed into the pickup and backed it up right to the edge of her garden. A flurry of May's hands and shouts told him when he'd gotten close enough to her precious flower beds. Seth heaved himself back out of the truck and walked to its rear, hitching up his pants and lowering the truck's rear flap. Then, to May's clapping hands, he brought out boulder after boulder of white marble and stone, setting them down in a neat line bordering her front garden. Each rock had been carefully chosen to be as uniform in size as nature had made them. Each rock had been washed.

By the time the last of the boulders was set in place, May's hands were coupled by her trembling lips and tears glistened in her eyes just like the water glistened upon the rocks in the late afternoon sun.

"They're from the sacred grove," she murmured.

"Yeh-up," replied Seth, breathless and brushing off the dirt from his hands. He reached out his hand and placed it upon his sister's shoulder. A pronounced crease etched his brow, and beneath it, his eyes darted sheepishly.

"I know how much you loved Tom. You miss him as much as I do. You always loved all of 'em like they was your own. I should'a noticed you couldn't get to the grove no more. It took a stranger to point it out to me."

May patted his hand on her shoulder and gave him a look that said she was as glad to hear him say it as he was glad to get it off his chest.

"Come on inside," May replied gravely. "It's time we talked about something else."

Seth followed May into the trailer and the two took either side of the round café table. They sat down in the same fashion, age and bearing being similar: they gripped the sides of the table and lowered slowly into the chair. After tea was poured, May told Seth all about Esther's rejection from New York.

Seth reacted precisely as Esther had predicted. New York was no good for his daughter, he said. Why'd she want to go there when she could live here with her family? he asked incredulously. His stress on "here" and "there" implied his well-known feelings of city versus country. May let him go on, quietly listening to how Esther was being mule foolish not to hitch up with John Henry and give him some grandchildren, like was expected.

That's when May jumped in.

"Expected by who?"

Seth met her gaze with raised brows. "John Henry, for one."

"And you?"

He flushed. "Everyone. They been together since they was six. His family treats her like their own." He rubbed his jaw and mumbled, "They been carryin' on like they been married, that's a fact."

"Well, they're not. And maybe they oughta not be."

He cupped his jaw and rested it, elbow bent on the table, as he eyed her speculatively. "What're you getting at?"

May brought herself up to full height in her chair, her ample bosom swelling to awesome proportions. In a firm voice she said, "Esther ought not to get married yet. She ought to go to New York."

"I never told her to stay. Never tell any of my kids how to live."

"You don't have to."

Seth shifted his gaze toward his sister. Confusion mingled with surprise in his eyes.

"Your kids love you," she said. "They flock around you like bees to honey. And I'm not sayin' that's bad. It's good fer some. Take Frank. Ain't nothin' he wants more than to live his life on this land. Sarah's just a bit mixed up now, but she'll turn out all right. She don't wanna go nowhere else. Her life is here with Grace and Timmy, and Zach too, once they settle up. And you know they will if'n you stop coddlin' her and boot her out."

Seth raised his chin high and furiously scratched his neck.

"Junior." May paused while her face eased. "Well, Junior may be simple but he's all heart and he'll live a good life here. Frank will always look out for his brother."

"That's how it should be." Seth was looking out the window.

"Yeh-up." May paused and made circles with her two thumbs. "Esther, though, is a maverick. She can't live by the hand-me-down values the rest of us live by. For you it's always the boys that go off huntin'. And it'll be the girls that tend the home. Well sir, Esther ain't like most women. She's slender in the hips. Esther's got to go out and stake out her own territory."

Seth dropped his hand down on the table. The spoons rattled on the metal table.

"So let her go! The gate's wide open."

May shook her head and turned sad eyes toward Seth. He had a look of resolution on his face she knew too well.

"She can't," May said gently. "The gate might be open, but the electricity's still on. She's scared of gettin' zapped." May's eyes flashed and she leaned as far forward over the table as her bosom would allow.

"Seth, you got to give your daughter permission to leave. You got to turn off the fence."

Seth angrily pushed himself away from the table, the chair scraping against the floor. For a moment he stood looking down at his sister. His face was flushed, and his lips tightened and loosened, fishing for the right words. May waited, then frowned when Seth merely brushed his hand in the air with a frustrated swipe and strode over to the door. He rested his hand on the handle a spell, pondering, then turned to face her. His face was resolute.

"I reckon she's old enough to turn it off herself."

17

—

ONE GOOD TURN deserved another in her book. Nora wanted to show her appreciation in ways that counted up here. In action. First on her list was C.W. Nora appreciated his kindness in the barn, his loan of books, and his driving her to town, knowing full well he counted the minutes until they got out of the town limits. C.W. was always doing that, giving up his time to help someone. How often had she seen him rush to Seth's side to carry a heavy bag or a tool for the old man? How many hours did he spend tutoring Frank in business? Esther was like a sister to him. They parried and shared barn chores in a way that would have made her jealous were it not such a friendly exchange to witness.

As she clambered across the meadow, the little red wagon filled with shopping bags bumping along behind her, she wondered about her elusive hired hand and his penchant for secrecy.

She came upon the little gray cabin suddenly. It sat on a rounded hilltop in the middle of a grassy clearing. The sun shone straight upon the tin roof without the hindrance of maple, birch, and cherry branches. It had been her cabin once. Nora had added flower boxes under the four-square windows, a slate front stoop, and to the left side of the cabin, the rising hill was held back by a boulder retaining wall.

The cabin sat on the border of the Johnston land, giving the cabin full view of Esther's small Christmas tree meadow and below that, Seth's marvelous Skeleton Tree Pond. Nora had built the cabin on this picturesque spot as a place to paint. That, she thought sadly now, was another dream that had died up here.

She pushed open the door to the cabin; it creaked loudly, making her cringe thinking the entire forest could hear the high wail. She peered around the door into the room. Motes of dust floated in a single ray of sunshine that filtered through the southern panes of glass. Nora hesitated, her hand resting on the knob. She didn't want to invade C.W.'s privacy. But hadn't she promised to help fix up the place?

Her mind made up, she hoisted the bundles in her arms up with her knee and walked into the one-room cabin. His room, now.

Her first thought was that C.W. lived like a monk. Four straight-backed chairs. A faded sleeping bag on the black iron bed. Dishes stacked on a shelf, collecting dust. Everywhere else lay books. Piles of texts tilted in the corner. Sheep and farming magazines were neatly stacked under the bed, and a long row of old, leather-bound volumes crowned the mantelpiece. Nora ran her finger across the crinkled leather as she browsed: Lao-tzu, Jung, de Tocqueville, Thoreau, Mark Twain. Her brow rose. Pretty sophisticated reading for a laborer.

On the table, one book, The I Ching, lay open beside a piece of paper and three pennies. Intrigued, she walked over for a closer look. He had drawn some kind of hexagram on the paper and beneath it scribbled notes in a tight, illegible script. Something about "the wise man and perseverance."

Another torn scrap of paper was sticking out from beneath the book. On this sheet, one word caught her eye. At the bottom of the paper, encircled so many times the tip of the pen had scraped through the paper, was the name *Nora*.

She caught her breath and stepped back from the table. This was too private. Sure, she was curious about the private Mr. Walker, but she wouldn't pry.

So Nora set right to work. Out of the shopping bag she pulled a freshly laundered down quilt and crisp white cotton linens. She approached the bed with militaristic purpose, but as she bent to fold up the sleeping bag, the musky, stale-sweet odor of his bedding arrested her. The scent was as identifiable as his signature.

Absently, she ran her fingertips atop the sleeping bag's flannel lining, along the cold jagged edge of the zipper, and finally, traced the depression on his pillow. Nora gathered the faded green sleeping bag to her face, sniffing tentatively, then rested her cheek against the soft flannel. This was as close as she might ever get to holding him.

Nora jolted back.

Back to work, she ordered herself, shaking the thoughts away firmly as she shook out the sleeping bag at arm's length. In like manner, Nora efficiently made the bed, dusted the furniture, swept the floors, and washed the grimy window-panes. It brought her pleasure to take care of him. She told herself it was because she was grateful for all he had done for her, but her heart didn't buy it. Smelling his scent, touching his books, making his bed—all these intimate actions hinted the truth. She was falling in love with him.

After a few more trips back and forth from the wagon, Nora was finished. Arms akimbo, she surveyed her work. It would do, she decided, pleased. The bed was now comfortably made up with fresh linens and a down quilt of slate blue. Curtains hung at the windows. A round, brightly colored braided rug stretched out before the wood stove, and sitting on the iron stove sat a new tea kettle and a selection of instant tea and coffee. Still, something was missing.

Her eyes scanned the room and were drawn to the far corner. Tilting against the wall, behind a pile of dirty laundry, rested a canvas. The scene depicted a shepherd, whose familiar hands-on-hips stance suggested alertness yet calm. He stood on a bluff overlooking a field dotted with white-fleeced sheep. Nora sighed. The painting was magnificent; Esther's talent undeniable.

Nora grabbed hold of the large canvas and lifted it high atop the mantelpiece, shoving aside the books to make room. There was no competition here. Nora knew raw talent when she saw it, and respected it. Standing back, she nodded firmly.

"I've been meaning to do that for some time," C.W. said from the doorway.

Nora whirled around, her eyes wide and her mouth agape. "What are you doing here?" she gasped.

C.W.'s brows gathered and he folded his arms across his broad chest. "I was about to ask you the same question."

A great whoosh escaped from Nora's lungs as she flopped her hands upon her apron. Her gaze circled the room, then shyly returned to his. What could she say that her actions didn't already scream out? She could feel a hot burn rising on her cheeks. The way he was staring at her, she felt certain he understood every secret that her work implied.

He remained silent, waiting, and she knew him well enough by now that he could stand there forever.

"I'd promised to fix things up," she started.

No reply.

"I picked up a few things in town..."

He still stood there, like a stubborn mule, not helping her out of this awkward situation in the least. Embarrassment, frustration, and pique all flared at once, prompting her to hustle over to her cleaning supplies and begin stuffing them back into the bags.

"Oh, forget it," she said without looking back. "I just wanted to say thanks. So thanks."

Her back to him, she didn't see him smile.

He scanned the small room, picking up the myriad details of change. The effect wasn't frilly, but homey. The blue-checked curtains matched the tablecloth, and there was no doubt in his mind she'd sewn them herself. The floors smelled of soap and the windows sparkled. And seeing the tea, he realized she'd noticed that he preferred herbal. C.W. was touched, much more than he cared to admit.

"It looks quite nice, Nora."

Her hands stilled upon the brown bags. Without looking up, she murmured, "Thank you."

He watched her as she bent over the bags. Her softly rounded bottom was so womanly, complementing her actions. How could a woman like her have been married to a man like Mike MacKenzie, he wondered for the hundredth time?

"Nora," he said, stepping inside, "why do you never speak of your husband?"

Nora stiffened, caught off guard, and quickly finished collecting her supplies. "It's too painful," she replied, not looking at him.

He winced, thinking that he'd been wrong. That she still mourned him. "Yet you said you didn't miss him. At all."

Nora heaved a sigh, one that spoke of frustration and impatience. She slowly rose to her feet, all the while wiping her hands upon her apron.

"By the time Mike died," she explained in a matter-of-fact voice, "there was nothing much between us to miss. He thought I'd failed him, not having his baby and all."

Nora walked over to the window and stared out over the bluff. But rather than pines and hills, in the vista Nora saw shapes and figures of her past.

"As he...went out more, I buried myself in my work on various art museum committees. People said I should have left him. They called me a fool, laughing behind my back. Did they think I didn't hear?" She grasped the curtain tightly in her hand. "But that's not my way. Not the way I was raised. I believed in my marriage vows—for better or for worse. I just got a little more of the worse."

Nora's shoulders slumped as she slowly untied her apron and lifted it over her head. C.W. watched as she folded it neatly, pressing the creases in the fabric while lost in thought. Then she walked back and tossed it carelessly into the bag.

"I spent a lot of time at our house in Connecticut," she continued. "In my garden." She lifted her brows, daring him to question. When he didn't, she said, subdued, "I guess I was hiding from the truth."

Nora met his eyes. "What about you, Mr. Walker? It's obvious you're not some uneducated laborer." She waved her hands to indicate the stacks of books all over the room.

"When we were in town, did you think I didn't notice the way you tugged the brim of your hat over your sunglasses? I've never known a man to check over his shoulder as often as you did. What are you hiding from?"

C.W. walked over to the table, allowing his hand to rest upon the opened book. Nora tracked each movement. C.W. appeared to read a line or two of it, then moved his hand the few inches over to the paper that held her name. It lingered there, the tip of his index finger tracing over the circled name. Then, very slowly, he crumpled the paper into his large hand.

"Have you ever killed a man?" he asked, slowly raising his eyes to hers.

Nora paled. Old suspicions flashed through her mind. "No," she replied softly. "Of course not."

"Of course not," C.W. repeated. "Neither have I. At least not directly. But indirectly I caused a man's death. And the guilt is just as strong." He raked his hair with his fingers, leaving paths in the gold like plowed fields of wheat. "Does one ever escape from that?"

Nora was struck with the pain in C.W.'s eyes and she knew, for certain, that she'd never have to fear this man.

"It doesn't pay to hide," she told him. "I've tried it. The problem doesn't go away."

Silence settled in the room as peacefully as the sun settled in the western sky. A pinkish pall flooded the gray cabin. Off in the distance, the birds sang out a mournful call, sounding the end of another day.

"It's getting late. I'd better go," said Nora, gathering her things. As she lifted them she felt his two strong arms hoist the bags from her. He walked to the wagon and was about to put them in when, resting the bags on his bent knee, he carefully removed a grapevine wreath from the bin.

"What's this?" he asked, settling the bags in the wagon and lifting the wreath.

"Oh, it's nothing," muttered Nora, rushing over.

"Not so fast," he said in a teasing voice, raising it out of her reach. "Let's take a look." The rough grapevine wreath was adorned with dried flowers and milkweed pods. The effect of the soft gray puffs against the curling, woody vine was exquisitely natural. Like Nora.

Nora's cheeks were flaming. She had made it for him.

Compared to Esther's powerful painting, however, it seemed so naive. Yet, it was her best, and that was all she had to give.

"It's quite nice," he said, admiration in his eyes. He grabbed a hammer and nail from his tool chest and headed straight for the door. With three firm taps, the nail was in and the wreath was up.

Nora walked over to the wreath and ran her fingertip through the downy seeds. "Now, it's home," she whispered. "You can stay here, C.W.," she added, eyes on the wreath, "for as long as you wish."

Behind her, she sensed him shorten the distance between them until he stood inches away from her. His breath was warm upon her head. She could smell the musky scent of his skin. She recognized it, like a pheromone, and it sent her blood racing and her heart palpitating.

She waited for what seemed an eternity, listening to his breathing grow labored behind her. The fine hairs on her head tingled as his lips lowered to lightly graze in the soft gold. His breath was warm. His fingertips lightly cupped her elbows, then stretched out to caress upward along her arms to her shoulders. Suddenly, his grip tightened, even as his lips lowered to her head and he pulled her back against his broad chest. She closed her eyes and arched her neck back like a swan. For a moment they stood there, as the birds called, as the sky darkened. For a moment they were not Charles Walker Blair and Nora MacKenzie, nor boss and hired hand. They were simply a man and a woman.

C.W. released her shoulder to grab the door and give it a closing shove. But Nora flashed out her own arm, stopping its swing shut.

"I'm not ready for this, C.W.," she hammered out.

Feeling his hands drop away from her, Nora moved away and hurried from the cabin. She couldn't look back. Grabbing hold of the wagon's handle, she hastened her trek back across the meadow. The little red wagon wobbled behind her. Nora heard the *clunk, clunk, clunk* of bottles banging in and out of the bag, but she didn't dare look back to see what she had lost.

Junior and Frank sprawled across the front seat of their Impala not saying anything, just staring out the left side of the car toward the plate glass window of the Look, a small dress shop in Rutland. The dress shop sat between Putnam's Ace Hardware Store, with a few snow shovels and snow blowers in the window, and the Green Earth health food store that stuffed every square inch of their display window with tea, vitamins, and assorted snack foods. The tiny shops clustered together in the dirty stone federal building like war veterans at a parade. They were old, run-down, and had seen former days of glory. Not one had "the look" that would stop the parade of cars from passing.

Except one car. In it, Frank wasn't thinking about the chipped paint or the outdated neon sign as he stared at the plate glass. Inside the window, Katie Beth Zwinger was busily laying out the new display: a couple of classic wool skirts with coordinating orange and yellow sweaters. Colored paper leaves that were ragged and curled at the edges were tacked on the window in a disappointing attempt at fall frolics.

Frank thought it was all grand as he watched Katie Beth's long fingers work rapidly over the mannequin. He studied the way she carefully plucked out the straight pins from her pursed lips. He eyed with stilled breath the slight length of thigh that crept into view as Katie Beth lifted a knee and stretched to pin the back of the kilt.

"She sure is good at her job," Frank said with awe.

Junior shrugged. He couldn't think of much to comment about.

"Why'd she start goin' out with John Henry, do you think?" he asked anxiously, swinging his head to face his brother.

Junior shrugged again, shifting his gaze, knowing for sure what he'd like to say but didn't dare.

Frank's gaze strayed back to Katie Beth. "We've been datin' for four years now."

"Five."

"Yeah." Frank scowled. "It must be that dairy farm John Henry got. Shoot. If I had that dairy farm, Katie Beth wouldn't be lookin' around."

"You got a farm, too."

Frank shook his head and ran his hand along the back of his neck. A dull ache throbbed. "Do not. Neither do you. We're just like Esther said, two bachelors without a dime to rub between us. Pa ain't never gonna let me run things. He never wants to see the land split up."

"You can have my piece, Frank. I don't care."

"Don't matter none," he said morosely. Frank glanced quickly at his brother and saw the hurt shining in Junior's eyes. He gave him a gentle shove. "Hey. You and I are always gonna be a team, right?"

Junior's eyes brightened and he bobbed his head. Frank ventured a lopsided smile, then sunk his chin in his palm and stared back out at Katie Beth.

Junior gathered his brows in worry. "Don't worry. Katie Beth ain't that way. She's real nice. She dances good, too."

"I know it," replied Frank, looking at Katie Beth with a new sadness in his eyes. It occurred to him that life wouldn't be worth much without Katie Beth, and his face fell farther into his hand at the thought of losing her.

"I want to marry her," he said, real slowly, the idea cementing in his mind as he spoke the words.

Junior shifted and grimaced as if he was sitting on a burr.

"If'n you marry Katie Beth, I know you're gonna want your own house and all. And wanna be alone. You won't want me hangin' around all the time. And that's okay and all. But, what'll happen to us? I mean, you know?"

Frank jabbed at his brother's rib. Then again. "Come on, whaddya think? Nothin's gonna change. Like I always say, we're a team. Katie Beth'll be, you know, at home. You and I'll work together and go out sometimes like always. Shoot. You can come to our house anytime," he said, swelling his chest and warming to the idea of him and Katie Beth having their own home after all. "Maybe someday you'll get married, huh? What about that?"

This time Junior jabbed at Frank, then Frank jabbed back again, and after a few more punches and laughs, Junior decided it would be a good thing after all if Frank married Katie Beth. He said as much to Frank.

Frank's smile fell and he nervously shifted his eyes toward the display window. He watched as Katie Beth neatly gathered up her supplies in a box and crawled out from the window, real dainty-like, he thought. The full window looked empty without her. The mannequins, dressed in their autumn colors, seemed to Frank like every other girl in the world: fake and wooden. Only Katie Beth held any life.

"A girl like Katie Beth wants more than a poor boy like me can offer," Frank said, his voice trembling with emotion. He jerked his arm down, rammed the key in, and fired up the engine.

Junior may not have been able to understand all the details that people sputtered, but he was astute at picking up the bottom line. He braced himself against the dashboard as Frank spun the tires and squealed away from the curb. Junior knew that he had to help his brother, somehow. Or someday, his brother was gonna crash and burn.

18

—

NORA'S FIRST MONTH passed in relative peace in the country. Down in the pen, Nora developed an air of camaraderie with C.W. and Esther. They worked in harmony to usher into the world sixty-two more lambs. Witnessing another creature slip into the world and wobble to its feet on its own strength instilled in her an awe and renewed respect for God and nature. The experience grounded her to the power of life: that which was around her and within herself. As each day passed, her confidence and self-esteem grew as steady and sure as the lambs she cared for. By the close of her first month, she was completing her chores with the same confidence that she had admired in Esther only weeks before.

Her routine was sacrosanct. She spent the morning feeding the barn animals and the afternoon doing house chores and paperwork. Seth joked that he gave up wearing a watch; he could tell the time by what Nora was up to. Winterization of the house was also coming along nicely. Freed from the chores of the pen, Seth drove his sons at a steady pace, all the while keeping an eye on the skies above. Within the month floors had been laid and the walls and ceilings had been Sheetrocked. Even a few closets and shelves had been installed.

Nora worked overtime vacuuming up all the dust that fell onto every surface, picking up the nails and wood chips, and moving furniture from one room to the other. She never complained. The work had to get done, and time was of the essence. Quietly and quickly she worked, figuring that not only did it speed things up, but that in fact, no one worked harder or did the job better than herself.

Frank, Junior, and the others called her the Whiz. No sooner would they set something down than she'd whiz by, offer a cheery comment, then clean it up. The guys no longer maintained a deferential distance. Her superior air had long since vanished and she laughed at their jokes. That they could talk freely with her in the room was testimony to her acceptance. She delighted in it.

Esther had finally come around, too. In painting, they had found that common ground, and from it they were building, albeit slowly, a working relationship. Not a friendship yet, but as always, Nora was optimistic and willing to work hard.

It was the work at night, however, that Nora enjoyed the most. Each evening, at precisely seven o'clock, C.W. knocked on the kitchen door. And each night, Nora felt a thrill of anticipation. He never failed to fill the doorway and her heart with his presence. For the first several days his manner was cool and indifferent. They sat, head to head, toe to toe, at the dining room table, careful not to accidentally graze a finger or bump a thigh. They were accountant and client—teacher and student.

Each night, with slow deliberation, C.W. took his wire-rim glasses out from his pocket and hooked them around his ears. Then, one by one, he spread the books before them. Nora sat, hands neatly folded, and watched how his hair fell over his broad forehead, just touching the thin wire-rims, which rested on and accentuated his broken nose. She thought the flattened bridge did not detract from his handsomeness but improved it. Without this flaw, his striking good looks would be too perfect, like a model's. That, she would have found boring.

C.W.'s small imperfection, however, sent her imagination running. Perhaps he'd been a football jock in high school, or maybe even college? Was it some rough and tumble barroom brawl; if so, who'd started it? Was the fight over some woman? Or maybe some horse kicked him during a shoeing?

Nora enjoyed creating a past for the private Mr. Walker. He held his cards tightly abreast. Every once in a while he'd discard a tidbit of information that Nora quickly picked up and sorted. She discovered he was intelligent by his vocabulary. It was rich with multisyllabic choices that came naturally, without the millisecond pause of pretension. His breadth of knowledge on a wide array of subjects revealed a strong education. And although he wore worn and torn clothing and could throw hay as far as Frank, C.W. could not disguise his quiet aura of quality. Nora paired these pieces of information together but as yet could not play out her hand.

As the nights grew colder, the kitchen became the only room cozy enough to work in without fingers and toes freezing. Nora tacked up large pieces of thick plastic at the stairwells to keep the wood stove's heat from dispersing throughout the house. It worked like a charm. C.W. noticed it the first night. Although he didn't comment, Nora caught his nod of approval.

With the same patience he had shown down at the barn, C.W. laid out the figures and explained what they represented. As he did so, he also taught her the ins and outs of sheep farming: the variable and fixed costs, and the high risk ventures versus the tried-and-true ones. Sometimes Seth and Frank would join him, and together they'd describe, with the excitement of a pack of inventors, the new crossbreeding they were trying out.

She sat back and listened with rapture, getting sucked into this world of sheep, hay fields, and wool. Here, as in the barn, Nora proved an apt pupil. She had a decent handle on the math, but she surprised C.W. with an extraordinary grasp of concept and management.

For the first several sessions, C.W. had maintained an employer-employee rigidity. He had seemed intent on getting a fix on her personal finances, offering to balance her books, referring often to any other ledgers she might have. But she demurred, returning instead to ideas and dreams for the farm. As the hours and days passed, however, their formality dissipated and a friendly exchange developed.

By the end of that first week, C.W. had decided to stop pressing Nora for more of Mike's records. She would confide only when she was ready and not before. He'd have to be patient. In truth, however, he was grateful for the reprieve. Without the pressure of a mission, he could relax and concentrate on his second goal: to get to know Nora better. After a while, he stopped gathering his papers at the hour's close and stayed for that cup of coffee.

During the second week, they settled into a peaceful pattern around the fireplace after their work—he with a book, and she with her sewing machine. They talked about everything: from Lenin to Lennon, grass roots to the ozone layer, Buddha to Christ, and apples to zucchini. They discovered that they shared numerous opinions and viewpoints. So rather than debate from opposite poles, they parleyed from the same side of the fence.

He also started noticing the floral arrangements and wreaths she created from the wild vines and flowers she gathered. Bread baked in the oven, soups and coffee simmered, water steamed on the wood stove, fresh towels and a space heater warmed the bathroom. This house was becoming a home. He felt invited here, even welcome.

From behind his book he stole glances as she sat bent over her sewing machine, wrestling with yards upon yards of thick, insulated fabric, pins protruding from her lips. He marveled at her industry—she was always working. Too often he was caught spellbound by her gentle beauty, so like her gentle spirit. Her blond hair was always swept up, either in a braid or bun, and it symbolized to him her struggle to maintain control over her life. He longed to loosen the bonds from her hair and watch it fall freely around her shoulders. It took all of his self-control to be patient, to wait for a sign from her.

On this last evening of Nora's first month on the farm, a gusty wind whipped over the northern ridge. C.W. walked the distance between the cabin and the house in record time. In one hand he held a stack of ledgers. In the other, a package wrapped in tissue and tied up in a bright bow. Before knocking, he adjusted the bow and stuck in a sprig of pine.

The door of the house swung open and Nora met him with her usual welcome. He held his breath, as he always did, when he first spied Nora's smile. Her eyes were as bright a green as the bow on his package, and they warmed him more than any fire could.

She wore jeans and a repaired navy turtleneck of cashmere. Brown leather at her waist and feet was the only contrast in color, giving her an aura of quiet elegance. Her long hair twined in a French braid, and gold French knots adorned her ears.

He looked over his faded flannel shirt, which was worn under another shirt of denim, and the torn pocket on his jeans.

Next to Nora, who looked great even when covered with mud, he felt shabby. Once he had taken great pains with his appearance. His suits and shirts were custom tailored, his ties were designer made, and his shoes were of the finest leather. Lint on his jacket used to distract him.

C.W. shrugged and smiled inwardly. He liked it better this way. He was confident with the knowledge of what was quality and what wasn't—and when it mattered. Wiping his feet on the woven mat, careful not to muddy her clean floors, he handed her the package.

"What's this?" she asked in surprise. "It's not my birthday."

"It's not a birthday present," he replied, gazing at his shuffling feet. "It's sort of a housewarming present. And given that gusty wind, you can use this one."

Nora's expression changed from surprise to affection, and he felt a blush rise from beneath his shearling collar.

"Well, open it," he said gruffly. "I'll lay this stack of books down on the table."

Nora followed him, gently fingering the sprig of pine. She stared at the package in her hands for a moment. "I love it already."

"You don't even know what it is." He was pleased.

Glancing up at him with a tease in her eyes, she gave the package a shake.

He gave a look that said, Will you just open it.

"Okay, okay." She giggled. Carefully, she took off the sprig and set it into her water glass. Then in a rush, she tore open the paper and opened the box. With a confused look on her face, she pulled out a pair of gray thermal bib overalls.

"I—I don't know what to say," she said, turning the overalls from front to back.

C.W. smiled and coughed back a laugh. "They may not

seem much now, but I promise you. Before you know it, you won't step foot out of this house without them. They're insulated and you'll be able to hike down the mountain and do your chores at the barn without freezing that pretty—your legs off."

"My legs," she repeated with a sly smile. Holding it up, she asked, "How does it look?"

Had he known she was going to model his gift, he would have bought something besides bib overalls, he thought.

"Fine, just fine," he replied.

"I'm truly touched," she said, holding the overalls to her breast. "As presents go, this one ranks right up there with Oma's pearls. You must have really thought about what I would need up here in the winter. And, I take it as a vote of confidence." She felt like giving him a big hug but offered a smile instead. "I love them. I don't know what to say. Thank you, C.W."

"Check the pockets."

With a raised brow, she fingered the bibs. "What could this be?" she asked tapping a lump in the pocket. "It feels like a small box, a jeweler's box, perhaps?" She winked and he held back a laugh.

She dug in and pulled out a small green tin. Casting him a suspicious glance, she read the red-and-green label.

"Bag Balm?" she said looking up at him with a blank face. "What's Bag Balm?" She read the small print on the label, then her face went aghast.

"This says it's for udders! Cow's udders!" she cried with an expression of incredulity.

He merely shrugged in defense and cast a wary glance at her breasts.

"C.W.!" she shrieked in mirth as she held the overalls over her chest. "Thanks a lot."

At last he burst out laughing and shook his head. "You'll need it. No, I'm serious." He reached out for the tin and she crouched in a defensive pose.

"Come on." He laughed as he took the tin from her hands. "It's the best thing for chapped hands." Then he added, without lifting his eyes from the tin, "Whatever else you use it for is strictly your own business."

"You, you, cowhand you."

"I'll show you how to handle a cow," he threatened.

Nora squealed as he grabbed her, held her in a neck lock, and administered tweaks to her ears and nose. It was almost more than he could manage not to tweak her bottom and udders. When he finally released her, she leaned against the brick wall and held her sides.

"I hurt from laughing so hard."

He stood with his hands on his hips while controlling his own laughter and catching his breath. He watched Nora as she laughed. When she brushed the golden hair from her face and looked up at him, her face aglow with happiness, he felt as if someone had punched him a good one in the solar plexus. The smile disappeared from his face and his breathing pace increased again.

With his thumb, he snapped the tight lid from the tin. Taking a sample from the balm, he held out his hand to her.

"Come here. I'll rub some on you."

Her smile faded slowly as she held out her hand. He grabbed it and pulled her close, then, ever so gently, applied the balm to her hand. It was glutinous and smelled medicinal. Nora stood without moving a muscle as his large hand massaged her small one, engulfing it as her nearness engulfed him.

He turned her palm up and, looking into her eyes, rhythmically rubbed the balm up and down her palm, from her wrist to her fingertips. Back and forth. Glide and press.

His breathing grew labored and his fingertips burned.

Her lips parted and she panted shallow breaths. And still his eyes held hers, never wavering.

"C.W.," she said, more in a moan.

He stopped but kept his hold on her hand. Spreading his own palm he gazed at her hand, as though it were a rare flower. Standing there, frozen for seconds, his stillness belied the war raging inside him.

He released her hand and still without speaking, tucked the tin back into the bib's pocket.

"Hope it helps you out there." His hands were back in his pockets and his eyes averted from hers. The air in the room seemed colder.

Nora tucked away her gift in a bureau and gazed around the room at nothing. Her lips were clenched, keeping in words she wanted to say.

"Well, let's get to work," he said.

Her heart sank. She nodded.

His gut wrenched. He nodded.

Neither moved.

"Thank you again for my gifts," she ventured in whispers. "I should have given you one for the cabin."

"You've done enough. Besides, I won't be there long. Lambing is almost done."

She swallowed and blinked. "Are you really going to leave?"

"Have to."

She looked up in surprise.

"Getting too cold in that cabin," he added.

"Well, you can stay here. I've told you that before."

His eyes burned into hers for what seemed an eternity. "I can't. You know I can't do that. Especially now."

She mouthed, Especially now, as she leaned slowly against the brick wall.

He paused and rubbed his cheek in consternation. Then, eyes on her, he took three steps toward her. She measured the distance with her breaths. As he neared, she pressed back against the cool brick with her fevered hands. Now, in the few inches that remained between them, the heat from his body seemed to scorch her own, and his breath was like a flame of fire upon her head. He pressed still closer.

She uttered a soft cry and raised her palm against his chest to stop him.

"Shhh," he murmured as he lowered his lips to her head. Slowly, he traced a fiery trail to her temples, to her cheekbone, to her ear.

Her knees grew weak and her shoulders slumped. Her palm was resisting nothing and beneath it, his heart beat harder. She felt his head turn and his nose press against her cheek nudging her face upward to where he could continue his trail to her mouth. His lips teased hers like a butterfly, alighting here and there, until with a soft sigh, she relinquished and allowed the seal to open. The tip of his tongue slowly slid along the tight aperture, moistening her parched lips, then darted inside and eased them fully apart.

Then his lips possessed hers—cool and dry, then warm and wet—as their excitement leaped. His palm slid to her breast. Whimpering softly, she inched away.

"Let me touch you," he entreated, his voice husky. "God, you're beautiful."

Reassured, she relaxed and, sliding her arms around his neck, stood on tiptoe to meet him. Openmouthed and eager. She tottered back, but his hand grasped her bottom and anchored her firmly against him.

Fused together, his flame struck deep and low, and she felt

the rekindling of a fire she had thought long extinguished. Searing, swirling sensations traveled from her lips to her breasts to her belly, where they churned then shot back up to her brain. There, they wreaked havoc on her common sense. From somewhere came the message to slow down…to stop. But another, more urgent ache screamed to be fulfilled, drowning out any warnings for prudence. She felt starved for his kisses and hungrily sought his mouth for the passion he delivered.

He crushed her against the wall, and she felt, for the first time in many years, the long hard pressure of a male's passion. As his hips began to move against hers, she was curious, even desirous, to feel again that passion between her legs. Slowly, tentatively, she moved her hips to his rhythm. Their music synchronized and they began to dance to the beat of their passion.

"Nora, Nora," he whispered against her hair.

The sound of her name snapped her out of rhythm and she stiffened. Mike's image flashed before her. Her lips shut tight and she clumsily pushed him back. For a moment, C.W.'s arms held tight, as though he would not let her go. Then he dropped them and took two steps back, leaving her trembling against the warm brick wall.

The heat of his kisses still smoldered on her lips as she took deep breaths of the cool evening air. Her heart was hammering the tale of her unabashed desire and though she shook her head in denial, she heard its truth.

She closed her eyes in shame and confusion. A part of her soared with joy at the spark he had ignited, but another, more practical side wanted to shove it back into hiding. She had no business getting involved with anyone right now, much less some handsome drifter. And—she remembered Mike.

When she opened her eyes, he was standing upright with his hands in his rear pockets and his gaze like flint.

"Just so I know," he said. "Who are you pushing away? C.W. the man or C.W. the hired hand?"

Her mouth dropped open and she cocked her head. "What do you mean?"

"I open a door and you slam it in my face. Why, Nora? Is it because you still mourn your husband? If so, tell me. That I can understand and respect."

She stiffened. "It's not that," she blurted out.

He didn't think so. "Then why, Nora?"

"I don't know who you are," she explained. "Where you're from—"

"Or what I have to offer."

Her voice caught in her throat. "Just what is that supposed to imply?" Her voice rose as she did.

"I think you know."

The silence spoke for itself.

"I'm sorry," he said, abruptly turning and grabbing his coat. "It won't happen again."

She sighed deeply, whether from relief or disappointment she wasn't sure. Her head back against the wall, she closed her eyes. "No, it won't," she agreed softly. The air was heavy with repressed desire.

He turned to leave.

Let him go, she told herself. It's better this way. But as his hand reached for the doorknob, her resolve fled and she pushed herself from the wall.

"C.W.!" she called.

He stopped and swung his head, hand still on the door.

"This has nothing to do with you. I—I just don't want to get involved right now."

He shifted his weight and took a deep breath. Disappointment etched his face.

"I wish I could believe that." Then he turned and was gone, taking the warmth of the room with him.

She stood beside the fire, rubbing her arms against the cold. How could he understand, she thought in dismay? He probably moved from place to place as the whim struck him, depending on his strong back and his incredible appeal. But not her. She wasn't going anywhere. She wasn't looking for a good time. She wanted security at last.

C.W.'s questions flared up in her thoughts. What did he have to offer? Who was she pushing away: C.W. the man or C.W. the hired hand? She covered her face in her hands. "Both," she said aloud. Nora wept bitterly against the rosy brick, cursing the ghost of her husband. She was afraid to take a risk again. Even after death, Mike could manipulate her rejection.

C.W. crossed the meadow with an angry stride. But by the time he finally reached the cabin, his anger had subsided into mere frustration. After all she'd been through, he could understand her hesitation, but not her fear. Nora, he thought, don't be so afraid.

He pushed open the door and stood in the entry, hands on hips, lost in thought, while the night air blew in.

There were choices he could make, if only she would give him a sign. Some indication that she wanted him. *Him*. The man. His fortune had already attracted far too much female attention in his life. He wanted a signal that she loved him and the future his love alone could provide. Until then, and until he could clear his name, he had to keep his identity a secret from her.

But his patience was wearing thin, his passion was harder to keep under control. He slammed the door and kicked the pot-belly stove, stirring up the embers and sending sparks flying.

The Long Road Home

He'd had about enough. Time was running out. His patience with Sidney and Nora was running out. He had to find a way to wrap this business up and find it quick.

Then, he'd never cross that damn meadow again.

19

—

IT RAINED FOR two days straight, making everyone feel as overcast as the skies. The earth turned to mud that clung to the heels of boots, the bottom of jeans, and the fleece of sheep.

Junior stood ankle deep in mud outside the Zwingers' two-story redbrick house. He was soaked to the skin and valiantly trying to muster enough courage to knock on the Zwingers' freshly painted white door and speak to Katie Beth. He knew she was in there: he'd waited across the street until she returned home from the dress shop. At least she wasn't driven home by John Henry, he thought, puffing his cheeks in relief.

His toes were numb and his fingers were like icicles hanging from a low-pitched roof. Junior stomped his feet, succeeding only in spraying more mud on his jeans.

"Shoot," he muttered under his breath. He might as well get this over with before he froze out here. Taking a deep breath, he rammed his hands into his jacket pockets and marched straight up the stairs to the front door, glancing nervously over his shoulders at the trail of mud he tracked across the freshly painted Victorian porch.

The door was opened promptly by Fred Zwinger, Katie Beth's father. He was big shouldered and tall and had a bristly black mustache that dark eyes glared over. Fred Zwinger had made Junior shrink in his boots ever since he could wear them. Seth had always said Fred's stern ways was on account'a him havin' five pretty girls to watch out for. That thought sure didn't make asking to see the baby of the girls any easier for Junior right now.

"Seth Jr., what are you doing standing in that rain?" Fred asked, his dark brows bobbing.

Junior hunched and nervously stamped the mud from his boots. No one but Fred Zwinger and the reverend called him by his proper name.

"I come to see Katie Beth. She in, sir?"

Fred's brows arched high in surprise. "*You're* here to see Katie Beth?" He swung his head farther out of the door to check the curbside. "Where's Frank?"

"He ain't here. Just me, sir."

Fred Zwinger stroked his mustache, perplexed. "Well, come on in. I'll get her."

"No, sir. I'm full of mud. I'll just wait here."

Katie Beth appeared as promptly as her father, with as much question written on her face but a lot more kindness.

"Come on in, Junior. You'll catch your death." She wooed a backstepping Junior into the tile foyer, where she assured him the mud could get wiped right up without fuss. Junior sneezed loudly and backhanded his nose.

"See, you're catching a cold. Let me get you some black-berry brandy. It'll take the bite off."

"No, no," Junior stammered, waving his hand before his mouth. "I never touch the stuff. Makes me sick."

Katie Beth cocked her head and waited to hear what Junior had to say that would bring him here even in the cold rain. Her eyes were shiny and she seemed nervous, as if she anticipated that the news had to do with Frank.

Junior colored, held his breath, then blurted out what he had to say like a trumpet blast.

"Frank loves you and you oughta marry him but he's afraid to ask you 'cause he thinks you love John Henry and he's got nothin' and thinks he's not good enough for you but he is." Junior stopped, breathless, with his eyes wide, staring at Katie Beth.

Katie Beth's mouth was hanging open and she stood quiet so long Junior began to shuffle his feet.

Her mouth gradually closed, and Junior was relieved beyond belief to see that her lips closed in a smile. He let loose a tremendous sigh.

"Is that so?" Katie Beth replied slowly. Her face softened. "You're a good brother, Junior. And a good friend to me, too."

Junior turned redder and made a dash for the door. "I gotta go now."

Katie Beth put her hand on his damp coat sleeve as he reached for the door knob.

"Tell Frank I think he's got everything a girl like me could want."

For two nights, since the kiss, C.W. did not walk over to the big house for their usual seven-o'clock meeting. Instead, he stayed in the cabin poring over his files and creating a farm budget that would coerce Nora MacKenzie to reveal her financial situation. To do that, C.W. needed to keep his feelings for Nora separate from the job at hand. He needed the cold approach to carry this off.

But at what cost? That morning, a dull ache formed in his chest as he approached the barn's entry. Despite himself, he hoped that he'd spy her blond head bent over some lamb. Regardless of his resolve, he realized that he missed her.

It was clear that Nora had made her own decision to back off, and he had to admit he was burned that she'd decided to ignore him completely. Although she was polite when they fed the ewes, prompt to help repair the grain feeders for winter, and agreeable to his opinions on balancing the sheep rations, no sooner was Nora done than she ducked out like a bat out of hell.

Esther, too. Like Nora, Esther showed up for her chores, did them efficiently, then darted away with scarcely a hello. It was clear the two women wanted nothing to do with the men around here.

C.W. spotted Nora in the barn, filling the feed box with confident ease. He stepped back in the shadows and watched. Nora was learning fast and already doing a number of chores that Esther used to do. Given the chance, she might just make it on this farm, C.W. realized with appreciation. He leaned against a timber and crossed his arms and legs, considering again how the hell he'd manage using MacKenzie's secrets without destroying his widow's chances.

It had been hell watching Nora blossom from city flower to wildflower. From pale and skinny to pink and rounded. Her cautious guard had dissipated to reveal a spontaneity that lured his own wounded spirit from its shell. Her mellifluous laughter was luring out his own.

And through her eyes, he viewed day-to-day chores with renewed awe. Each birth was a miracle, each lamb assigned a personality. Even hauling hay was done with a lighter heart.

Nora moved away from the ewes and headed toward the creep for preweaned lambs. C.W. straightened quickly, tucked in his shirt, buttoned his sleeves, then entered the barn a man with a mission.

C.W. approached the creep and abruptly cleared his throat. Nora looked up at him with eyes filled with an inner peace. Seeing it, his own shaky peace was rocked.

"I've been looking for you." He rested his hands on the rail and lifted a boot on the creep's runner. "I've got that budget information you requested. Whenever you're ready."

Willow stood up at the noise and slipped through the panel that lets lambs in but keeps ewes out. Nora walked to the lamb and plopped down cross-legged next to Willow.

"That's great, C.W.," she said, looking at the lamb rather than him. The runt was growing heavy and strong between milk and high concentrate rations, and Willow had a definite preference for Nora.

"Never saw a lamb take so to a human," he said, moving closer to the pair. "Maybe you're right about him being exceptional."

"At least he knows what a nipple's for. Isn't that right?" she asked the lamb, scratching behind the lamb's ears and neck.

When was she going to stop talking to that infernal lamb, he wondered with another scowl? He moved still closer.

"Do you think Willow understands English?"

"Oh, I'm sure of it," Nora said, finally looking up. She seemed pleased to be exchanging her first joke with C.W. in days.

A smile escaped C.W.

Nora smiled back, quickly, before looking back at the lamb.

"Willow tells me you're loafing off down here and only work this hard when I'm here watching you," she said with a soft laugh.

"Does he now?" he replied gently. C.W. bent down and

patted Willow's head. "Well, little fellow, did I ever tell you how much I like lamb stew?"

Willow looked sleepily up as C.W. stroked his chin.

"I can see you frighten him," Nora said in a whisper.

"Yes. It's obvious I have this effect on people." C.W. turned his head to face Nora. On bent knee, his face was inches from hers, and he could feel her warm breath against his cheek.

"Do I frighten you too, Nora?"

Her mouth opened but no response formulated. Her lips, now centimeters from his own, slowly closed. Her breath stilled. The air grew thick. Closer they drew, their lips almost touching.

"Ahem. Am I breakin' up something here?"

Seth stood at the far railing, hands in his pockets, smiling a toothless grin.

Nora jolted back while C.W. jumped up and stepped back a pace or two, shuffling his feet in the straw.

"Nope," C.W. replied, running his hand through his hair. "Just talking to Nora, that's all."

Seth raised his brows and offered a doubtful expression.

"Can't say as I ever knew she was so hard of hearing."

C.W. grimaced and knew there was nothing he could say to change what the old coot was thinking. And hell, he was right. He was about to kiss her. He peered over his shoulder and found Nora's eyes still on him.

"I hear you're ready to start work on the insulation," Nora said shifting her gaze to Seth. "None too soon. It seems to be getting colder by the day."

"I thought it was getting warmer," Seth replied.

Nora blushed, and C.W. rocked on his heels and whistled a silent tune.

"I got the batting and some drywall," Seth mumbled, pulling out ragged papers from his equally frayed jacket. "Joe

Cronin brung it up. You know Joe. Does construction. Lives in the gray cape by Squire's place. Married to Fred Zwinger's little girl, Elsa."

Nora couldn't keep all the names straight but nodded anyway. She'd know Joe and Elsa, and Fred, "the pump man," well enough by the time the house was finished.

"Got the figures too," Seth continued. "We'll do the work for a good price, but it ain't going to be cheap. There's lots of floors and walls in that big house, and gettin' it ready in time for winter will take full-time work."

Nora sighed and chewed her lip. "Everything is a lot of work and a lot of money these days," she replied. "Still, we've got to do what we've got to do."

That comment played right to C.W.'s hand. "Speaking of money," C.W. said, drawing Nora's attention back.

Nora set Willow down off her lap onto the hay, ignoring his bleats of protest, and proceeded to rise. She shooed away C.W.'s hand. No more nonsense, her eyes told him. C.W. felt properly chastised.

"Well," she said to C.W. "when can we meet? I'd like to get started as soon as possible. How about four o'clock?"

"I'll be tied up all afternoon. Why not the usual time. Seven o'clock?"

"It's a date," she replied, then stammered. "I mean, yes. That would be fine."

Nora left with Seth, unaware or uncaring that C.W. followed her every step out of the barn. C.W. ground his teeth as he stared at the emptiness left by her departure. If he wasn't careful tonight, that emptiness would be all he'd have left.

C.W. and Nora sat in agitated silence across the long mahogany dining table. It was seven-fifteen and they were meeting as planned to discuss the budget. It was clear that they would not discuss what had almost happened between them. Yet Nora could think of nothing else.

C.W. was thinking only of business. He quickly glanced at his watch. There was no putting this off. He had to get his hands on her books. Time was of the essence. He covered all the angles to ensure the result would be the same. How many times had he designed an interview in his career? More than he could count. And he had always emerged the victor. Yet never before had his emotions been involved. Never before had the outcome been so important.

"Well," he said, sitting straight and slipping on his wire-rim glasses. "Shall we get started?"

Nora nodded and brought her chair closer to the table.

"This is a good lambing," C.W. began, pointing to the column of figures. "Lots of twins. Few deaths. All together Seth expects to bring your flock up to about one hundred."

"That's good," Nora said, her enthusiasm sounding false in the tension. He was being exceptionally formal again.

"Yes, but not good enough."

C.W. went on to carefully review the fixed and variable costs, the depreciation, and discussed in detail the profit-and-loss statement. The situation was bad, but C.W. had deftly maneuvered the numbers to paint the picture bleak.

He tapped his pencil across his palm. "The bottom line is you're facing more losses. In the past Mike covered the losses with a check. No questions asked." He sighed and leaned back in his chair, then shoved over a sheet of paper with long columns of his calculations.

"The farm will not push into the black. You'll need to do likewise."

Nora's mouth gaped open as she read the amount. It was staggering. More than she had left in her account after the winterizing of the house and the pricey new ram. She slumped in her chair and rubbed her temples with shaky fingers.

"I don't have it."

C.W. slowly removed his glasses, folded them, and laid them parallel to his pencil before looking up again. This was it. She had finally admitted financial trouble.

"Are you saying that your husband's estate can't balance this budget?"

"What estate? I don't have the capital. It's gone."

There was a long silence. Gone? It was worse than he'd thought. Go on, he silently urged. Let's get this out in the open and done with.

Nora shook her head and slumped down in the chair. "When Mike died, the outstanding debts were enormous," she replied with a voice that had lost its enthusiasm. "It's too hard to explain. Some of it is beyond my own understanding."

C.W.'s fingers drummed on the table as he watched her stare in silence out the window while her chest heaved.

Nora looked over at him, her face clouded with in-decision.

C.W. stilled his fingers.

She wrapped her arms around her chest. She seemed to be fighting an inner battle. Then, dropping her chin to her chest, she released a ragged sigh.

"I need your help."

C.W. exhaled slowly. He hadn't realized he was holding his breath. Folding his hands tightly before him, he asked in a low voice, "What do you want me to do?"

Nora looked at his face, and in that moment he saw her make a leap of faith. It made him sick with guilt. Rising with resignation, Nora walked to the maple sideboard, and from its center drawer she pulled out a long leather volume. He craned his neck for a better view.

Nora held the book in her hands, absently rubbing the leather with her thumb, then slowly paced back to C.W.'s side, holding it out before her. It was thin, burgundy, and it was a ledger. His tension doubled.

"After Mike's death," she began slowly, "his lawyers, accountants, everyone, started ripping through his things, searching for something. Mike didn't trust them, so neither did I. I found this in his desk at home, hidden in a secret portal. It's his private account book—a kind of cheat sheet that he used for himself only. Somehow I knew that this was my only weapon against them so I took it. Until I understood what was happening to me, I wasn't about to lose total control."

Smart girl, C.W. thought to himself. He would have done the same thing.

"I've read it through a number of times, trying to make sense of it, and the only connection I can make is with the Blair Bank." She shook her head and wagged a finger. "They are somehow tied in with this mess. Mike hated Charles Blair," she said, her fingers making deep indentations in the supple leather. "I'm sure he was responsible for Mike's fall."

She gritted her teeth and said with a conviction that chilled C.W.'s blood, "I'd like to get even with him. And if I can—I will."

C.W. sat frozen in his chair. Any hope he'd harbored for avoiding deception withered with her words. She despised his very name.

"This is hard for me, giving this to you." Nora looked at the ledger, as though reconsidering. When she looked up, she appeared resolute. Without another word, she stuck out her arm and offered him the ledger.

C.W.'s nostrils flared and he sat straighter in his chair as he looked at the book held out before him. He felt like a cad;

this was stealing candy from a baby. Suddenly, he stood up, angrily, and turned his back to her.

"What's the matter?" she asked, eyes wide.

"What the bloody hell do you expect me to do?" he returned, swinging his head around to face her. "I can't promise to save you. I am not your knight in shining armor." He slammed his hands behind his back and stared intently into the fire. Inside, he raged at the Fates.

Nora saw only his stiff back and the way his hands clenched and unclenched.

"I don't want a knight in shining armor," she said softly. "I only want a friend I can trust." She paused. "I thought that was you."

His shoulders lowered. Slowly he turned around and stood for a moment, looking at her. There was no way she could understand why her trust had cut him so deeply. Nor was there any way he could explain it now. That ledger was the reason he was here tonight. Not her offer of friendship. Nor his feelings for her. She was Mrs. Michael MacKenzie, and that book in her hand could save the neck of her hated enemy, Charles Blair.

In his usual understatement he said, "I've made you anxious, haven't I?"

Nora looked at the ledger in her outstretched hand, and raised it a fraction.

C.W. took the book.

The leather was soft and supple, from ample use, and in the firelight, its burgundy color glowed in muted reds. He knew without opening it that his instincts had been correct. His wait was justified, his quest was complete.

C.W. lay the ledger carefully before him on the table. Once opened, the die was cast. He drew a deep breath. Would this information be akin to opening Pandora's box? He knew evil lurked in these pages, but did he have the power to conquer it?

With disciplined determination, C.W. drew the ledger close, opened it, and began his study.

The minutes passed to an hour, then two, with C.W. bent over the books and Nora sitting silently beside him staring into the fire. Occasionally the papers would rustle as he sifted through them, checking a fact, noting a date. The fire popped and crackled. The wind sighed a high-pitched wail that shook the windows.

C.W. read the tale of greed, dishonesty, and ruin. The plot was not unique; he'd read similar tales before. This one, however, was personal. He read in the erratic words, in the doctored columns, and between the lines, the desperation of a dead man. Finishing, C.W. resented MacKenzie, deeply, not only for what he had done to him, but to Nora.

When at last he lifted his eyes, C.W. was mute with exhaustion. He slowly closed the ledger and stared at the burgundy leather under his hands. After all this time and anguish, he had his answer. C.W. knew why Michael MacKenzie had chosen to kill himself in front of Charles Blair.

C.W. rubbed his eyes. He felt like laughing, he felt like weeping. The whole thing was all a ruse! They had both been duped. Mike had mistakenly believed that it was Charles Blair who had deliberately destroyed him. By blowing his brains out, Mike had chosen a brutal form of revenge. Two lives senselessly destroyed.

C.W. came close to approaching the level of anger that Mike MacKenzie had once felt against Charles Blair. C.W.'s mouth went dry. Remembering the hatred he saw in Mike's eyes, he wondered if in fact murder had been on MacKenzie's mind that ugly morning, not suicide.

C.W. rested his large hands flat upon the ledger and turning his head to Nora, said quietly, "That son of a bitch."

Nora looked at him without expression, blinked, then returned her gaze to the fire. "Yes, I suppose he was." Her tone was flat, void of any feeling.

His ire rose as he did. Slamming the book on the table he shouted, "I can't believe how high-handed he was."

Nora looked up, visibly shaken at C.W.'s rare show of anger.

"MacKenzie didn't give a damn who he hurt! Only a man without honor would gamble with stakes so high on a game so risky without first ensuring his family's security. Wasn't he concerned about leaving you destitute?"

"Please. Don't yell."

C.W.'s mouth tightened and his nostrils flared. Of course Mac didn't care. Not only did Nora not have a penny—she owed one! She owed more money than most people dreamed of earning in a lifetime. Nora was in trouble. Big trouble.

He looked over at her small frame slumped before the fire. It pained him to see it. It also pained him that it fell to him to spell out her precarious position.

"Tell me how you kept the farm." His voice was sharp.

She spread out her palms. "The lawyers sat me down, explained that I had lost virtually everything, then stated that I could scrape out a small amount from what was left. I immediately thought of the farm. It was one of the few places I really loved, and I thought, Aha, land! The most tangible form of security. So, thinking that with the sheep operation I could live a simple life up here, I negotiated for the farm over cash."

"And they deeded it to you outright?" He cast her a dubious glance.

Nora shifted her weight. "Well, not exactly."

He groaned inwardly but maintained his poker face. "What, exactly?"

She fidgeted and her voice took on an irritated tone.

"Exactly—the lawyers are holding the deed until after the auction. That will be the final step before our estate is settled. With all the loans, the taxes…it's taken months to work through."

C.W. kept his face still.

"I thought I'd use this time to see if I could in fact earn enough on the farm to live here." She rubbed her temples. "That's why I studied the books, learned the business, was in such a hurry. Only eight weeks."

His fingers stopped tapping. He sat back down and leaned forward in his chair, hands clasped between his knees and his eyes inches from her own.

"Look at me, Nora, and listen." He took a deep breath and forced his voice to a gentler note. He spoke slowly. "I am not telling you this to cause you pain. I am telling you this because I am your friend. And you have not been dealt with honestly or fairly by those in whom you've placed your trust."

Her eyes were wide and bore the hunted look of a rabbit caught in a snare.

"I'll try to explain this as simply and clearly as possible."

She nodded in mute understanding.

"Your husband's financial machine was built on paper. For this last venture, he borrowed under the guise of false companies and finagled from every bank he could. The man was a series of wallets. He created a web so complicated that only he knew how flimsy it really was. It was genius, I admit. It was also foolhardy. He risked it all. But the rug was pulled out from under him and he lost."

"I already know that," she replied in level tones. "But who pulled the rug?"

He cringed. That was exactly the question he needed to answer.

"I don't know. What matters is that the banks that he borrowed from are calling in his debts. The total amount is substantial."

"That is true," she responded. "But the estate could file for bankruptcy after the auction."

He reached out and cupped her chin, redirecting her gaze from the fire to him. She had to understand.

"You'd lose the farm for sure, then. Mike also owed back taxes. You realize that the IRS will stop at nothing to collect their due."

She stared back at him.

"They'll come after you. And if they can take the farm, they will."

"The auction!" she said, jumping to her feet. "The auction should bring me enough money to pay the debts, cover our taxes, and keep this place afloat. At least for this year. That would buy us time. The auction will bring in a fortune," she repeated. "After all, I have a van Gogh."

C.W. was unimpressed. He looked at her with a worried frown and ran his fingers through his hair. "Now *you'll* have to back up. Explain to me about this auction."

She paced to the windows and back. "Next month the estate is auctioning off my worldly goods, such as they are. My antiques, jewels, and most importantly, my art collection. You know, the kinds of things a big auction house dies for. I have some wonderful pieces. I should do well."

He took a deep breath. "Nora, I don't know what you have to auction off. Frankly, it could be worth many millions and might not be enough."

"It's got to be." She chewed her lip and held her palms together, giving the impression of a woman in prayer. "Don't you see? That's why I have to be so secretive about the bankruptcy. If scent of this leaks out in New York, the auction is doomed. The dealers will know there are no reserves set and they'll snatch up my things for a song. I'll lose everything." Her voice choked and her hand flew to her mouth to cover her quivering lips. She fought with herself, taking deep breaths to maintain control.

"Now do you understand?" she asked in a monotone. "I have to pretend everything is fine." She looked at him with a level gaze. "But, I can't balance that budget," she said dispassionately, shoving the paper back to his side of the table. She lowered her head and sat quietly in her chair, beyond the reach of his words.

C.W. was beginning to understand everything all too well. The pieces of Nora's puzzle began to fit together. He reflected on her comments and quips about Mike and understood that no love was lost between them after all. The Big Mac was the Big Loser. Who the hell cared about the money? That flagrant womanizer lost the one treasure worth keeping.

"Well, I won't let them take it!" she said, suddenly sitting upright and pounding her fist on the table. "Damn Mike and his problems. This is *my* farm. I paid for this land myself, with Oma's inheritance. Didn't know that, did you? I've worked too hard to sit back and let those damn lawyers take it away. I've sat back too long. There are some things worth fighting for. Give me those figures!"

Her eyes were like two green flames leaping high. Sliding the papers over to her, he sat back and watched her attack them as if her life depended on it, which in many ways, he realized it did.

"There's always a way," she muttered, more to herself as she checked figures and scribbled numbers in long columns. "If we rent out that new stud, put off the tractor repairs, stop all work on the house, rob Peter to pay Paul…" She scribbled a few more figures on the paper, checked some notes, and re-totaled the columns, working quickly and with focused attention.

"It might just work," she said pushing the paper back to C.W.'s side of the table with a challenge in her eyes. He didn't miss her smug grin, either.

C.W. scanned the figures, added a few more, then lifted his head. "This might work," he agreed cautiously. "But, Nora, it's only a delay."

"I'll deal with that after the auction. It'll give me time to come up with something new. I have to have faith the auction will pull through. Then, I'll think of something."

Yeh-up, C.W. thought with admiration. She wasn't the runt any longer.

"Thank you, C.W. You've been a bigger help than you know."

C.W. remained silent.

"I hope you understand that what we discussed here is strictly confidential."

He nodded his head. "I agree. Absolutely no one should know about this ledger."

Nora stuck her hand out across the table. "Partners?"

C.W. stared at the outstretched hand for a second, reluctant to take it. My God, he was about to use the information she'd just dished out.

Across the table, her eyes were aglow with determination. In her eyes, he saw a chance to do the right thing. In her outstretched hand, he saw the chance to regain trust in himself. His future hinged on this decision.

He grabbed her hand and held it tight. "Partners," he replied with conviction.

20

——

LOOKING AROUND THE deserted gas station, C.W. punched the number of a trusted associate at the Blair Bank. He'd found what he needed in MacKenzie's ledger: proof that the defaulted loans were all fronts for MacKenzie. Knowing that, he could begin his campaign. One other fact on MacKenzie's ledgers stood out from the rest. One reality that heightened the stakes for him. Nora might owe money to several banks, but the lion's share was owed to his.

Someone had set up not only himself, but MacKenzie as well. It was positively Machiavellian. But who? Sidney or Agatha? Nowhere in the ledger did Mike name his accomplice at the bank. Mike was clever. He had written in code. Only at the end, when he lost caution to mania, had he written a name. Charles Blair.

Mike believed Charles Blair called the loans in. Without proof of the real accomplice, the damn ledger would only incriminate him further.

He decided to call an independent.

"Strauss here," came the affected voice on the phone.

"Blair here."

There was a long pause. "Charles?"

"Hello, Henry. You sound as if you've heard from a ghost."

A faint chuckle sounded on the line. "I thought maybe I had. It's been a long time. I was beginning to wonder if you were alive."

C.W. let that one pass. "Henry, we have a war to wage."

There was another pause, and C.W. could envision Henry's face turning cold. "Yes, sir," he replied evenly.

C.W. smiled. He could depend on Henry Strauss. "I have information on twelve businesses that were lent loans from our bank. These businesses were all fronts for Michael MacKenzie."

He heard Henry suck in his breath.

In rapid-fire order, C.W. listed the names of the businesses and the dates of the loans. "I want the status quo of the Mac-Kenzie estate. I want full reports on these loans and the businesses. And," he said for emphasis, "most importantly, I want the name of the person who issued them. I warn you, my name may be on it, but that's a red herring. Someone has been manipulating for my removal. It's either Sidney or Agatha. I want you to find out who." He paused, letting Henry absorb the implication of the risks he would be taking. "I need your best work here, Henry."

"You can count on me, Charles."

It was the first time C.W. could ever remember hearing a tremor of emotion in staunch Strauss's voice. Good ol' Henry.

"How long will it take you to dig this up?"

"This will be buried deep. MacKenzie's estate has a battalion of lawyers to get past." He coughed. "I'm on the outside now."

"How long?"

"Two, maybe three weeks."

The Long Road Home

C.W. thought of Sidney's warnings, of Nora's bills, of the upcoming auction. "You've got seven days. Tops. Or this thing's going to blow."

Agatha Blair peered out from one of a long row of Palladian windows at Stoneridge, the Blair estate in New Jersey. The sky was as black as ink and the wind rustled dry leaves against the pane. She was irritated to be receiving visitors so late, but Henry had insisted. At first Agatha had hesitated. She despised those horrid cellular phones that enabled people to call en route and be at the door within minutes. Henry must have been sure she'd receive him. His voice had actually trembled like an old woman's when he mentioned the one name that would drag her from bed at any hour: Charles Blair.

Agatha had wrapped herself quickly in a long silk receiving gown and ordered tea brought to the library. Standing by the window, she sipped cognac. Her nose lingered at the snifter, the heady scent cleansing her of sleep as steam would a cold. Within minutes, Agatha spied a pair of headlights winding up the long private drive to the house. She dropped back the lace curtains, took a long swallow of her cognac, and sat in a pre-selected chair. The cognac's fire began to burn in her belly.

Peacham, her butler, showed Strauss into the library with the proper degree of decorum, despite the irregular hour. Henry Strauss was eager but nervous. When he spotted Agatha seated in a particularly high-backed, arched wing chair, Strauss paused. Agatha's eyes gleamed from her petite form and her hands stretched out upon her cane. Strauss was struck by how much she resembled a bat about to take flight. It was damn disconcerting. He straightened his tie as he walked across the room to take the seat beside her. He did not move his chair nearer.

"You've news of Charles?"

"He telephoned me tonight."

Agatha's surprise could not be concealed. Henry smiled.

"Well, go on, man. It's late." She tapped her cane.

"Charles knows about the loans to MacKenzie. He had the names of the shell companies." Strauss leaned forward. "He had the dates."

Agatha's face pinched as if she'd just tasted something sour.

"How?" she whispered.

"I traced the call back to some public phone in Vermont. Ring a bell?"

Agatha shook her head.

Henry leaned back in his chair, rested his elbows on the armrests, and crossed his legs. Agatha eyed him shrewdly.

"Vermont struck a chord with me," he said with a hint of conceit. "I thought about that, for quite a while actually, and then it hit me." He paused while his fingers rubbed the velvet armrests.

"Oh, for Christ's sake, cut the theatrics, and spit it out," Agatha snapped.

Henry frowned, offended. Flattening his palms on his lap, he continued in a more strained manner. "Do you remember I told you that Mrs. MacKenzie had left town? You were not interested in that at the time, I recall." He delighted in the short stab, searching Agatha's face for any clue of displeasure. Agatha peered over her cane, her face more stringent. Strauss continued without further delay.

"Mrs. Michael MacKenzie went to Vermont. Her farm is in the same town as the phone booth. Interesting coincidence, wouldn't you say?"

Agatha paled. Her breathing pace increased slightly even as her mouth tightened. She made a snorting kind of sound from her nose.

"I knew it! I knew MacKenzie had papers somewhere.

Damn his soul to hell. Now Charles has them." Her voice rose in anger and she stomped the cane hard upon the floor. "I want them. Do you understand, you blithering fool? If we don't get MacKenzie's papers we're ruined."

"I don't believe those papers exist. Even if they do, they are not as incriminating as you believe," Strauss countered. He kept his voice calm, enjoying this peek at Agatha's violent temper. "Else why would he call me and enlist my help?"

Agatha stilled. "Your help?"

"Precisely. He wants me to do homework for him. It's all guesswork on his part. He doesn't know names. I'm to keep his call a secret, you see. Charles suspects you…and Sidney."

Agatha leaned back in her chair and smiled broadly, revealing a line of small, even teeth under a thin upper lip.

"Sidney, you say? How perfectly marvelous."

"Quite so."

Agatha allowed herself a moment of humor, then felt very tired. She rose to her feet. Henry immediately followed suit and accompanied her to the door.

"Thank you, Henry, for this most important information. You were quite right to see me immediately. You will have the information I need on my desk first thing?"

At the door her hand lifted in a discreet signal. Peacham suddenly appeared with Henry's coat and hat.

"I truly doubt your search will turn up these mysterious papers, you know," Strauss said.

"We must know for certain what we are dealing with, don't you agree? Of course you do." Agatha turned toward the wide circular staircase. Her gaze swept up the walls of the staircase, lined with portraits of the illustrious Blair family.

"Charles suspects Sidney? Perfect."

Turning her head to Strauss, she added, "Calm, Henry. We must remain calm. The house of Blair is soon to take a fall."

21

—

"STAND BACK, LADIES, here he comes!" called Seth from the barn entry. Nora and Esther turned their heads, but it soon became obvious Seth wasn't calling to them. At his side stood a magnificent ram, all bulging muscles, flaring nostrils, and the largest testicles Nora had ever seen.

Seth strode as proud as the ram into the barn. Close behind sauntered Frank and Junior, jabbing each other's ribs and pointing to the suddenly alert ewes. Lastly, C.W. entered the barn. His hair curled askew and his muscled arms, still tan under rolled up sleeves, carried a large load of equipment. Nora couldn't help comparing him to the great ram.

"What are you gonna call him?" asked Seth, bringing the ram around to Nora.

Caught off guard, Nora mustered her thoughts and perused her new prize ram. She imagined all the fine lambs he would sire; rams with great balls of fire and ewes that gave birth to twins and triplets. Fat and healthy, every one of them.

"Studly," she declared in a clear voice.

C.W. broke into a wide grin and offered her a nod of approval.

"Yeh-up. Suits him," declared Seth. "Well, Studly. Go live up to your name."

With a wide swing of the gate and a formal bow, he escorted the ram into a large pen where several ewes waited with ears pricked and eyes flashing.

The ram rushed into the pen with sureness and majesty. As he surveyed his harem, he jutted his jaw forward, lifted his nostrils high into the air, and curled his lip far back, revealing his lower teeth.

"He's a magnificent beast," C.W. said as he walked up beside Nora.

"He should be," she remarked in her best business tone. "He cost a fortune."

"A wise investment," C.W. countered. "The best ram you can find will be the cheapest in the end. This ram will sire above-average lambs, who will, in time, become more than half the flock."

He leaned over the fence, resting his boot on the railing. Nora looked straight ahead but could feel his gaze on her. Lowering his head close to her ear, he said softly, "You know, Nora. One must be cautious when choosing the right ram. And when found, be decisive."

Nora continued staring at the ram, trying to ignore the comment so laden with innuendo.

Seth, Frank, and Junior gathered around the pen in unaccustomed silence, watching the ritualistic performance of the ram. Breeding happened each spring and fall, yet there was always a fascination with the raw beauty of nature. Perhaps even with the dawning of next year's lamb crop.

"You get what you pay for," commented C.W.

As the ram confidently approached a ewe, Nora's mouth went dry and her body moist. She ventured a bored look but she felt sure she wore the same rapt expression as the others. In time, she no longer was aware of anyone's presence save C.W.'s. His arm edged over along the fence, just enough to lightly graze her own. His thigh rested beside hers.

So close, she smelled the pungent sweat on his skin. The soft hairs on his arm tickled her own as she leaned closer to him, millimeter by millimeter. From under her lashes, she saw the rapid rise and fall of his chest. There was a chemical exchange between them. Undefined, but very real, very there. With each violent thrust of the ram, her gut tightened and her throat constricted.

Several ewes now had a blue smudge on their rumps.

"What are those?" she asked, her voice a dry whisper.

"Crayon marks," answered C.W., his voice husky. "See that harness Studly is wearing? It's a marking harness. Each ram has a different color, and it identifies who mounted the ewe. For records."

"Sounds efficient," she replied, relieved to be discussing the operation.

"How about you," Frank called out to C.W. "When're you gonna get off this farm and service the ladies?"

Junior leaned over and whispered in C.W.'s ear loud enough for all to hear. "Maybe you don't need to leave the farm after all."

Nora died on the spot. Through lowered lashes, she noticed a red flush creeping up C.W.'s ears.

He calmly shook his head, appearing mildly amused by the boys' antics. To his credit, despite the snickering around him and the color on his neck, his voice assumed a deep, resolute quality when he answered.

"This is one stud who will choose but one mate for life." He raised his eyes to Nora, a direct message sent in a direct line. And a warning to all witnesses.

Nora tried to look away but instead found Seth's keen eyes upon them, never missing a thing. Her blush deepened.

The Long Road Home

In a rush she turned away, but C.W. straightened and brought his boot down from the rail with a thud. Reaching out, he grabbed her elbow. Nora jerked his hand away, but he stubbornly refused to yield. As he led her to a private corner of the barn she shot him a fiery gaze, but he ignored it and only tightened his grip till she thought her bone would snap.

The heat in the barn was oppressive, and it exacerbated the heat of the moment. As C.W. swung her around to face him, Nora's long braid slapped her face. Her back was against the wall and she felt the dry wood scratch through her denim. Clenching her teeth, she yanked her arm free, but before she could skirt away, he arched over her, leaning both arms against the barn wall and covering her like a tent. In defiance, she tightened both arms around her chest.

"I'm not one to mince words," he said. His blue eyes flashed and demanded her total attention.

"Don't say them," she pleaded with closed eyes. The afternoon had been too tense, nerves were too frayed. At times like this, secrets could be exposed.

His sigh rumbled in his chest. "Nora, Nora, Nora. Don't deny what's between us. Closing your eyes to it won't make it go away."

"I thought you said this wouldn't happen again."

"I know. You make me a liar. I can't stop this."

His intensity invaded her and she shook her head in denial.

As if physically to change her mind, he grabbed her chin. She opened her eyes, now inches away from his, and gasped in the humid, charged air between them.

He released her chin and let his fingers slide down her neck and rest upon the gentle curve along the shoulder. Nora traced each centimeter along her nerve endings, and the pulse in her neck throbbed against his thumb. He offered not a hint of pressure, yet she felt choked with desire.

"Stop. Please."

His hand stiffened on her shoulder then slipped away as he stood straight. Cool air slipped between them, though the breathing came no easier.

"I'm not a teaser ram," he said bluntly.

She blinked and stood straight herself. "And I'll not have crayon marks on my back."

His eyes narrowed; the blue fires raged. "What's that supposed to mean?"

"It means you'd better realize I'm not just another mount." She turned her head, embarrassed by her crude analogy.

"Nora," he said as he leaned over her again and brought her eyes to his, "I don't think of you that way."

His nearness was suffocating and her nerves snapped. "I don't want you to think of me at all." She swallowed in the dry air as she grappled for the right words. The distance he created after stepping back gave her the chance to gather herself in a proper stance.

In her best employer-like tone she declared, "I don't think it's wise for us to start a personal relationship."

He stood as straight as the wall. "Because I'm a farmhand and you're a New York socialite?"

Nora closed her eyes for a moment. His question stung and dissolved her control. "No," she cried, "not because of that. Because I have nothing and you have nothing, and I'm afraid of what that adds up to."

When she opened her eyes again, the fire in his eyes still smoldered. She had admitted far more than she had ever intended.

"Let's just be friends," she whispered.

He looked around the room, then raised his eyes to the ceiling as his fingers drummed his hips. All the while Nora saw a muscle twitching furiously in his cheek.

"Please."

When he lowered his eyes, his face was carved in granite. "Yes, ma'am."

"See you tonight at seven—friend?" she persisted.

He swung his hands into his rear pockets and stared at her with squinted eyes, considering. His brows created deep creases in his tanned skin.

"Seven sharp." Then he turned and walked to the tractor parked at the barn's rear entry. She watched him tinker with the engine for several moments, but it was obvious he wasn't getting much accomplished.

Steeped in frustration, Nora turned and marched out of the barn and up the long road to her house. The house was dark and the kitchen door was ajar. That was strange, she thought, and she felt a sudden prick of fear. Oh well, she reassured herself. I must not have closed it tight enough. Nora slowly climbed the steps and gave the kitchen door a quick push. The swing was cut off by some resistance on the inside. She pushed harder. The door scraped open, pushing a fallen trash can along the floor. Her stomach tight, Nora reached her hand along the inside wall and flicked on the light. She stood listening intently, ready to flee. When she heard no response, she peered around the door.

Her furniture, dishes and pots—everything—were scattered across the floor. Nora's hand flew to her mouth and she ran out.

The men returned to the barn from her house, somber faced. Esther and Nora sat together, trying to figure out who could have robbed her place. There had been a couple of robberies in town lately; TVs and guns were the prime targets. When the men approached, they stood up for the news.

"Someone's done a good job tearin' up your place," said Frank.

"A real mess," added Junior.

Seth remained silent but watched C.W. carefully.

"Nora," said C.W. "Can I talk to you a minute?"

He led her to a far corner and said, in a low voice, "Do you know who could have done this?"

"No. Some local robber, I guess."

He shook his head. "It wasn't a robbery. Your pearls are still there, right on top of your bureau. And the TV. This wasn't the job of your everyday robber."

Nora's eyes widened. "Oh my God. The ledger!"

C.W.'s eyes were calm. "It's in my cabin. I checked." He drew her farther away from the others. "So, you think they were after the ledger too?"

Nora's knees felt weak. She leaned against the wall with a sigh of resignation. "It wouldn't be the first time. Some goons ripped apart our apartment right after Mike died. They want that ledger."

And they want me, C.W. thought, grinding his teeth. His phone calls to New York had led them here. It had to be.

Nora looked up at C.W. She had never seen him so angry. He looked as if he was ready to kill.

"Nora, who do you think wants that ledger? Any names?"

Her face hardened. "Charles Blair. Who else?"

He studied the contempt so clear in her flashing eyes. Un-adulterated hatred. And misplaced.

"Go on up," C.W. said, his voice controlled but weary. "No one is there now and they won't return." He put his hand on her shoulder. "I'm sorry, Nora."

"You're sorry? Whatever for?"

His eyes flickered and he dropped his hand. "It's a mess up there. I'll do your chores. You'd better get started."

"I'll help," called Esther when Nora started to leave.

"Thanks. I appreciate it."

When they left, C.W. leaned against the barn wall, eyes shut. He was a fool to put the hounds on the trail. Bastards. The ante was up; they knew where he was and what he knew. They didn't, however, know for sure if there was proof. He ran his hand through his hair. This was a damned dirty campaign.

Someone tapped his shoulder. C.W. jerked his head up and opened his eyes in time to catch Seth jab a digit toward the exit. Without a break in his stride, the old man kept chugging out of the barn to the tractor. There, he leaned against the green metal, pushed back his visor, and waited.

C.W. followed with long strides and faced him squarely—no head bobbing, no wayward glances.

"Expecting unwelcome company, Charley?"

"One never knows what to expect."

Seth nodded. "Yeh-up. Other than death and cold winters." He turned his gaze to the mountains. "If you got problems I need know about, I'd appreciate you lettin' me know."

C.W. leaned against the large curved fender and rested one boot atop the other. "I can deal with any trouble that comes, I assure you, Seth."

"Don't seem that way. You got trouble with the law?"

C.W. emitted a short laugh. "If it were only so easy."

"Well, who're ya runnin' from?"

"My family." It sounded childish, even to himself.

Seth guffawed. "Who isn't?" He slapped his knee. "Might as well stop running. They always find you." When C.W. didn't reply, he added, "Never took you for the kind'a man that was tied to the apron strings."

"I'm not," he barked. It was a knee-jerk reaction and he felt guilty for cutting Seth off. "It's not my family I'm running from, it's the business we're in." He sighed. "What can I say? You know I was on Wall Street. Well, I ran a bank—my bank.

We bought and sold businesses not just for the money but for the power. People got hurt who didn't need to…" The words trailed off.

Seth stood there, staring out over the fields, ruminating the confession with the bored look of a sheep.

"Are you listening?"

"Yeh-up. I hear you. Ain't nothin' to say."

"How about that I've lied to you, pretended to be a hired hand."

"You are a hired hand. Best I ever hired. Way I see it, you never talked about your past and I never asked. That ain't lying. That's keepin' to yourself."

C.W. leaned back against the tractor and joined Seth in staring out over the fields. For a while, neither spoke.

"When my father died," C.W. began at last, "I became head of the family, and the family business. I was never asked if it was what I chose to do. It was assumed. I had my duty to fulfill, and I fulfilled it beyond anyone's expectations.

"I could be as cold and calculating as the best of them. MacKenzie and I were a lot alike, except that he enjoyed it and I, eventually anyway, didn't."

"That'd be right," Seth agreed. "So, what's the problem?"

"The problem is there's trouble at the bank, and it's somehow tied up with MacKenzie."

Seth hoisted up his pants. "You ain't spying on the missus, are you, son? That why you here?"

He let his head fall back as he took a deep breath. "No, that's not why I'm here, and yes, I do need information from Nora. Believe me, Seth, I would never hurt her. In fact, I can help her. But my feelings for her and my duty to the bank are all tangled up."

He drew a deep breath, deciding. "Seth, I have to go back

to New York, right away…tomorrow. It's time to settle my accounts. But I won't stay there. I don't belong there anymore." He shook his head. "The question is, where do I belong?"

Seth kicked a few stones. "Son, God gave each of us a field. It's our job to find a way to live in it."

"It's hard to live in a field that one doesn't belong in."

"Life is hard, son. But it don't have to dictate how you live. A man's got to work out his own system. He's got to make it work in a way that gives him satisfaction but don't rile everyone else."

Seth rubbed his chin, then moved his hand over to scratch behind his ear in thought. "I wanted to die when my Liza did. And my boy. But I learnt you can't run from life. We enter and exit one by one. It's all we got. And I like knowin' the sun's going to rise in the morning and set in the evening and who really cares whether I believe it rises on an earth that's flat or round? I do my work, help my neighbors, keep the kids straight and true. I miss wakin' up to my Liza, though. No doubt about that." He sighed heavily, and C.W. sensed the loneliness of the old widower.

"But," Seth concluded with a slap on his knee. "I'll see her and Tom again when my own time comes." He rested his hand atop C.W.'s shoulder in a rare show of physical affection.

"Find your field, son."

22

———

NORA PICKED UP the broken china, carefully examining each piece to see if she could repair it. Chest drawers and boxes and books were strewn across the floor, which was littered high with practically everything she owned. The assassins, as Nora called the thieves, had a hurried search. Their target was obvious. Too obvious, Nora thought. They were trying to frighten her.

Well, they did not succeed, she told herself, rolling up her sleeves.

Esther and Nora worked together in the house as they did in the barn, efficiently and without idle gossip. Nora felt intensely violated by the robbery, and it was comfortable having Esther here with her now. They had reached an accord through their painting, and at times like this, Nora even ventured that she had a friend. She watched Esther lift up a huge box and carry it down the stairs.

Nora took the chance to sneak quickly up to her closet. She pulled out several dresses and pairs of shoes and added them to the piles already heaped across the floor. She cast aside a few pieces of luggage and grabbed a small tapestry suitcase from the rear of the closet. Unzipping it, she flipped up the lid.

"Thank God!" she exclaimed, releasing a long sigh. Mike's papers were still there. It was the ledger the thieves had been looking for, but these papers, memos, and his diary would surely have been taken if found.

"Anything missing?" asked Esther as she came up behind Nora.

"No," Nora replied, flipping the lid shut and zipping it. "Everything is here. Either those bozos were lazy or I scared them out when I came back early."

"I hate to think they were here when you were."

"I don't want to think about that. Lord," she said, wrapping her arms around her bended knees, "I'm so tired, I don't want to think about anything else tonight."

"I'm sorry this happened to you, Nora. You've worked so hard, and now this."

"It could have been worse, but thanks."

Their eyes met and they smiled.

"Here," Esther said, handing Nora a padded envelope. "Found this on the table. It's from New York."

Nora set the envelope beside her without looking at it. "It's probably more paperwork. It can wait." She shifted her gaze to Esther. "Speaking of work," said Nora, "I appreciate the way you've been teaching me your jobs."

"I never liked to do them anyway."

"That's hard to believe. You're good. I could spend a lifetime here and still not know as much as you do."

"I doubt it," Esther said. "You're learning about things I don't know beans about. You see, the difference is you want to know about this stuff. I know it because I lived it, but it's a drag. Pa gets real angry at me, though he doesn't say it. I've seen the way he watches you work. He knows you love it, same as him. Same as C.W."

"And you."

"Me? No. I stay because Pa needs me here. Never wants any of us kids to leave the farm. But I swear, sometimes I feel like I'm chained here, and if I just pull hard enough, the link to him will break and I'll be free." She sighed. "I used to watch you all pack up and leave at the end of summer—God, I envied you when I saw your packed luggage, ready to go."

Esther's voice trailed off as her gaze fell to her boots.

"Remember how once you told me you wished you knew what you were good at?"

"Yes, of course."

"Well, now you know. Sad thing is, the table's turned. Now I don't know."

"What do you mean? You still have your talent."

Esther leaned back against the wall, arms tight across her chest. "I have nothing."

It shocked Nora to see her lip tremble. Esther, who never revealed a chink in her armor.

"I know about the school. I'm sorry."

"It might all be for the good. Kinda knocked the dreams right out of me, you know? I can go back to John Henry now, if he'll have me. Get married. Have kids. Do what's expected." Her eyebrows lowered over her closed eyes and clenched lips.

"Esther, don't," Nora said with deathly cold. "Don't marry a man you don't love. You will regret it. I know."

Esther stared at her wagging boot.

"I might have another choice to offer you. I've made some calls to New York, to contacts I have in the art business, and who knows? Something might turn up. Hang in there awhile longer."

Esther's mouth fell open. "You did that for me?"

"I've done nothing, yet. Unfortunately, I can't offer you financial help. Contacts I have. Money I don't."

"I'll get it from somewhere," Esther replied, full of enthusiasm. "I have some saved. At least enough to get me there and settled. I heard how expensive things are in New York."

"It's true." How ironic life was, Nora thought. This was one of the times having money would be fun, not to hoard it in a bank but to give it to someone who really needed it.

"Talk to your pa and Aunt May. I think they have a few ideas on that."

A cloud settled over Esther's face. "Excuse me for asking," Esther asked guardedly, "but…what happened to all your money?"

"Mike spent it."

The look of perplexity on Esther's face made Nora laugh. She must have worn the same expression herself months ago when the lawyers told her she was broke.

"Really," said Nora. "I'm poor."

Esther's face gathered into a picture of doubt. "Come on. You're not poor like I'm poor. You still have this house, this land. Shoot. You have those 'contacts' you can call."

"Poor is poor. No use splitting hairs."

Nora watched as comprehension registered, then another undefined emotion grabbed hold of her features.

"So," Esther said with finality, "Mike left you with nothing too."

Nora swung her head around. "What?"

Suddenly, Esther's face mottled and she looked away.

"Esther?"

Esther turned to face Nora again. All her previous joy had fled. Now her features were set in seriousness.

"Nora, there's something I have to tell you. You've been

fair with me, and I can't accept your help without your knowing the truth about…" She took a breath. "About me and Mike."

Nora's breath felt caught in her chest as an old, too familiar, suspicion took hold. She recognized this look. She had seen it far too many times to miss it now. Her heart tightened in a vise.

"Esther, what about you and my husband?"

Esther's face suddenly appeared haunted. She took a deep breath and when she spoke her voice took on a faraway quality.

"He used to like to watch me paint."

Nora's heart skipped a beat. With a sense of impending doom, she huddled and rested her chin on her knees. In her mind's eye she recalled how Mike used to watch *her* paint, back in the early days of their marriage. She could still picture him lying in the fields beside the canvas, eyeing the brush as it brought a blank canvas to life with hues of blue, yellow, green, and red. Only this time the woman holding the brush wasn't herself. The hair blowing in the wind wasn't the color of wheat but of strawberries.

For the first time, she studied Esther's long hair, her peaches-and-cream complexion, and her intense green eyes with a critical eye. Esther had an earthy beauty—very alluring. Her flame-colored hair matched her passionate nature as well as the color that now rose upon her cheeks.

Nora chewed her trembling lip. Esther's former disregard, her jealousy, her referrals to Mike: all the pieces fell into place. The clink clamored in Nora's brain. The realization was deafening.

"Oh, Esther," she whispered.

The color spread from Esther's cheeks to cover her entire face. Centimeter by centimeter her chin jutted forward, by small degrees the flame in her eyes heightened, breath by breath her breathing hastened. Nora braced herself for the explosion.

"What do you know of it?" Esther shouted at Nora. "You left him!"

"I did not leave him!" Nora shouted back, scrambling to her feet. "I did not leave him!" She choked on a sob. "He drove me away!"

Nora was so angry she was trembling and her hands made small fists at her side. She could not contain herself. She was like a bantam: pacing, fluttering her wings, beak forward, ready to strike. "Who the hell are you to throw this up at me now? What right have you?"

That brought Esther to her feet and she towered over Nora by a good five inches. Esther breathed heavily, and Nora saw a wild anguish in her eyes as she stood there, mouthing but not making a sound. Nora glared back; she was not afraid.

Then Esther's rage disappeared as quickly as it had come. Her face stilled, then contorted, and she slumped to the floor, covering her face with her hands. Small, short cries escaped as her shoulders rocked.

"I have no right," Esther blurted out. "None at all. Except that I loved him."

Nora stood rooted to the spot. Oh, please, don't let me hear this, she cried to herself. Not Esther. No, not Esther too. Pain, jealousy, betrayal, all stabbed her heart and it hurt. It hurt so badly.

Nora slipped to the floor beside Esther. She did not reach out or try in any manner to comfort her. Compassion was beyond her. Still, she saw in the weeping, pathetic figure a mirror of herself a year ago. She could not help but pity Esther.

"Why?" Nora asked in a husky voice. "Did Mike lure you

out? He was like that. Esther, you know there were others. Many others."

Esther wiped her eyes and sniffed as she nodded her head. "But not right away."

Bit by bit, Esther collected herself, pulling the damp hair from her face and wiping her nose. Red face, red hair, and now red eyes. Nora waited. She didn't wait long. After a deep, shuddering breath, Esther continued.

"He—he said you didn't love him. Tha-that you and he weren't, you know, weren't together anymore."

Nora closed her eyes in shame. "That's right," she whispered. "We weren't."

"I couldn't help loving him. He was so different from the men I knew. Then he—he just stopped coming up. I waited and waited. It was so hard. I never dared try to contact him. Not ever. I knew he was married." She blushed and cast a nervous glance at Nora.

"Then one summer night he did come back. I saw the Jaguar go by. I was breathless. I hurried so to get cleaned up. Then you drove by too. I was terribly disappointed, but you left again, in a real hurry. I figured you had another row. Mike told me you used to fight a lot. So up I went, all dressed and excited to see him again." Esther sniffed and let out a shaky laugh. "Well, I got what I deserved."

Nora remembered that night. Esther must have seen the same tawdry scene that she did. Probably felt the same shame. No, she thought again. Not quite the same. That particular shame was reserved for wives only.

"It's cruelly ironic."

"Yeah. He got two birds with one stone." Esther covered her face with a hand and looked away. "I am so ashamed."

Nora was unmoved. She rubbed her temples. She felt like a piece of glass about to break into infinite pieces.

"He wasn't exactly your type." Nora's voice was hoarse in the strain.

Esther sat up wiping her eyes and gathering herself together. "It's not because of who he was but because he represented New York."

"I don't understand."

"I only understood it recently myself. It's not an excuse, but... You see, all I've ever wanted to do was paint. I teach at night at the country college and show my work in local shows that no one ever comes to. But I dreamed of going to New York. Mike used to say he'd help me get there."

Nora hardened her heart. "So. You did it for the money."

Esther paled and her mouth dropped open. "No! It wasn't like that at all. I thought I loved him. Really."

"And that makes it right?"

Esther shook her head and looked at her hands. "No. I'm sorry. I am so very sorry."

"Yes, well." Nora started to get up, but Esther shot out a hand to restrain her.

"Please, let me explain."

Nora coolly looked down at the hand, then at Esther. Esther dropped her arm, recoiling.

"I cannot discuss this any further," Nora said, unconsciously assuming her haughty tone. "If you would be so kind as to leave now."

Esther looked completely defeated as she nodded. Her pride had been humbled. Picking herself up from the floor she slunk away, repeating, "I'm sorry" once more at the door.

Nora remained staring at the floor, completely drained. It didn't matter, she told herself again and again. Mike was dead. It was all over.

But it wasn't. Like an insidious snake, the truth danced before her, weaving, spitting its venom, mesmerizing her into depression. Nora leaned against the wall, exhausted. She gazed absently around the room. Tonight it looked tawdry and unkempt with its plywood floors and plastic-wrapped ceilings. Books had been knocked off the dusty cinderblock shelves and the makeshift closet of nails and clothesline sagged in the middle, threatening to topple more of the iron hangers. The place was a mess. Who did she think she was kidding?

She flopped her hands upon the floor, hitting the padded envelope that Esther had brought up to her. With little care and less interest, she picked out the four staples and pulled several papers from the envelope. They were from Ralph Bellows.

Nora skimmed the first page. Then, sitting up sharply, she raced through the second, the third, and the fourth. Nora's insides felt sore and raw, as though she'd just been mugged.

Slowly, as if each movement brought pain, Nora doubled her knees and hugged them tight against her chest. Her vocal cords strained to keep the cry in, but the timbre of anguish grew louder than she could control. It escaped as a high hum from her tight lips. She began to rock back and forth as she tried desperately to lull the misery to sleep. Misery never sleeps. It welled up larger and larger inside until her chest swelled, pushing painfully against her rib cage.

Crumpling the pages in her fists, Nora moaned. "I cannot bear any more." Unable to stop the flow of misery, she buried her face against her knees and unleashed the avalanche of tears.

A sweet-smelling wind was blowing in from the south as C.W. hiked up the mountain for his appointment with Nora. A sweet smell for a foul day, he thought. This late in the fall, dusk set earlier in the evening. Already, the vibrant pink and blue sunset was lowering in the western sky. As he walked the gravel road, equally vibrant colored leaves fell around him, twirling in the breeze.

Turning the final curve, he spied the big house over the field of purple heather. Though night was setting in, the house was dark. Not a single bulb shone. He panicked, thinking himself a fool for leaving her alone. He broke into a run. As C.W. approached, the melancholy music of Ravel poured out loudly across the mountains.

C.W. entered the house with caution, holding the screen door with his hands to prevent it from slamming. He could hear only the music. Looking around, all was back in order, yet not. She had evidently cleaned up the mess, but no dinner was on the stove. Only an opened wine bottle sat on the counter.

"Nora?" he called. No response. Only music. He followed the sad strains through the kitchen, up to the great room, but it, too, was empty. Fear gripped him. He was about to head up to Nora's room when from the corner of his eyes, he spotted a shadowed movement out on the deck.

He strode across the room and slid open the glass doors. "Nora?" he bellowed.

"I'm here." It was a hushed response from a dark corner.

Relief flooded him as he crossed the distance to her side. Nora was curled up under a blanket on the wooden bench, resting her chin upon her knees. Her eyes were on the sunset, now but a long, thin pink line in the valley.

He lay his hand upon her shoulder. "What's wrong?"

She didn't speak immediately but waited until the waning sunset sank into darkness. Then, when he could no longer see her face, she answered.

"It's all over. I've lost."

His fingers tightened on her shoulders. "The auction is two

weeks off. I thought we decided we'd have time to come up with something."

She reached out and handed him a large padded envelope. "Everything is gone. Here. Read it. It's from Bellows. The Blair Bank won't wait two weeks. I can't make it. I can't balance that budget without my account."

C.W. shook open the papers as he paced to the window where light shone out in a narrow beam.

Dear Mrs. MacKenzie (Nora):

It is my unfortunate duty to inform you of the latest development concerning your estate. After reinvestigation, the estate is compelled to rescind the interestbearing account established in your name. Apparently, a loan made to Sav-Mor, a MacKenzie company, has suddenly been refused a delayed repayment schedule by the Blair Bank. (See attached letter.)

It is most unfortunate, but the money is required immediately. There it is. I wish it were not so.

I hope that this transaction does not inconvenience you too greatly. Please inform me if I can be of any assistance.

Sincerely,
Ralph Bellows

Another page briefly described the SavMor property, and another was a copy of a letter from the Blair Bank, signed by Sidney Teller.

C.W. carefully and with precision folded the crumpled papers and slipped them into the envelope. His hands shook in anger.

C.W. leaned against the window, his head falling back against the cold glass. So, it was Sidney. Sidney was behind the MacKenzie deals. Sidney had orchestrated the robbery. Sidney was bringing him, and his family, down. C.W.'s anguish redoubled. Why Sidney? His brother-in-law, Cornelia's husband, his colleague, and friend. He had hoped it was Agatha. But all fingers pointed to Sidney.

He swallowed the news; it was bitter. Now he was alone in this fight. He felt like the leader of a retreating army. The ammunition was stolen, the morale was low. He released a laugh, for fear he might cry.

C.W. lowered his head to gaze at Nora. His eyes acclimated to the dark, giving him full view of her slumped shoulders and sagging jaw. She had once said, with such spirit, "There were some things worth fighting for." He had taken that spirit to heart; it was his rallying call. Where was that spirit now, Nora? The *I Ching* taught that adversity breaks the inferior man's will but only bends the superior man's spirit. How far could Nora bend before she broke?

"Do you know what the real kicker is?" Nora asked out of the blue. Her voice was laced with uncharacteristic bitterness. "First I put my trust in Mike, and he died leaving me worse than penniless. Then I put my trust in this farm, with an almost religious zeal, and it can't break even." She let out a sharp laugh. "I sure know how to pick them."

C.W. gathered his wits and moved to sit beside her on the bench. He gripped both her shoulders, giving her a gentle shake.

"That's the problem, Nora," he said slowly. "You're not picking. You've been drowning in rough waters and are grabbing for anything that remotely resembles a lifeline. What you need to do is learn how to swim. And to do that you have to put the trust in yourself. Otherwise your trust will always be misplaced."

She looked at him with a queer expression on her face. "I

could have chosen a little cash, you know, but I picked the farm. This was going to be my security. My future."

He dropped his hands. She wasn't listening. "Security, huh?" He shook his head. "Anyone who depends on a farm for his security is nuts. First of all, it has one of the lowest rates of return on the market. Second, and this is important, so listen up, boss lady.

"Second, security doesn't come from a profit margin, whether it be a farm or a restaurant or a bank. Security is the knowledge that whatever happens, whatever garbage fate throws your way, you trust in yourself."

She tossed a dubious glance his way. "But what happens when you don't know who you are, and you don't trust in yourself?"

"Then you've got a problem. A serious one," he said without missing a beat.

"Right," she replied dourly.

He ran his hand through his hair. "Nora, it's only one farm."

She stood up and glared at him. "Only one farm!" she shouted back at him. "It's *my* farm. It's all I have left in the world."

He was glad to see her spirit, yet she was missing the point. "It's not all you have left. You have yourself!" He held back from adding that she also had him. He was certain she did not want to hear that now.

Suddenly her face twisted and she buried her face in her hands. "Damn these tears," she cried. "I hate them. I am so damn tired of crying. I am so tired of being hurt."

He sat and watched her suffer, suffering himself. He rubbed his large hands together, then looked at them with disgust. What good were these big, strong hands when they couldn't patch up her battered soul?

She wiped the tears away with determined strokes and

smoothed out her hair. After a quick wipe of the nose, she straightened and faced him.

"Listen, it's getting late. Let's call it a day."

"If you'd like to talk…"

"No, I wouldn't. I've said enough already."

It was a dismissal. He knew she was shooting from a point of pain, but it still hit its mark. He gathered his books and grabbed his coat. She hadn't turned to walk him to the door, or even bid him farewell. She sat on the deck, arms folded and chin back to her knees. Her only movement was an occasional wiping of her eyes.

"Nora, look at me. I have to leave. Tomorrow. Just for a few days. But I won't leave you like this."

She lifted her eyes. Even in the dark, her despair was easy to read.

"It'll work out. Trust me," he demanded, his finger jabbing the air.

"I trust no one," she said in a thin voice.

"Such cold words. Not even a good-bye."

"The truth is cold. Farewells are bitter. I have learned this too late in my life."

Hoisting his books with a frustrated yank, C.W. marched away, his heels reverberating on the wooden deck. At the stairs, he stopped, his hand gripping the railing. Damn fate, he thought, his face contorting in anger. Tomorrow he was taking a chance that could spin his life into orbit. He didn't deserve this treatment. Neither, he decided, did she.

Spinning on his heel, he swept down upon her like a March wind, lifting her in his arms and kissing her, long and hard, with a passion born of desperation.

"Do not give up hope," he said, squeezing her tight.

Then he turned and disappeared into the darkness.

Alone and breathless, Nora shivered in the night air.

23

———

SIDNEY TELLER HAD been sitting on the edge of his chair ever since Charles Blair walked into this hastily rented conference room on the outskirts of the city. When he first saw Charles walk in with his faded jeans and checkered flannel shirt, he had been appalled. The Charles Blair he knew had always been an impeccable dresser. That wasn't the only radical change.

Sidney noticed dark circles under Charles's angry eyes and the pallor of his skin, despite the tan. Emotion from a man whose stone face was legendary. Charles Blair was a changed man. Sidney was unnerved.

Charles approached the conference table with the same authority he always had; his shoulders were straight and while he didn't linger, Charles Blair never hurried. He rested his long fingers on the table while he paused to study Sidney seated at the far end.

Sidney ventured a smile. "Welcome back."

"Yes, thank you."

A smile did not crack Charles's iron composure. He sat down and methodically folded his hands.

Sidney shifted his weight and reached for the briefcase at his feet. It was to be business as usual, he thought with a pang of disappointment and a twinge of fear. Not even cordiality, after all this time. Sidney yanked the briefcase to the table. The click of the polished brass latches pierced the strained silence between the two men.

"I have only one question, Sidney."

Sidney's hand stilled on the many files he had begun to unload. His glance darted up quickly.

"Tell me about the SavMor loan." Charles's voice was threatening.

Sidney's face flattened. He cleared his throat. "SavMor is a small company that the bank loaned some $300,000. It's one of those faulty loans stamped with your approval." He waved his hand in a nervous, impatient manner. "It's a flimsy operation, way overdue on the repayment schedule. Of course, I've refused further delay requests."

Sidney's anger leaked into his voice. "I'm doing my job, Charles. And frankly, I'm trying to save your neck."

Charles considered this very carefully, as though weighing every word.

"And that was your sole reason for refusing a delayed repayment schedule?"

Sidney grew increasingly nervous. "Of course. What other reason would there be? It's a lousy company that never should have been granted a loan in the first place. There is no question here. We'll be lucky to collect a cent."

Charles looked at his hands.

"Did you know Mrs. MacKenzie's home was robbed?"

Sidney was confused. "Yes."

Charles's eyes shot up. His gaze was wrathful.

"It happened a year ago." Sidney's words poured out quickly, like water over a flame. "Right after Mike died. Why bring it up now?"

Charles visibly relaxed. He spread out his palms and dropped his head again. When he lifted his eyes, Sidney saw relief in them.

"Why, indeed," Charles said, a small smile at last easing across his face. He leaned back in his chair and folded his hands across his waist, eyeing his brother-in-law speculatively.

"Sidney, accept a delayed repayment schedule for SavMor." His voice was calm, though decisive.

"What?" Sidney blustered. "We have to collect on these bad loans. You'll go down. And I'll go down with you."

Charles nodded. "Trust me, Sid. I know what I'm doing."

Sidney considered. "Do you? Charles, come back. Take the helm. It's mutiny out there."

C.W. stood up and thrust his hands behind his back. "You know I can't do that. Not yet." He paced the conference room floor. With his wild, uncut hair, Sidney thought he looked like a caged lion seeking a route of escape.

"Is it the loans?"

"In part. Of course. Who is handling the repayment schedule?"

"Henry Strauss," Sidney replied lightly. "I've been after him for months to let me call these in. He's been holding on to these loans tighter than a miser holds a penny. Then last Thursday, he up and hands me the SavMor file and agrees I should go after them."

C.W. swung his head around. A fresh bolt of anger crossed his face. "Last Thursday?"

Sidney fingered his report. "Out of the blue."

C.W. immediately ceased his pacing. A lengthy silence ensued.

"Strauss. Of course. I understand," C.W. said slowly.

Sidney looked at Charles with apprehension. He had heard that tone in Charles only a few times before. Dry ice. A ruthlessness so cold it scorched those who were touched by it. An eerie calm settled in the room. At length, Charles took his seat and with precise movements, closed his hands on the table before him.

"Talk to me, Sidney."

Sidney stirred with excitement. He couldn't help it. This was Charles's battle call. War was being declared and Sidney was well armed and ready. "At last," he said as he dug into his briefcase and pulled out reams of pages of his investigations. Sidney's thoroughness had always been his best route of attack.

"As you've requested, I've looked closely into Michael MacKenzie's background," he said, handing C.W. one of several reports. Sidney picked out the vital points. "Only child of a small-time grocery chain owner, Catholic, born and raised in New Jersey. A poor student academically but labeled most likely to succeed. You know the type—a good-looking jock who was also in student government and several other organizations."

"A manipulator even then."

Sidney noticed the slight curl of C.W.'s lip.

While Sidney rambled on and on about details C.W. already knew, C.W. sifted through the collection of photographs of Michael MacKenzie that was included in the file. As a young man, Mike always sported a wide grin and a look of enormous "can do." The all-American boy, through and through. It was no wonder Nora had found him attractive.

C.W. stopped at one photograph and brought it closer to

his face. In it, a black-tuxedoed Mike, white rose in his lapel, had his arm wrapped possessively around his smiling bride. In her pouf of white lace, Nora appeared virginal. A shining Venus about to be abducted by Vulcan.

C.W. was stabbed with jealousy, though he would never have admitted it. His tense fingers curled the edges of the photograph. No, not jealousy, he told himself. C.W. attributed this galling feeling to anger against a man who did his friend wrong.

C.W. pushed away the photographs. Sidney stopped speaking and looked up from his report. He didn't like the morose look on Charles's face or the twitching in his jaw. It wasn't anger this time. In Charles's expression Sidney witnessed a personal struggle.

"Should I go on?" he asked, tentatively laying down his report. "Charles, are you ready for this?"

C.W. shifted his gaze, focusing intently now on Sidney. He knew that Sidney had been forthright about the loan. He wasn't hiding anything; Sidney was just doing an honest job. Agatha must have counted on his thoroughness. Sidney had not betrayed him. If he wasn't so involved with the war, he'd have felt joy at this victory.

Across the table Sidney sat, file in hand, ready to pit his brain and wit against their common enemy. All right, Sidney, C.W. decided. Loyalty wins out.

A slow smiled eased across C.W.'s face. "I'm ready if you are," he replied.

Sidney searched his eyes and found the old Charles. Sidney's own smile was filled with relief.

"Skip all this background," C.W. said with impatience. "I know it all. Let's get down to business."

C.W. then proceeded to deliver a complete report on the MacKenzie loans from the Blair Bank and all the pertinent details involved. His memory was photogenic. "I'm expecting a complete rundown on MacKenzie's business dealings for the past three years. Should be faxed soon," he concluded, looking away.

Sidney was aghast. His respect for Charles's cold logic and skill grew, as did his suspicion that this battle had become a personal vendetta.

"Unbelievable," Sidney replied with a gasp. "How did you get all that information? I've tried every channel, but it's been bottled up. There's a consortium of secrecy out on the Street."

"I've had some inside information. MacKenzie left behind incriminating information. It could be helpful." C.W. contained a tight smile. "Or it could nail me to the cross." He looked straight at Sidney, implying his own danger by association.

"I see," Sidney replied, a frown creasing his face. "We'll have to be all the more careful."

C.W. looked at his brother-in-law with respect and affection. Ah, Sid, he thought to himself. You're a good man. When this is all over, I'll make it up to you.

"Look at this," Sidney said, presenting a file. "Most of MacKenzie's wealth was a ruse. He shifted assets from one company to another. What I can't figure out is how he passed his annual audit."

"He used accounting tricks. He really was quite clever."

"More a mobster than a magician, I'd say."

C.W. held his tongue.

Sidney never sprawled, but he leaned far back in his chair, arms crossed. "I can see other banks being duped by MacKenzie. But Agatha? She's pretty shrewd, even if I hate to admit it. And why the forgery of your name?"

C.W. tapped his fingertips. "Consider the dates. Don't you

find it interesting that coinciding with the dates of the loans are significant rises in MacCorp. stock?"

"I noticed that as well."

"It's obvious. Someone was buying. Heavily."

"It had to be inside."

"Loans made in my name. Loans suddenly called in. Figure the results."

Sidney considered for a moment, then realization flooded him. "It was never intended for MacKenzie to repay the loans."

"MacKenzie went into a selling frenzy. His house of cards collapsed."

"Poor bully."

"Don't feel too sorry for him. I guess you could say he died by his own sword. Did you know that he illegally borrowed from his company's pension fund?"

"You're right. I don't feel sorry for him."

C.W. looked squarely at his brother-in-law. "I've confided in you about the MacKenzie–Blair connection because I trust you. I do not want the loans called in, not until after the auction. On that I must depend on you."

"Of course. Charles, what are you going to do?"

"I don't know. The pieces aren't fitting together yet."

C.W. saw the worry in Sidney's face. He stood and walked the distance to his brother-in-law's side and rested a hand on his shoulder.

"The family is in this together. Sidney, I warn you, events may occur that will shake your confidence in me. But trust me, Sid. I won't let you down."

Sidney's gaze rose to Charles's face. The doubt and anger were gone, replaced by an appeal.

"You can count on me. As always."

C.W. tightened his grasp on Sidney's shoulder. When he

released it, he went straight to the telephone. He dialed the number of a trusted associate, one whose power on Wall Street was unquestioned, whose resources ran very, very deep. This man was his godfather. He had sat on his knee, dated his daughter, raced his ponies. This powerful man came to the phone directly, straight out of a meeting, to take Charles's call.

After a brief, quite personal exchange, C.W. dove into the business with characteristic simplicity. "I need to know the income he declared to the tax authorities as well as the income actually earned. In particular, any stock profits. Dates, of course. I need to know of any concealed income and where he is currently invested. In short, I need to know what brand of underwear this man wears and how often he changes them."

Sidney chuckled and pitied, in a remote sense, the man targeted by Charles Blair.

"The man's name?" concluded C.W. He leaned back in the chair and closed his eyes. "Henry Strauss."

24

—

BACK HOME, NORA did give up hope. When he returned three days later, C.W. noticed the change right away. A pall was cast over the farm. Though the work continued, as it always must on a farm, the cheerful spirit they had enjoyed since Nora's arrival had slipped away. Nora appeared, precisely on time, to perform her chores. But she barely said hello and her pace struck him as slower than sap in January. She didn't seem to care anymore. Not even Willow got much more than a pat.

Things were just as sullen up at the big house. Frank and Junior exchanged questioning glances his way when Nora walked silently past them and into her room. Seth thought she looked older, the boys thought she looked tired, but they all agreed she didn't look the same. As they hammered in nails and measured drywall, Frank and Junior cast mournful gazes upstairs at Nora's closed door and worked without the usual jokes and banter. The aroma of coffee grew acrid as the day wore on, and the boys' stomachs grumbled for a slice of Nora's bread. Their nails and wood chips fell unnoticed. At the end of the day, clutter loomed in large piles across the floor.

As the day passed, C.W. made increasingly frequent stops at the house. Always to pick up this or drop off that, always glancing up toward the top floor. Seth held his tongue, biding his time, but C.W. noticed the scowl that deepened on the old man's brow at each passing.

"What'd you say to her, C.W.?" Frank finally blurted, his eyes skewered in accusation. Junior's head was bobbing in agreement, his hammer swinging in his hand. It was clear whose side they were on now.

Seth approached with a slow gait, rocking from side to side. When he stopped at C.W.'s side, he swept his gaze around the room, grabbed his belt, and adjusted his pants, a clear signal that he was going to talk turkey.

"What do you know about what's going on up here?"

"It's not for me to explain. She's just not herself."

The old man snapped his suspenders. "Not herself? Shoot. More like she done lost herself and she don't even miss it."

C.W. frowned and looked away.

Seth let a few minutes pass before speaking again. The younger men rocked on their heels and shifted their weight, waiting with respect for Seth to begin.

"You remember that ewe that got sick last July?" he finally asked.

C.W. nodded. "You mean the one that filled up with gas?"

"That'll be the one. Ate too much of the weed. Just swelled up like a balloon. Seemed 'bout ready to burst too. But she didn't. She dropped to her knees. And you know what happens when a ewe drops to her knees, don't you, boy?"

"Yes, sir, I do," he replied. "She'll die."

Seth nodded. "We didn't let that happen, did we? We

propped that ewe up and eventually she got better. Yes, she did."

C.W. nodded in agreement.

"When a sheep drops to its knees, it just quits the fight to live. If'n you leave it down in the fields, it's gonna die out there sure as the sun sets. But if you can get it back up on its legs, chances are it'll pull through.

"That's just the way sheep are, son. People too. You leave one out in the fields, alone, without the will to live and she'll die too. Maybe not so we can all see it and mourn it, but deep inside she'll wither up and the life just gets snuffed out." He blew a puff of air for effect. "Nope. Gotta find a way to prop her up."

Their eyes met in understanding. C.W.'s lips tightened and the muscle in his jaw began to work. By the spark in Charley's eyes, Seth knew he had lit a fire.

"Listen, Seth, keep an eye on things for me, will you? There's something I need to take care of."

"Yeh-up," replied Seth, grabbing hold of the tools and swallowing back a smile. Yeh-up, he thought to himself as he watched C.W. sprint up the stairs. He fairly lit a bonfire to that boy's butt.

C.W. took the stairs two at a time and pounded three times on Nora's bedroom door. "Nora MacKenzie. Come out here. I need to talk to you."

"Go away," she called back.

He turned to see Frank and Junior jab each other in the ribs. Seth twisted his lips and snapped his cap on his head.

C.W. pounded again on the door. "Open up, or I'm coming in. We can talk in there as well as anywhere."

From behind the door he heard the padding of feet. In a moment, the door swung open just wide enough for C.W. to catch a glimpse of Nora. She looked awful. Her eyes were puffy and her hair, which had lost its golden lustre, hung limp and in disarray on her shoulders. He had always wanted to see it down, but definitely not like this. Seeing her so apathetic, his demeanor changed from gruff to gentle.

"Come on, Nora. Grab your coat. Let's go for a walk."

"I don't want to. I'm busy packing."

"Come on," he persisted. "It'll do you good." He coaxed her out of her room, into her jacket, and out the door toward the east meadow.

The October day was masquerading as summer; the sun shone in a crystalline sky and the air was warm and moist. C.W. thanked Nature for her help. Who could be depressed on such a beautiful day? He said as much to Nora, and though she nodded in agreement, he wasn't sure she felt it. Still, he persevered. He took her on a long walk down the road to the eastern border of the property.

"C.W., where are we going? Let's turn back. I'm really not in the mood," she protested.

He offered her only a squeeze of the hand and a wink for an answer.

Up the steep mountainside they climbed, slowing just to remove their jackets on this Indian summer day. After an arduous climb, they reached a ledge that looked out at a view that lured the eye. Above them stretched an expanse of brilliant blue sky. At their feet, acres and acres of fields spread out, golden where shorn, deep brown, magenta, and burnt orange where wild. How could Nora's sagging spirit not be revived?

C.W. wrapped an arm across her shoulder and had her follow his pointed finger to where natural spring water came rushing down the mountain. He traced its gurgling path into a recessed field where it sat, marshy and dark.

"There," he said grandly, "is where you can build not one

but two ponds—maybe even three, one atop the other, like steps. And in them you can raise trout, bass, even crayfish for harvest and sale. I'm convinced there is a market for it, and it can be profitable."

Nora looked at him as though he had gone mad. "Ponds? Marketing fish? What are you talking about?"

"Making this place work, Nora. We can do it."

Anger flashed in her eyes. It was the first emotion he had seen so far.

"Stop it!" she cried. "I don't want to hear it. No more plans, no more dreams. Not for this farm. Not for me."

He stood back. He hadn't expected her to be so defiant. "So, you're giving up?"

She threw up her hands. "No, I am not giving up. I never had anything to give up. They'll take this place anyway."

"We don't know that yet. Have faith that the auction will pull through. To give up on the farm now will ensure that even if the bank doesn't take it, you'll lose it anyway."

"I don't care anymore."

"Is that so?" he replied, grabbing her elbows and holding them tight before him. He wanted both to shake her and to hold her. "I don't believe you."

Her shoulders slumped as she stared back at him. She wanted to feel the same enthusiasm, to rally, but she just couldn't. She felt drained.

"I believed it could be done…once," she replied.

Her voice was as soft as the breeze. He saw her head-bent profile, her lashes blinking quickly, and her lips quivering the way they always did when she tried to prevent tears. He hoped she didn't see his shudder or the swelling of his chest.

"Diversify," he said.

"What?"

"We have to diversify. Then we can minimize our risks and

increase the farm's output at little or no extra cost." He was gesturing with his hands, then wrapped an arm around her shoulder, giving her a gentle shake. "Look again, Nora. See all the possibilities here. We've been talking about this—let's do it! Your idea of expanding the sugaring business is a good one. And look at all this lumber! Then there's fish farming, specialized crops—"

"Where's all the financing for these operations coming from?"

He heard the doubt in her voice and persevered. "It won't take a lot and with robbing Peter to pay Paul, as you said, I think we can swing it. The secret's in the management. Besides, I'll take a cut in pay." He held up his hand against her objections. "Don't worry, I'm no martyr. I'll buy into the business. It's a great opportunity for me, and who knows, maybe Frank and Junior will follow suit."

Nora listened and he saw a flicker in her eyes.

"And we should plan an intensive management for the sheep," he continued in a rush. "Their wool, freezer lambs, replacement lambs, and such. We'd have to bring up the flock number. By half at least."

"Possible. Yes." Her foot was tapping. "But cost control is the first factor. We'll have to pay strict attention to expenses like fuel, repairs, utilities. And I'll have to let people go. The gravy train is gone. No more submitting a bill and expecting a check to be written."

"You bet."

"You know, I have one idea that really appeals to me."

"What is it?" he asked, thrilled to catch her interest.

"Well," she began slowly. "I could spin wool. Make better use of our own wool to increase the value of the lamb. May and I have talked about it. I know it's not much, but…"

He stood with arms akimbo, a grin stretched from ear to ear. "It's a wonderful idea. Let's do it."

Her eyes opened wide and the hope he read in them was humbling.

"I want this farm to succeed," she said, hope daring to enter her voice again. "I want, very much, to make it my home. We will make it. Won't we?"

His face grew solemn. "You will. You will succeed at anything you work at. I truly believe that." He saw her frown.

"What's the matter?"

"You won't be here?"

He walked the few paces to her and cupped his palm along her chin. The wind gusted, stirring the goldenrod clusters gone to seed, blowing the white puffs of exploded milkweed pods, and tossing curled, brown maple leaves in a swirl around them.

"I will be here. If you want me to be."

"The other day you said you were leaving." Her voice was a whisper. "Now you want to stay. Now you have wild and wonderful plans and really seem to care whether this place makes it or not. Why?"

He stared into the depths of her green pools until he felt he would drown in them. "Nora." He sighed, standing before her. He worked his mouth but the words didn't come.

"Why?" she repeated, mouth open, eyes wide. He could see the pearly ridge of her teeth, and between them the pink moist mound of her tongue.

The exhilaration of the afternoon spearheaded the assault on his resolve. Perched high on the bluff, the air was charged. It gusted around them, snatching Nora's hair from its hold and sending it whipping freely in the wind. C.W. was undone.

He stepped closer, gripping her slight shoulders, and held her close.

"God help me," he said, pressing his lips against her head. C.W. lifted her face and held it between his palms. Her gaze was trusting, her face pale. "God help us both."

In one swoop, his mouth sealed hers in dominant possession.

She felt his wave of passion sweep her up like a small piece of driftwood, tossing her senses in a turbulent swirl that left her dizzy. She could drown in his kisses and drew back, gasping for breath. Her hands rested upon his cheeks, stalling his advance with her fragile resistance. Every fiber in her body desired him. That he wanted her was clear.

Yet where did this tide come from? That her passion could ignite so quickly, so unexpectedly, frightened her. Of what she wasn't sure. Rejection? Regret? Deep down, she knew she hadn't resolved her greatest doubt: Had Mike reason to turn away? Was something wrong with her?

These fears and questions swirled in her brain so fast they left her trembling. She could only back away. She tried, yet his arms held her close.

As if he heard the questions, C.W. quieted his approach. Taking her hands from his cheeks, he kissed the tip of each finger while his eyes smiled on. She stilled, her breath in her throat.

"You're beautiful," he whispered as he slid her arms around his neck, and his own down her arms to wrap around her back.

Hearing the words, she felt beautiful.

"I want you," he crooned as his lips met her ear. She felt his tongue trace the delicate folds of her inner ear and his hot breath seemed to blow her fears from her brain.

Hearing the words, she felt desirable.

"God, I need you," he murmured as his lips met hers once

again. Their trembling gave credence to his words, humbling her with their honesty.

Hearing his plaintive cries, her heart denied her brain further resistance. With a surge of tenderness she relinquished. Shyly, she echoed his declarations of desire, her whispers mingling with sighs.

Hearing her words, he buried his head in her golden hair. His emotion brought him to the edge of pain. In a desperate rush he wrapped her in a grip so tight the air whooshed from her lips.

"I need you, Nora," he repeated. "I want you now... here."

His desperation excited her. His hands, shaking yet hard, raked her back, her buttocks, then traveled up her spine again.

"Yes, yes," she whispered.

He swept to her mouth again, moving his hand to crush her hard against him.

"C.W.," she gasped as her head fell back and her arms wrapped tight around his chest. He moaned her name in reply.

The sound of their names on each other's lips struck like a bolt of lightning, and like two dry tinders, they dropped to their knees in the meadow. The lovers stretched out upon the fields. His hands caressed her as they pushed her back until, at last, he covered her body with his own. Their clothing slipped away. She shivered as the colors of dusk deepened around them. His body became a shadow: dark, bold, full of mystery. Even in the dim light she could see the turbulent color of his eyes, more dusky a blue than the twilight. She read in them an understanding of what was to come.

Lips, tongues, bodies clung and pressed into one form. Their blood raced in a single vein. Their breaths mingled in a single cavity. Again the tempo increased. The coarse grass scratched, the sweat trickled between them, and their pants sounded in the night like wild animals. When at last she cried out his name, he shuddered, knowing she was his.

For several minutes after, they lay quietly, allowing the night air to cool their bodies. Then his hands gathered her hair and pulled her head slightly back so she could meet his gaze. A small, sly smile broke out on his lips, then on hers, then in unison they both were smiling wide, smug grins. They saw proof in each other's eyes that they had both felt it. That they both knew it had been all they had hoped it would be.

He squeezed her again.

Nora's hidden fears of inadequacy began welling up in an almost tangible form before her. Somehow, if she could address them, get them out in the open, she felt she could shut them out at last.

"C.W.?" she asked, resting her cheek against his chest. She couldn't look at him. "Was I...I mean, compared to other women..." She sighed. How could she ask this question? She was raised not to speak so casually about sexual encounters. But this was a special moment. There was a unique confidence she felt now, after the loving, that hadn't been there before. A mood that might dissipate when the moment passed. Compelled to ask, she racked her brain, but there wasn't a delicate way.

"What is it?" he asked.

"It's just that I haven't..." She paused, grasping. "Well, I haven't been with a lot of men, and Mike—" she blushed in the dark "—Mike could be cruel." She felt his muscles harden beneath her cheek and his hand stopped stroking. Nora couldn't continue and an awkward silence fell between them.

"What is it, my love?" he asked, stroking her hair again.

She took a deep breath. "Please be honest. I have to know.

Am I any good to make love to? Is there something wrong with me?"

He lay still for a second, unable to answer, unsure of the right words. Her seriousness, her shyness, affected him deeply. Part of him felt inordinate violence brewing. If MacKenzie was alive he'd have killed him. Another part of him was awash in the protectiveness he felt toward Nora. His Nora. As he peeled back the layers of her shell, he found more signs of beauty and more indications of abuse. Women, he knew, could be resilient. And in this way, Nora was exceptional.

He paused to turn her face to meet his. "With you, I made love. And I've never experienced the equal."

He felt her swallow hard and he heard her long, ragged sigh. Then, she rose up on her elbows and stared down upon his face. Her hair fell like a shimmering veil upon her shoulders. Behind her, the sky was purple and would soon cloak their nakedness in darkness.

So, in the last few moments of this precious day, she studied his face with a loving eye, committing each curve and angle to memory. He was studying her too, with the same calm intent, and neither felt embarrassed nor uncomfortable under the scrutiny.

The curtain of night slowly dropped, bringing to an end this act.

"Come," he said, his voice low. "Let's go."

Neither one moved to rise. Instead, she lowered to his embrace, each one clinging to the love found, neither one wanting to be the first to separate. A trigger of renewed passion flared.

"God, Nora," he murmured. "I'm as randy as a ram. I'll take you again if we don't stop now."

She cooed against his shoulder, pleased, and not unwilling.

Another wind gushed and sent goose bumps, not of passion but of plain cold, along her naked body.

"Oh, C.W. I hate to leave you," she said, burrowing.

"I have no intention of allowing you to. I'm merely suggesting that we dress and move to warmer quarters." He leaned forward and scratched his backside. "And these damn weeds are poking in all the wrong places."

She giggled again, and he laughed in low counterpoint. Then with a sigh, he rose to his feet and swung her up beside him. The wind picked up, blowing in a northern cold front, and they parted to dress in record time.

Nora finished first and in silence, watched his silhouette in the meadow. He stood, wide legged, his shirttails flapping in the breeze, while he buttoned his shirt and gazed out over the fields. He seemed so at ease in their new relationship. His fingers moved deftly. They did not shake like hers.

As he buckled his belt, she looked down at her hands and rubbed the finger that had once carried a gold band. He caught her motion, and with a taut heart, paced over and held her against his chest.

"What's the matter?"

She exhaled and brought her palm to his flannel shirt. "You'll probably think I'm old-fashioned. I know I'm awkward, but I've only made love to one man before in my life. And that man was my husband. I'm afraid I'm not very good at this. I don't know what to do next."

He held out his arm and a chuckle rumbled in his chest. "My darling, I assure you. You know by instinct exactly what to do." She slipped into the warmth and he held her tight, thanking God for this gift.

"Nora," he said, pulling her back and catching her attention, "I don't want you to make love to any other man save me."

"No. Never," she replied.

He swept her to his arms again, hugging her with such force she thought he would suck the air from her. That someone could be so strong, and still so tender, was bewildering. It also filled her with a singular sense of power and responsibility.

Not wanting the moment to end, Nora lingered in his arms for a final kiss, then held on again as he turned to go. "I'll let you go on one condition," she teased.

He raised a brow, his lips twitched.

"You'll come for dinner."

"You know, when the boss makes advances on the employee, that's called sexual harassment. I could sue."

"Go ahead." She laughed. "Join the crowd and see how much you'd collect."

"You've got a point," he said in mock defeat. "I guess I'll have to exact payment in some other form." He patted her bottom and released her before she could swat him away. "I have to finish my chores, first. Seven o'clock? I'll be there—and I'll be hungry."

He wrapped an arm around her and, bumping hips and matching strides, they headed home.

25

—

THE LOVERS PARTED at the barn. Nora raced up the mountain, adrenaline and happiness pumping in her veins, to start dinner. When she stepped foot in her kitchen, she came to a screeching halt.

She stared at the room in horror. It was Dresden after the bombing, Omaha after a tornado, Tokyo after Godzilla. Two Godzillas by the names of Frank and Junior. The boys had left their dishes and paint-splattered rags overflowing from the sink onto the counters. Chunks of stale bread and crumbs were in every possible crevice, and the acrid odors of stale coffee, sour milk, and rotting fruit peels permeated the air.

Nora walked through the house, tripping over drywall and sidestepping wood chips and nails, all the while collecting a film of white dust on her shoes and jeans. It was too much. Her house, her clean, orderly house. It had only been three days! She gripped the stair railing and let out a primeval scream.

She felt silly but better.

"Okay, Nora MacKenzie," she said rolling up her sleeves. "Let's see what you're made of."

Dust flew, water splashed, and garbage was slam-dunked outdoors into bins. She worked so hard her mouth went dry, but she didn't stop for water. With each pass through the kitchen she glanced furtively at the clock: 5:00, 5:20, 5:45, 6:00. At 6:10 she could delay no longer. She emptied her bucket, washed her hands and put on a clean apron. It was time to think about her dinner.

The refrigerator held little more than milk, butter, cheese and eggs: traditional dairyland fare. What to make, what to make? She settled on a classic: a soufflé. Out came the ingredients and she whisked the egg whites in tempo with her thoughts.

By 6:50, the cheese soufflé was in the oven, the table was set and she had just time enough to shower and throw on anything that was still clean. She frowned as she raced up the stairs. How many times had she imagined what she would wear for a dinner date with Mr. Charles Walker? Here it was and she'd be lucky if she wasn't wearing stripes and polkadots. "Life is difficult," she said as she stepped under the steaming shower.

"Anybody home?" C.W.'s voice boomed up the stairwell.

"I'll be right down," Nora called back, sputtering and grabbing a towel. *"Mi casa es su casa."* She cringed. How corny.

Down in the kitchen, C.W. smiled at her answer. He surveyed the room and maintained his grin of pleasure. The lady had style. She had pulled a leaf from the dining table, giving it a smaller, more intimate appearance. Covered with crisp, white cotton, white china, and an unusual arrangement of striated rocks and greens, it was elegant.

He knew if there was crystal and silver in the house, she would have used it. Thus he appreciated all the more her clever arrangement of fanned napkins in the simple glass cups and the obvious shine of the stainless.

Nora descended the stairs. She wore that gray wool dress as if she'd been poured into it. Although he had felt her curves with his hand, he never appreciated her body's symmetry more. Her hair, still wet, was clamped back with a black be-ribboned clasp, and C.W. promised himself that he'd free it before the night was through.

God, you're beautiful, he thought. He said, "You look lovely tonight."

She demurred. "So do you. And all this time you were a wolf in sheep's clothing."

He looked at his polished boots and cursed himself for his folly. He, too, had raced to shower after finishing his chores, but his sole recourse had been the Johnston house. He had to endure the suspicious glances of the whole Johnston family when he begged use of the shower.

Not to mention the raised brows and dropped jaws when he emerged from the bathroom in his creased corduroy trousers, cable knit sweater, and, worthy of the stares, an ironed shirt. He cast threatening glances at Frank and Junior as they practically injured each other with their guffaws and rib jabbing once they detected a whiff of his bay rum.

The sparkle of serious teasing was in Seth's eyes tonight, and he would be forever grateful to the old man for rubbing a palm across his smile and holding his tongue. C.W. offered a quick but polite good-bye to Seth, winked at Esther, and grabbing his dirty clothes, ducked out of there as fast as a fox from the hen coop. The glow of appreciation in Nora's eyes, however, made the fuss all worth it.

When she reached the bottom of the stairs and glided toward him, he fought the urge to grab her in an embrace. So he was all the more upstaged when she rested her hands on his shoulders and tiptoed to place a soft kiss on his lips.

Eyes twinkling, he handed her a brown paper bag.

"Here, these are for you. I didn't pass any florists on the way, and we're long past wildflowers. I thought you might use these someday."

She opened the crumpled bag. It was stuffed full of milkweed pods, their feathery contents overflowing into the bag.

"Thank you," she whispered, pulling out a few pods and running her finger in the silky seeds. "They're perfect."

He wrapped her in his arms, his thick sweater covering her like a blanket, and kissed her once, gently, on the forehead.

"You're welcome."

"Now it's my turn. Wait here," she called as she ran downstairs. In a flash she was back, carrying two bottles of wine: one white and one red. "This one," she said, handing the bottle of red to C.W., "is your housewarming gift. It's rather late, but it should help warm the cabin."

He accepted it and studied the label. He knew the vineyard; he knew the owner.

"It's an excellent year. I'm surprised you found a bottle."

Nora was taken aback by his lackluster thanks. "And this bottle," she continued holding up the white, "is for dinner." Her hand froze midair. "Dinner!" She handed him the bottle. "Open it, please," she called over her shoulder as she grabbed a mitt and ran to the oven.

C.W. held the bottle in indecision. He hadn't had a drink in a year—swore he'd never have another. With a determined yank, he uncorked the wine.

"Just in time," Nora sang as she carried into the room a puffy, golden-crowned soufflé. "Won't you please sit down? Once I light the candles we should eat. Soufflés collapse within min—oh," she said with a crestfallen look. "Even as we speak."

The puffy soufflé toppled and collapsed into a wrinkled, flat-topped casserole. So did Nora's smile.

"Not to worry," he said reassuringly. "I saw it in its glory. It was perfection."

"It should still taste good. Please." She extended her palm. "Won't you sit down?"

As she served the soufflé and salad, she tilted her head toward the wine. "C.W., would you please do the honors?"

He hesitated, then filled Nora's glass without pouring any for himself.

Once finished serving, Nora reached for her glass, noticing as she did that his glass was empty. "None for you?"

C.W. drummed his fingers on the table. "I don't drink."

Nora's glass stopped at her lips. She paused, then set the glass back upon the table.

"Don't do that," he said gently.

"Don't do what?"

"Don't be nervous. Enjoy your wine. It's all right."

She picked up her glass, took a small sip, then set it back down. She couldn't taste its sweetness.

"I don't miss it," he continued. "To tell you the truth, my life here is so challenging that I can't afford to be sluggish the next day. I could lose a finger or a foot in one of any number of ways here. Just like that." He snapped his fingers.

She fingered the long stem of her wineglass and watched shadows of emotion cross his face.

"My father drank," he said in way of explanation, "and as a result he made some mistakes. He died a broken man." His voice was low, and he used that tone people use when they're talking more to themselves than to anyone else.

"Tell me about him, about your childhood," she urged.

Placing his hand over hers, he pulled her closer across the

table. The candles glowed. Above them, his eyes shone with such intensity she could see his pupils flicker like the flame.

"My father was a decent man. A brilliant man. He worked at a bank, but home for him was on a horse. We used to go riding together early in the morning—he, my mother, myself, and my sister Nelly—before he went off to the city." He chuckled. "We'd laugh, swap stories—those were the best times of my childhood."

C.W. leaned back with a heavy sigh. "Then my mother died. I was about ten, and everything changed. Father was lonely and remarried. The classic evil stepmother. She hated animals, she hated Nelly and me—you know, I'm quite certain she even hated my father."

Nora reached out and patted his hand. "I'm sorry."

"Don't be. Nelly and I had each other and we did all right. But my father... You know, all he really wanted to be was a farmer."

"Like you."

He raised his eyes. "Like me. Now it's your turn. I imagine you were a sweet little thing with long, yellow braids, a kitten, and skinned knees."

She laughed and shook her head. "Oh, I don't know about how sweet I was." Her smile faltered and she absently traced a line along the damask cloth. "Actually, my father died when I was young too, so I know what it's like to lose a parent.

"He was a baker, a wonderful baker." She smiled. "That's all *he* ever wanted to be. When he died, the bakery died with him." She sighed. "Mother never reconciled to the fact that she was broke. Times were hard back then, harder for her, probably, than they were for me. Mother dreamed of the day she'd be 'back on top,' as she put it. I guess she saw me as her best chance."

C.W. pursed his lips, understanding. As the eldest and only

son of a financial empire, his family had pinned their hopes on him. It was a burden.

"Were you ever married?" she asked, changing from an unpleasant subject.

He smiled and shook his head. "Nope. Never did. Never wanted to. Yet."

"Oh."

He saw her frown.

"There is so much about you I don't know," she said.

The muscles in his jaw worked as he wiped his hands with deliberation. Then, with an air of resignation, he tossed his napkin upon the table.

"What do you want me to tell you?"

"Everything. The truth. Why you won't go to town, why you disappear for days, why you keep your past a secret?"

His hands moved to the cup before him and he studied the clear liquid. Nora waited, trying to be patient. Underneath the table her foot tapped.

Slowly, he lifted his glass and drank water from his cup. The ice clinked in the glass. "Do you remember when you chose this house site?"

She released an exasperated sigh. "Of course. What has that got to do with anything?"

"You had to build it near a water source," he continued in an even voice. "Throughout history, civilization has developed around a water source. Yet sometimes the well gets muddy. When it does, one has a choice. Either to take the time to clean it, maybe even rebuild its foundation, or to drink from tainted water—and eventually die of the poison. The wise man cleans his well."

He put the cup to his lips and took a long sip. "Ahh," he said with relish. "Fresh, pure, Vermont water."

"You're saying you took time to clean your well—up here— on my farm?"

"Something like that. Nora, I have my reasons for asking you to wait for an explanation, and one will come. I promise you."

"Why can't you tell me now? What difference will a week or a month mean? You want me to believe in you, in your plans for the farm. And yet, you can't confide in me about your past? What do you fear I can't accept?"

A long, strained silence reigned.

Leaning far back against the ladder-back chair, she said evenly, "You expect a lot from me, C.W."

"You're right. I do."

His tone changed and his gaze sharpened. "Do you want to know what I can offer you? Is that it? Nora, I thought you knew that by now."

She felt slapped but kept a resolute silence.

"Ah, this part of Nora MacKenzie I know very well," he said. "So stubborn. So persistent." He sighed. "Very well." Tilting his chair back on its hind legs, he stuck the tips of his fingers in his pockets. He looked to Nora like a gambler about to make a bet.

"What can I offer you? I offer you whatever I have. Right now in dollars that's…" He dug inside his pockets, pulling out a handful of dollars and some coins. Then, taking her palm, he carefully counted the sum into it. "I can offer seven dollars and forty-two whole cents, plus whatever I might have in the bank."

Sitting prim in the wood chair she faced him squarely. "No. This isn't about dollars and cents. I've learned that money isn't the root of security." She held out her palm full of money to him.

His eyes gleamed in satisfaction as he closed her fingers

around the coins. "What we have cannot be measured in dollars and cents," he murmured, looking deep into her eyes.

"You ask me to have faith in you. All right, I will. But is it wrong for me to ask the same of you?"

He didn't speak, but his expression told her he had listened. His sigh rumbled in his chest, then bubbled up to burst as a short laugh.

"Touché," he said, smiling and shaking his head. "Give me a week. Two at the most. Then I'll tell you everything you want to know."

"Agreed," she whispered.

His chair scraped the floor as he moved closer to the table.

"Nora," he continued, taking her hand again. He fiddled with her fingers, choosing his words, before bringing it to his lips. "I have to ask you to trust me a little further. I need to go away."

She sucked in her breath, but he held her hand firm. "Again? Now? After tonight?"

"I know what you're thinking, and stop it," he admonished, tapping her hand. "There's something I need to take care of." He gave her hand a reassuring squeeze. "I'll be back in two days."

"Oh, C.W.," she moaned. She turned her head, not able to hide her disappointment behind her hand. "Promise?"

"I promise. I couldn't keep away from you for more than two days."

Nora tried to smile, but it turned out to be more of a lopsided frown. "You know where to find me."

"Come on," he said, taking her hand with a wink of devilment. "Give me a good-bye kiss that will last me."

It was almost dawn and Nora was still wrestling with her sheets. Thoughts of C.W.'s leaving had teased her all through the night, creating nightmares of abandonment and heart-break. Turning on her side, she again ran her hand along his chest, its steady rise and fall allaying her fears. Memories of their lovemaking stirred. She had kissed him here, she thought, tracing the path with her fingertip to his still lips. And here… here… Her finger stopped and her eyes continued the path down the sheets. And there, she recalled.

How many nights had she reached out for her husband, eager to please him, her own desire prodding her courage? And how many ways had he rejected her? A turned back, a vicious remark, a swagger out of the room. Nora's hand slipped under her cheek. This man wasn't Mike, she reminded herself.

She listened in the dark to the sonorous sound of his snores. When she could lie in bed no longer, Nora sat up and glanced at the alarm clock. The hour glowed green in the early morn-ing darkness: 5:05. Nora had a flash of inspiration.

She crept from her bed, carefully covering her sleeping lover, and grabbed her robe. Her bare feet skipped across the cold floor as she tied her robe, rolled up the sleeves, and tugged on heavy wool socks. Until this morning, she had deliber-ately remained in bed until after C.W. had showered, shaved, breakfasted, and left. But today, she'd surprise him.

In the kitchen, instead of the usual welcoming aroma of fresh coffee, the air held the stale smell of cold ashes. It oc-curred to Nora that she had taken for granted all of C.W.'s thoughtfulness. The thought of preparing a meal for him, of warming the room for him, of showing in little, everyday ways that she cared, warmed her more than any fire could.

Nora measured the freshly ground coffee into the pot, then worked to the cheery tempo of the percolator. Soon, the smell of ashes was overpowered by the fresh smell of hot coffee. Next, she lit a fire, humming as she did so. Then with practiced efficiency, she pulled out the bowls, bins of flour and yeast she would need for baking bread.

She felt better the moment her hands were in the dough. This one skill brought Nora back to her roots more than any genealogical chart ever could. While she kneaded, memories of her childhood, of hours spent in the kitchen with Oma, drifted back.

Baking was in her blood; there had been bakers in the Koehler family for generations. Her grandfather took his family to America, setting up a bakery in Milwaukee, Wisconsin. Her father, Franz, carried on the tradition, and the name Koehler came to stand for quality bread and pastries in that Germanic city.

As the bakery expanded, Nora's care shifted from her mother to her grandmother. Oma was distraught to see her family recipes replaced by cost-effective, inferior ones. So she baked for her granddaughter, teaching her the family secrets, instilling in her a love and respect for the art of baking. She also taught Nora about perseverance, patience, and consistency.

"Life is like dis bread dough," she would tell Nora as she took a bowl full of risen dough from the oven. "Mit bubbles like a balloon, yah?

"But *liebchen*. Life is not alvays full of bubbles. Sometimes somezing vill crash down like dis." With that, Oma thrust a powerful punch into the dough. It collapsed around her fist. "But not to vorry," Oma said with a wink, reshaping the dough into formed loaves. "If you take ze time to vork mit ze problem, reshape things a bit, and give it a tincture of time—" she put the loaves into greased baking tins and set them back into the warm oven "—ze bubbles, they vill rise again and in ze end, you have somezing to be proud of.

"Life, it can be simple, if you do vat you believe is right."

Nora hadn't listened. At twenty-one, Nora had met Michael

MacKenzie—and he was everything her mother had ever dreamed of. Young MacKenzie was smart, driven, and poised for financial success. And at thirty-two, he needed a wife.

Nora still could feel the rush Mike gave her when he swept her up in his brawling arms and told her he wanted her to be his wife, the matriarch of his empire. He had called her "good breeding stock." Back then, she had laughed. Now, as she remembered his words, Nora's hands squeezed the dough till it oozed through her fingers.

"Ach, he is a swinehund, zat one," Oma had warned when Nora announced her engagement. Oma had reached out to touch her face with fingers worn thin from years of kneading bread and braiding her long, yellow locks. "This one vill punch down your bubbles. And *liebchen,* from zat kind of punch, it vill be hard to rise."

Why didn't I listen? thought Nora as she wiped away a tear with her elbow. She had loved Mike, sure, in a youthful passion. In retrospect, she realized she was wooed by his promise of security more than she was by him. How could she have been so naive?

Nora's still hands rested on the formed loaves of dough. Father, Mother, and Oma too—they were all gone now. She had only herself to listen to.

"What's going on in here?"

Startled, Nora turned to greet C.W. and stopped short of laughing. His hair was tousled and his cheeks bore bristle. Under his eyes, the dark circles attested to his not having slept as peacefully as she thought.

When C.W. saw her standing at the counter, with an apron and a smile, he didn't speak. He simply stood in the doorway with a look of sleepy stupor.

"Breakfast is almost ready," she called, sliding the loaves

in the oven. "I thought you'd want a good meal before your trip."

He walked around the kitchen, absently drumming his fingers near the percolator, over the wood stove, upon the neatly set table. "Are you always this domestic?"

Nora laughed and carried him a mug of coffee. "I haven't been. But I'd like to be."

"Busy and warm, wasn't that it?"

"Like Oma's kitchen. You remembered."

"It's an image I've kept pocketed away." His eyes were glowing over the rim of his coffee cup as he watched her wash dishes in the sink. "Are you really happy here? Living this life? Are you sure you don't miss New York?"

Nora's hands stilled and she looked out the kitchen window. The sky was pink over the eastern mountain range, a mist hung low in the valley, and she heard the bleating of her sheep in the distance. She thought again of Oma's words. Life could not be more simple, nor did it ever feel more right.

"I'm happy here," she replied.

He reached for her but the telephone ring cut him short.

"Who could that be at six o'clock in the morning?" she asked. The memory of Mike on the phone at all hours during his last months rushed by. "Phones are bad news," she muttered as she swung around and answered. She immediately recognized the nasal voice of her auctioneer in New York.

"Walton! Is everything all right?"

With a wave of his hand, C.W. headed to the bathroom.

"I know it's early," Walton went on, "but I thought you farmers rose with the sun anyway. Have you seen the *Times?*"

"I'm in Vermont, remember? What's so exciting?"

"The advance notices for your auction are out."

She paled and held the phone tight. "Already? What does it say?"

He read the short column, emphasizing adjectives and adverbs with a flourish. The article was brief, and to her relief, there was no mention of her financial status. Yet, the news was bittersweet. Pleased as she was at the rave reviews, hearing the description of her furniture, her jewelry, her private art collection was painful. So public. So much of herself was going up on the block.

"They're touting it as the biggest sale since Warhol." He cleared his throat. "It should bring in a fortune."

It better, she thought. From the walls Nora heard the distinct squeak and thud of the shower turning off. "I'd appreciate it if you'd clip that and mail it up to me."

"Why mail them? Aren't you coming to the auction next week?" Walton's disappointment rang across the wire.

Nora hesitated. Perhaps she should make a showing, to boost the sales. While she was considering this, C.W. walked into the room, rubbing his dripping hair with a towel. Nora remembered the first time she saw him. Smiling, she held out her hand to him.

"No," she replied to Walton. "I'm not going to New York. My duty lies here."

After a couple of bites of bread, several gulps of Nora's dark coffee, and a few comments from C.W. on how his hair would stand on end that day, they were off for a quick walk before C.W. left. Like two scouts out on a hike, they marched in synchronized rhythm across the gravel drive and down the mountain. When they reached Mike's Bench, C.W. halted, then led Nora toward it.

The bench could hardly be approached through the foliage and a thick blanket of colored leaves almost obscured the bench from view. Nora made her way to the marble and brushed away the leaves. The mud streaked across the marble's whiteness, lending it the appearance of a gravestone upon which was carved an epitaph for a season past. The ghost of the man who carved the bench rose and touched their thoughts.

"He must have loved this place to create something so beautiful, so personal," said C.W. He spoke in reverential tones, as though he stood at MacKenzie's gravesite.

Nora didn't respond for a moment. "I suppose he did love it. It was probably the only nonprofit-motivated, noncorporate thing I've ever seen him do."

"I find that difficult to believe," C.W. said. "There's too much of the man here: the design of the house, the bench." He shook his head.

Nora languished in her memories. Happier times with Mike in the early years of their marriage crossed her angry barrier and demanded to be recognized. Days full of poring over blueprints, walks along their border, and dunks in the icy water of the pond. Nights camping out in a tent, huddling against the cold and the strange noises, and counting dreams as numerous as the stars over their heads. Mike had so many dreams.

"He did love it here once," she conceded. "We both did." With a brash movement, she scraped away the *M* she had traced in the mud.

"Then it all changed. With success came an edge so sharp that he left bleeding all who ventured a touch. After a while, I didn't know who he was anymore. And he didn't care who I was."

"You speak of MacKenzie, your husband, so rarely. Was he always cruel?"

"No. He was, in the beginning, quite thoughtful."

"Did he ever physically harm you, in any way?"

"Not physically. Only verbally. In that he excelled."

"Did you share many interests? Your art? Love of nature?"

"My art interested him, especially at first. Then it bored him. Or perhaps not only my art bored him."

"I suppose he was cheap, penurious. Forgot your birthday, that kind of thing?"

"He was methodically generous. At first I was overwhelmed by the size and perfection of the jewels he gave me. Birthdays, Christmas, anniversaries...all marked by a significant gift. I never like to wear large jewels. I am too small boned and feel uncomfortable in them. On occasion, Mike insisted. Later, as I grew more knowledgeable, I came to understand that the larger stones were investments. He gave his lady friends the smaller, cheaper, clustered stones. I, however, was the investment."

Nora grew irritated. "I really don't want to talk about Mike anymore. Not this morning."

C.W. was haunted by a real, human Michael MacKenzie. "He must have loved this place," he repeated. "He must have loved you."

"No! I don't believe he ever really loved me."

"Nora, did you love him?"

She paused, knowing he waited on a personal precipice for her answer. "I thought I loved him. Once. But that was a different me. I didn't know what love was. Until now."

He took her in his arms and crushed her against his chest. She sensed in him an urgency she didn't understand.

"C.W.," she said as her head lay against his shoulder, "Mike is gone. I am only beginning to accept that it was his decision to end his life, not mine, or anyone else's."

C.W.'s tension eased and he released a long sigh.

"Nora," he said, taking her hands and holding them tightly,

"while I'm gone, come back here. To this spot. Remember Mike, the good and the bad, and put his memory to rest. There's no room for his ghost between us."

Nora leaned back in his arms to meet his gaze. "I'll try," she whispered. "I promise I'll try. Promise me, too, that wherever you're going today, you'll put your ghosts behind you too."

He hugged her to him, hard and suddenly, as though he was afraid of losing her. "I'll try, Nora. God knows, I'll try."

26

——

C.W.'S HAND BEAT the steering wheel to the tempo of the song. Why couldn't this Jeep go faster? His foot pushed the pedal to the metal, but the battered car wouldn't go more than fifty-five miles per hour. When he thought of the Ferrari in his garage in New York, he ground his teeth in frustration. Then laughed. He could see himself trying to explain to Nora how a farmhand could afford a Ferrari.

Nora. Her eyes stared at him through the windshield: soft and dreamy after his kiss. Frightened yet determined when faced with a bill. Hard and vengeful at the name of Charles Blair. Ah, but she would be a vengeful angel.

His hands tightened on the wheel. His deception was becoming a nightmare. He rubbed his eyes and grabbed for his coffee as the miles stretched out ahead. So far to go.

He had asked for her trust rather than appeal to her innate kindness. Was it the better course, or was he nothing but a coward? Trust me, he had asked. Yet, for her to do so, he had to watch her suffer in her financial debt. What kind of fate would set him up in a position of champion, when honesty would destroy any hope for their relationship?

Michael MacKenzie's ghost would be put to rest, he vowed. Nora would have to bury his memory in her own time. She was well on her way. And with the settling of MacKenzie's accounts, he would, at last, bury the ghost as well.

"Then, MacKenzie," he swore aloud, "leave us. And let the living live."

C.W.'s jaw set and he cranked his window flat down. He rested his elbow on the door and ran his hand through his hair. The sun was getting higher and burning off the fog along the valley roads. As he drove past the craggy horizon in his battered Jeep, his lone shadow etched across the mountain.

C.W. made it to New York in time for his appointment. The hotel room was adequate. A bed, two chairs, and a table. Not like his apartment—but it was beyond curious eyes. He flicked on the TV, flicked it off again, then stood before the window overlooking the traffic and congestion of the west fifties. Horns blared and the people traveled in packs as the lights changed from red to green. He stared at the throngs without emotion. A lifetime he'd spent in this city, yet today he felt like a stranger.

A knock sounded on the door and he straightened his tie. It was time for business.

"Good afternoon, Henry," he said as he opened the door. He did not extend his hand. "So good of you to come."

"Good to see you again, Charles."

C.W. watched his once trusted ally cross the room as he carefully laid down his briefcase and, without a pause for gossip, took out his papers. His movements were those of the efficient executive getting down to business. His face was impassive. Nothing Strauss did or said gave the impression he had anything to fear.

"Here are the reports on the twelve businesses you requested," Strauss said, straightening. "As you suspected, they were all lent large loans from our bank." He coughed. "From you, actually. They all defaulted on the loans, and—" he slowly turned his head "—they were all fronts for MacKenzie. How did you know?"

C.W. cocked his head. Henry was here to learn, for certain, if he had MacKenzie's ledger, he thought. C.W. walked over to the small table and took a seat across from Henry.

"I wasn't sure," he replied evenly. "I've been thinking about this for some time. Putting two and two together. I followed a hunch. As you know, I've long been the Captain Ahab to MacKenzie's whale."

Henry's eyelids fell to half-mast and he nodded slowly. He was buying it, as C.W. knew he would, because he wanted to buy it.

After briefly scanning the summaries, C.W. leaned back and, bringing his fingers together under his chin, asked, "You realize what this means?"

"You'll be forced out."

"And most likely you as well."

Strauss took off his glasses and rubbed them furiously with his linen handkerchief. After returning the heavy glasses to his face, Henry sat straight in his chair and faced his former boss.

"I've been doing everything possible to ensure that the extent of MacKenzie's ruin remains quiet. At least until after the auction."

"You have not been entirely successful, have you?"

Strauss's eyes were haunted. "No."

"The stock is falling."

"A few points. It happens."

"We both know that is only the beginning. The pattern is too obvious. They will plummet."

Color rose along Strauss's collar.

"Has it not occurred to you, Henry, that someone is deliberately leaking this information? That someone wants me out?"

Strauss's silence spoke volumes.

"I see that it has. Well, that someone is going to a lot of trouble for naught." C.W. proffered a cold, silent stare. When he spoke his voice was hard. "I have returned to New York because I have made a decision."

Henry leaned forward slightly. His ears almost wagged in their attentiveness.

"I intend to resign from the bank."

The surprise was evident in Henry's face. He was, for the moment, speechless.

"The fact is the loans bear my name. The bank cannot afford another scandal." He leaned forward on the table. "Nor, frankly, can I."

Relief visibly flooded Strauss's face. His chest actually heaved. "I am sorry it came to this," Strauss said. "Your immediate resignation may very well prevent further action." His eyes widened slightly. Henry had slipped, for a fraction of a second, but it revealed too much knowledge. They both knew it.

C.W.'s response was visceral. He wanted to go in for the kill.

"Somebody set you up," Henry said quickly, offering C.W. a look of conspiracy. "I'm sorry. I wish I could have found out who."

C.W. tapped his fingers together. "That somebody is either Sidney Teller or Agatha Blair. Any comments?"

"Sidney Teller. Got to be. He's had a bad year, and his name will be tied to this MacKenzie fiasco as well."

"Yes, but I'll take the fall for the MacKenzie scandal. With my sister's share of stock, Sidney would be able to pull out from under and rebuild the stockholders' confidence."

"That may be a problem. Apparently—" he shuffled his papers "—their marriage is in trouble."

C.W.'s gaze sharpened. He observed the slight smugness in Strauss's features. Gossipy old woman, he thought with distaste. Still, the comment rankled.

"Yes. Well. My resignation should ensure that no scandal touches the bank." He paused to capture Henry's full attention. "You'll pass the word on, I trust?"

Henry Strauss did not even shift his weight. C.W. realized that the man was incapable of feeling guilt.

Henry waited, with surprising calm, for Charles's next move.

C.W. leaned back and crossed his ankle over his knee. He wanted to enjoy the moment. "I'd like your resignation," he said in an icy voice.

Henry sat up straighter in the cheap chair. "What do you mean?"

"Don't be a fool, or take me for one. You were the one who processed the loans."

"You have no proof of that."

"No, that is true. But it's only a matter of time."

For the first time, Henry smiled. It was a faint, sickly move of his muscles. The smile of a man pulling his last trick.

"You're finished, Charles. Your reputation's shot. Nobody would consider risking their neck for you. Quite simply, dear boy, you can't do anything anymore." He eased back in his chair with relaxed arrogance.

C.W. gripped the arms of the chair lest he reach out and grip

Strauss by his fat neck. Fury surged through his veins. At his peak Strauss would never have dared such a comment. That he dared now meant he was confident of the power behind him. Fool.

Strauss was watching him now, with those pale gray eyes, gauging his reaction. C.W. would not give him the satisfaction of revealing his anger. He stood up, abruptly terminating the interview. When he turned to face Henry, he offered not anger, not fear, only boredom.

"You are a small fish, Henry. As I said, I am after the whale."

Henry's lids fluttered, but he staunchly fixed his smile.

"And what is that supposed to mean?"

"I should think it was rather simple. I no longer need you. You are entirely expendable, which I am sure someone else figured when he—or she—sent you here today."

Henry shifted his gaze to the TV and stared at the blank screen with seeming avid interest while a small muscle worked in his cheek.

C.W. closed the books on the table before him and neatly stacked them. When he spoke, it was as in summary of a long, unspoken lecture.

"I cannot put you in jail, where you belong. So instead I will personally see to it that you are never hired in a position of trust or authority again. To put it simply, you are through." C.W. paused, briefly, changing to a menacing tone. "I will destroy you."

Henry looked back now and C.W. leaned forward slightly.

"Investment by investment, dollar by dollar. You will never realize your newfound profits. I shall pursue you, relentlessly, until you truly understand the meaning of *finished*. You know me, Henry. You know I can do this. Easily. You know I will."

For the first time, Henry Strauss looked afraid.

Now, only now, did C.W. ease into a smile. The knowing smile of a man with great power and wealth. Of a man in complete control.

"You may go now."

C.W. didn't watch Strauss leave. Whether he ran under the skirts of Agatha Blair or off the nearest bridge, he didn't care. Soon, it would all become perfectly clear.

C.W. walked again to the window and looked out at the blur of traffic lights. Slowly, he brought his hand to the curtain and squeezed the grimy Herculon fabric into a tight ball in his fist. A gut-wrenching realization surged through his veins.

My God, he had enjoyed it.

Watching Henry squirm. Playing with him like a cat with a fat mouse. He had relished the power that only his immense wealth and influence could wield. It was like a drug, an addiction. One entirely more seductive than alcohol ever was. Tonight he tasted it again, after a year, and it was intoxicatingly sweet.

He brought his hand to his forehead and rubbed it hard.

"I've got to get out of here," he swore under his breath. "Got to get out of this business. If I don't, I'm going to kill someone else."

C.W. stood and stared out the grimy hotel window at the autumn moon. He wanted to go home.

Miles away, Nora stared out at the same moon. The air outdoors was too temperate for October and too inviting for a troubled soul. She couldn't breathe in the stagnant air of the house. Three times she paced the floor. On the fourth round she grabbed her jacket and headed down the dark road. She walked fast, her boots kicking rocks down the steep incline. The sound of her footfall in the gravel echoed in the dark.

It was a black night. The moon, shadowed by the drifting clouds, left eerie patterns upon the woods. Only the light from her flashlight cut through the darkness, bobbing on the road ahead as she marched down the hill. She didn't know where she was going. She wasn't afraid. Whatever menace this mountain held was minor compared to the disaster that loomed outside it.

As she rounded the final curve and entered the lower pasture, she passed the rams, Studly and Brutus, in their small fenced partition. The stud and the teaser—what a pair, she thought as she stopped to flash the light upon them. Studly stood at attention, ears pricked. Beside him, lying in the tall grass, Brutus eyed her lazily. Which was C.W.?

As she approached the barn, she heard the rustle of a large animal along the fence. The hairs on her neck stood as she stopped short and swung her flashlight toward the noise.

"The Bible says not to hide your light under a bushel, but you don't have to blind a soul with it, neither."

"Seth," she cried in relief. She moved the light away from his face and walked toward the figure leaning on the railing of the fence. She wondered how the rotted wood supported his heavy frame. "What are you doing out here at this time of the night?"

"I might ask you the same question."

"I needed a walk."

She sensed his nod in the darkness.

"If you flick off that light, your eyes will get used to the dark and your senses will pick up the rest. Go ahead. Trust your senses, like the animals do."

She clicked off the light and closed her eyes while she took long, deep breaths. The pounding of her heart subsided and she stood, motionless, in the darkness. As she stood, she became aware of a new world of sounds and sensations. The wind caressed her cheeks with its cool, dry breath. The air smelled sweet, like water.

And she heard the nightsongs. The sheep were quiet, and from the distance she heard the music of Seth's coon dogs baying at the moon and the mysterious, atonal cry of an owl. When the howling ceased, to her ears sprang the raspy sound of dried stalks rustling in the wind. A branch snapped to her left—a rustling beyond. The quiet was so intense she could almost hear the clouds move in the sky.

When she opened her eyes again, the darkness was not nearly so black. In the distance she could make out the conical forms of pines, the lines of fence posts, and scattered within their borders, round bales of hay resembling sleeping beasts in the fields. She followed the shadows as they crept across the pasture to Seth's face. He was watching her with eyes as knowing as the owl.

"I see. It's beautiful here at night, so peaceful. Do you come out often?"

He turned to lean again over the fence. "Most nights. Nights like tonight. Something's in the air." He turned his face toward her. "What do you hear?"

She pricked her ears and closed her eyes. After a moment's silence she replied, "I hear—or feel—change."

He didn't reply but brought his hand to his chin and looked up at the sky. Slowly, his gaze shifted from the sky to her face. "Some people have an instinct about Nature, her animals and her garden. They're just born with it. Sure, anybody can learn her signs and signals. But some, well, they can hear her direct. I like to think I can. I think you do too."

She looked up, surprised. "Me?"

"Yeh-up. I've watched you with the animals. You and them understand each other. Go with your instincts."

"I don't trust them."

"If'n you can't trust yourself, who can you trust?"

She thought of C.W.'s same words. And Oma's.

"When I close my eyes like this, I feel a peace so deep it stretches beyond this world. I feel if I can just go on living like I am now, working hard, loving hard, all will be right. But then the outside's realities hit hard. Bills to pay, pipes to fix, my problems with the estate, New York. Doubts. Before I know it I'm caught in the grind, and I'm struggling so hard to keep it going that I forget the inner peace I had. And I'm lost. I make mistakes." She shook her head. "I'm rambling."

"When you get all screwed up inside, that's when you should git your nails into the soil. When you're busy, the whole world may be going to hell, but you ain't got time to worry about the details."

"Seth." Nora laughed.

He pursed his lips and scrunched his weathered face. With his missing teeth, Nora thought he looked like an ancient wise man or a shaman.

"When you gonna ask me what you really want to know?"

Nora's head bobbed up. "What do you mean?"

"A ewe don't butt against a bucket lest she wants some grain. You've been walkin' around, kickin' up the dirt, and sniffin' for something. I can't give an answer lest I knows the question."

Nora blushed in the dark. It was no wonder his family adored him. "Seth, how well do you know C.W.?"

"Well enough."

His answer was quick, his lips tight. She shuffled her feet, knowing he wasn't going to offer details even if he knew them. "Do you trust him?"

"With my life." He rubbed his bristle and gave her a quiz-zical look.

She needed someone to talk to. Some sage advice. Yet, what could she ask? Does C.W. have a dark past? Should I link my future to his? All were questions she had to ask herself.

"Well." She paused, letting him know she understood his re-luctance to talk about C.W. "It's late. I'd better get going."

"Yeh-up."

"Good night, Seth. See you in the morning."

"Bright and early."

She turned to walk back up the mountain.

"It's a long road up," he called after her. "Take small steps."

She nodded and savored his words.

On the way up the mountain, she felt the strain of the climb, pausing as she rounded Mike's Bench. Moss clung thick to the marble. Like a silent film, visions of her years with Mike played in her mind. The early, happy years, when love was so easy to give and take. The later years, when ambition domi-nated, when time together grew short and silences grew long. Their love was lost before either of them realized it, and once realized, apathy gave rise to cruelty. In war, there can only be the victor and the vanquished.

Love wasn't all that was lost in those years. Nora lost her values, her dreams, and worst of all, her self-esteem. Now she had them back; she'd worked hard for them.

Tonight she felt she was standing with one foot in her past and one foot in her future. It was time for her to listen. It was time to trust her instincts. It was time to forgive and, though not forget, to move on.

Nora looked at the bench, and like a visitor at a grave, made peace with her past. She forgave Mike. She forgave Esther. Mostly, Nora forgave herself.

The Long Road Home

"Ah, Mike," she sighed, no longer feeling anger or resentment against him. "I'm sorry that your life ended the way it did. I'm sorry, too, that our marriage was not the heaven we envisioned. I don't blame you entirely. We were both to blame. But you're gone now. And I am stronger. I have to climb this mountain on my own."

She ran her fingers along the bench, creating two long streaks in the mud. Against the black, the gold on her right finger caught the moon's light, giving it an eerie patina. Looking at it, Nora knew what it was time to do.

Slipping to her knees, she dug through the rocks, creating a small hole in the mossy soil. Then, with a religious intensity, she carefully removed the ring and laid it in the hole. Nora stared at the bit of gold until a night cloud covered the moon and left her in darkness.

"Good-bye, Mike," she whispered, sprinkling the dirt over the ring and patting the mound firm.

Nora hiked up the mountain, feeling every step. She was bone weary, putting one foot in front of the other with effort. When at last she slipped off her clothes, turned off the light, and pulled the covers to her chin, she felt freed from a burden that she had carried for years.

Nora shivered under the down coverlets and tucked her hands between her knees. "Small steps," she whispered as she fell into a deep sleep.

C.W. woke early to the sound of honking horns on the street below. He had several visits to make that day, and time was of the essence. He dressed quickly, hailed a cab, barked out the address, and with a lurch, felt the hum beneath his feet.

C.W. approached his sister's house after watching Sidney depart for the office. The butler greeted him warmly.

"Mr. Charles, sir! Oh, yes, do come in, sir. Mrs. Cornelia

will be so pleased, Mr. Charles." The old man's hands shook with excitement as he took C.W.'s hat and coat, allowing himself the personal transgression of a gentle pat on C.W.'s sleeve.

C.W. smiled warmly at Aengus, remembering the days when he was Master Charles, still in short pants. Aengus had been the family butler since Charles's mother was alive, and he'd later guarded the motherless brood from Agatha's sharp tongue. Agatha was no match for Aengus's dry Irish wit. Aengus had the children doubled over with suppressed laughter as his zingers went clear over Agatha's head.

This morning it was bittersweet to see Aengus again. He was old and thin, and his once regal stance had been reduced by age to stooped sentimentality. Cornelia, of course, would never let him go. Years ago Aengus had, in his inimitable snobbish way, refused Agatha's lucrative offers and had gratefully accepted a position in Cornelia's new home. Aengus deftly guided the young bride as to the proper management of houseguests, the preferred weight and engraving of a lady's stationery, and the disgrace of polyurethane finishes on antiques of quality.

Aengus ushered C.W. into the foyer with as much decorum as the excited man could muster, then hurried off in search of Cornelia. C.W. scanned the dome-topped foyer with its intricate murals and marble floors. The room resembled a Fabergé egg, and was almost as priceless. A perfect introduction to Cornelia's eastside brownstone, he thought.

Each room was lavishly, yet tastefully, decorated and furnished. Magazine editors clamored for permission to photograph the unique rooms as representative of the epitome of style and grace. And yet, he had never felt at home here. No children ran across the polished floors. Not a single fingerprint or a bit of chipped paint let him know this museum was a home.

Having grown up with Cornelia, with her toys, horse gear, sports equipment, clothes—and even boyfriends—thrown every which way, her perfect house seemed an incongruity. And their mother would have felt like a caged bird in this house. Stoneridge, their family home in New Jersey, was always comfortable and relaxed because of, not despite, the antiques and richly colored carpets. It was, he knew, a matter of attitude.

It had to be Sidney's influence, he thought with a frown. He was such a perfectionist. Good for business, but a man shouldn't bring his business home. He had always liked Sid, and he'd thought Cornelia was loosening him up a bit. Henry Strauss's words came to mind: "Their marriage is in trouble."

"Well, look what the wind blew in."

C.W. looked toward the familiar voice. Cornelia was leaning against the door frame, arms crossed, and wearing an expression of mock displeasure. Tall and slender, with her short blond hair wisped around her face, she appeared a cocky youth. But when he crossed the distance and took her hands, closer inspection revealed new lines at the eyes and forehead, and her eyes had lost their usual brightness.

"So, tomboy. You've forgotten your big brother already? Seems cheeky."

"Forget the boy who tortured me for most of my life? Never! I still owe you. So come here and collect your punishment."

She gave him a tight hug, one that lasted longer than a mere hello, the one she always gave him when something was wrong. He squeezed back and looked searchingly into her eyes. How true was Henry's gossip?

"How're tricks?"

Her smile faltered, but she rallied. "Oh, the usual. Dinners, parties, more parties. You haven't missed a thing. Except maybe Louellen's facelift. Makes even Agatha look good!"

Laughing, they moved to the morning room, where they talked of days long gone until the conversation's calendar moved forward to the present. C.W. coaxed and listened, until Cornelia finally remembered that he was her brother.

"I hear your marriage is rocky."

Cornelia's eyes flashed. "What gossip told you that?"

C.W. only shrugged, but his eyes stared straight into hers.

Cornelia flopped back onto the upholstery with total disregard for grace or decorum. "It's just like you, Charles, to come back after almost a year of hiding to hit the nail on the head."

"I'm worried about you, Nelly. What's up?"

"It's really all your fault. I should be mad at you, except—" she flipped him a glance "—I've been worried about you too."

C.W. felt a rush of affection for his sister.

"Sidney's under the gun at the bank," she confided, serious now. "Ever since you left, pressure's been building and his way of dealing with it is to take it all inside." She pounded her fist into the silk upholstery. "If only he'd confide in me, trust me enough. I'd stand by him. I don't give a damn about the money."

"Have you asked him to confide?"

"Of course. He can't talk about it. Or won't."

C.W. knew that Sidney had kept his silence, and his word.

Cornelia leaned far back and stretched her long legs out beside her brother's, the way she'd done as a kid.

"See," she said, folding her hands across her belly. "Ever since you left there's been a power struggle at the bank. Sidney feels abandoned by you, I'm sure. And the others. It's got to hurt. He's built a wall of secrecy to protect himself. The bigger it grows, the more even I am shut out. And if he won't talk to me, then his worst fears will come true. I will stop believing in him. Then—what's the point? My biological clock is ticking. I'll leave for someone who will."

C.W. realized if Sidney didn't confide the truth soon, he'd lose his wife. And there was a lesson there for himself.

"Why don't you step back in the bank? Become a partner? You were good, you know."

She lifted her shoulders. "I stepped aside to let Sidney take the lead. It was hard on him, having his wife more influential than he was."

"It's time to step back in."

Cornelia gave him a queer look. "I know that tone. What are you scheming in that brain of yours, Charles?"

C.W. leaned far forward, bringing his fingers to his chin. "This isn't just a friendly visit, Nelly. It has to do with Sidney... and the bank."

She sat up but, like a Blair, remained quiet.

"Tell me the truth. I need to know. Does Sidney harbor any jealousy or even hatred for me?" he quietly asked.

"No, of course not!"

"In your opinion, is he intrinsically honest. Can I trust him, against all odds?"

"Yes. On both counts."

"Would he stab me in the back to gain control of the bank?"

Her eyes widened, then narrowed.

"No. Absolutely not. He thinks of you as a friend. As the brother he never had."

The air blew out of C.W., and with his elbows on his knees, he studied his shoes. He could trust Cornelia, not only for the truth, but for the brains to discern it.

"Will you take your place in the bank as a Blair? If not before, then beside your husband?"

Her face hardened in determination. "Yes, Charles. I will."

"Then I need your help. Keep Sidney out of this one for now. I'm sorry, but it's for his own protection. I may take a fall and he's safer at a distance. And I believe Agatha has spies in the woodwork," he said, eyeing the walls of the room.

"Agatha! I should have known. That bitch."

"This is business," he replied evenly. "Are you willing to risk a fortune?"

"For my husband, yes."

"Then fasten your moneybelt, sister, 'cause I've got a plan."

27

—

"COME ON, YOU ALL," called out Seth. "There's a flock of ewes and lambs what needs movin'." He strode over to the barn door and stood at its entry.

Nora walked up beside him and tilted her head back to peer at the sky. She felt the moisture in the air and didn't like the look of the dark fast-moving clouds. A broad, gray front was moving in over the mountains like a lid being pulled over the earth.

"What do you think?" she asked Seth.

"Hard to say. It's been a cold summer and a warm fall. The weather, she's been moody." He seemed pensive. Seth's eyes screwed up, making a prunelike face, then he donned his cap with a decisive snap. "Best get those ewes to the north pasture before the weather hits."

Seth divided the work crews into two typical groups: the men and the women. Seth, Frank, and Junior were to move the ewes to their new pasture. Nora and Esther were to lead the weaned lambs to the lower barn.

Willow was in this group. Nora watched with pride as her

runt, filled out and strong, trotted with his cousins behind her grain bucket. His hooves pranced with a jaunty air.

Over her shoulder, she watched the men spread out in the fields to escort the ewes to their winter pasture. The windbreak of pines and maples that surrounded the northern pasture would buffer the ladies from the blustery cold winds. Frank and Junior clanked their grain buckets and sang out, "Come on, girls. Come on!" in their melodic voices while Seth led the way.

The ewes pricked their ears and trotted in a herd beside the men, occasionally nudging their legs and butting the grain buckets. The sun shone warm and bright, coloring the men's fading tans.

Nora witnessed their male bonding and thought them akin to their Neanderthal ancestors out on a tribal hunt. They joked, laughed, and shared the success of the job. As she watched them disappear behind a cloak of trees, Nora felt a twinge of envy.

"Come on, babies," she called out, shaking her grain bucket and leading her first group of fledglings to the lower barn. They rallied behind her, one or two catching up and butting her legs.

"That's not polite." She laughed as she marched on.

The moment she entered the lower barn, she sensed a dark mood. Esther was leaning against the gray barn wall, staring out the door. Her flop hat was in her hands and her hair was pulled back in a ponytail that was off center and already losing most of its hold upon her slumped shoulders.

From behind, the lambs bounded into the barn. They gamboled as they raced down the alley.

"Ready or not, here we come," shouted Nora.

Esther didn't respond to her gaiety. She picked up the

rear, shooing in with her hat the hesitant ones. Without their mothers to follow, the lambs bleated piteously.

Nora lowered her voice to a soothing croon, calling the lambs into the pen with a gentle shake of her grain bucket.

"Poor babies," she sang in low, soothing tones. "Where did your mamas go? Don't you worry. Nora's going to take good care of you. Yes, she is." She talked and patted while Esther closed the gate behind her with a sullen face.

"I don't see why they don't go out to pasture with the ewes like they always done," Esther muttered.

Nora looked up slowly and saw Esther's combative pose and heard the resentment in her voice. She let a moment pass before responding in the respectful manner C.W. had always shown her.

"As you know, this is a late lambing. These babies would have a hard time of it out in the pasture. We're going to try something new this year."

Esther snorted and gave the feed bunk a shake.

"C.W. and I have discussed this in full," Nora explained. "Frankly, Esther, I have to try a more economical system." She kept her gaze steady.

Esther's face twisted and she looked away. "Well, whatever you say. You're the expert at my jobs now. Seems I'm not needed here anymore."

"As a matter of fact," Nora said, closing the pen gate and gathering her wits. "I'd like to talk to you about that."

"So. This is it. You're letting me go."

"Yes."

Esther paced back and forth, firing up her resentment.

"Well, it took you longer than I figured. So. How does it feel giving your husband's girlfriend the boot, huh?" Esther's anger made her mean. Her lips turned down and her nostrils flared as she stopped in front of Nora.

"I guess you could say I got screwed by both the MacKenzies."

Nora flinched but salvaged her composure. "Sit down, Esther. If you would be so kind."

"Up yours."

"Sit down, Esther," Nora's voice rang out. She took a deep breath and restrained her temper. "Please."

When Esther didn't move, Nora walked purposefully to a bale of hay and sat down, patting the bale beside her. Being in the right gave Nora strength. "This is just as difficult for me, I assure you. But we need to settle a few things between us, and it might as well be now."

Esther crossed her arms and considered this a moment.

"You owe me that much."

Confusion registered on Esther's features, and a shade of guilt. She agreed with a brief nod and seated herself on the bale of hay with as much esteem as she could with mud on her clothes and her spirit.

"Esther, I'm sorry for taking over your job. I don't have a choice. I'm trying to make a living for myself and the decisions I make are sometimes very hard."

"Okay." Esther was looking off at a distant point, and Nora saw that she was struggling to get through this. To prove she could if Nora could. Although Esther was taller and broader, Nora felt larger. She edged forward on the bale of hay to better catch Esther's expressions.

"I am not letting you go because of your relationship with Mike. I know that you've suffered enough. This is simply a matter of economics. I can't afford to pay you. I bear you no grudge, Esther."

Esther brought her focus to Nora's face and their gazes locked: Esther's searching, Nora's telling. Nora could see the battle going on inside Esther. She couldn't quite believe that Nora was being honest.

"To prove that," Nora continued in a steady voice, "although I am taking away one job, I am offering you another. One that I think you may be very interested in."

Esther shook her head. "No, thanks. I'm not interested in any more farm jobs." Esther slumped in defeat. "I've decided to marry John Henry."

This was the last thing Nora had expected to hear today. "What? When did you decide this?"

"Today. I'm going to tell him tonight. At the dance."

Nora let loose a long stream of air. She stood up and walked over to the feeder, gave it a shake, then turned and leaned against it, facing Esther squarely.

"Then I guess you're not interested in the job offer I had, or rather that Jenny Gold had."

"Who's that?"

"Jenny is a friend of sorts. She owns an art gallery in SoHo."

Esther bolted off the bale of hay. "New York?"

"Of course."

"What job? I didn't know about this job. In New York?"

"What does it matter? If you're going to stay here and get married…" Nora brushed dirt off the bunk.

"It matters! You know it does. Nora, don't fool with me. Tell me."

"Jenny was interested."

"She liked my work?"

"Of course she did. But it's young. Raw. You need to develop it, but you'll be able to work at her gallery and take classes during off hours. The atmosphere, the peer criticism, the exposure—you'll never get another opportunity to equal it.

The plan is that you live in her loft as part of the arrangement." Nora paused.

"I'll be totally honest here, Esther. I called in a lot of favors. And with Jenny, it took some doing. Otherwise the loft would never have been included. It's a real coup, a morsel she dishes out carefully. In the end, she'll come out the winner. She knows it, too, but will never admit it to you."

"I can't believe it."

"Jenny Gold will earn her keep from you, believe that."

Esther was standing perfectly still, as one in shock. "I can't believe it," she kept repeating, her voice rising in excitement. Then her excitement ebbed and she turned to face Nora.

"You made those calls, spent that effort, all for a woman who'd slept with your husband?"

"No. I did it for a friend."

"This is too much."

"It isn't too much. I also did it for Seth, for the boys, and for May. You're like family, the only family I have."

Esther looked down. "I'm sorry I gave you such a hard time in the beginning."

"Forget it."

"I thought you had everything. The rich and pretty blond girl from New York with her perfectly polished nails, matching her fancy outfits." Esther chuckled, holding up Nora's dry, tanned hands with their chipped nails. "I have to admit, you fit right in, now."

Nora smiled awkwardly but retracted her hand, putting it to her hair.

Esther eyed Nora's hair and twiddled her fingers. "I don't even know how to do one of those fancy braids."

"Such a little thing. It's not hard to do. I could teach you. Would you like me to braid your hair?"

Esther moved uncomfortably. "I guess."

The Long Road Home

Nora walked around behind the bale. Standing close behind Esther, not seeing her face, she felt it was an odd truce for their rivalry. Nora hesitated before putting her hands on Esther's head. This was a personal move, one that required either friendship or apathy. Deciding on the former, she began braiding Esther's fabulous red hair.

The ritual of preening was relaxing. They began to chat.

"You know," Esther ventured, still looking down, "I never had too many friends. The girls up here never took much to my liking books and painting instead of boys. I like boys, mind you, but I never wanted to stay home and take care of one."

Nora thought how she had always wanted to take care of someone.

"What about you?" Esther asked. "Do you think you can stay here or will you go back to New York?"

Nora puffed out her cheeks and exhaled. "I wish I knew. I thought I was going to die in New York. It's so loud there, horns honking, people shouting, and everybody in such a hurry."

"Sounds great."

Nora looked over at her and wagged her head with exaggerated sympathy. "You're a born city girl, I guess."

"Thanks."

Both women nodded, smiled to themselves, then nodded some more. Nora finished Esther's braid, then sat comfortably beside her on a bale of hay. "You know what this reminds me of?"

"No, what?" Esther answered with ease.

"My favorite childhood story, *The Prince and the Pauper,* by Mark Twain. Did you read it?"

"I saw the movie."

"Right. Then you know how they switched places, each one thinking that the other had the better life. After they tried it, however, they couldn't wait to go back to their own worlds. Maybe that's us."

"No way. I know the story, but it's not mine. I've got to get outta here. Really, Nora, you saved my life."

Nora looked at her chipped nails. "There is one other reason why I did this for you." She looked up to see Esther nervously shift on the hay. "I feel responsible to fulfill all Mike's debts."

"You didn't have to."

"Yes, I did. As much for me as for you. But it's done now, and let's never talk about it again."

Esther put her hands under her arms and shifted her eyes lest the flash of tears show.

Nora jumped up from the hay bale. "Ain't nothin' worth doin' here, as your father would say."

"Let's go and get cleaned up. Tonight's the Harvest Contra Dance. Those brothers of mine are croakin' like two horny toads and can't wait to borrow some of C.W.'s bay rum. Frank's in a rare mood for celebrating." Esther stood and brushed her pants, pausing when she caught Nora's bewildered expression. "You heard about Frank, didn't you?"

"No," Nora replied openly. "What?"

"He's gone and asked Katie Beth to marry him."

"How wonderful! There certainly will be celebrating tonight!"

"You coming?"

"I wasn't invited."

"You're invited now."

Nora smiled gratefully. "Thank you, Es. In that case, I'd love to come. I could use some dancing."

"I don't know how much dancing I'll be doing." Esther rubbed her hands together and Nora could feel the tension pour out of her. "Frank's getting married won't make John Henry any happier. He's still hurting."

"Better now than after you're married."

Esther shook her head, mumbling to herself. Nora closed the gate and trotted to catch up with Esther. They walked, side by side, toward the road.

Above them, the darkening clouds swirled and gathered in a storm pattern.

In the northern pasture, Seth extended his hand to Frank. Frank took it gladly, then Seth grasped his son's hand between his two.

"That's good news, son," he said, his eyes gleaming. "Katie Beth will make you a good wife, and a good mother to your children." Seth brought a hand to Frank's shoulder and gave it a firm shake.

"You're a man now. And a man needs his own place."

Frank's eyes widened and he rushed to close the gap between himself and his father with a grateful hug. Junior stood nearby, swinging his arms at his side and smiling from ear to ear. He wanted this feeling to go on forever.

In the Zwinger household, the feathers were flying. Emily was pulling out wedding dress patterns from her sewing box and fussing about how she was going to make her daughter's dress herself, as she'd done for the other four, and Katie Beth most certainly was not going to wear some store-bought wedding gown!

Fred Zwinger closed the door that separated the kitchen from his back room study and sighed in the resulting peace. He strolled casually to his favorite chair, sat down in it, and lazily stretched his feet out, one upon the other, on the ottoman. Then, in no hurry, he reached for his newspaper and reading glasses. Even though it was midday and he had more work piled up than he could handle, Fred sank back into the soft leather with a grunt of satisfaction and opened up the paper before him. Five girls married, he thought to himself. Now, for the first time in thirty years, Fred Zwinger felt he could relax. His stern face shifted to a boyish grin that would have hushed Emily right up in amazement if she had seen it.

Naomi Thompson heard the news from John Henry. He was halfway out the door on his way to the milk house when he glanced over his shoulder and, trying to sound casual, said, "Oh, yeah. Frank Johnston's getting married to Katie Beth Zwinger." His expression dared his mother to make some comment. The years had taught Naomi never to speak her mind where the Johnstons were concerned. So she swallowed her disappointment and smiled, saying, "Isn't that nice," before returning to pickling her cucumbers.

May welcomed the news with customary gusto. She'd been plucking dead heads off her mums when Sarah came rushing over brimming with smiles.

"That boy finally became a man!" May bellowed, clapping her hands together and chuckling out loud.

"Maybe that'll bring two spring weddings," Sarah said, smoothing out her skirt nervously.

"Nope, it won't," May said, shaking her head at her niece. "Your sister ain't making any plans to marry John Henry. You know that."

"I wasn't talking about Esther and John Henry."

May liked to think that she knew everything that was bubbling under the surface in her family, but this news burst that bubble and her shocked face showed it.

"You and Zach make peace? Praise the Lord!" May bellowed even louder than before, making sure He heard her through the black clouds gathering in the heavens.

The Long Road Home

★ ★ ★

Late that same afternoon, Seth drove the pickup straight across the trickling stream that flowed from Skeleton Tree Pond to the roadside creek. He parked a scant few feet from the family's canopied picnic bench. Seth had built it for Liza when she was pregnant with Tom. Over the thirty-odd years, the redwood posts had tilted, generations of spiders had come and gone, and coats of red stain had been applied and chipped off. The covered table was still the favorite family meeting spot.

Esther was sitting there now, alone. She saw her pa drive up and wondered why he never walked where he didn't have to. It seemed to her it might work off some of the fat he grew more and more each year. A small twinge panged her heart when she saw the truck door swing wide and Seth struggle to push himself from the cab with a hefty grunt.

Esther knew why. She knew her pa's breathing came harder these days. Seth let C.W. and the boys do more of the leg work during the day, and at night, he took to watching TV more than walking the land like he used to. A worried frown creased her brow.

"I thought I'd find you here," Seth called as he strode in his wide, swinging gait to the bench.

"Hi, Pa," she called back, her heart happy to see him.

Seth's eyes sparkled with joy as he approached, and Esther knew that Frank had told him the good news. Seth eased down on the bench beside her, rocking it, and settled in to join her at staring out over the pond.

"Yeh–up," he said with a contented sigh. "This is the best pond for miles."

"I love this spot," she said, meaning it.

"Yeh–up," he replied, knowing it.

Seth and Esther sat comfortably together in silence, as they had often done in the past. This pond was a private link between them. They'd meet here before dinner on most warm nights, just to sit, talk a little, and share each other's company. Neither one knew which one started it. It just happened and they'd kept it up over the years. Until the Michael MacKenzie trouble, when Seth stopped coming altogether. That was how Esther figured out her pa knew about her and Mike, and how deeply he disapproved. Though he never once mentioned it, not even after Mike MacKenzie died.

So Esther was all the more moved that her pa would seek her out at the pond, with a cold wind coming in from the north, wearing a smile on his face. Her own smile trembled with emotion.

Seth rubbed his thighs in thought, then leaned back, resting his elbows on the old redwood picnic table behind. His belly spread out before him like another table, and Esther noted that his leather belt was let out clear to the last notch. Esther didn't tease her pa about it, as she might have done. The time wasn't right for teasing. Instead, she waited patiently.

"Got a letter from Squire," Seth muttered. He casually reached into his inside pocket, pulled out an envelope, and gave it to Esther.

"From Uncle Squire?" she asked, surprised. Esther opened and read the letter, then the amount on the check enclosed. It was written in her name, for more money than she ever thought she'd see at one time.

"May told him about you wantin' to go to the city."

Esther was speechless, and her pa, sneaking glances at the tears running down Esther's cheeks, wasn't up to words either. Esther reached over and clutched her pa's hand. The wind tugged at the papers, but she held on to them, and to her pa, so tight her fingers turned white.

Then they let go, at the same time.

28

———

THE SKY HAD long since darkened and the clouds overhead were transformed into battleships of gray and black. They sat in readiness, an armada of awesome proportions with an unpredictable captain at the helm. C.W. stood alone in the fields. Hands on hips, he screwed up his nose and sniffed, slowly turning his head from side to side. Moisture was in the air; he felt it on his face and in his bones. A cool, heavy presence, laden with a whiff of snow.

In the distance, the bleating of ewes echoed against the mountains and floated back to him. Its sweet familiarity sang across the pastoral scene like the hypnotic song of the sirens. How good it felt to be back home.

Behind him, the sound of heavy footfalls broke his concentration. Turning, he saw a shadowed form approach with a wide, swinging gait. It could only be Seth.

"Glad you're back, son," he called.

C.W. met up with him and shook his hand with strength and warmth. "Strange night," he said, returning his gaze to the sky.

"You feel it too, huh? I've lived through many an odd season, but I ain't seen the likes of this before." Seth scratched the hair under his cap. "Heard tell of a freak snowstorm in Grandpa Wade's time. October, same as this. Never heard of another." Worry creased his brow as he looked again at the sky.

C.W. continued the sky watch. The hills were cloaked in suspenseful silence. Far off in the northern pasture he heard a low, worried bleat. "Is that Brutus?"

Seth chuckled and nodded his head. "You old cow!" he called out to the teaser ram with affection. Seth took one last sweep of the threatening sky, listening to the rumble with a frown.

"Best go get the kids, son," he said, scratching his bristle. "Gotta shore up the hatches. They're at the Harvest Contra Dance in Clarendon Springs. They won't like it none, but hell, what's one dance more or less in the face of a storm?"

"You be sure and wait," replied C.W. "The boys and I will round up the ewes to the lower pasture."

"So who's givin' the orders around here?"

C.W. smiled down at the scowling, toothless face. "I'm not giving orders. But with your heart, you have no business up in the north pasture. Now please, go on back and sit tight. I'll go get the kids and come right back. We'll get it done."

Seth grunted and wiped his lips with his palm. He was about to leave when he turned back and asked, "You find your field, son?"

C.W. nodded. "Yes, sir. I believe I did."

"Good," Seth replied. After a moment, he hitched his pants up a notch and, head down, added, "You oughta talk to that girl of yours, son. She needs to know you more to love you more. She's a good'un. And seems only fair."

"I will, sir. Thank you." There was much more C.W. would

have liked to say, sentimental words of gratitude and affection. Like a son would say to a father. But of course he didn't. Men didn't speak such things. He could only nod his head and tighten his lips, letting his eyes translate the message of his heart.

Seth did likewise.

Shifting his weight, Seth pointed toward his house and began the trek home. C.W.'s last sight of him was his rocking gait steadily plowing through the waving fields like a barge headed toward the light.

Over the stairwell leading to the church basement, a long banner announced in orange and brown: Harvest Dance Benefit/Wallingford Rescue Squad. C.W. followed the music down the rear stairs to where the moist heat of forty twirling, laughing couples enveloped him. On one side of the room, long tables were laden with coffee, soda, homemade brownies, cakes, and cookies. On the other side of the room sat two fiddlers, a piano player, an accordion player, and a bass player.

The rest of the room was filled with long lines of couples. Facing west, the women glowed in the moist heat, their eyes sparkling in anticipation. C.W. spotted Nora easily. Dressed in a long flared skirt of green cotton and a white ruffled blouse, she was shyly, even flirtatiously, swishing back and forth in time to the music.

C.W. automatically looked four steps to the east to check out the man who dared partner his Nora. He was as broad and tall as Paul Bunyan, and ruggedly handsome with his starched white collar unbuttoned and his sleeves rolled up over muscled forearms. The man's eyes were firmly on Nora as he pounded his boot and clapped his hands, obviously eager to have east meet west.

For the first time in his life, C.W. understood jealousy. It cut through reason like a knife, leaving him irrationally angry and decidedly possessive.

The intro sounded and the caller sang out his prompt, "All forward, bow and back!"

Hands touched, feet shuffled, and the dancers moved through the phrases. C.W.'s foot began to tap, but not because of the heady rhythm.

A couple came dancing down the long line toward him. When they reached the end of the line, they separated and marched back up the outside. Next Junior and some red-haired, freckled beauty promenaded. When they reached the end of the line, C.W. tapped Junior's shoulder and called him out. Not far behind, Frank and Katie Beth danced down the line, flushed with happiness and clearly the Young Couple in Love. Frank rolled his eyes as he was waved over.

C.W.'s smile froze, however, when Nora and her Paul Bunyan sashayed down the line. The man's eyes were as tightly fixed on Nora's face as his hands were around her waist. Did she have to smile up at that clown so fetchingly? C.W. thought bitterly. Jealousy flared anew, then consumed him as he watched the eyes of each man she passed follow her down the line.

C.W. scowled as he passed through the crowd with an un-daunted gait, meeting up with Nora as she reached the end of the line of dancers. He grabbed her arm with a possessive yank and firmly planted his own hands upon her waist.

"Come on," he said harshly. "Let's go."

Nora's face darkened. She backed up, resisting his direction.

"Who do you think you are, treating me like this? I'm not going anywhere. You go! You're good at that."

He swung around to face her. "I'm back now. And you can tell Paul Bunyan over there to keep his hands off."

"Tell who what?" she sputtered, straining to keep her voice low. "Listen, I'm having a very nice time, or at least I was. And as for keeping hands off..." Nora's eyes sparkled in defiance as she pointedly looked at his hands on her waist.

C.W. did not move them, but from the corner of his eye he spotted Nora's enormous partner shouldering his way toward them, sporting an enormous scowl. Instinctively, C.W.'s grip tightened around Nora's waist.

"This guy botherin' you?" the man said, eyes on C.W.

"Beat it, Paul," C.W. ground out, not taking his eyes off Nora.

Nora opened her mouth to speak, but the man had already stepped forward and pushed C.W.'s shoulder back.

C.W. slowly turned his head toward the man with a deadliness Nora had never seen in him before. His shoulders were drawn, like a big cat's, about to pounce. Her partner noticed it too, and though taller than C.W. by a few inches, he backed off one step, then stood his ground.

She jumped between them, swinging her head from one to the other. "Stop it. I forbid it."

The tension began attracting curious looks. "We're creating a scene," Nora muttered. Putting her hand on his shoulder, she turned toward her partner and said, "Thank you, Andy. I'm fine. I have to go." The fight in his eyes smoldered and, with a shrug of disappointment, he turned away.

Nora's gaze swept the crowd. She had handled the stares of curious gossips for years, and many far more shrewish than any in this crowd. Gradually, the music resumed and the couples returned to their food.

"Look," C.W. said, checking his anger. "There's a storm coming. Seth wants us all back, pronto. Where's Esther?"

"She's over there, fightin' with John Henry," said Junior as if this happened every day.

"Go get her, Nora, and meet us at the farm. Come on, guys." He turned abruptly and marched out of the room, Frank and Junior following in single file behind him.

Nora had enough of his imperious tone but sensed the impending emergency. She'd settle this with C.W. later. Now it was time to be cool and follow orders. She turned and rushed through the crowd to gather Esther. She found her, alone, leaning against the rear wall with one knee bent, her foot against the wall, and her arms across her chest. Esther's cheeks were as red as her hair and her eyes flashed with angry tears.

Nora delivered the message quickly. Esther responded with equal alacrity, pushing off from the wall and jogging to the door. Nora had to run to keep up, hearing dancers mutter something about "pushy out-of-towners" in her wake. She kept plowing through the crowd, up the stairs and out the door.

The snow hit her face like a thousand minuscule snowballs. The silent, heavy flakes blurred her vision, disorienting her. Around her, a white blanket, already over an inch thick and sticking, covered the ground, the bushes, and the cars, altering them to various-sized humps of white.

Where did it come from, she wondered in a panic? Where was everyone? She called out but her voice got lost in the deafening stillness of the heavy flake-filled air. Suddenly she felt an arm around her, pushing her back.

"Get inside! Hurry!"

She recognized C.W.'s voice and immediately turned and hurried down the stairs.

Within minutes, C.W. stopped the music and alerted the crowd of the storm. With practiced alacrity, farmers, their wives, and their children hastily grabbed their coats and hustled like seasoned veterans toward their cars, pickups, and home. The refreshments were hurriedly scooped up amid worried comments: "Freak storm!" "Never seen it like this," "Could be trouble."

C.W. grabbed Nora's elbow and pulled her aside to the dark corridor leading to the restrooms. His jaw was set, his mouth was drawn tight, and a look of no-nonsense shone.

"Listen, Nora," he said in low tones. "I want you to be prepared. A storm like this could dump a foot or two of wet, heavy snow in no time. The leaves will catch the weight and bring down branches and tops. The sheep are far off in the north pasture, and surrounded by all those trees, they may be hard to get out. Especially in the dark." He took a deep breath. "There may be losses. Can you handle that?"

It hurt that he had to ask. "Of course," she replied tersely and moved to go. He held her back and leaned closer to her in the darkness.

"Nora, no more games. Life is a tough enough game without adding to it. We're either together in this fight or not, but let's decide where we stand before we leave this place."

His closeness was suffocating. The fur of his sheepskin coat brushed her face, and she recognized the sweet smell of his skin and soap. They had shared so much in the past few months: working with the sheep, struggling to balance the books, even daring to envision a future together. He had been there for her when she needed a friend. She wouldn't allow whimsy to destroy all the trust they had struggled so hard to build.

"I'm with you," she whispered.

In a sudden swoop, he crushed her body against the wall and drew her mouth to his. The kiss was as brief as it was passionate. They clung tightly for one moment. For one moment they offered what the other lacked, supported each other's weakness, accepted each other's fears, and shored up their confidences. In the darkness, against the pale green tiles of the church basement, with the snowstorm gaining strength outdoors, time stood still as she sealed this precious pact with C.W.

Esther called for them in a shrill, anxious voice. C.W. pulled back and guided Nora to the hall where Frank and Junior were stomping their feet and clapping their hands to an inner music of anxiety.

"Reverend Wilcox got a call," Esther cried, the freckles on her face standing out against her pale skin. "Pa up and went out for the sheep. Alone."

"Let's go!" shouted Frank, his face grim.

Nora ran with the pack, slamming open the church door and slipping on the slick pavement toward Frank's Impala. The storm had picked up and the wind howled so loudly, she had to cup her ear to hear C.W. shout, "Meet you at the farm. Take it real slow!"

She squeezed in beside Esther upon the torn, smoke-smelling seats. As she closed the door, she saw C.W. pull out of the lot in his four-wheel-drive Jeep, taking the boys ahead. Esther gunned the engine and tried to follow, but the Impala started to skid on the wet, greasy snow, forcing her to slow to a crawl.

"Goddamn bald tires. Who'd have thought we'd need god-damn snow tires tonight!"

Someone pounded the roof of the car and peered through the driver's window. "Stop!"

Through the snow, Nora saw John Henry's anxious face. Esther stopped and John Henry swung open the rear door and jumped in.

"I heard. Let's go."

Emotion charged the air between John Henry and Esther, but neither of them spoke. Esther clenched the wheel, gunned the engine, but crept forward slowly, guiding the wheels over the slick streets.

Nora's gaze focused on the Jeep's two red brake lights as they disappeared into the storm. Here and there the wheels spun and Nora's knuckles whitened, but they continued on at their snail's pace, not speaking, each praying that they'd make it home—fast. That the storm would end—soon. And most of all, that Seth would get his butt out of the fields and back in the warmth of his home.

Seth reached the northern pasture before the storm turned mean. No sooner had he left the road and trudged past the windbreak of pines than the sky opened up and dumped its load of heavy, wet snow. He could barely see his hand in front of him, but he raised it anyway in a clenched fist at the sky. "That was a cheap trick, you old bastard."

He looked around and saw how the snow was already clinging to the branches and covering the black dirt with a coat of white. The temperature was dropping by the moment, and the wind was picking up the snow and whipping it into his face. He bent his head and closed his mouth. While raising his collar, he lifted his feet to check how wet they were getting. He couldn't see much over his girth, but already his toes were tingling.

"Dang it all. I could'a took two minutes to put on my boots. Well, pay the piper, you old fool," he scolded himself. He shook the snow off his feet with mulish kicks. In retreat, he headed back toward the road, muttering obscenities about his own stupidity. Each step through the thickening snow was harder than the next and his breathing became more labored. Steady as she goes, he told himself, and he paused here and there to catch his breath. At one stop, he heard the frantic bleating of a sheep. The sound was low and gravelly, and he recognized it immediately as Brutus's.

"You found your way out, you old cow!" he shouted with a measure of surprise and pride. Then he thought of his ewes in the northern pasture, and his smile fell. If this snow kept up, all the trees and branches'd be bent over with snow. They'd be corralled up there, unable to roam back to the barn, unable to graze. They could all die.

Seth looked back toward the road. A few feet more and he'd be out of the field. His heart was chugging like a locomotive pulling a full freight, and sweat was dripping down his back. He knew the thing to do was wait for C.W. and his sons to get here. He just had to get to the road, then it'd be downhill all the way home.

"Baaaaaaaa," came the call from Brutus. Farther away he heard the feminine, higher-pitched bleats of ewes.

Seth shook his head and made up his mind. This was his battle and he meant to fight it. There wasn't time to wait for C.W. and the boys to get back. His girls had to be freed before the trees started falling. They were up there because of his decision and he'd be the one to get them out. Same as he'd always done.

"I'm comin', Brutus," he called. "It's up to you to settle the ladies." He turned his back to the road and headed up into the northern pasture.

He wasn't stupid, he took it slow. Trudge, trudge, trudge, and it was time to take a breather. The storm fought him each step of the way, throwing snow in his face, blowing away his scarf and blanketing the moon and the stars. Trudge, trudge, and he heard Brutus calling nearby. Encouraged, he pressed on, walking uphill against the wind toward an area of thick brush. It was so steep here he had to grab tree branches to steady himself against the incline. A branch snapped and scraped his face.

"Where are ya?" he called out, winded. "Come here, you old woman or are you gonna make me fetch you in that jungle?" His heart was pounding painfully. He brought his hand up to rub the soreness beneath the folds of fabric and fat. Around him, the wind gusted, catching him full in the face and causing him to swallow in the cold. He couldn't catch his breath! A stir of panic brought up the hairs on his neck. Despite the cold, he broke out in a sweat.

"Brutus!" he shouted, "if you ain't one stubborn old…"

In one agonizing, bursting sensation, death strangled his heart and radiated down the left arm. Seth blindly reached out in the darkness, took one final step forward, then collapsed upon the earth. Gasping, his face against the ice, he clawed through the several inches of snow with his bare hand, down to the black soil beneath. Clenching a fistful, he brought it up to his heart and held it there, close, while he suffered his last spasm.

Then Seth lay still, at peace. The earth at his heart and in his nails.

In somber silence Nora and C.W. searched for Seth in the blizzard. Tied at the waist with rope, they headed toward the northern pasture, where the sound of frantic bleating could be heard over the roar of the storm. In the distance they saw the lanterns of the Johnstons bobbing in the dark mountains like a string of holiday lights.

Nora stopped and pulled the rope. "C.W., listen. That bleating is coming from over there."

C.W. closed his eyes and moved his hat from his ear. "That's Brutus. Let's go." Holding her hand tight, he guided her at a steady pace up the steep incline.

Even with C.W.'s help, it was a difficult climb. With each awkward step her ominous feeling of dread increased. Nora's instincts alerted her to what lay ahead in the quiet darkness, beyond the brush, pierced only by the occasional guttural cry from the teaser.

As they approached the pasture, Nora balked. The atmosphere of death was overwhelming. "C.W.," she said, pulling back.

He turned to meet her gaze. Snow and ice hung from the rim of his hat and littered his reddened face. From beneath his brows, C.W.'s eyes shone bright blue with pain.

"I know. I'll go."

Nora shook her head and raised the rope that bound them. Squaring her shoulders, she took a step forward, even as waves of fear swept over her.

"Oh, Seth," was all she could say when she found him, sleeping in the fields, covered with a white blanket of snow. Brutus stood beside him, shaking his head, nudging Seth's shoulder, searching for grain from the old shepherd who would not awaken.

Nora knelt beside him and gently brushed the snow from his face. He looked peaceful, she thought. Then she saw the earth in his nails, and with a trembling lip, she knew she'd carry that image in her heart for the rest of her life.

"Sleep well," she whispered before placing a kiss upon his cold cheek.

Turning slowly, she rose and moved toward C.W. The stark pain on his face arrested her advance. He stood, ramrod straight, with his hat clutched in his fists. Snow gathered on his head and ears without notice.

"We must get help," she said, reaching out for his hand.

He did not seem to hear her but stood still, save for an occasional twitch at the corners of his mouth and the quivering of his pupils.

"C.W.?" she called.

He took a deep breath, nodded, then grasped her hand. As he led her out of the thicket, she looked once more over her shoulder, marking the spot where Seth lay in the field.

The snow had already covered his face.

Good news and bad news travel fast in the mountains. Neighbors left their own troubles to suffer the storm and bring Seth home. John Henry Thompson, Fred and Emily Zwinger, Joe and Elsa Cronin, Darryl and Debra Weaver, and others. Kind words, pats, hugs, and tears were shared within the Johnstons' pale green house. No one sat and commiserated. A storm raged outdoors and there was work to do. Though the feelings ran deep, the words were blunt and to the point. Seth would have approved.

The Johnston family, with the exception of Frank, had retired to Seth's room to mourn in private. Frank surprised everyone by assuming his role as Seth's eldest with the dignity and finesse of the old man himself. He and C.W. worked together to organize the following day's chores and tools. Junior and Zach signed up the volunteers. Dawn was a few hours away, and a full day of bringing in the sheep from the north pasture lay ahead.

"All right everybody, listen up," Frank called out when he caught sight of a sagging May emerging from the bedroom at one a.m.

C.W. looked for Nora and found her standing at the sink, washing cups and spoons. She had changed into a pair of Esther's work clothes and resembled a waif in the oversized, folded-up overalls.

"Go on home and get some rest," said Frank. "There's

nothing worth doing around here tonight." Frank's voice choked on the final word.

Everyone noted Seth's epitaph in silence and quietly filed out the door. In admiration Nora turned and watched them leave. They were a fine people: unafraid of hard work, accepting of life's joys and difficulties, and in tune with nature. They formed a family for her, and she felt included in their protective circle.

Seth had left a place for her to fill. She'd worked hard for the spot—she'd earned it. It felt right. With her, the circle would remain unbroken. She could hear Seth smile and say, "Yeh-up. Life is like that."

C.W. approached her and gently tapped her shoulder. When she faced him, she offered him a reassuring smile. His hand moved from her shoulder to her face, and she rested her head in his palm, eyes tightly closed. "Let's go home," she whispered.

There was nothing he wanted more.

29

—

NORA AND C.W. LEFT the Johnston house together to climb the mountain to the big house. They cut deep strides through the snow that now reached her knees. In silence they climbed, C.W. pushing back bent branches for her, holding her lantern while she crossed a broken limb, and grabbing hold of her hand as she struggled through drifts.

A quiet peace had settled in the mountains. The battle had been fought, the howling wind was spent. Over her head the clouds slowly dispersed to the south, leaving a hazy moon and a few stars to illuminate the snow below. The ice crystals sparkled in the shafts of light like millions of infinitesimal diamonds.

As the hike grew long and weary, Nora was conscious only of the loud crunch of their footfalls. The steady beat acted like a drummer, keeping them trudging forward in the night. Occasionally, the sharp crack of a snow-laden limb rifled through the still air, followed by the muffled thud of its graceless landing.

They made it to the house after an hour's climb. Nora was

too numb with cold and grief to care that the electricity was out, the phones were dead, and the temperature inside was as frigid as it was outside. Yet, despite their exhaustion they set to work. They lit fires, lugged logs indoors and hauled jugs of water up from the root cellar. It could be days before electricity was restored. Survival was an automatic response.

Upstairs in her room, Nora sat on her haunches before her rosy-brick fireplace. She carefully laid out a few logs, stuffed newspaper between them, and struck a long match. It left a long trail in the damp flint but did not ignite. She tried another, then a series of them until the logs were littered with thin wooden twigs tipped in red, blue, and green.

Behind her came the sound of a match taking light.

"Allow me." C.W. bent over and put the small flame to the paper. The dry wood took to the fire immediately, its bark curling in the heat and snapping out bright sparks.

Nora sat back on her heels, absently staring at the leaping flame. Depression numbed her of all the problems that faced her tonight, tomorrow, and beyond. Her lids began to droop and she swayed off balance against C.W.'s legs.

"Come on," he said gently, taking her by the shoulders and raising her up. "Your teeth are chattering. You must be freezing."

"I'm okay. Really," she chattered back.

"Then why do you sound like a locomotive?" His eyes were teasing as he rubbed her shoulders and hands vigorously. "Let's get you dry." The teasing in his eyes turned to a warmth that rivaled the fire. He pulled off her jacket, then guided her feet out of the bib overalls, one foot, then the other, rubbing each one in turn. Then he released each of the long row of pearl buttons on her ruffled blouse, his tapered fingers nimble with the tiny plastic disks.

Nora closed her eyes. Half-awake, half-asleep, she felt both the gentle tugs at her chest and the radiating heat of the fire. Her teeth still chattered and her body shivered, but she let the blouse slide from her shoulders, down her arms, and onto the pile of clothing at her feet.

For a moment nothing else happened. She pried open her eyes. C.W. stood before her, mute, but obviously not blind to her milky white breasts covered only by the intricate design of her lace bra.

"Where are your pajamas?" His voice was as raspy as the wind outside the window.

Nora pointed a shaky finger to the large armoire in the corner. C.W. walked to the chest, yanked open the second drawer as if he knew where they were stored, and pulled out a long, pink flannel gown. He rolled the soft fabric in his palm before handing it over to her.

"Thanks," she whispered before slipping it over her head. He sighed and turned to go but she reached out quickly to clutch his hand.

C.W. turned, so slowly, that it seemed each degree of the turn was measured. When he faced her, his brows were so closely knit that they formed a long shadow over his doubtful expression. C.W. was still fully dressed for the outdoors in his layers of flannel shirts and socks, covered by a midlength lambskin jacket.

"Where are you going?" she asked. Her shivering stopped.

"Perhaps I should sleep elsewhere. So much has happened. So much to think about. I don't want to confuse you at a weak moment."

"It's too cold out there," she replied.

He looked at her face, drawn and pale in the flickering light. Her eyes held no promise of passion, but they were warm and welcoming. Her voice was not trembling with desire, but cajoling, like a mother's to a favorite child.

"I don't want to be alone tonight," she continued. "Won't you stay by me? Keep me warm?" She paused, whether in indecision or fatigue, he couldn't tell. "Please?"

He squeezed her hand and held it, searching her eyes for some answer.

She squeezed his hand in return, then quickly turned and scrambled onto the king-sized bed where the mountain of covers invited her in from the cold. She pulled them back and crawled under their folds upon the icy sheets, rubbing her feet together.

Trying to keep her teeth from chattering, she lay back and listened to the rustling noises of C.W. as he removed his layers of clothing. Two thuds, one boot after the other, the slide of his leather belt, and the scratchy hum of jeans falling off of his long legs.

The sound of a man undressing in her room was still somehow unfamiliar. She peered over her blankets at the shadowed figure. In the darkness it could have been Mike, broad shouldered and tall. But when the figure bent to pick up the clothes and lay them on a nearby chair, she knew the athletic grace was C.W.'s. And for sure, Mike would never have bothered to pick up his clothes.

"Come to bed," she called out to him.

The bed bounced with his weight as he lay down. Then he swept her up in his arms, tucking her bottom close so they lay like spoons. They cuddled in the shared warmth, neither speaking. This was good, thought Nora. Too much had happened tonight. They were tired. They needed to sleep. Yet she was aware of C.W.'s chest rising and falling behind her, and the breath he expelled was too ragged for him to be asleep. As the minutes passed in agonizing slowness, she could feel through her gown the bristle of each of his chest hairs and his arm felt like a hundred pound weight over her shoulder.

Suddenly, a tremendous crack exploded in the woods. The windows rattled. Nora jumped, and C.W. tightened his arm around her. The ripping noise that followed told of a mighty tree crashing against its brothers, bringing a number of their limbs down as well. It hit the earth with a resounding thud not far from the house, and the aftermath rustling and snapping continued for seconds more. Then all was deathly still.

Nora's heart still pounded in her ears.

"That must have been a big old tree," C.W. murmured in reassuring tones. "I doubt it could stand up against the weight of the snow."

Nora imagined the old tree. Probably one of the ancient maples, she thought, with roots deep in the earth, many rings around its center, father to scores of saplings.

"Like Seth," she whispered aloud.

She heard him swallow.

Saying Seth's name brought to surface all the buried sorrow. The darkness heightened the pain and brought back to Nora ghosts of a lifetime of partings: her father, her mother, her grandmother…Mike. Her shoulders shook as she wept, feeling no shame for these tears.

C.W. gently turned her toward him and cradled her head upon his bare shoulder. Nora felt her tears pool against his skin. As she wept, his fingers ran along the fuzzy fabric, gently caressing. She nestled in his arms, gradually settling, rocked by the steady rise and fall of his chest.

"Why did he have to die?" she asked so softly he had to tilt his ear toward her mouth.

His shoulders shrugged under her head. "It was his time." He gently stroked her arm. "Seth was an old man with a heart condition. He knew better than to go out there. He took a risk he shouldn't have, but he wasn't afraid. He did what he felt he had to do. Seth often said he wanted to die in the harness.

"But Nora," he continued, giving her shoulder a gentle shake. "We're young. We must take risks—risk it all. Don't you see? Life is a series of risks. Trust, and you'll sometimes be hurt. Love, and someone will die. Life is joy and pain. If you don't risk the pain, you lose out on the joy. This was Seth's final lesson to us."

Nora swallowed hard. "I'm afraid to die," she confessed.

C.W.'s fingers stopped stroking. Slowly, deliberately, they traveled up to her face. With his thumb he wiped the tears from her cheeks. With his hand he swept the hair from her face and tilted her chin. She stared into his eyes.

"Don't fear death. Death is life's companion. If you fear death, you fear life." His hand tightened on her chin. "Nora, don't be afraid to live."

Her breath stilled in her throat. Suddenly, it was all so clear. What did it matter if she made a life for herself on this farm, if that life didn't include this man? When she died, what would matter except that she loved and was loved in return?

Nora brought her arms around his neck. "Oh, C.W.," she cried, her broken voice barely able to speak his name. The emotion was too strong. "Oma and Seth both told me to trust my instincts. I won't be afraid any longer. I don't need to know anything more about you than I do right now. Love me, C.W."

"I love you." In a rush of emotion, his lips met hers and the vows were sealed.

C.W. lay awake for the remaining hour before dawn. Rubbing his weary eyes, he prayed he'd have the strength to get through the day. He had loved Seth like a father, and he mourned Seth as any son would. His death turned a page in his life. It was time to write a new entry.

And Nora's name would be the first word on the blank page. Forever after, what was written about him would include her. Each pronoun would be plural: we, our, us, they, their.

He watched her sleep upon his shoulder. Her hair was golden in the firelight and soft upon his skin. A primal urge surged unbidden. She was his. He wanted to protect her, to ward off others, and to breed within her yet another generation. This feeling stirred in his gut with the knowledge that this commitment to her was not for one night or one year.

His teeth clenched and he resisted the urge to hold her tightly against his chest, to keep her physically close even as her mind drifted far away. He couldn't imagine life without her. She had come to him like a gift during his bleakest hour, and nothing—not a dollar, not a word, not an act of God— would take her from him.

Yet, his heart was heavy knowing that though their commitment tonight was very real, the play had not yet ended. Tonight she had loved a man called C.W. Until the mask was off, until she knew that Charles Walker Blair was not the villain but the hero, then the play had to continue. Though his intent was good, his lines were false, and still he had to perform. What else could he do? Another act followed, just one more, and he prayed the ending would follow the script.

A wave of weariness swept over him as he heard the throaty call of the bluejay outside the window. The room was dark, and the stillness of the earth sleeping under a blanket of snow gave an aura of peace.

He knew it was just a facade.

Nora woke to a gentle shaking of her shoulders. Roused from a druglike sleep, she was vaguely disoriented. In the fireplace, the flames had diminished. Beside her, rumpled and with dark circles against his pale skin, sat C.W.

"I know it's early," he began, "but we've got to get a head-start on the day." He brushed the hair from her face. "Are you up to working in the fields? I'd understand if you weren't."

"No, no. I want to. We're in this together, remember?"

"Of course."

He tapped the tip of her nose with his finger. The kiss he bestowed on her head was chaste. What she wanted, what she really needed, was a tremendous bear hug and some assurance that everything was going to be all right. She swallowed back her words and told herself to be brave. Yet it was with dismay that she watched him climb from their bed.

"I can't make you coffee this morning," he said, scratching his head with vigor. "Hardly the honeymoon. We'll have to hike down to the Johnstons' and hope they have electricity. We could be out for days up here." He walked to the window and looked out. "Do you want to move down the mountain?" he asked in a serious tone.

The gray veil of cold, and the muffled silence told her without even looking that the snow outside was deep. The electricity could be out for days, and there would be precious few comforts after their long hours struggling in the snow. They would, however, be alone. And this was home. "No," she replied. "Let's manage up here."

She stretched then, sat up, and wrapped her arms around her shoulders. The memory of their lovemaking was as fresh as the scent upon her sheets. So was the memory of Seth's death. She closed her eyes and shielded them with her palm.

The squeeze he gave her chased away her worries like a specter at dawn's light. That single clutch conveyed the affection Nora craved following a night of lovemaking and commitments.

"I needed that and I feel better."

"Now, up and at 'em, old girl," he said with a smile and a tug on her arm that sent her flying.

In minutes Nora was slipping into her outdoor armor: layers of long underwear, multiple pairs of socks and pants, topped with her new thermal bib overalls and a down jacket, two pairs of mittens, a lambskin hat, and a wool scarf.

"You look like the Michelin man." C.W. laughed.

"I don't care if I look like the abominable snowman. I'm warm."

"How are you ever going to survive a winter up here?" He was smiling, but his worry was real.

"Looking like this," she answered.

"Hmmm, I guess we'll be spending a lot of time in bed. I'll keep you warm."

"Is that a promise or a threat?"

They were parrying, trying to keep the mood light. For outside, they both knew disaster awaited them.

Nora's stomach was growling, her head was screaming for coffee, and moisture was already gathering on the scarf across her face by the time she waddled to the door. C.W. was right behind her. With a deep breath, she pushed the door and stopped with a throaty "whoof!"

It took a heave from C.W. to scrape the door open against the built-up snow. When Nora stepped out, the brilliance of white reflected on white blinded her, forcing her to raise her gloved hand as a shield. Gradually she grew accustomed to the brightness, but she was unprepared for the sight that met her.

As far as she could see, oranges, yellows, and reds of peak foliage sparkled against a crisp white backdrop so deep that it distorted her perspective of space and distance. Like a Bosch painting, the scene held beautiful yet queer tableaux. Limbs emerged from the snow, twisted and gnarled, yet tipped in glory. Majestic pine trees stood stooped and dwarfed by their white robes. Above her, in a brilliant blue sky, birds circled and called, no doubt as confused as she was by nature's trick.

"Let's get started," C.W. said, taking her hand and making the first indentation in the deep snow. He turned to make sure she made the first step safely. His physical strength was needed now to carve out a rough path through the drifting snow to the Johnstons'. From deep in the woods they heard the distant sound of high bleating. To Nora, it was a pitiful wail. She clenched her jaw and quickened her pace.

At last they reached the pale green Johnston house at the bottom of the mountain. Enveloped in fresh snow and surrounded by tall pines, it looked like a Vermont postcard. Smoke curled from the chimney, and as they approached a dog barked. No one would guess, she thought, that within that domestic picture, grief and death dominated the scene.

"Perhaps life and death are companions," she said, pausing at the front door. "The flip side, like black smoke and white snow. Good and evil."

"Yin and yang," he answered. "It's all a matter of balance."

"Remind me of that later today."

"I'll try to remember it myself. Listen, before you enter..." He put an arresting hand on the doorknob. "Today will be tough, you know. Whatever comes from all this, remember what you said earlier. We're in this together."

A nod was her reply. How could she forget?

She needed him the moment she entered the Johnston house. Few lights lit up the dim front room, making the faded wallpaper and worn furniture appear dingy. The family clustered in the kitchen, no one cooking, no one eating. The strained silence froze them into a staged grief.

The Long Road Home

"Here, let me help you get breakfast," Nora said with mustered enthusiasm as she quickly shook off her coats and kicked away her boots. Tossing away her scarf, she reached out to grab the frying pan that hung uselessly in Esther's hand.

"Where's May?"

"Tending Pa. She wants to do it herself." Esther stepped close. "They gave Sarah a sedative; she's pretty much out of it. May won't take anything of course, especially not from a doctor. I'm concerned about her. She's been sitting beside Pa all night."

Nora cast a worried glance at the bedroom door, then to Sarah seated on the quilt-covered sofa. Sarah wore a black dinner dress, hardly suitable for the rigorous day ahead, and leaned against the arm Zach had protectively wrapped around her. Grace lay with her head in Sarah's lap, and Timmy cuddled between his parents with his skinny arms tight around Zach's neck.

Nora donned an apron and hustled up a breakfast of eggs, sausage, pancakes, and maple syrup. The smell of hot coffee and food revived the spirits in the room. Grace and Timmy tugged at Nora's apron for a sausage while Zach and Esther began setting out plates and cups. As she cooked, Nora watched C.W. confer individually with members of the family. He was kind and gracious, leaving each of them with an encouraging smile. His gaze always returned to her, however, and when their eyes met, they were alone.

Esther kept busy and her comments were short. Nora knew she would mourn Seth for a long time but would, eventually, settle her grief.

But the older boys... Nora wondered how Seth's death could affect two seemingly inseparable men so differently. Frank and Junior: the names rolled off the tongue as one. No longer did they stand side by side, jabbing and sharing remarks.

Frank stood tall by C.W. He was steady and mature in his replies, ready to oversee the day's work. It was clear Frank would assume confident command of his family.

Junior, however, leaned against the far wall with his hands in his pockets, staring out the window. Nora walked to his side and handed him a cup of hot coffee. When he turned her way, his eyes were bloodshot and he reeked of booze.

By eight o'clock the near neighbors and friends began to arrive. The snow outside was deep and treacherous, not fit for travel. Katie Beth immediately went to Junior and sat by him, cajoling him to eat his breakfast. Everyone brought food and supplies.

May at last opened the door to Seth's room. May's cheeks seemed to hang in long folds from her cheekbones, making her eyes appear to protrude even farther under creped, drooping lids. Death was hard for May to bear. The final ailment that went far beyond her help.

"Come say your respects," she announced gravely. Her voice was unusually low but could easily be heard over the hushed voices. "Then be about your work. He'd want the sheep tended to first." May stepped aside and called over Sarah and the little ones to enter first.

Nora and C.W. followed the family into the back bedroom, barely big enough for Seth's double bed, a small bedside stand and lamp, a narrow walnut dresser, and a wooden chair. On every tabletop, candles burned beside freshly cut pine and yew branches. At the foot of the iron bed, May had placed two boulders from Seth's sacred grove.

"Smells like Christmas," whispered Grace. She was quickly shushed.

Everyone filed in and out quickly, only a few people pausing to touch Seth's folded hands over a patchwork quilt. Esther laid a sprig of evergreen beside them. Frank bent down to kiss his father. C.W.'s face was stony. Junior lurked at the door. Nora escaped the trapped air of the small dark room with barely a glance. She couldn't reconcile seeing Seth lying in bed rather than working in the fields.

Frank and C.W. organized a work force of thirteen: eight men and five women. No matter that the neighbors had their own troubles at home, they always came to help a neighbor in need. Word was, John Henry's place was hard hit, but he was here for Esther today.

"Thank you, gentlemen and ladies, for helping us today," C.W. began. "We all recognize the respect you pay to Seth and his family. I'm sure he appreciates it. We all do." He looked over to Nora and she nodded deeply.

He shifted his weight and stood straight. He seemed accustomed to command, and this was immediately sensed by the men and women in the room. Point by point, he ticked off the list of tasks that needed doing, organized work teams, and tallied up the supplies.

"We've got a major problem here," he concluded. "Most of our flock is caught up in that field. Unless we can get them out soon, they'll be unfit to breed. If we can get them out at all. The brush is thicker than a hornet's nest. What can I say?" He shrugged. "It's October. We didn't foresee the magnitude of this storm. Nobody did."

C.W. leaned against the table while his eyes swept the room. "The storm came, but it did not conquer. Let's give it our best."

The room echoed with calls of "We can do it!" "You bet!" "Let's go!" Nora sensed the solidifying of spirit. They'd work for the sheep, for the farm, for Seth, and most of all, to prove man could emerge victorious over nature.

Armed with chain saws, grain buckets, and rope, the teams headed across the deep snow to the northern pasture. Nora plowed through snow up to her knees before catching on to the trick of stepping in another's footprints. The snow and leaves that had seemed so beautiful to her just hours before were now their greatest enemy. The sun was shining bright. Wet and heavy, the melting snow sent branches falling dangerously near.

Within minutes of reaching the pasture, the mountains rang with the buzz of multiple chain saws. The men manned the saw while the women worked alongside, pulling aside the severed limbs. Brittle branches scratched Nora's face, leaving her skin raw to the biting wind. She lugged limbs twice her weight through the wet snow, and with each tug, more snow fell down her neck.

Everything was cold and wet. In her soggy gloves her fingers grew icy and in her boots her toes felt numb. Still, she kept to her task, never slowing, never complaining. Nora worked on C.W.'s team and shoulder to shoulder they kept the pace, working that much harder than the rest.

Hours of buzzing and pulling passed before they cleared a ragged path through to the pasture. A few ewes bolted out of the brush, ears up and eyes bulging in panic. The deep snow made it hard for them to run and easier for Nora and Esther to catch. Keeping the ewes herded with the grain bucket, Nora waited in the cold, stomping her feet, while C.W. took a crew into the area. Soon, a few more sheep straggled out behind C.W.'s banging grain bucket. He approached with a grim face.

"Where are the others?" she asked, giving voice to her worst fear.

"I can't see them. It's a sea of fallen branches and brush in there. It'll take hours, maybe even days to get through." He put his hands on his hips and clenched his jaw.

"Twelve sheep saved? We can't quit. They're in there!"

He snapped his gaze toward her. "Quit? Who talked about quitting? We'll work till we drop."

She recoiled and reached for his arm. "I know. I'm sorry."

C.W. wrapped his arm around her, their thick coats padding his hug. "The snow is making us all irritable."

"It's okay. I understand."

"Go on down and bring these ewes in. I'm going back in. Maybe a few more will hear the bucket and find their way out. No use everyone freezing up here. I'll send the crew down for lunch."

Nora turned her face up and he kissed her. Their lips were cold and parched, but the touch bolstered their spirits.

"Don't be too long," she called out. "I'll keep the soup hot."

"That's not all I want you to keep hot."

She almost smiled but her cheeks were too icy to move. His good nature was back; it would keep them all going.

"Come on, girls. We'll be all right," she crooned to the ewes. Then, giving the grain bucket a good shake, she led the lost dozen down the mountain.

C.W. never did come down for lunch. May and Katie Beth served up pots of thick chicken soup. The Zwinger family brought casseroles and cheese sandwiches, and Naomi Thompson delivered hot coffee, cookies, and carrot cake. Nora carried a thermos of hot soup up the mountain to C.W. and wouldn't budge until she watched him drink the whole thing.

Day turned to dusk, and the laborers' shadows stretched long down the graying slope. Shoulders stooped as heavily as the pine boughs, the jokes had long since stopped, and fatigue etched deep lines upon their faces. It was time to quit. The neighbors exchanged handshakes, but victory was not theirs.

Only forty sheep had been rescued so far, and tomorrow the crew would dwindle back to the original five.

That night Nora and C.W. made love with a tenderness born of mutual respect. Side by side they had worked, glancing at each other over the scraggly brush and shoring up their conviction with a smile. Simple gestures became meaningful symbols of their union: his arm around her shoulder, her brush of snow from his hair. They were as intimate in the fields covered with layers of wool as they were in bed, lying naked in each other's arms.

Mates in the field, mates in the bed; their forces merged into one.

30

———

SETH'S FUNERAL WAS QUICK and to the point. He would have approved. There was no church service, but a few words were spoken at the gravesite by the Reverend Wilcox. Despite the rain that would not let up, a large group gathered, ankle deep in mud, in the small Johnston family plot. The Johnston family had settled in these parts generations ago, and by virtue of many children and marriages, the family stretched for miles in these mountains. Neighbors, associates, and friends, dressed in their best suits and dresses, braved the gusting rain and leaves to stand in tribute to Seth atop the rolling hill overlooking Skeleton Tree Pond.

Squire had flown in from Florida. May flustered about him like a plump hen seeing to his needs. Squire was short and wiry, unlike Seth and May, but he had the same warm blue eyes and unassuming manners of his younger brother. He stood ready to support the family in any way he could, emotionally and financially.

Afterward, the mourners were invited for coffee and cake at

the Johnston house. Everyone talked in hushed tones and were courteous to Nora, many meeting her for the first time.

"I'd like to thank you for what you did for our Esther," Squire said when Nora met him. The way he said it made Nora sure May had told him the full story. He meant it kindly, but Nora colored, muttering how she would like to have done more.

Frank stood stoically between Katie Beth and Junior, arms linked.

Sarah did her best to be helpful, but her eyes still held a look of bewilderment. Zach picked up her slack with the children and stood by her side.

May announced that she'd move back into the house to look after Frank and Junior, just for the winter. Come spring, she declared loud enough for Katie Beth to hear, she'd move out. May surprised everyone by saying how she might move down to Squire's place in Florida, explaining how these northern winters were getting hard on her and her ailments. Despite Katie Beth's protests, May was sure the last thing a new bride wanted was some maiden aunt living with them.

Esther disappeared somewhere in the mountains. John Henry stood by the window, looking out.

C.W. stood quietly in the background during the funeral. He never intruded and barely spoke a word. Nora approached him often, squeezing his hand, bringing him coffee. He assured her she needn't bother with him and said appropriate phrases of encouragement. Yet his heart wasn't in them. Nora decided she wouldn't burden him with her own sorrow, or her desperate financial straits or even the lost sheep remaining in the mountains.

Seth used words sparingly in his lifetime, so it was fitting that a discreet marble headstone, engraved only with his name and the dates of his life, mark his grave. "Just let the grass grow over me," he'd said in life, but May had insisted on at least the small marble slab. Frank and Junior carried the two rocks from Seth's bedroom to sit on either side of it.

C.W. stretched his long legs out before the wood stove and laced his hands across his stomach. What a weekend, he thought with exhaustion. But it, like the storm, had passed. In only four days, he had watched the fields of white snow change to acres of black mud—and the mud was worse. All of them were slipping as they continued their dangerous routine of chainsawing and pulling. Rubbing his back, he wondered if he had ever been so exhausted. Squash, tennis, football—all those sports paled next to logging.

His glance returned to Nora. She was back in her usual position of late, hunched over her desk scribbling and erasing, poring over various books, papers, and letters. She drank too much coffee and ate little food. She was losing weight, and she was losing her farm. Of all of them, this fight would be toughest for her.

The sharp ring of the telephone pierced their temporary peace. Both C.W. and Nora jumped up, for it was the first time in days the reconnected phone had rung.

"At least the phone's back," he said, grabbing the phone.

Nora leaned back in the swivel chair, her face open.

"Hello?" C.W. asked, mugging curiosity to Nora.

"Charles, is that you?"

His face dropped as he swiftly turned his back to Nora. He could feel her gaze upon his back and his muscles stiffened.

"Hello, Charles?" the voice repeated.

C.W. hesitated, debating whether to answer the familiar voice or hang up. "Yes," he responded after a painful interval. He was almost whispering and he cupped the receiver tightly near his mouth.

'It's Cornelia. I'm sorry to call. You said I could in case of an emergency. This is an emergency."

The tightening of his muscles progressed from his back to his neck. "Go on."

"At today's board meeting, Agatha presented her 'discovery' of the numerous bank loans that defaulted. She's calling for an in-house investigation. Your signature has been exposed and your head is on the block. I've heard rumblings about asking for your resignation. Agatha's licking her chops."

C.W. ground his teeth. Damn Agatha. She must have a sixth sense for an opponent's moment of vulnerability.

"Have the loans been traced?" he asked, looking over his shoulder. Nora's eyes were still on him and she was chewing the end of her pencil. He looked away, avoiding eye contact.

"Traced back to MacKenzie? Not yet. But it's only a matter of time. This in-house investigation will leak outside in a matter of days. Once it does, everyone will know. New York is a small town that way. Sidney has done his best to keep it quiet, but Agatha is determined."

C.W. cursed under his breath. Nora's auction was this week.

"You should know. Sidney is your staunchest defender. He is calling foul play and initiating his own in-house investigation. The two of them are head-to-head on this one. And right now, I'd bet on Agatha. Sidney's going to take the fall with you. He isn't giving any sign of abandoning your ship to save himself."

C.W.'s chest swelled at the clear signs of loyalty in his ranks, and in his family. Despite the mess he was in, he greeted his brother-in-law's support with relief and pride. This was going to be a tough fight: for him, for Sidney, and for Cornelia. He knew what he had to do. God willing, it would be enough.

"Charles, the situation is bleak. The bank is losing confidence in you. They'll turn to Agatha and you know she'll push for your resignation. You must get back here. Now."

The situation was more bleak than Cornelia realized. The plan he'd been setting up hinged upon locating proof of Agatha's duplicity. He didn't have it—and time was running out. The ledger connected him to MacKenzie; he wouldn't be able to prove his innocence. Who'd believe his word? MacKenzie's suicide acted as a finger pointed his way, and his alcoholic binge would only be interpreted as guilt. He'd be forced to relinquish control to Agatha.

And worse, Nora would learn who he was and what he supposedly did. She'd think him a liar and a cheat—she'd never forgive him. A veil of dismay dropped over him. This one worry, more than any bank problem, more than any strenuous labor, caused his shoulders to droop.

"I'm on my way," he said with resolution. Then hung up the phone.

"Who was that?" Nora asked, turning a suspicious glance his way.

C.W. leaned over, hands on the kitchen counter, eyes down. What was he going to say? He, Charles Walker Blair, the master planner, was totally stumped. Would she believe it if he said, "Wrong number?" He snorted and shook his head slowly, realizing that with each moment of his silence, Nora's anxiety increased.

"Someone I know," he replied evenly, straightening and turning a gaze to meet hers head on.

He challenged her with his eyes to ask another question—dared her to. Nora clenched her jaw, as though to keep the question in. He saw her eyes flash and the muscle twitch in her jaw.

"Oh," she said pointedly, then swung around and furiously began to erase a column of numbers.

C.W. crossed the room to place his hands upon her shoulders.

Nora tensed at his touch.

He dropped his hands.

Nora sighed and tossed the pencil on the table. "I don't have it in me to fight you. I'm too busy fighting banks and Mother Nature. If you feel the need to keep secrets, go ahead. I'll give you the time you need."

"Don't you think you should stop and get some rest?" he asked, rubbing her neck once again.

"There's no rest for the wicked," she said, tilting the back of her neck.

"Why do you say that?"

"I'm being punished for something, but I can't figure out what." She groaned. "Too many sheep are lost. It's all there in black and white. Or should I say red and white? The dream is over."

His fingers dropped away. Nora had put to words his greatest fear. "What do you want me to say?"

She rubbed her eyes. "Oh, what I want to hear. That you'll make it all better. That I won't lose the farm. That you have some new scheme."

She heard C.W. sigh and turned in her chair to see him standing, hands on hips, staring into the fire.

"That's not fair of me," she said with an apologetic tone. "I'm sorry. I don't expect you or anyone else to rescue me." Reaching out, she took his hand and kissed his palm. "You've taught me to rely on myself. And I am. But damn it all…" Nora muttered, reaching for a handful of papers.

"I've been trying to be clever. I keep going through these old letters and papers of Mike's. I don't know what I'm after exactly, but I have a hunch there's something here I'm missing. With all his deals, I keep hoping for some hidden asset."

C.W.'s head swung sharply around. "Those are old papers and letters of Mike's?" He kept the urgency from his voice. Stepping closer, he peered over her shoulder. "What's in them?"

"Some are personal—his journal, letters and such. He described various deals, loans... It gets pretty complex." Nora sighed and dropped her handful of papers on the desktop.

"Deals and loans? Anything curious or interesting."

"Mike keeps referring to someone named Agatha."

C.W. lost all caution and swooped down to stare at the littered desk.

"Where?" he demanded, forcing back his rising excitement.

Nora lazily shuffled the papers. "Here," she said, handing him a memo, "and here, and those over there. I wonder who she is."

C.W. didn't answer. He studied the memos, his eyes narrowing as he scanned the information. A faint blush spread along his ears as he pored over the memos. When he bent to search through the letters, his fingers began to shake. He couldn't believe it. It was all here: deals, loans, illegal banking activities—all in cahoots with Agatha Blair. He had the proof he needed! And it was better than he had hoped. He had to hold himself from laughing out loud.

C.W. pounded his fist in his cupped hand like a baseball pitcher about to throw the winning pitch. Nora recognized that glint of triumph and slowly straightened in her seat.

"What's going on here?"

He paced the floor, still rubbing his hands. Lady luck had at last surfaced; the final piece was in place. All he needed to do now was get to New York and start the game.

"C.W.?" Nora's voice was more insistent.

He stopped his pacing and stood before her, searching for the words to reassure her. No matter what excuse he came up with, it wouldn't suffice. At this point, he had to open the window to truth. Running his hand through his hair, C.W. walked to her and squeezed her shoulder.

She raised her beautiful eyes to his; small worry lines pinched at their corners.

"I think I have a way to ease your difficulties at the bank."

Nora stiffened in surprise.

C.W. swung around another chair to face hers and clasped his palms together, leaning forward on his knees. "Some of Mike's bank activities were clearly illegal."

"Good God, what's next?"

"A lot, if this is uncovered. He dealt with one bank in particular, one person in that bank. And these—" he grabbed a handful of papers "—are the proof."

"It has to be the Blair Bank," she exclaimed. "And Charles Blair...I knew he was connected with this! Is this Agatha connected with Blair? If so, let's go after them."

C.W. lowered her back into her seat with a gentle pressure from his hand. "Slow down. This is extremely delicate. It could all backfire, and with Mike's implication, the authorities could seize all your personal assets. That would include this farm."

He saw confusion then alarm register on Nora's features and he inched his chair closer till their knees touched. "I've told you before that I'm working on this farm while I sort out my life. I'm not a farmer or a hired hand."

"That much I figured out."

"I thought as much." He patted her knee. "I worked at a bank. Yes." He nodded. "I knew of your husband—who didn't?

The Long Road Home

I left New York and I never wanted to return. But I will. I must. I know people in the business and have connections."

"But how will any of this help me?"

"Silence is a precious commodity, Nora. You owe the Blair Bank tons of bucks. These papers can buy plenty. Could save you this farm."

Dawning slowly reflected in her eyes. "Silence is golden."

"Exactly. I'll need to bring these papers to the right people and negotiate for you. Trust me, Nora. This is my bailiwick, I know what I'm doing."

"I should come with you. It's my problem."

"No. You're too vulnerable, and frankly, I'd do better alone. Will you let me take these papers?"

Nora could not quite believe what he was asking. Take Mike's personal papers to his New York connections? She always suspected that C.W. was educated, sophisticated. But a New York banker—with connections?

"Lord, Mr. Walker. You certainly know how to drop a few bombs. This is a lot to swallow all at once."

"I know. It's not by choice, but time is of the essence here."

"Was that one of your 'connections' on the phone?"

"Yes, it was."

"I see." Part of her was glad he admitted that much. "You really think you can do this…without my help? After all, I *am* Mrs. MacKenzie. Mike's name still opens doors."

Slams them, more likely, he thought. "I'm quite sure."

Nora looked at her hands. Mr. Walker, the banker, wanted her to hand over the only protection she had: Mike's papers. By doing that she gave him custody of her future.

"I don't know," she said.

"Nora, listen to me. Think about what I'm asking. This is

not just about the bank. It's about us. It's about trust. Trust me, please. Trust yourself—trust us."

A moment passed without words. Part of her wanted to accept his plea, to trust the man she had come to love. Another part called her a fool and warned her to guard against her nature. Mike's last words haunted her: "Don't trust anyone."

But there it was. "Trust me." A covenant offered, a promise begged. Nora closed her eyes. How far did trust extend? She raised her gaze and looked across the short distance at C.W. With this man, trust extended as far as it took.

"Yes," she agreed hesitantly. "You may take them. Except the journal. There are some…well, it's too personal."

"I would never do anything to hurt you."

"I know."

"Agreed, then. With the exception of the journal, I'll take these papers and memos, and the ledger, to New York. But I may need access to the journal later."

"The ledger too?"

"Most definitely. Is that agreeable?"

"Yes." The word rolled off her tongue, leaving her without anything else to say.

C.W.'s chest expanded. Nora's love for him manifested itself in that one word: *Yes*.

"I realize," he said, taking her hand, "believe me, darling, I do, that you have been patient with me and that this constitutes blind faith."

"There are some things worth fighting for."

The light in C.W.'s eyes brightened at the rallying call, then changed from warm to hard as he tapped his fingers in agitated thought. Nora saw immediately that he was already in New York.

"I'll leave tomorrow. I don't know how long I'll be, but I'll be back to you, and to our farm, just as soon as I can."

C.W. was using that deep slow voice he always used when the issues were important and he wanted to be sure he was understood. He brought her to him and wrapped his arms around her shoulders. Tonight they seemed even more thin and frail.

"Ah, Nora," he said against her temple. "These separations are no good for you. You will analyze and mull over your problems and eventually try to distance yourself. Yes, you will. I know you too well."

"I love you," she murmured brokenly against his chest.

C.W. closed his eyes tightly. He'd make this period of suffering up to her, he vowed. And he prayed it would take him the rest of their lives.

They walked out to the deck and stared up at the sky. The storm was long gone and October's normal crisp air made the stars shine like brilliants. Tonight, they could even see the Milky Way streak a quarter moon.

Nora and C.W. stood together, arm in arm, each praying that wishes did come true.

Two days later, Nora raced for the phone, thinking that it might be C.W. with some news. "Hello?" she gasped, out of breath. It was her auctioneer in New York.

"Walton! Is everything all right?" She glanced at the calendar; only two days until her auction.

"I only wish, darling."

She swallowed hard and leaned against the counter. From the corner of her eye she saw Esther turn around and raise her brows. Nora waved her back with a shaky hand.

"Spell it out," she said.

"D–I–S–A–S–T–E–R. Word's out that you can't set a minimum bid."

"No." Nora's knees felt weak. "That secret was buried deep."

"Dealers live under rocks. And they thrive on secrets. The phone's been ringing off the hook for tickets to the advance showing. And all from big name dealers. Darling, it's going to be a bumpy ride."

"They'll set the prices."

"It's already happening."

Nora didn't know whether to laugh or cry. After Mike's disaster, then the farm disaster—was this a trend?

"What do you suggest?" she asked without much hope.

"You've got to squelch the nasty rumor that you're broke. I don't know how, but if you don't, it's all over."

"How can I squelch it? It's the truth!"

"Can't you talk to someone at the bank? Cry? Plead? Good God, sweetie, blackmail them if you have to."

"Hold them back, Walton," she said, an idea formulating in her brain. "I'll leave today. And don't worry. I'll think of something."

Nora hung up the phone, amazed at how still her hand was.

"Are the auction people causing a problem?" Esther asked, wiping her hands.

"Unfortunately." Nora rubbed her temples.

"Too bad C.W. isn't here to talk to. He has got lots of good ideas."

"Uh-huh," she agreed, keeping his whereabouts a secret. C.W. hadn't called and she didn't know how to contact him. She desperately needed to talk to him. What did he say? Silence could buy plenty? He had all her main papers, and the ledger was gone. That was the bulk of her ammunition.

Nora's heart skipped. She still had the journal.

The Long Road Home

Nora scooped up the dishes and tossed them in the sink. "Pies can wait, Esther. I'm going to New York."

Esther jumped from her stool. "Take me with you!"

"Oh, Esther. This isn't the time."

"Yes, it is! For me. Please, Nora." She clasped her doughy hands together. "I stayed for Pa, but now he's gone. Frank will handle things here just fine. I've got enough money. For the first time in my life there is nothing holding me back. If I don't get out of here right now I might never have the courage again. Please, Nora."

What else could she do? Esther was her friend. "All right," she said, giving Esther an impulsive hug. "I only hope you have a better life there than I did."

"Oh, God. Thanks, Nora. I will. I know I will."

"Say your good-byes to May and the kids. And to John Henry."

They gripped each other in a sisterly hug. Nora could smell the country in Esther's hair and, for a brief second, prayed it would always stay there.

31

———

SIDNEY NERVOUSLY ARRANGED the files on the surface of his black desk, checked the Windsor knot of his tie,
then eyed the clock for the third time in as many minutes. At
precisely two o'clock his secretary notified him, in an awed
tone, that Mr. Charles Blair was here to see him.

Quickly, Sidney touched his damp palms to his wool trousers and stood as his office door swung open. He stepped
around his desk, grin wide and arm outstretched to his colleague, brother-in-law, and president of the bank.

To his credit, Sidney did not break his stride when he saw
Charles walk in. Gone was the wild-haired, lumberjack appearance. Charles was immaculate, even elegant, in his navy
double-breasted suit. His hair and nails were trimmed and
polished, he was freshly shaven, and there was no trace of the
dark circles under angry eyes that Sidney remembered from
their last meeting. Charles had the sleek, dangerous look of a
shark in shallow waters.

Greetings were brief. Charles did not take a seat. Sidney was
so unnerved by Charles's cold demeanor that he didn't know

whether to sit or stand. He stuck his hands in his pockets and ended up standing by default.

"I'll be brief and to the point," Charles said, holding his hands behind his back and standing with his feet an arrogant distance apart.

Sidney nodded in compliance and wondered how the hell this man could walk back in after a rocky scandal and a year's mysterious disappearance and still have the bearing of a king. For despite the current turmoil, Charles Walker Blair was still the king inside this bank.

"This unfortunate affair with the bank loans has grown out of my control," Charles said evenly. "I intend to resign."

Sidney's mouth dropped into a silent *no,* then he cleared his throat. "I don't think it's come to that yet," Sidney said, his panic rising.

"I wrote the ethics code for this bank. No one has to tell me I'm out," Charles cut him off.

Sidney's face tightened.

"I have a proposition for you, Sidney. The MacKenzie collection will auction off a van Gogh. I intend to offer the successful bidder my controlling interest in the Blair Bank in exchange for that painting."

Sidney paled and his hands lifted from his pockets. "Are you mad?" he burst out before he could stop it.

Charles reacted with an icy smile. "I am sure there are those who will claim so, but no. I am not mad. I am quite serious."

Sidney decided to sit down. He stared at his shaky hands, and when he looked up at Charles again, he searched the face of his one-time friend for some clue as to how he should react. Charles's face was devoid of any expression, but his eyes held a strange gleam.

"Controlling interest in the bank in exchange for a painting?" Sidney asked, not believing what he'd heard.

"The MacKenzie van Gogh. Yes," Charles confirmed.

"In the name of God, why?"

"For the name of Charles Walker Blair, that's why." Charles continued in a louder voice, enunciating clearly. "It's simple. I want the loans cleared because I want my name cleared. I'm willing to trade my stock for that."

Charles turned and walked to the door. "May the best man—or woman—win," he said graciously. Before he left, he looked over his shoulder at Sidney. His blue eyes were intense. Then he was gone.

Sidney leaned back in his chair, feeling bewilderment before hurt and anger. What was that all about? What the hell was that final look? Was it some secret message that he was supposed to interpret?

Or, was it a warning?

C.W. stretched and looked out his window toward Central Park. Encircling the park, building after building of granite, marble, and glass—symbols of all he had rejected—cast shadows upon the foliage. He rubbed his eyes and turned to look around his apartment. The antique Mahal rug, the onyx table, pre-Columbian figures, European paintings, Italian Renaissance chairs—all reflected a personal, educated taste. One that he still admired but no longer felt akin to.

The clock read 3:00. One more visit. He had made many visits today, battening down the hatches, as Seth would say. His head was on the block; the directors at the bank were up in arms, and Agatha was poised with the dagger. C.W. smiled. He excelled at these eleventh-hour takeover attempts.

After plugging in the coffee machine, he jumped into the shower to wash away the day's grime. By three-thirty he was dressed in a conservative dark suit and drinking coffee; by four he had made two more calls and was reading the catalog of Nora's auction. C.W. studied each item, its description and provenance. The estimated values were fair, but a few items were so spectacular in style and form as to be without a real price. He had to pause and admire their photographs.

"Not bad, old girl," he mumbled. No doubt about it, Nora had a great eye. Under ordinary circumstances she would have an important sale. His second visit that morning, however, informed him that she had a fiasco. Sidney couldn't keep a lid on MacKenzie's impending bankruptcy. The dealers swarmed down and had already divvied up the goods and set the prices, knowing the MacKenzie estate could not set a minimum bid.

C.W. made a fresh pot of coffee and set out another cup. This time, the second cup was not for Nora. He wished it was. The door buzzer sounded. He glanced at his watch again: 4:25.

"Fashionably late, Agatha," he murmured in distaste as he crossed the floor. Pressing the intercom, he ordered, "Show her up."

C.W. held his hands behind his back as he stood before the window, reviewing his plan. Two knocks sounded on the door. He knew no more would come.

"Agatha," he said politely after showing her in.

Agatha Blair held out her gloved hand and turned her cheek toward him. C.W. refrained from kissing it. Her eyes flashed and again their yellow hue reminded him of a snake's.

"Son," she said with a flourish.

C.W. cringed, as he did every time his stepmother used that endearment. She was a shrewd opponent and he'd have to be on guard.

Agatha strode past him into the drawing room, eyeing

him over her shoulder while her elaborate cane clicked on the marble tiles. "You look fit, all ruddy and tan. Mountain air?"

"Honest living."

"Hmm." Her eyes raked him from head to toe. She was tiny and thin and her charcoal-gray hair was swept up in a matronly bun. But he was not fooled. Beneath her petite exterior and Chanel suit lived the heart of a corporate raider. Agatha held her own against the toughest on Wall Street, and usually emerged the victor. If a deal was cut, Agatha knew about it. If a hand was shaken, she set it up, and if a secret hid in the walls of the bank, she sniffed it out. C.W. knew it and counted on it.

"Coffee?" he asked, stepping back.

"Please. Black. No sugar."

"Nothing sweet. Of course."

Agatha sank into a silk-upholstered chair, keeping her hands tight upon her ornate cane. "It was quite a surprise to receive your call," she said, accepting the cup and saucer. "It's been almost a year. We were all quite worried. The bank was in an uproar, but we managed." She took a small sip.

"I had no doubt."

"It was irresponsible of you, nonetheless. Where was your loyalty? Or did you down it with one of your bottles of scotch?"

The stab was quick and clean; she could have been discussing the weather.

The cup stilled at his lips. Swallowing the bitter brew, C.W. slowly placed his cup upon its saucer. "My loyalties have always been to my family."

Agatha's eyes widened a hair and he knew he'd hit his mark. She had never been accepted as family by himself, Cornelia, or the relatives.

"Furthermore," C.W. continued, "as you no doubt are aware, I settled with Sidney before leaving."

Agatha set her cup down with a small clatter. "Sidney." She spat out the name in disgust.

C.W. raised his brows.

Agatha visibly reined herself in and lifted her cup again. After a pause, she raised her eyes to his. "Taking an interest in art lately?" she asked.

C.W. leaned back in his chair and crossed his legs. "Not generally. No."

He noticed her foot tap twice. "Offering stock in the family bank for one painting constitutes an interest, I'd say."

C.W. sipped his coffee.

Agatha's voice rose in pitch. "An avid interest."

He held back a smile. "It *is* a van Gogh."

"*Controlling* interest!"

C.W. let his smile loose and slowly, with deliberate ease, placed his cup on the table next to hers. Not a drop spilled.

"Well, Agatha. Talking to Sidney, are we?"

"Everyone is talking to Sidney! That ineffectual school-marm. His clumsy attempts at learning why you want that painting has everyone stirring. That bloody auction will become the social event of the season. How dare you make such a spectacle of our business? How dare you make such an offer to Sidney without first speaking to me? You know as well as I, he'd never be in that position if he wasn't married to your sister."

C.W.'s eyes narrowed. She had slipped. His offer to Sidney was too fresh for gossip. C.W. abruptly stood and crossed the distance between them, allowing his size to add strength to his argument.

"To begin with, Agatha, it isn't our bank. It's mine. I still have controlling interest. Secondly, I do not remember ever requiring your permission for anything I decided to do. Thirdly, I don't believe Sidney is the only one to have married into the business."

"How dare you!"

"This is business, Agatha. I invited you here today not to discuss family, but to make you a proposition." C.W. placed his hands behind his back and coolly eyed his stepmother.

"The invitation to bid for the painting is open. The one who acquires MacKenzie's van Gogh at the auction acquires my controlling interest in the bank. A simple trade."

Agatha's eyes glared and she pinched her lips. He knew she could not refuse.

"It'll be bid up into the millions."

"Cheap at the price, wouldn't you say?"

"This is absurd! Why this painting? What game are you playing?"

"What's the matter, Agatha? Can't you play a man's game?"

She leaned forward upon her cane, clutching it so tightly that her hands resembled the wooden ball and claw feet of her chair.

"You impudent pup. I can play any game you set up. And I play to win. I don't give a damn why you want this painting. You probably owe some Colombian drug dealer a clean payoff. Game—hah! You ought to know. You played at every bar in town after that fool MacKenzie blew his brains out in your office."

C.W.'s face turned to stone.

Agatha's mouth twitched into a thin smile. "What's the matter, Charles? Was that a tad too rough for you? All that mess, and all that scandal... *Tsk. Tsk.* Finance is a dangerous game. You shouldn't play with the big boys unless you can play rough." Her eyes shone.

C.W. stretched his fingers at his side to calm the anger that was rising. Very good, he thought, sizing up her skills. She knew where to strike. Now it was his shot.

"You may be right, you know," he replied evenly. He spread his jacket and stuck his thumbs in his belt. Then, looking at his shoes, C.W. gave his head a weary shake.

"It's not a game," he replied evenly. C.W. moved to a chair and sat down, staring at his hands. "Let's be honest. For once. It cannot be news to you at this point that I intend to resign. We both know the bank cannot afford another scandal. Nor do I wish to endure one. I'm wealthy enough to walk away, and that is exactly what I intend to do." He lifted his eyes to Agatha's and his voice rose in warning.

"I do not, however, intend to walk away with my reputation in tatters. I want MacKenzie's loans paid back and my name cleared. It was either you or Sidney who set me up, and I don't give a damn which of you buys me out. The hell with both of you. As soon as I know the bank is solid, I want out."

Agatha's hands stilled on her cane while her eyes studied him through narrow slits. Then she stomped her cane.

"It's a done deal. As if Sidney could do anything."

C.W. tilted his head. "A done deal? My brother-in-law is a well-educated, shrewd banker. Don't underestimate him."

"You *are* out of touch." She clucked loudly. "The Mac-Kenzie scandal almost drove the stock down. Then you disappeared. People lost confidence in you—and your sidekick Sidney Teller. They came to me. *Me!* If it wasn't for *my* intervention, *my* planning, the bank would have gone under."

Her fingers clasped and twisted up along the cane as she shifted her weight. "And now you have the audacity to come back from some drunken binge and tell *me* that you're offering controlling interest of *my* bank to that loser."

"You're having trouble with pronouns, Agatha. The possessive can be tricky."

"I've never slurred my words," Agatha parried.

C.W. leisurely walked over to the Sheraton sideboard and poured himself another cup of coffee. It was clear that she had set up Sidney as neatly as she had set up MacKenzie—and himself. It was a shame she was so brilliant. While pouring, he stole a glance at his watch. Time was running out. He had to finish this in a hurry.

"You wouldn't be afraid to lose to Sidney?" he asked, returning to their arena around the coffee table.

Agatha rose and stomped the floor with her cane. "Lose to Sidney?" She laughed with the screech of a crow. "I? You must be spiking your coffee. I haven't lost one round with Sidney yet. You don't think for one moment I'd give him the chance to amass power over me. I'd see the bank go under first. Afraid of Sidney. Hah." She waved her hand again and muttered something under her breath.

C.W.'s eyes glowed over his steepled fingers as he sat, listening deeply.

"Do you fear me perhaps?"

"Fear you?" She studied him again for a long moment, then slowly shook her head. "Once, perhaps. When MacKenzie killed himself, you couldn't stomach it. It revealed a weakness in you. Call it a human weakness, it doesn't matter. Human qualities are not valued in business. And your sister! Cornelia clings to that failure of a husband. If she had any spine she'd have thrown him out long ago. Him and that mindless butler."

Agatha picked up her purse and threw a final disparaging look his way. "No. I'm not afraid of you. You are not ruthless. Neither was your father, or your sister. It is your Achilles' heel, and it will be your ruin."

She turned and without another word paraded from the room, not bothering to close the door behind her.

C.W. strode across the checkered floor to the door, catching a final glance of her withered features before the elevator doors closed.

She didn't see him smile.

Fate decreed that Nora's auction would be the playing board upon which not only his own problems would be resolved, but Nora's problems as well. Knowing that, he did not challenge fate. He used it to set his strategy. The players were on the board. The first move had been made. He had to finesse the black queen—and the game was his.

"Checkmate," he said confidently.

He didn't know that his own queen was already on the move.

Late that night, in another part of Manhattan, Sidney and Cornelia shared their bed but not their thoughts. They lay side by side, neither attempting to cross the five-inch gulf that separated them. Over dinner, Sidney had cursed Charles Blair's black heart and his own blind loyalty. That Charles could offer controlling interest of the bank to Agatha was bitter. It made him physically ill. Better to sell public than offer to Agatha.

Cornelia had listened silently, not touching her plate, not offering even a syllable of rebuke or defense of her family. With a strange look of anguish on her face, Cornelia had spoken of patience and faith. Trust and loyalty.

Empty words, Sidney thought, lying in bed with his mouth twisting in anger. He stared at the blackness.

Charles was ever the calculating shark, he realized with cold logic. Charles must have known that things were tense between Nelly and him. He wasn't cutting him a deal in case the marriage fell apart. That had to be it. He wouldn't even offer to his sister.

Damn, but Charles was really going for the highest bidder! Sidney, intensely hurt, hadn't thought that really possible.

To hell with the whole Blair family, Sidney muttered as he rolled angrily on his side, presenting Cornelia with his back. He'd buy that stock if it took every penny he had, and it no doubt would.

"Sidney?" Cornelia's voice was soft with sadness.

He didn't respond. His voice caught in his throat. He heard her sigh heavily and turn to her side, careful not to let her body brush against his. The distance between them pained him. He missed his wife. He loved her still. All it would take was a stretched-out hand, one touch. But no. Impossible. The gulf was too wide.

Sidney tossed and turned for hours, wondering if Charles had really betrayed him. Hadn't Charles warned him of rough days coming? Of doubt and the need for trust? Was this offer to buy the van Gogh the last trick of a desperate man, or another ploy of the unpredictable Charles Blair?

Possible. He remembered the intense stare in Charles's eyes. The recollection gave him hope.

Then Sidney shrugged the emotion away. It didn't really matter. This was business. Every man for himself. Let the bidding war commence, he decided with more aggression than he'd felt in years. The bidding would go high, he figured, but he knew what the bank was potentially worth, and it was more than even Agatha knew. They'd underestimated the bank, Sidney thought, jutting out his jaw and clutching his pillow tightly.

And they'd underestimated him.

32

———

NORA TOOK A LONG, last look at her mountain before climbing in the Volvo beside Esther. The Johnston family was there to wave them off, sharing a look of sadness and shock as they clustered on the front lawn. In only twenty-four hours, Nora and Esther had closed up the big house, designated their chores, packed, and said their farewells. All that was left was to leave.

Esther's eyes were moist but she waved heartily from the window. When she turned and faced forward, her eyes sparked with excitement.

Nora started the engine. In so many ways, this was going to be a long journey to New York, for both of them. She backed out slowly, careful not to hit any dogs, cats, or junk on the front lawn, and eased onto the road. Frank, Katie Beth, and Junior walked the length of the front yard after them, waving. May, Zach, and Sarah watched with solemn faces from the front porch, while Grace and Timmy chased the car down the road calling out, "Bye, bye!"

They hadn't traveled more than a minute when Nora spied

a blue pickup speeding down the road after them, honking. She pulled to the side, recognizing the truck as John Henry's. From the corner of her eye, Nora saw Esther's face pale and stiffen.

John Henry parked on the side of the road, just ahead of them. He leaped from his truck, leaving the door wide open, and ran toward Esther's door.

"Oh, no," Esther moaned, with more sadness than irritation, as he approached and yanked open her door.

"Esther, we gotta talk."

"I tried to yesterday but you wouldn't come out. It's too late now. Let it go."

"Es, please. You can't go like this."

Esther glanced at Nora, who promptly nodded and lifted her hand in a signal to get out. She did, reluctantly. They walked a few feet from the car.

"I know you're doing what you always wanted to do," John Henry began, marshaling all his reserve. "I respect you for that."

"Thanks," she whispered, holding herself taut.

"I'm sorry I've been so hard on you—"

"You haven't," she interrupted.

"I have, but it's because I love you so much."

Esther wouldn't look up, afraid to see the pain she heard in his voice. "I care about you too."

John Henry cleared his throat of the cry that suddenly shot up. He stood ramrod straight and he spoke forcefully. "I don't know when you'll be comin' back, or even if you are. Even if you do, I don't know if I'll be waitin'." He paused. "Es, look at me."

Esther raised her eyes, and in the man, she saw the boy. Esther shuddered and willed herself not to cry.

The Long Road Home

The wind streaked John Henry's brown hair across his cheek.

"Before I go I want you to know that, no matter what, I'll always be here for you, Red. Know that John Henry Thompson will always be your best friend."

Esther stepped forward, slipping her hands from her pockets to go around his neck. She couldn't tell him that she loved him too, for fear he'd take it the wrong way and start to hope again. So Esther just whispered, "Thanks," against the fine short hairs along his neck.

They sealed their pact of friendship with a hug, neither knowing how long it would be before they would see each other again, or whether they would ever be able to touch each other again with such intimacy.

John Henry was the first to break away.

"Good luck, Red," he said heartily with a brave smile and a hasty wave of his palm. Then he retreated to his truck, his pace far too quick for indifference.

"God, I hope you know what you're doing," Nora muttered when Esther slid back in the car beside her.

"Me too," Esther said gruffly, thinking of the water that pooled in John Henry's eyes as he turned away. She leaned back, rested one worn shoe across her knee and stared out at the mud ditch that John Henry's tires dug in the road.

"Let's go," she said.

Nora had driven this route many times, but the New York Thruway had never before seemed so long. Each mile brought a new knot of tension along her spine, at each exit she fought the temptation to turn around and head back home.

The mountains shrank in size as she headed south. They were sparse of trees and thick with ski runs. The traffic picked up and the drivers were more aggressive as the scenery changed from rural to suburban. Nora cut through Westchester, past rows of middle-class postwar houses. Then she hit the New York City limits and the scenery changed drastically.

She was back, she realized with a small shiver. She had thought she was ready to face that metropolis of memories, but now, speeding toward its skyline, she wasn't sure. New York, for Nora, was a melting pot filled with too many ingredients. Rich, spicy, hot, sour. She just couldn't digest it.

Esther sat up in her seat and gawked like a tourist at the billboards, the boarded-up buildings, and the high-rise, low-income housing. Nora's face was grim as realization of the transition she must face hit full force. Here she was Mrs. Michael MacKenzie, with all the history that name evoked. Nora hardened her heart, sharpened her wits, and toughened her hide.

This was more than a change in scenery. This was entering another world.

Big-city driving is as much a learned arrogance as an acquired skill, but once you have it, you never lose it. Nora bumped over potholes, cut across lanes, and shot down to the south of Houston.

Jenny Gold came out to greet them and Nora hastily made the introductions. Jenny and Esther stood eye to eye at the gallery's threshold. Both women were tall and angular, but the similarity ended there. It was city mouse and country mouse. Jenny Gold's kohl-lined eyes shrewdly evaluated the simplicity and utter lack of chic in Esther's severe black cotton dress and worn leather flats. It pained Nora to witness Jenny's subtle sneer and hear the thinly veiled contempt in her welcome. Nora closed her eyes, inexplicably weary of the significant subtleties of this world.

To her credit, Esther was neither mincing in manner nor

shy. It was as though by her very arrival in the city, Esther had validated her talent and her dreams, cloaking her with a unique aura of confidence. Nora thought Esther was like a brilliant red rose: magnificent, straight, and thorny.

It was Jenny Gold's job to recognize uniqueness in any form, and she was good at her job. Her sneer shifted to a wide, toothy grin and she swung wide the gallery door.

"Do go off to wherever it is you have to go," she blithely informed Nora with a wave of her hand. "I'll see to Esther."

As Nora drove away, Esther flashed her a delightfully discreet thumbs-up sign.

In contrast to Esther's confidence, Nora was shaking in her boots. She parked her luggage in a modest, discreet hotel, then headed straight for the Blair Bank, before her nerves failed her. She had carefully chosen a conservative, well-cut suit of dove gray, a white silk blouse, black low-heeled pumps, and matching black purse, and of course, Oma's pearls. It was her intention to confront Charles Blair with the journal and insist that he pass out the word that the MacKenzie estate was indeed solvent. As the elevator passed floor after floor in the Blair skyscraper, Nora counted reason after reason why she had to face her enemy.

The doors slid open, revealing a long, well-lit corridor of highly polished wood and stark walls covered with a breathtaking collection of Hudson Valley artists. Along the walls sat sleek desks and behind them sat equally sleek and polished secretaries. This was the anteroom of the executive offices, the inner sanctum of the Blair Bank. Nora smoothed her French twist, clutched Mike's journal, and stepped forward.

Her heels clicked along the bare floors as she walked down the long hall. The eyes of the secretaries discreetly followed her as she passed each desk. Their expressions were curious, and Nora knew they were evaluating the expense of her suit and the millimeter of her pearls. Undaunted, Nora continued walking until she faced the largest desk at the end of the hall. Behind it was an imposing wooden door with a discreet brass plate: President.

"May I help you?" The secretary was a big woman: eyes, bones, belly, and all. With her dark suit, her severely pulled back black hair, and her sharp expression, the woman looked like an SS guard off rations.

Nora raised her chin and spoke with authority. "I want to talk to Mr. Charles Blair. I am Mrs. Michael MacKenzie. It's urgent."

The woman raised her brows and clasped her hands firmly upon her desk. "I'm sorry. Mr. Blair will not see anyone without an appointment."

Nora bristled. "Announce me, please."

"I'm sorry. Mr. Blair will not be disturbed."

"Is he in?" she asked in her most imperious tone.

"Yes." The word was a dismissal.

Nora studied the pinched face of the secretary and knew there would be no coaxing this gatekeeper. She had bigger battles to fight than with this battle-ax. Holding her purse and journal tightly, Nora swung on her heel and swept past the desk.

"Mrs. MacKenzie! Stop! You can't go in there. Mrs. MacKenzie!"

The cries of alarm spurred her forward. She didn't look back. Eyes on the door, heels clicking, she grabbed the door handle, swung wide the door, and marched into the private office.

Light poured in from the large windows. Blinking, she made out a very long, highly polished desk. Behind it was a high-backed leather chair. Nora blinked again, focusing on the man slowly rising from that chair. His long fingers rested on the desk as he stood to face her. A tall, broad silhouette; a familiar image. The seconds seemed like minutes, the minutes like eternity, as her mind recognized, then questioned, then painfully accepted the sight.

They stood separated by the desk, neither moving, neither speaking. Only the secretary flustered about, muttering, "I tried to stop her, Mr. Blair. She stormed right past me!"

"Leave us," he commanded, eyes still on Nora.

The secretary sucked in her breath, clasped her hands again, and scurried from the room, silently closing the door behind her.

Still no one spoke. Nora searched his face. The eyes were the same blue ones she had stared into. The nose was the same angled one she had mused about. His skin was the same tawny fabric she had kissed.

But his wild blond hair had been slicked back and trimmed. His wool suit was expensive, his white shirt was crisp, and his tie had just enough panache to be fashionable yet conservative. But it was his hands that arrested her. Those long, tapered fingers that had explored and excited every inch of her now rested confidently upon the desk of Mike's hated rival.

"C.W. Charles Walker. You left out Blair, didn't you?" Her voice sounded lifeless, even to herself.

"Yes. My full name is Charles Walker Blair."

She raised her eyes to his. When they met she felt burned by the intensity he wore whenever he was reining himself in. He held out his hand to her. A sudden memory stabbed deep. She remembered for an instant how much she loved him.

"I hate you," she whispered.

The pain and hate in her eyes stopped him dead in his tracks. His face mirrored the anguish. "Nora, you must listen."

"Never. Never again!" She thrust her finger out, pointing to the desktop. "Trust me, you said! You deliberately used me to get your hands on those ledgers and papers. To save your own neck, and your blessed bank's, you twisted mine."

Her voice was low and cold. He tried to explain.

"I did need the papers," he said evenly. "But it's much more complicated than it appears. Sit down and—"

"How could you have?" Her chin trembled. "Couldn't you have just stolen the evidence and left? What kind of perverse pleasure could you have gained from working your way into my life? Did you have to pretend you loved me? Did you have to make me love you?"

"Nora, I—" He swept around the desk.

"Stop! Stay away from me!" she shrieked, stepping back with an arresting hand outstretched. She felt her anger rising up and she couldn't stop it. She hated him—she loved him; the two emotions churned in such tumult they overpowered her. She gulped huge breaths of air as she hunched over the journal and stared at him with wounded eyes.

"My God, you're worse than Mike," she cried. "He used and abused me, but at least he was open about it." The tears were flowing down her cheeks. "At least he didn't sleep with me."

C.W. visibly cringed.

"I hate you, Charles Walker Blair. Not for what you did to Mike. But for what you did to me. Take your evidence," she said, throwing the journal at him. As he ducked, she swept her hand across his desk, sending the papers and ledger crashing to the floor. "Keep them, I don't care."

She squared her shoulders and stared into his eyes. She saw his pain, she saw his desolation, and it took every ounce of strength to muster hatred instead of love.

Nora turned sharply and walked to the door, each click of her heels sounding like a death knoll in her ears. With her hand on the handle, she turned and faced him one last time. He hadn't moved a muscle.

"Don't worry about your reputation," she said, her voice even. "My shame has bought my silence."

She swung open the door and fled down the corridor, oblivious to the open-mouthed stares of a long line of secretaries.

In desperate silence, C.W. watched her run down the hall. He stared without moving as she turned in the elevator and faced him, chin trembling but high. The bronze mirrored elevator doors silently closed.

He stood there for several minutes, staring ahead at the doors that had closed tight against him.

"Excuse me, Mr. Blair. Should I clean up the mess?" asked Mrs. Baldwin.

He looked at her face and saw no one. Around him C.W. saw only the rows of meaningless diplomas and awards, the shelves of unremembered books, the walls of an impersonal bank that seemed to be closing in on him. At his feet, Mike's papers lay scattered.

33

———

"THERE IS NOTHING MORE I can do."

It was the first day of her auction. Nora stood at the door, dressed in funereal black, with Oma's pearls at her neck and ears.

"I see," replied Walton. His gaze swept the sparse crowd milling about the room seeking out seats. "Pretty straight group," he summed up. "A few artsy types, a few private shoppers." He shrugged. "A lot of top dealers."

Nora glanced at the dealers. Some of them shot speculative glances across the room, a few pairs huddled together furiously scribbling notes in their catalogs. Still others, the well prepared, sat with impassive faces waiting for the auction to begin. Clearly, this was an "inside" crowd. Most of the seats were unoccupied.

"It's my worst nightmare." Her hand briefly touched her forehead before she collected herself and stood straight once again. "I went to every bank involved," she stated, a flush creeping along her neck. "They wouldn't see me."

Walton frowned, guessing at the truth behind the gross understatement.

Nora read the understanding in his eyes and her color deepened. Would her shame never end? Bank presidents, men she had entertained in her home, had turned her away without so much as an interview.

The two that did see her spent the time in a tirade against Mike and his schemes until she managed to excuse herself and leave with her tail between her legs. At least as the grieving widow she had been inviolate. Now, however, they'd felt justified in venting their anger against Mike, demanding their pound of flesh. What they didn't realize was that her heart had already been torn out.

The image of C.W. standing behind his powerful desk flashed through her mind with a blinding pain. Closing her eyes tight, she felt physically ill at the memory.

"Are you all right?" asked Walton.

"Yes, quite. I'm just tired. It's been a long couple of days."

Walton reached out and touched her elbow.

She smiled gratefully. "Shall we start?"

Mustering her courage, she put on her mask and paraded past the hushed whispers to her seat. Once there, she pretended to study her program, ignoring the naked stares, praying for the auction to be over with.

It began late. At 10:05, Walton stepped forward before the beige-curtained stage where some of Nora's antiques of assorted pedigree had already been set up. He silently acknowledged her presence. His thick shock of white hair fell over his equally white collar as he perused the crowd above his bifocals. After a final glance at his watch, he cast a frustrated look at Nora and raised his thin shoulders. Despite the house's careful marketing and publicity, the audience remained far below expectations.

Walton stepped to the auctioneer's post to the far right. He bandied with his assistants, cajoled the bidders, and drew attention to whimsical details on vases and furniture, hoping to lighten the mood. The crowd twittered and bidding commenced.

The jewelry went first. Mike's gold cufflinks, tie clasps, watches, cigarette cases. Nora remembered how he'd looked in each of them. Her collection of Victorian jewelry followed, then her Russian vermeil eggs. The bidding was slow but steady. When her personal jewelry was presented, she began to harbor hope. Her spectacular pearl and diamond necklace neared its estimated value; she felt her first rush of relief.

Suddenly, a broad-faced woman with a short blunt haircut stomped into the room with a bold bid. All heads turned toward the woman as she marched to the table, nose up, glasses down, and made a show of studying the pearls. Then, with a dramatic shake of her head, the woman found a seat and refused another bid.

Immediately the bidding slowed. Nora was furious. That dealer had deliberately cast doubt on the pearls' quality. Again and again as the bidding rose, so rose the henchwoman to the table. And as before, as she declined, so did the bidding. It was as though the strange woman was reminding them of a previously arranged deal.

Nora's furs and lesser furniture were all sold for a song. Her china was stolen, and by the time her oriental porcelains were presented, Nora knew she had lost.

"God," whispered a young man behind her. "I can't believe we got it."

"A real find!" squealed a woman to her right.

"A real steal," was her friend's rejoinder.

One by one whispers of disbelief and triumph reached her ears. By the end of the morning, the auctioneer's calls garbled with the buzz of the crowd, becoming a white noise in her own head.

For the afternoon's set, rows of chairs remained empty and those that weren't again held dealers. Nora acknowledged with polite nods a few discreet greetings, but was not taken in. Her hands were tied; the lady would burn.

As if on cue, Walton stepped forward, graciously nodded her way, then let his gaze sweep the crowd. She saw in his eyes the same sense of futility that she herself felt. He raised his palms up and shrugged as though to say, "Is there no champion?"

Nora's carpets started the afternoon's auction. She examined them in a detached manner, allowing her critical eye to catch their merits or flaws. The bids, she ignored. They were too ridiculous to contemplate.

With her silver, she recalled the many dinner parties she had presided over. Her better porcelains, china, and curios came and went. Her furniture was spectacular, and well received. How many letters did she write on that tiger maple desk? How many dinners served on that Sheraton table? Remember the hours spent reading in that Chippendale wing chair?

A chill ran down her back when her elaborately carved four-poster was carried on stage. The bed didn't do well, nor, she decided, did it deserve to. The gavel sounded. Sold.

She leaned back and closed her eyes. Watching her merchandise pass by was endurable, but reviewing the memories that they provoked was an ordeal.

Walton finally rose to the podium to call an end to the fiasco. Only a few dealers were left in the cavernous room. "Thank you for the competition," he said, giving the sparse crowd a cold stare.

Nora rose and ducked out of the room, not caring who saw

her retreat or what they said. Yes, she had expected a bad show, but not this preordained disaster. Out of all her things, only one piece did well: Oma's mine-cut diamond ring. It had been Oma's engagement ring, the one she never took off. Nora's only smile of the day came when the auctioneer called, "Sold!" after an astonishingly high bid. Yet her revenge was not sweet. Oma's ring, like so many other of her personal things, were gone. Nora stopped short and rubbed her temples.

"I'm sorry, Oma," she whispered as she strode out over the blood-red rug.

The following morning was rainy, and the cold wind whipped the wet into her face. Nora walked the distance to the auction house nonetheless, feeling the need for fresh air to bolster her courage. At the entry, however, she stopped and wondered if she'd approached the wrong building. Inside, the auction room was packed. Not only dealers volleyed for seats but society's elite elbowed their way through the crowd. They smiled and waved to her like old friends at a party. Walking to her reserved seat, Nora felt the fine hairs rise along her neck.

Walton stepped forward and clasped his hands before him, like a man about to sit down to a feast. He welcomed the crowd and gave a brief yet elaborate presentation of Nora's art collection. He deftly reminded the audience of the art's importance and drew attention to specific pieces in the vast collection.

After a gracious acknowledgement to Nora, the auction commenced with her Haitian collection. She was delighted when the bidding was as brisk and bright as the colors on the canvas. The same held for her early American works. Her biggest thrill, however, was the enthusiasm engendered over her collection of relatively unknown artists. These were the pieces that she was especially proud of. She thought of Esther and knew that if her work had been in this collection, it would have stolen the show.

Her collection was vast and the auction was long; still, the crowd remained strong. As the auction drew to a close, however, the festive mood of the room altered. Excitement grew as the crowd thickened to standing room only. The heat rose, the amalgamation of perfumes choked, and still the tension mounted. Quickly pulling out her pad and pen, Nora calculated the day's intake. She sucked in her breath. Her art collection had come through for her. The collection was her work, her ability, and no one else's. After a lifetime of dependency, she had succeeded on her own merit in the end. Nora held herself proudly in the pressing crowd. She realized that though she was far from out of debt, at the very least she could pay back a goodly portion of it with honor.

By God, she would restore honor to her life.

The lights dimmed and a hush fell over the crowd. Only one painting remained, and it was Nora's last hope.

With ceremony and care, two uniformed men carried her van Gogh out to the blue velvet-draped stand. The brilliance of the master's colors and the power of his brushwork jumped out under the expertly staged lights. The crowd let out a sigh and Nora smiled.

Walton stepped forward and delivered a dramatic introduction. Then, without a trace of emotion, he called for the first bid. Nora held her breath.

"Five hundred thousand dollars."

The crowd grumbled their disapproval and Nora's mouth fell open.

Walton looked as if he sucked a sour lemon. "We have a conservative bid of five hundred thousand dollars on the floor. Ladies and gentlemen, may I remind you that this painting is without question. It is a verified van Gogh. Let's hear a bottom bid of one million."

"I have a million," called out the woman at a special booth for telephone bidders.

"I have one million. Two? I have two, two million five. I have a new bidder. Three million."

The bidding picked up. Hands raised, the phones lit up, and discreet signs to the auctioneer kept his head bobbing from left to right. Nora couldn't see who bid what, but she perched on the edge of her seat as the bidding crossed into its fifth million.

In this new arena, old bidders dropped out and new ones stepped in. The phone bids increased and the bidding passed mark after mark. The excitement hushed the crowd as they inched to the edge of their seats. Up went a card. Up went another. The bidding maintained a heady pace. Nora's fingers flew across her paper as she did her calculations. Hope bubbled in her veins. Higher and higher soared the bidding, beyond most of the crowd's limits. A few runners fled the hall to reach a phone.

Eventually, Walton's head swung between only two bidders. The phones sat silent and the crowd's attention focused on the remaining pair. Dealers both. The whispers started as to who they represented. The Getty Museum was hungry for a van Gogh. A Japanese businessman had a penchant for the artist. Who?

After a particularly high bid, one of the pair of dealers swung his head around and searched the crowd. He had obviously reached his limit. Nora followed the dealer's gaze to the rear of the room. There was a long pause. Walton raised his brows. Up came a hand. The crowd buzzed the name: Sidney Teller.

Nora chewed her lip. She knew the name. He worked

for the Blair Bank. He was married to a Blair. Of course, Charles Walker Blair's brother-in-law! She gripped her pencil tightly.

The dealer and Sidney Teller parried higher. Heads volleyed back and forth like spectators at a tennis match. Nora's eyes remained on Teller.

After a satisfactorily high bid, the match seemed to end. The bid was out of the dealer's bounds. He paused. Sidney Teller smiled.

Now the second dealer craned his neck to the far side of the room. Once again, like a wave, all the heads followed his line of vision. Nora inched herself up for a better view.

From the side rose a cane.

A wave of shock swept the room. Agatha Blair bidding against her own son-in-law! What a story. The crescendo of wagging tongues rose to such a point that Walton had to strain to follow the bids. Nora sat stunned as the bidding shot back and forth, with fury. Neither Teller nor Blair cast a glance away from the auctioneer, but sparks of hostility and competition filled the room.

As the bidding surpassed the estimated value, Teller's face grew ashen and sweat formed on his brow. Nora's mouth went dry. She glanced at Agatha Blair and saw on her face the cruel grin of a victor without mercy. Her heart fell as she made the connection with the journal. The Agatha of Mike's journal was Agatha Blair. Further proof of C.W.'s duplicity. And now he would have her painting. How she loved the van Gogh, and how she despised Charles Walker Blair.

The whispers ceased into silence as it grew clear that Teller could not meet the new bid. Heads turned from the side of the room to the rear, searching for a signal, any small movement that would indicate another bid from Teller. None came and Walton met Agatha Blair's gaze.

"I have my high bid," Walton said. "Do I hear another?"

A new bid sang out, piercing the silence in its clear-toned soprano.

As one, all the heads in the crowd swung toward the voice in the rear of the room. One woman stood at the door. She was young, blond, tall, and attractive, and on her face she wore a look of fierce determination. The room was in an uproar. Nora strained to hear the comments, trying to ascertain from the crowd who the mysterious woman was. She looked vaguely familiar, but Nora couldn't place her.

"I thought that marriage was on the rocks," she heard a man mutter behind her.

The crowd's buzz echoed one name: Blair. It must be Cornelia, she thought. Teller's wife. Another Blair had entered the bidding! Like the rest of the crowd, Nora sat flabbergasted at the unusual turn of events. This was turning into more than an auction. A family's saga was unfolding before the crowd's eyes.

Walton put his derailed auction back on track. In a monotone that belied the flush on his cheeks, he reopened the bidding. Immediately the crowd hushed. Cornelia took a step forward and searched the crowd. Her gaze rested on Sidney Teller, and Nora read on the woman's face an expression of love and loyalty that she envied. Then Cornelia turned to Agatha Blair and stopped, hard, with a cold stare. A cough sounded in the silent crowd.

Walton focused on Agatha Blair. She sat stiffly in her seat; only her hands moved while they squeezed the ball of her cane. Nora looked from Cornelia to Agatha, then back to Cornelia.

Agatha Blair raised her cane. Cornelia smiled and bid again. The murmurs of the crowd rose in volume. Up came the cane, up again came Cornelia's hand. Up went the bid. Agatha was visibly upset. The skin on her face was as taut as a drum. When Agatha raised her cane to make the record bid, she looked ready to club someone with it.

Walton looked to Cornelia. Cornelia Blair Teller gave her head a discreet shake no.

"Sold!" Walton announced with a tremendous pound of his gavel.

The crowd erupted in surprise and delight. People were on their feet, clapping their hands, slapping backs. What a good show; there would be fodder for the gossip mill for months. Men and women who had ignored Nora the day before rushed over to congratulate her now. Nora was in a daze, totally unprepared for the tumult.

Between the squeezing of her palm and the cool kisses on her cheek, she followed with her eyes Cornelia's path to her husband. No one stood in Cornelia's way as she wound through the aisles to where Sidney stood, silent and transfixed. Husband and wife met hands and without a word exchanged, walked together, uninterrupted, from the riotous room. Agatha Blair was gone.

Buffeted by well-wishers and gladhanders, Nora finally made her way up to Walton. He hugged her and led her from the throng into the privacy of his office. There, sitting like vultures upon the tapestry chairs, sat her lawyers. Ralph Bellows was noticeably absent.

"Well, gentlemen," Nora began as she proffered a steely gaze. "Let's settle our accounts, shall we?"

Agatha strode past Mrs. Baldwin's odious expression into C.W.'s office with the attitude of a victor surveying her spoils. She paused to study the Rothko abstract on the wall, ran her hand over the Rodin sculpture, then sauntered her way toward C.W., her cane clicking on the wooden floor. Finally, she settled herself with a satisfied grunt in the deep leather chair opposite his desk, keeping her hands tight upon her ornate cane.

"Son," she began.

C.W. was sitting in a dark leather chair before the large expanse of his polished mahogany desk. The wood was void of even a single sheet of paper. His eyes coldly swept over her, then he nodded.

"Isn't it a tad dark in here?" Agatha asked. "Why are the drapes drawn?"

"There's light enough for this afternoon's work."

She smacked her lips, savoring the moment. "I do hope you are not too disappointed that I won the van Gogh instead of Sidney. It was foolish of you to waste your time offering him the same deal. Even though you did send your sister in reserve."

His eyes narrowed, but he did not move a muscle.

Agatha's cane lightly tapped the floor. "Yes, yes. Thought you had me there, didn't you? But the three of you combined could never outwit me."

C.W. saw the glimmer in her eyes. She was truly enjoying this. He wasn't. "Let's get on with the business at hand," he said wearily.

"Don't take it so hard," she said as she pulled out the auction papers from her bag and set them on his desk. After a dramatic pause, she inched the papers toward him with the tip of her polished finger. "You offered your controlling interest of the Blair Bank in exchange for the van Gogh. That was the deal. The deal is done. Here is the van Gogh. Now…"

C.W. leaned back in his chair and brought his fingertips to his lips. Staring over them, he impassively studied her greed and malice.

"Why do you hate me so much?" he asked calmly.

She cocked her head, obviously surprised, perhaps even amused by his question. Then she slowly spoke.

"I hate you because you always had my number. Even as a child, you were lurking, hawking my every move. You even tried to talk your father into divorcing me—of course I knew about that." Agatha's fingers tightened around her cane as if she were strangling it. "You never accepted me. Neither did your sister. None of the Blairs did." She stomped her cane. "Hah! Who needs you?"

Agatha resettled herself in her seat, gathering herself as she looked to her left and her right, finally raising her nose in a haughty stare.

"Enough of this mother-son banter. Here is your painting," she said, reaching out with her cane and tapping the auction papers atop his desk. "I want *my* stock."

C.W. slowly ran his finger along his jawline. "The bank, the house, the name if I can help it—nothing will be yours. Nor will it ever be."

The smile froze on Agatha's face. "You wouldn't go back on your word. Not you. Not a Blair."

C.W. slowly shook his head. "No, I wouldn't." Sitting up abruptly, he opened his desk with a sharp pull, took out a pile of papers, and set them in a neat pile atop his desk.

"I had in mind a trade."

"A trade? What trade!"

"Instead of controlling interest in the bank, I thought you might like to buy my silence instead."

Like a flustered crow, Agatha spread out her elbows, then brought them tightly back to her sides. "Silence for *what?*" she shrieked.

He took one memo from the top of his pile and eased it toward her. She grasped it from the desk to her face. He saw her eyes widen, then narrow. He watched as her jaw clenched and her fingers whitened on her cane. She reminded him of a gargoyle he had once seen in Paris.

"Where did you get this," she hissed.

"Does it matter? What matters, dear stepmother, is that I am in possession of Michael MacKenzie's private papers and journal. You thought they existed, didn't you? Sent your minions to search. But they never found them. They were never discovered because MacKenzie's wife was too smart for the lot of you. She suspected foul play all along and took them as her only protection against your backstabbing maneuvers."

He flattened his palms upon the papers as he leaned forward. "You led MacKenzie on, creating a web so intricate that neither he nor I knew what was going on. Then, like the black widow you are, when you were done with him, you took everything he had and killed him."

"He committed suicide."

"There are many ways to kill a man. I know."

He leaned back in his chair, but he was clearly angry now. He studied Agatha's pale face closely.

"You have been caught in your own web, Agatha. What I have here—" he tapped the papers with the tip of his finger "—will not only take everything you have, but it will put you in prison for a very long time."

"You do that and it will ruin your bank!"

"I doubt it. Shake it up a bit, perhaps. But ruin it? No."

"But the van Gogh!" she shrieked. "Why the game?"

"Ah…the game. As I said, it wasn't a game. I knew I would win. You are incredibly avaricious, Agatha. I knew it, and I counted on it to set my strategy."

Agatha's voice lowered to a husky whisper. "What strategy?"

"You do play chess, don't you? Sidney wanted control of the bank. Desperately. He bid up the painting enough to ensure a fair auction; he was my knight. Cornelia then moved in to push the bidding higher, and the auction into a success; she was my bishop. And Nora, my queen, will now step forward and repay the bank loans, clearing both her name, and my own."

C.W. leaned far forward over the desk and stared deep into Agatha's gray eyes. "You do remember those loans, don't you? The ones you forged my name to?"

Agatha paled and her lips parted.

"It seemed only fitting that you should pay back the money you stole," C.W. continued, sitting back and screwing the cap to his black fountain pen with quick twists of his wrist. His business was almost completed.

"So now the accounts are balanced, MacKenzie's debt has been repaid and you, dear Agatha, have purchased a fine painting."

"My money!" she cried, rising.

"Why, Agatha. You never liked cheap art."

She began to rail against him, calling him names from the gutter and cursing him, his family, and MacKenzie. But when her slurs turned to Nora, he cut it short.

"Enough!" he called sharply, fixing her with his famous cold stare. She shrank back against the wall.

"Don't you ever refer to Mrs. MacKenzie in those terms again," he warned. "In fact, I don't want her name to be fouled by so much as crossing your lips."

C.W. paused to collect himself. He was very, very angry and ready to lash out. After a slow breath and straightening his tie, C.W. gathered Agatha's purse and cane and, politely taking her elbow, steered her across the room. He waited until they reached the door before speaking again in a low voice, careful to enunciate clearly.

"I will not press charges if I have your resignation on my

desk by six tonight. You're out of the bank. You're off the board. And, you have one month to clear out of my family home." He swung wide the door, handing her the auction papers. "Your painting, madam. Study its message well."

Agatha, seeming dazed, turned slowly and, without another word, left. He heard the faint *click, click, click* of her cane dissipate down the hall, then the velvety swoosh of the elevator, and she was gone.

C.W. lowered his head and released a deep sigh. The deed was done. Yet, he felt no joy in this victory. Revenge was not sweet. God, he thought bitterly. Was he cursed to live out this routine again and again?

He remembered Seth's words: "God gave us each a field. It's our job to find a way to live in it."

C.W. tightened his fist. He'd come too far to return to despair. He'd found his field, and it wasn't this one. His business here was done—the lot of it. Sidney had been put to the test and passed with flying colors. His sister had proven herself a Blair and stood by his side. She would stand by the bank. Everyone, even old Abe, all had come through. Family and loyalty—that was all that mattered. The rest he could sign away, with a smile on his face. He wanted to go home.

He almost ran to the phone, picked it up, and dialed his sister's number. Sidney answered.

"Sid, I know it's short notice. May I come over?"

There was a pained pause. "You're always welcome in our home."

"I'll be right over. Brother."

C.W. scooped up Mike's papers and shoved them in his briefcase, grabbed his coat, and raced out the door. He never looked back.

34

—

A NOVEMBER RAIN PELTED the windows of Nora's hotel room, a mean, cold kind of rain that she felt even indoors. Nora rubbed her arms and turned away from the window. *Let the world cry,* she thought bitterly to herself. *I've cried enough.*

The morning's weather suited her mood. She closed her suitcase, clicked the latch, and with a heave, hoisted her suitcase from the bed. Then she rang for the bellboy. One more bill to pay, and she was out of New York for good.

The last two weeks had been purgatory, with no heaven in sight. The auction had ended well, thanks to the van Gogh, but not well enough. Her debts were paid and she'd come out of the skirmish with her head high. Yet, personal honor came at a high cost.

That thought brought back to mind the farm and the fifty-two ewes that hadn't survived. Those that had were unfit to breed. Even a number of her "babies" had died of pneumonia during that freak storm. They just hadn't made it. Neither had she.

Nora slumped upon the bed and rested her arms upon her

knees. The carpet blurred, yet there were no more tears to fall. The farm felt so far away now. A distant place in another time. Nora understood that life was difficult. Yet she'd always believed that somehow she'd save the farm. She'd believed that she'd found a place, at last, that she could call home. That dream was hard to let go of.

And she had to let it go. The auction hadn't brought enough capital to cover the looming farm losses. When she could admit it, she didn't have the heart to start again from scratch without C.W. So she had put the farm on the market and it sold quickly.

It almost killed her to sign the deed. She was glad Seth hadn't lived to see the sheep dead and the farm sold. Frank and Junior could make arrangements with the new owner; they'd make out all right. Yet, from some deep recess in her mind, Nora knew the old shepherd wouldn't have quit. Seth would have tried again. "Life is like that," he would have said with a shrug.

Nora's cheeks burned. What choice did she have? She had done her best at the farm, and she was through being sorry. It was time to face facts. Without the dream, the farm was just geography. She'd find some place to live—any place—it didn't matter. She'd get some job. Her life would go on, without childish dreams.

Nora brushed away a lock of hair from her face, along with the thought that the dream had lived with C.W.

"You don't love him," she told herself. "You don't even hate him. You feel nothing for him. Nothing." She repeated it again and again like a mantra, hoping to convince herself of its truth. But the void left by his absence these past two weeks proved her a liar.

Three knocks sounded on the door. Startled from her bleakness, she shot upright. "Come in," Nora called, wiping her cheeks.

The bellboy stepped in. He seemed so young. She felt so old.

"Here for your bags, ma'am. And," he added, handing her a large padded envelope, "this came for you."

"I thought I was finished with all these legal papers," she muttered, tipping him and taking the package. Reading the return address, she stopped midstride.

"Where did you get this?" she demanded.

"From the front desk," he answered defensively.

It was from Charles Walker Blair. She ripped it open, spilling out a small green-and-red tin.

Bag Balm.

She stared at the tin with wide, disbelieving eyes. Was this some kind of sick joke? Attached by a piece of tape was a small, heavy calling card. She twisted it over, recognizing at once his tight, scrawling script. "Thought you might need this. I do."

"Should I take these down, Mrs. MacKenzie?" The bellboy's voice filtered through the layers of her confusion.

"What?" she asked, her voice distant.

"The bags. Should I take them to the lobby?"

"Oh. Yes, of course. Here," she said, giving him another tip. She looked again at the tin in her hands. "Bring them to the front desk. And please, watch them for me."

The bellboy left, shaking his head at the dizzy blond. When he counted his tip, however, he called out, "Thanks again!" and whistled down the hall.

"Why is he doing this?" Nora asked herself as she fingered the tin. She refused to believe he might be sincere. He had to be after something. What more could he want from her? She opened the envelope and reached through bits of torn padding searching for something…anything. Her fingers brushed against a thick fold of paper. Yanking the plain envelope out, she unsealed it and, hands shaking, scanned the papers it held.

Her mouth went dry as she read the papers. It was the deed to her farm, purchased in her name.

Nora tapped the papers against her hand. Thoughts were racing in her head so fast she couldn't make sense of them, so she had to physically burn off the confusion. A few laps around the peach carpet and she caught hold of one idea—and it stuck fast.

Charles Walker Blair was paying her off. That had to be it. This was her little stipend for a job well done. No strings attached.

In a rush of self-righteous fury she threw the Bag Balm across the room. The little tin bounced from the wall, clattering loudly, popping its lid. Instantly the room reeked of its antiseptic odor.

"Well, Mr. High and Mighty Blair. This is one girl who can't be paid off. If you think you can ease your conscience this easily, you've got another thing coming!"

As Nora drove up to the huge black iron gates of Stoneridge, the edge slipped off her nerve. In the center of the gates, one on each side, the initials C.B. were embellished in an elaborate script. These had to be the initials of the founding father of this dynasty, she thought. Another Charles Blair, no doubt. And now here she was, off to do battle with his heir and namesake. Sitting in her dented Volvo, relatively penniless, she felt shut out by the power and wealth on the other side of those gates. And to think she'd believed Charles Walker Blair was a drifter. He must have had a lark playing the role.

The Long Road Home

She felt her anger boil again and she stoked the fire. Anger was good now; it gave her courage.

The two imposing letters separated as the gates opened. "Remember who I am," the bold initials seemed to call in the squeak of moving iron.

"Oh, yes, I remember who you are," she whispered as she maneuvered past. Her hands tightened on the wheel.

The driveway was not nearly as long or as winding as her road to the big house on the farm. But it was paved and neatly edged by a labor force only considerable wealth could afford. The parade of trees, lined straight and tall like silent sentinels, were bare now. Beyond them, acres and acres of rolling pastures, dotted with horses and cattle, lay exposed to her view. It was incredible that here in the heart of New Jersey, where a small plot of land cost more than most houses alone, rolled a vast tract of prime real estate. The discreet yet significant display of wealth fed her disquiet. It was as though the long, winding driveway was designed to confirm the real distance between the powerful Blairs and the common man.

The gravel changed from gray to red as the drive circled before a stately brick Georgian colonial. The house stood alone. Not a tree or shrub dared to interrupt its isolation. Only in the center of the driveway circle did an immense flower bed hint at life. Yet even this mound was covered now with brittle flower stalks and molded leaves. Nora found the effect mournful. The aura of the whole estate was like the garden: a place of beauty long past its peak of color and vibrancy.

She shuddered in the November wind and clutched at her thin coat, looking again at the frost-bitten landscape. How fitting that she should end her relationship with Charles Blair while the earth lay barren and spent.

The engine was off, the deed was in her hand—there was nothing left to do but confront C.W. for the last time.

"Yes?" asked the waxen-faced, faultlessly neat butler at the stately front door.

"I'm here to see Mr. Charles Walker Blair on personal business. I am Mrs. Michael MacKenzie."

The butler raised his nose. "I am sorry, madam. But Mr. Blair is not in residence at present."

Nora chewed her lip. Her phone call to the Blair Bank had confirmed that Mr. Blair had returned home. She was not to be put off by the elusive Mr. Blair again.

"We shall see," she said through gritted teeth as she pushed past the butler and stomped into the marbled foyer. This was becoming a familiar scene, and as such, she was more bold.

"C.W.! Come out of hiding! Charles Walker Blair, you come face me!" she called, wending through the rooms, head turning and eyes searching. All the while, the butler chased her about like a shadow, not really speaking but muttering something about "most unusual," and how she'd "really have to leave." Nora pressed on, striding through the elaborate rooms, calling for C.W.

When she came face-to-face with his visage at the end of a long row of portraits, Nora's voice caught in her throat. She stood silently before the gilt-framed portrait, gulping back the sudden tears as she gazed upon the likeness of the man she had once loved more than herself. The artist had caught the gentleness that lay behind the steel blue eyes. Only the nose was different. It was as yet unbroken.

"Peacham, who is making such an ungodly racket?"

Nora heard the husky, slurred voice of an old woman echo from the hall, then the tight reply of the butler. "I'm sorry you were disturbed, madam. I've already called security. Some woman is here for Mr. Blair."

Click, click, click. A cane sounded along the marble, followed by a shuffling of padded feet. Nora did not move, save for the squaring of her shoulders. As she gazed at C.W.'s portrait, she calmed her nerves, gathered her resolve, and prepared to meet the dread Agatha Blair.

"That won't be necessary, Peacham. I'll see the woman."

"Very good, madam."

"Well, well, well," came the heavy voice from behind her. "If it isn't the indomitable Mrs. MacKenzie."

Nora's stomach tightened as she slowly turned toward the voice. She couldn't abide drunks; their belligerence and vulgarity turned her to stone. Facing Agatha, she saw an old woman stooped at the entry, swaying slightly over her cane. Her cloying perfume filled Nora's nose, but that scent was overwhelmed by the bitter smell of gin.

"I'm here to see Charles," Nora said.

"First-name basis, is it? But of course it is," Agatha slurred with a wobbly wave of her hand. Then her eyes formed two thin crevices on her deeply lined face. "Well, your lover isn't here. You'll have to do your gloating elsewhere!" she spat out.

Nora stiffened and marched toward the door.

"Does your revenge taste sweet?" Agatha cried after her. "You got your lover to avenge your husband. Not bad, not bad. I underestimated you."

Nora stopped dead in her tracks and slowly turned on her heel. Agatha was still facing the portrait of C.W. and seemed to be talking more to him than to her.

"What do you mean?"

"Once you found out that I used your husband, you lured a bigger fish for your rescue. Hah! Even the lofty Charles was a sucker for a blonde." She shook her head in a drunken swing before rambling on to the portrait.

"I thought MacKenzie's suicide finished you off. I was a fool." She spat out the word, ignoring the spittle on her chin. "Well, you got me, you son of a whore. You got me good. And you!" She swung around fast, nearly losing her balance, to face Nora.

"You spurred him on, didn't you? Showed him those papers against me. Did you whimper and cry? Or did you seduce him first?" Her voice attempted a singsong tone, but it came out like a macabre wail.

"You got your money back from *me*—damn you. Paid your loans back with *my* money. I suppose you think that's only justice, right?" Her face constricted. "Well, it's lousy."

Realization set in. The weight of it caused Nora's knees to weaken and a fine sweat to form along her brow. "Why Mike?" she asked, breathless.

Agatha turned her head and stared with gimlet eyes.

"Why Mike? Why not?" Agatha snorted. "The Big Mac… Hah! He lost all caution in his lust for power." She waved her cane around the elaborate, richly appointed room. "He wanted all this! I saw it all over his face, and I used it.

"He was convenient," she said with a lift of her protruding shoulder blades. "I didn't care about MacKenzie, you fool. He was cannon fodder for my campaign against Charles. To make the bank mine."

Her lips lifted to form a sinister smile that sent a chill down Nora's spine. "And the beauty of it all was that Charles didn't trust your husband. He saw him for the high roller that he was. Refused him all loans. Oh…" She groaned like one starved before a feast. "I set it all up soooo beautifully. It would have been so perfect."

Agatha traveled slowly to the sofa and dropped into the deep upholstery. Swinging her ivory-headed cane from left to right between her bony knees, she moaned again, then muttered to herself in an alcoholic slur, "He took it all away. He took the bank from me. He took this house from me." Her face hardened, and in that glimmer Nora saw the depth of her hatred for Charles.

"I should have strangled him in the cradle."

Nora stepped back, so appalled was she by the woman's bald-faced evil. What C.W. must have endured living with her, growing up with her, calling her Mother.

Nora's heart lurched. She now heard C.W.'s words to her from a different perspective. "Trust me." She saw his actions from a new angle. "Trust me."

My God, she thought in stunned horror. What had she done? He was her knight in shining armor—her champion. He picked up her glove while all others trampled upon it, and she threw it back in his face.

He had signed over the farm to her. This was no act of conscience. It was an act of faith. And of love. She remembered the Bag Balm. She remembered the note. Was there some hope after all?

Nora cast a final glance at Agatha. She looked wizened and spent, sitting there rambling, awash in self-pity. Nora could almost pity her, but then remembered Mike and C.W. and the countless others who had suffered by her quenchless thirst for power.

"Good things come to good people," Oma had always said. It was true, she knew now. For in the end, Agatha's spiteful tirade brought Nora her greatest triumph: she knew that C.W. had been trustworthy. She felt free from the worries about money, success or failure that had plagued her all her life. The only thing that grounded her in this life was one man.

Someday, she knew, she herself would be old and wizened, poised for leaving something behind. And she had just seen what could happen if she built her life on money and power.

She left Agatha in the big, isolated house, mumbling curses at a portrait.

Her first stop was to the Blair Bank. She ran down the long corridor, straight past the row of secretaries, to the large desk before Charles Blair's office. The stiff-backed Mrs. Baldwin didn't make a move to stop her but merely waved her by. Nora swung wide the heavy wooden door and stormed into his office.

The man sitting behind the desk wasn't C.W. This man was tall, but his body was slender, not broad like C.W.'s. His hair was dark and thin, and he wore tortoiseshell glasses over eyes that were a paler blue.

"Where is he?" she asked in a high voice.

Sidney Teller stood and indicated the chair with his hand. "You must be Nora. I've heard quite a lot about you. Won't you sit down?"

She shook her head. "Where is he?" she repeated.

Sidney held back a smile. "I wish I knew. He left the bank. For good this time. Before leaving he signed over controlling interest of the bank to me and to Cornelia, Stoneridge, the family estate. Gave it all away. Said he wanted to go live on some sheep farm."

Nora's heart leaped as she did. It beat as fast as her feet upon the corridor as she raced to the elevator. She punched the button and tapped her foot. "Hurry, hurry," she pleaded. "I'm going home."

The sun shone straight above her as she crossed the border into New York State. She passed toll booth after toll booth, tossing coins into metal bins and squealing tires when the light flashed green. With her foot flat on the accelerator, she pushed past the outlines of cities and moved into long stretches of open highway. Buildings gave way to houses, which gave way to rolling hills and mountains. The color gray was pervasive: gray skies, gray trees, brown and gray earth. She had fallen in love among the bountiful colors of harvest. Now she had to learn if the colors of winter were the colors of rest, or of death.

Charles Walker Blair. The name rolled off her lips with a strange feel. Blair; one syllable that added so much. That changed so much. How Mike had hated him. And how she loved him.

He had to still love her, she prayed. Wasn't he there, at their farm, waiting for her? She would make him forgive her, make him love her again. Once before she had fought for a loveless marriage. And though perhaps it was a losing battle, some things were worth fighting for. This time Nora knew, in every ounce of her body, that C.W. was the whole war.

Nora prayed and vowed as the sky turned dusky and she crossed the Vermont border. The highway changed to gentle roads that curved and dipped along farms, silos, herds of black-and-white cows, and quaint white houses with green shutters. She knew the markers: turn left at the green warehouse, turn right at the Poultney steepled church. Up past Ed's syrup stand, then straight on to the marshy pond. Then, at last, it was a left turn onto the dirt-and-gravel road that bordered her farm. The window creaked as she rolled it down, allowing the crisp fall air to fill the stale compartment. It smelled of snow and pine. She could almost taste it.

She grew excited now, even as she slowed to a crawl on the bumpy road. As she drove past the lower barn she doubted whether C.W. would really be waiting for her. She told herself she had imagined the whole thing. Passing the pole barn, quiet now without the hungry ewes, she remembered the first day she spent there with C.W.: his patience and her incredible naivete. How far she had come since then.

Nora turned onto the drive then, seeing the condition of the road, and slowed to a stop. Deep ditches had been dug by the storm and coursed along both sides of the road. The narrow strip remaining was humped and littered with patches of ice. Her heart rose to her throat and her stomach tightened into a knot. In the distance, Seth's coon dogs began howling at the sound of her approach, their incessant wail drowning out the bucolic bleats of the remaining ewes.

The engine purred in gear as she stared at the road and chewed her lips. Already her fingers were cramped around the wheel. Like a déjà vu, the mountain symbolized her fears. They were mighty indeed. Yet forward was C.W. Beyond the icy patches, around the dangerous curves, lay her happiness. She gripped the steering wheel and shifted into low. Easy and calm, she told herself. Small steps.

Despite the icy patches, gullies, and pits, Nora climbed the mountain road steady and sure. Her wheels hit a soft spot and spun, but she kept climbing up, up, past Mike's Bench where she had at last made peace with her husband, past the stooped maple where she had had her accident, and beyond. The foliage was gone now, and the craggy limbs of the barren trees seemed to point the way. "Go on," whispered the wind. Her dented Volvo wheezed and whined, but it limped to the top like an old dog finding its way home.

At last she saw the sharp angle of the slate roof, the broad smiling deck, and as always, she smiled back. But her smile froze as she perceived a figure on the desk. A single, tall figure, standing in his familiar stance: hands on hips.

Her own hands shook as she pulled up to the house, turned off the engine, and pulled up the brake. He did not rush down the deck steps to the car, as he had the first time. He stood still, watching, waiting for her first move.

Nora sat in the car, staring back. He was there, just as she'd known he would be. He was there for her. With a deep breath she swung open the car door and stepped out upon the gravel. Her legs felt weak and shaky, whether from the long ride or her apprehension she didn't know. She stood, hand on the car door, staring up at the figure. He remained standing high up on the second-story deck, looking down. The thought of backing off, of playing a game, never occurred to her. She had come too far, climbed too high, for false pride. This move was hers to make.

Nora slammed the car door shut. Step by step she climbed the stairs, under his watchful gaze. Step by step her confidence grew.

He was smiling now, and his eyes were filled with love. Her heart swelled and she thought she would die. He opened his arms to her and she ran into them, laughing, crying, calling his name. No words were needed, nor were they sought. She felt his arms around her, smelled the sweet scent of his skin, and then, oh, yes, his lips were again on hers.

She felt grounded by his kiss. The current flowed and sparked her to life. Nothing had ever felt so right. She never knew she could love so much.

"How did you know I'd come back?" she asked.

He cupped her face with his hand, his thumb wiping away a single tear. "There's an old Chinese saying: If a horse is truly yours, do not chase after it, for it will return on its own accord.

"I knew you loved me, Nora. And I always trusted you. I just had to wait until you trusted yourself."

"I trust us."

He smiled and pressed her head to his shoulder. "That sounds right."

They stood for a while, shivering in the cold wind as the sun lowered, neither daring to move and break the moment.

"You made it up all right. The road's getting pretty bad."

"Yeh-up," she replied.

He gave her a squeeze. "You got my package?"

"You mean the Bag Balm?"

"Yes. And the deed?"

"Yes. I got them. It's an interesting story. I met Agatha."

He stopped stroking her hair.

"I see why you left New York."

He laughed and kissed her head.

"I can't accept the deed," she said, leaning far back and looking him full in the face. "It wouldn't be right."

C.W. released her and reached into his jeans pocket. After a brief dig, he pulled out a ring, and taking her hand, he placed a large mine-cut diamond on her left finger.

"If you wear this," he said, "I can't see what the problem is."

"Oma's ring!" she cried, grasping her hand and staring at the treasured family heirloom. "How did you get this? When?"

"So many questions. And you know the answers. Let's see," he said, taking her hand. His lips turned into a smug grin. "It fits perfectly. Fate."

"Destiny," she replied, delighted.

His eyes glowed warm against the cold night air. Their talking ceased, the birds stopped their song, even the coon dogs ignored the early moon. Nora and C.W. stood, holding hands, in a deep mountain silence. Above them, night clouds moved over the mountain ridge, like a curtain closing the final act.

Nora lowered her shoulders, her lips parted, and her mind emptied to receive his words.

"Nora Koehler MacKenzie," he said, speaking in his deliberate style, "I love you. And loving you has made me whole again. Will you marry me?"

Joy leaped to her throat and expressed itself in one word.

"Yes," she replied, and buried her head against his chest. He squeezed her so tight she could say no more.

"Come," he said, taking her ringed hand and leading her indoors. "I've missed you."

★ ★ ★ ★ ★

New York Times
bestselling author

Mary Alice Monroe

They are the Season sisters, bound by
blood, driven apart by a tragedy. Now they
are about to embark on a bittersweet journey
into the unknown—an odyssey of promise
and forgiveness, of loss and rediscovery.

Jillian, Beatrice and Rose have gathered for the
funeral of their younger sister, Meredith. Her
death, and the legacy she leaves them, will trigger
a cross-country journey in search of a stranger with
the power to mend their shattered lives. As they
search for the girls they once were, they find what
they really lost—the women they were meant to be.

The **F O U R** Seasons

Available now wherever books are sold.

MIRA®

www.MIRABooks.com

MMAM2684TR